By the same author

U.S. Grant in the City
Jesse and the Bandit Queen (a play)
The Last Days of Alfred Hitchcock
A Hollywood Education
A Hollywood Life
One of Us

It's All True

A Novel of Hollywood

David Freeman

Simon & Schuster   New York London Toronto Sydney

SIMON & SCHUSTER
Rockefeller Center
1230 Avenue of the Americas
New York, NY 10020

Parts of this book were previously published in *Written By,* the magazine of the Writers Guild of America, West; *Projections 10,* published by Faber & Faber; and *ZYZZYVA,* a journal of West Coast writers and artists.

SIMON & SCHUSTER and colophon are registered trademarks of Simon & Schuster, Inc.

For information about special discounts for bulk purchases, please contact Simon & Schuster Special Sales: 1-800-456-6798 or business@simonandschuster.com

Manufactured in the United States of America

10 9 8 7 6 5 4 3 2 1

Library of Congress Cataloging-in-Publication Data is available.

ISBN 0-7432-4975-5

To Judith Gingold

Contents

What was your name in the East, boy
Oh, what was your name in the East?
Did you murder your wife
Or run for your life?
Oh, what was your name in the East?

—Gold Rush tune

Now

1

Finding Home

As he drove his aging green Jaguar through the Hollywood Way gate and onto the Warner lot, a bit of movie business folklore bounced through Henry Wearie's head: If you have a hit when you're young, you'll never leave. The business was full of homemade salami like that. Because most everyone was flying blind, any ten-cent aphorism that had been around for a while took on an air of biblical infallibility.

The Jaguar was about two dings away from being a used car that once was fashionable. Henry didn't need reminding that he was once a fashionable writer who came to work through this gate every day. The guard didn't recognize him and gave him a parking assignment that Henry judged to be a half mile away. Might as well park in Glendale and take the bus. Make it as hard as possible for the writers, Henry thought. That was the real Hollywood way. Just as well. It wouldn't do for some studio pirate to see him driving a beat-up car. Henry was going to Projection Room Ten on the old part of the lot, the section that still looked like the 1940s with low-slung vanilla buildings and red tile roofs. The guard had offered a map to the distant parking space and directions to Room Ten. Henry passed on that and left the car in the first empty spot he saw. The hell with it. What were they going to do, arrest him for illegal parking?

Henry knew well enough where Room Ten was and he climbed the outside stairs at the rear of the building. It might have been easier to go through the front door but using this shortcut would demonstrate his familiarity with the place in case anyone like the guard at the Hollywood Way gate was watching. Oh, me-oh, my-oh, he thought. Coming here is making me unhinged. Madeleine, his ex, used to say that Henry thought too much about things that didn't matter. It never seemed like a fair complaint to him. He stopped for a moment and contemplated the cast-iron stairs of this fire escape, or whatever it was meant it to be, because the little ridges and bumps in the steel reminded him of a serrated bread knife. Oh, dear. Maybe later he could call Madeleine and tell her she was right after all, except they weren't speaking. Maybe he could send her an e-mail and then pretend not to notice if she didn't answer. Oh, me-oh, my-oh.

Henry found his way to the booth and asked, "Do you have *Finding Home*?" The projectionist was a young guy who looked eager to please. That was new. When Henry first worked at Warners, the projectionists, who sometimes called themselves engineers, were a prickly bunch, usually older men, lifers at the studio who were only too glad to tell you how they used to run dailies for Ronald Reagan. The booth looked the same, though, still piled high with film cans and cartons and old paper coffee cups.

"Got the studio print," the guy said. "From the original neg. I'm cued up."

"Did you check it?" Henry asked.

"Color's perfect. You could eat it with a spoon."

"I'll remember that if I get hungry."

"Mr. Desantis is on the way."

"Thank you." Ah. Held up once again by a studio executive. No doubt because he's busy writing cheesy notes for somebody's script. Easy, Henry, he thought. Desantis is just acting like what he is. Don't get your dukes up over any of this stuff.

Henry let himself into Room Ten, a little theater with a red curtain in front of the screen that was more ceremonial than useful. Henry knew it would groan as it opened. He sat down in front of the control panel. It was one of the old-fashioned kind. Just a few buttons and switches. He tested the intercom and fiddled with the volume dial. Henry liked these old panels. He never did more than adjust the sound or tell the projectionist to skip to the next reel, but operating it made him feel as if he was in control. It wasn't a feeling screenwriters often had on studio lots. Henry glanced around, feeling like a burglar in an old Warner Bros. picture. He was casing the joint, stealing a look. There were twenty well-padded leather chairs, though the leather was starting to crack in the ones next to the control panel. The screen was big enough to handle any format. The place had been painted since Henry was last here but other than that, the room looked as he remembered it, which was essentially the way it had looked since the days of Ronald Reagan and his dailies. The air had a damp and clammy feel. Henry remembered that as well. Probably from all the years of scared, sweaty people watching their fortunes rise or fall in all those formats on the screen in front of him. Now Warners was going to put *Finding Home* out in a DVD that would include an interview with Henry. *Finding Home* had been his first public success. At the time it felt as if it would be the first of many. Henry had arrived in Hollywood to join the parade when he had just turned twenty-one, young enough to squander a few years without noticing. He kicked around for a while writing scripts that didn't get made and rewriting other people's scripts until *Streets of New York*. He'd written it without a deal because no one had wanted it enough to hire him to write it. It wasn't his first spec script, but it was the first one he sold. Henry was paid $250,000. He had repeated that sum to himself again and again. He'd find himself in traffic or at a screening and $250,000 would float into his mind. Sometimes he would think, $100,000 two and a half times in a row. Other times it would be, A quarter of a million. For all that, the script never became a movie, which was a great disappointment at the time. Despite that annoying detail, *Streets of New York* was a hit of sorts, though its reputation didn't go past the city limits. Still, it took Henry from the fringes and put him in business. "A hit when you're young" drifted through his mind again.

The studio had sent Henry a tape of *Finding Home* but he had refused to look at it, telling Desantis that videotapes were tiny and blurry and not worth his time. Then, in case Desantis had missed the point, Henry told him videotapes looked like lousy impressionist paintings. They could interview somebody else for the DVD, which was no way for a screenwriter to talk to a film studio. It was just that anything to do with *Finding Home* still irritated him, all these years later. Desantis offered to set up this screening, saying he would watch it too. Henry stopped being so cranky and said, sure. Later, when he thought about it, he realized that they needed him because he was the likeliest suspect who could put a few coherent sentences together. Art Lesser, the director, would be interviewed. If Henry didn't participate, whatever self-serving lies Art came up with would become the record. Henry knew Warners would edit whatever he said, but a screenwriter ought to be able to work around that. Art Lesser had been hired when the picture was already in preproduction. He shot it, but that was about all. Still, the press always wrote about "Arthur Lesser's *Finding Home*." It irritated Henry, but it also amused him. Art was doing television now and whenever Henry ran into him he made a point of calling him Monsieur Auteur. Morty Elfman, who had produced the picture, would be interviewed. He'd do okay. At least he wouldn't make any excessive claims for himself. The other candidate was Blake Porter, who played the lead in the damn thing. The picture had made Blake an even bigger star. DVD viewers would expect to hear from him. Even if Blake wasn't stoned, without a script he'd just babble. He was probably in some other time zone anyway. They'd find him, they'd interview him. They'd interview the whole pack. Henry knew he'd best calm down and participate because whatever future life the picture might have would be in this DVD. The thought that Art Lesser would have the final word was appalling. So despite his unease with the movie, Henry was back at Warners, if only for a few hours.

Bob Desantis finally rolled in, fifteen minutes late. He had been the executive on the picture and here he was, still at Warners, still tall and geeky, though now with a bit of a paunch that looked as if it had been strapped on, like a little pillow. "Henry, Henry," Desantis said as he plopped down. "So. 'Sup, bro?" Oh, me-oh, my-oh, Henry thought. He's still using street slang. It worked for him twenty-five years ago when such terms were thought arcane and certainly unknown to studio executives. Now, for a movie executive, a season running with the Crips was as good a credential as the USC film school. Still, it sounded bizarre coming from middle-aged, pale-faced Bob Desantis. "Roll when you're ready," Desantis barked into the intercom. As the lights went down and the credits came up, he said, "So here we go. Our triumph."

"Yeah," Henry muttered, keeping his eyes on the screen. He knew he should be blasé about seeing his credit, but he couldn't help feeling anticipation. He knew he'd be tense until he saw it up there.

"People really like this picture," Desantis said. "*Beaucoup* rental numbers with men twenty-five and up." Henry knew that was true because the residual payments were good and because Warners was spending money, not something they tended to do if they weren't assured of a return.

"My old song," Henry said as he watched *Finding Home* again, trying to let it unfold anew for him. It was about a cop who put a man on death row and then discovered the guy was innocent. The cop worked to undo his great success. For the first time in all the years since he had written the movie, Henry saw that it could have been about himself. Not literally—Henry wasn't a cop and the only killers he knew were more along the lines of Bob Desantis—but he saw a parallel that wasn't there when he was writing it. Had Henry worked to undo his own great success? When the cop was on the screen, Henry felt uncomfortable. Handsome, sinewy Blake Porter as Lionel Detweiler. He had to laugh at that. Henry had spent a lot of time with the real Officer Detweiler and even brought him to Warners to meet Desantis. That little escapade was what closed the deal.

"This thing's not bad," Desantis said. "That was a time, huh?"

"That it was."

"We go back, Henry. We do. The battle of the Oakdale." Henry and

Desantis had been neighbors at the Oakdale Apartments while they were going through their divorces. All this bonhomie and talk of old times was fine, but when Henry had last called Desantis to pitch ideas, he had been fobbed off on an assistant so young that Henry thought the guy should have had a permission slip from his parents. *Finding Home* and the breakup of his marriage were jumbled together in Henry's rag-bag of unpleasant memories. He tried to dismiss his ruminations and settled in to watch the picture that once was the center of his life. Desantis was already talking on the phone and only occasionally glancing up at the screen. Henry could see the mistakes in the movie, the overwriting and reaching for effects. It was as if he had wanted to put in everything he knew for fear that he'd never get another chance. Despite that, there was a passion in the script that still felt vital and that overcame some of the florid writing. Blake Porter was good. He couldn't have done it without the script, but Porter had breathed life into the movie. Henry always thought of Blake as a dimwit, but on screen he came alive, his every thought and hope clear. A real star turn. Watching the picture now was like seeing himself again in a distant time. It fascinated him and yet it also rattled him to sense the presence of the young man he once was. What ran through his mind was that this picture was an early draft of himself. The beginnings of what he had become were now visible, though at the time the picture was made, they couldn't be seen. There were some ad-libbed lines that made Henry wince. Blake's changes sometimes had grammatical errors along the lines of "between you and I," which made the character appear illiterate. Henry had argued with Art Lesser about it at the time. Art had said not to worry, they would fix it in the edit or dub it later but of course that never happened. It irritated Henry no end. The quality of the picture wasn't the problem, nor was it that his career hadn't been as big as this picture would have suggested—hell, he lived with that fact every day. It was thinking about Lionel Detweiler again that was bothering him. The circumstances of their temporary alliance had been difficult. Recalling it now broke Henry's concentration. To calm down, he reminded himself that there was at least one promising possibility ahead for him. He was to have lunch soon with Maggie LeMay, a studio executive who was interested in an idea of his. Maybe he could winkle the story of this screening into an anecdote for Maggie. Charm her. Amuse her. Remind her that he was in business—well, sort of—and ease his way into the script idea he was pushing. The lunch was to be at La Plume. A good sign. The thought of Maggie brought on more memories of his divorce, which made him think about the Oakdale. Then, with his movie and his younger self washing over him, his mind leapt from the past to the present and the studio's parking arrangements and the Hollywood Way gate and this damp screening room, all of which led back to *Finding Home*. Everything turned in on itself, each thing reminded Henry of something else. His mind felt like a movie, though not a studio picture, more like an independent film.

When the action on the screen lagged, Henry snapped his fingers as if that might help the actors pick up the pace or perhaps restore his concentration and bring his meandering mind back to the present. Desantis, still yakking on the phone, glanced up thinking that Henry was snapping his fingers at him. If Henry was impatient with anything besides his old dialogue, it wasn't Bob Desantis. As Henry watched with his thoughts ricocheting across the years, he felt like he was in the picture, not one of the characters, but a sort of presence hovering over the story trying to steer it and keep it under control. He tried to focus again on the actual movie in front of him and to push all the other thoughts from his mind. He was going to have to think of something clever for the DVD interview. No dust on it, he would say. Screwed me up for years. It was one of the reasons my marriage went bust. Well, maybe he wouldn't put it quite that way. He'd mention the no dust and then he'd trick up something about Lionel Detweiler's moral choice. He could use the same salami he had used to sell the movie in the first place. He wondered if Desantis would remember any of it.

"Great to see you, dude," Bob said as he finally put down the telephone. "You're looking way fine. I have to boogie."

Henry was tempted to say, you're putting on weight in a really unattractive way. Instead, he turned down the volume, let the picture run, and said, "Nice to see you, Bob." Alone again, Henry rewrote some of the dialogue in his mind, perking it up here and there, well aware that only a writer looks at a movie this way. Henry knew that except for the occasional clever bits, the dialogue was like wallpaper to an audience. Henry knew he couldn't change the dialogue any more than he could change Desantis's unthinking rudeness or repair his broken marriage. It was the past that he couldn't change. Maybe that feeling of impotence was why he was so unsettled and out of season. Desantis's exit had broken Henry's reverie. He told the projectionist to skip to the last reel because no matter how many years had passed, no matter what memories were evoked and no matter how good the color was in the studio print, *Finding Home* still gave Henry the creeps.

2

A Place at the Table

Henry parked in the Sunset Plaza lot, the one that looked out over West Hollywood, the only lot in town with a view. He didn't leave the Jaguar there for the scenery but because it was free and if he used the valets at La Plume it wasn't. They parked all the cars in the same place, anyway. It was a small risk to leave his poor dented Jaguar on the Warner lot where it was unlikely anyone would know it was his. La Plume was a society parade and everything was on display, every possession was an advertisement of its owner's station. Henry walked up to Sunset, glanced in the cafés and didn't recognize anyone, went past the Armani Exchange, which reminded him once again that the lapels on his blazer, his last good jacket that still fit, were shiny. He had rubbed them gently with very fine sandpaper to reduce the glare. He'd done it before. If he did it again, the threads would probably show. At fifty-three, studio gigs were hard to come by. His Writers Guild health insurance had lapsed and the Guild only let you buy it for a limited time. The limit was in sight.

The story Henry had pitched to Maggie was about a salesman who gets mixed up with some aliens. When he'd told her the general idea, he had been uncertain about the aliens, it seemed like such a pathetic attempt to be hip, but she had liked that part. His second choice had been werewolves. He was holding those in reserve. She'd thought it over and then her office had called to arrange this lunch. Very promising. Even a low-end development deal would mean he could pay off his damn credit cards and replace the blazer. And get the Jaguar fixed enough so that he could again call it a classic. The green paint had faded in the sun. Getting a Jaguar repainted was an expensive proposition. Henry told himself that if he could make this deal, one more score, that would be it. He'd get out. Maybe go back to New York. Spend some time with his father. Well, not too much time. Felix could be hard company. Maybe London.

As he walked toward the restaurant, his mind ranged back to how he had met Maggie LeMay. It was a few years ago, when things were going well for him. Maybe more than a few. He was hot for a while, in demand, thinking about farming out some of the scripts. It could be done. Say yes to any offer, no matter how unlikely the project, take all the meetings, spin out a story line, and then hire somebody to do the rest of the work under his supervision. He had done it before—from both ends. When he was starting out, before he sold *Streets of New York* for his famous quarter of a million, he would occasionally ghost scripts for older writers. He'd been glad to get the work. When he was the one doing the hiring, he always polished the script himself. Then he'd put his name on it, collect the money, and pay the guy about a third of the fee. Oh, me-oh, my-oh, he thought. Maggie. Henry and Maggie. Wearie and LeMay. That "and" reminded Henry that in a screenwriting credit "and" means separate writers. An ampersand means a team of writers. He and Maggie were once Wearie & LeMay. He had met her when his marriage had collapsed and he was living at the Oakdale. He was working from morning till night as a way to avoid thinking about his life. To calm down, usually after about eleven o'clock, he would putter around his apartment. Some guys drank, others smoked dope. Henry built bookshelves. Once, at about midnight, he had gone to the Home Depot in Hollywood to buy paint or lumber or some damn thing. The Home Depot was open late in those days. It had become something like a singles bar. Except there was no bar, only walls of nails in little packages and aisles of hand tools. Maggie, who was a script reader, was trying to buy an electric drill. Henry offered to help. She was quick and funny and had a habit of running a hand through her thick dark hair. She was a lot younger than Henry but she could pin him in her gaze from the moment they met over the electric drill. They both knew they were living a cute meet and that was enough for them to start going out. She got her first promotion not long after they met. They had a good time for a while and then one day it stopped. They lost touch and then a year or so later, Maggie was in the trades for a promotion and then another and now she was the vice president of a studio. Henry didn't have to be reminded that he was worried about his health insurance and his shiny lapels.

The patio room, which was what La Plume called a glassed-in section that had once held outdoor tables, was already busy, the air filled with ambitious chatter. The tables were larger than the ones inside so meals were more comfortable, though everyone knew the really prime tables were in the dining room. Henry saw the screenwriter Paul Baron sitting by himself, apparently waiting for his lunch date. There had been some animosity between them over a script of Paul's that Henry had rewritten. The job had involved a location trip to Mexico. Henry went and Paul stayed home. It made for a certain resentment. It was a long time ago but Henry didn't think Paul had forgotten. Henry nodded to him and held up a finger meaning he'd be over in a minute and checked in with Alphonse, the philosopher doing the seating. Alphonse wore an Armani suit, a black silk T-shirt, and a gold chain. He looked like an extra in a disco movie, circa 1972. The regulars often slipped Alphonse a folded twenty when they shook his hand. Henry was inept at it. He knew Alphonse held him in contempt for his lack of skill at bribery. Once, in his nervousness, Henry had called Alphonse "Gaston," and the guy had never forgiven him. He always acted as if Henry had just stepped off a tour bus, but he perked up at the mention of Maggie's name. Oh, me-oh, my-oh, Henry thought, that girl's now a name to conjure with. Her office had called, she'd be a little late. Would Mr. Wearie like to go to the bar? That was the last thing Mr. Wearie wanted—to be associated with people who drank during the day and at the bar of La Plume no less. "I want to say hello and then I'll go to the table," Henry said, assuming the authority of someone there to meet a personage.

Henry strolled over to Paul Baron and shook his fleshy hand. Paul was always about fifty pounds overweight and usually in the throes of one faddish diet or another. Today he was swishing chunks of La Brea Bakery bread in olive oil so glossy and gold that Henry thought about stealing a carafe of the stuff and putting it in a safe deposit box at the bank, except he didn't have a safe deposit box because he didn't have anything valuable enough to keep in one. For a moment he pictured a dish of olive oil, gathering dust in a dark vault. It seemed perverse in a way that interested him. Paul was in his usual getup of bib overalls and Hawaiian shirt. Today he had added a denim railroad cap, a little striped job. His wiry gray hair stuck out on the sides of his head like aerials. All he needed was a red bulb on his nose and a seltzer bottle or maybe a ukulele and he could be Clarabell the clown. Still, no one forgot who Paul was, weird duds and weight trouble or not. Paul had been having some luck lately. At least he'd been making deals, though as far as Henry knew none of the scripts looked as if they were going to be made. The guy had to be solvent and Henry would settle for that, even if it meant he had to wear a clown suit to La Plume. Well, maybe not that. A man had to draw the line somewhere. Henry hoped that Paul would ask him who he was meeting so he could drop Maggie's name, or better yet, perhaps Maggie would arrive while they were talking and Henry could introduce her casually. Of course if that's what happened, it would be better if he were talking with somebody a little higher up the food chain.

"So, is there going to be a strike?" Paul asked, bringing up a favorite topic of all screenwriters.

"Probably," Henry said. "The companies get to clear out the dead-wood and dump all their writer deals."

"Right," Paul said. "If it happens, I'm leaving the country till it's over. No more picketing for me." Henry laughed and then Paul said, "Nice to see you." It was a dismissal. Paul Baron telling him to shove off. He must have seen his lunch date arriving and didn't think Henry was hot enough to introduce. Henry knew enough to move on. He nodded to Alphonse and said he'd go to the table now. A waiter tall as Charles de Gaulle and about as welcoming led the way, striding through the dining room, a colossus of the menus. Henry followed, but not too closely, because that would surely make him look like the guy's aide-de-camp.

Henry knew he should be concentrating on who was already seated, where he might stop, how long he might linger, what he might say. Instead, he found himself musing again about the Home Depot days. Maggie was different then of course, but Henry had been different too. Things were easier for him then. He told himself the business had changed. Well, of course it had changed. It was always changing. That was its nature. New. New. New. That used to be easy and natural for Henry. He liked it that way. He was new. Henry didn't exactly feel old, but now the idea of all that change, that constant turmoil, gave him a headache.

When Henry and Maggie were in the sweet grip of their romance, when everything that happened to them was new, new, new, Henry had helped her with a few household chores. Being handy around the house wasn't a skill typical of his profession. Screenwriters tended to be clumsy and awkward while all the while dreaming of themselves as graceful and athletic. Maggie sometimes called him Handy-Writer. Henry and Maggie had gone on a few weekend expeditions. Once to San Francisco, where they had stayed in a little hotel off Union Square and wandered around the city visiting galleries, and in those pre-Starbucks days, laughing about how many coffee shops there were. Henry had insisted on calling the city San Cappuccino. He told her that actors called a cappuccino an Al Pacino. She had loved that and told Henry he should specialize in coffee jokes. At the time, Maggie was reading scripts for the Morris office and scheming to become an assistant, which was just becoming the term of preference for secretary, which now seemed to be something of an insult. Henry was writing long form, mostly movies of the week, for the networks. You had to turn them out fast because the up-front money wasn't much. In those days the networks made most of what they commissioned so the residuals were good. The trouble was most of the pictures were lousy and then that market dried up or at least it dried up for Henry. After the sale of *Streets of New York,* Henry had assumed he'd be in demand with all the work he wanted. It didn't happen quite that way. When the picture wasn't made and was soon forgotten by everyone but Henry, he started pursuing jobs of any sort. He didn't care which ones had status. He'd slide from TV movies to feature gigs to rewrites. If somebody had asked him, he'd probably have tried writing cartoons. Henry was in love with the action and he was learning how to play the game.

He'd heard about Maggie's promotions. One minute she was covering scripts, the next she was answering phones, and then she was booking writers. Once, after she got her first studio job, Henry had called her Mrs. Norman Maine. She didn't get it. As far as Henry knew, Maggie hadn't seen any movie that was older than she was. A few promotions ago, she'd stopped taking his calls. Not all at once. It started to take a day or two for her to call back. Then three. Then Henry didn't call anymore.

"Hey, Henry Wearie—back from the dead?" Henry looked up, jolted out of his reverie, to see a face he knew but couldn't quite put a name to. "Hello, amigo," was what he managed. The mystery diner was an agent who had once represented him. He had sold *Streets of New York,* which had made Henry hot for a while, some $250,000 ago. He had been Henry's agent right through *Finding Home* and now Henry just couldn't pull up his damn name. The guy was having lunch with an Asian woman who was surely in her twenties. She was small with a face that looked like the handiwork of a studio makeup artist. Her dark red lips were out-lined in a perfectly drawn black line and something had been done to her eyes that made the pupils seem the size of quarters. Her breasts were too large for her frame and seemed to jut out in an arrangement unknown in nature. Henry wondered if she could keep her balance when she stood up. Mr. Mystery Agent was about sixty. He was wearing an Italian suit that probably cost as much as the paint job Henry's Jaguar required. The guy knew Henry couldn't come up with his name and Henry knew that he knew. The babe was oblivious.

"Karen Tanaka, meet Henry Wearie. Henry wrote some movies you probably never saw. Remember *Finding Home?*"

"I've heard of it," she said, using the California interrogative tone that turned declarative statements into questions, a formulation that could only arise in a place where no one was certain of anything. It's bad enough I can't think of his name, Henry thought. Now he's talking about a movie that came out when this girl was in grade school.

"It did some business. I made the deal for you, remember?"

"Sure. I just saw that picture the other day. For the DVD. It was okay. The deal was pretty good, too." All Henry could think was that instead of reminding this man of his presence, he was pissing the guy off. Then the name Howard Lathrop drifted into his head, curling down from the ceiling like a feather. "You were a great agent for me, Howard. I liked those days."

Howard smiled, suggesting that it was fine that Henry recalled his name, but it was too late. The only reason Henry could imagine that Ms. Karen Tanaka was hanging around with an old goat like Howard Lathrop was because he knew most everyone. If everyone didn't know him, he would be at a disadvantage in whatever campaign he was on with her. Ms. Tanaka, on the other hand, struck Henry as deeply indifferent to the fine points of such matters. "Good to see you, Henry. Stay in touch."

Henry had now been dismissed by two of these rascals. Maybe coming here wasn't such a good idea. If you're out of practice, maybe you had to work out first. Flash cards of everyone in the business until you knew all the names and a couple of recent credits. Walking through the long dining room with tables on either side of him, Henry felt he was running the gauntlet in an old Western. At any moment people would start flinging food at him, pelting him with tiny pink shrimp and their Cobb salads—no bacon, no cheese, thank you. General de Gaulle led him to a table for four, not far from the round table in the back that could seat six, but of course never did. The point of such a table was to use it for two, though not just any two. Henry's table was impressive enough. Perhaps Maggie had come up in the world even more than he knew. Henry was aware he was wool gathering when he should be concentrating on the lunch ahead, on just how to tell his story to Maggie. She'd want to hear more but not too much more.

"You see Howard Lathrop over there?" Henry looked up to see Rick Moses, his oldest Hollywood pal.

"I couldn't think of his name."

"I bet he loved that. Does that kid think he can do something for her?"

"He was selling. She was buying."

"This your Maggie LeMay meeting?"

"Yeah. Who're you here to be abused by?"

"Agent. I'm going to the table. Kill the bitch."

Henry laughed as Rick moved into the other room, beyond the bar. Rick had made his name with a series of novels about a Las Vegas comic who was also a private eye. The books were still popular, but after seven of them, Rick had lost interest and was now determined to be a director. Henry had always admired his friend's ability to act and make decisions. If a script wasn't going right or if he ran into a roadblock, Rick just said "Next" and moved on. Henry and Rick looked somewhat alike and people often thought they were related. Henry said all it meant was they were both losing their hair at about the same rate. They had once collaborated on a script. The very Howard Lathrop had made the deal. It was about runaway teenagers. The script was good, but it wasn't as flashy or as hot or as something as the studio was expecting so they dropped it. It felt like a failure to Henry and he brooded on it. Rick hardly noticed.

"Would you care for something to drink, sir?" It was General de Gaulle again.

"Iced tea, please." Henry didn't even like iced tea. It just felt better than asking for the damn bubble water that joints like this pushed. Must be all profit for that stuff. They order a few hundred cases with an Italian name and then deliver it a bottle at a time with an 1,100 percent markup. De Gaulle asked something about passion fruit or mango. Henry just nodded and said fine. As the guy went off to rustle it up, Henry watched Alphonse himself seat a silvery gent at the big table. It took Henry a moment to recognize Milt Arkadine. It was Ark who had turned *Streets of New York* into the $250,000 package that Howard Lathrop sold all those years ago. Henry should have been pleased to run into two of these guys from his past—that's why people came to La Plume. It sure wasn't for the service. Henry knew that not recognizing both of them instantly was a measure of just how distracted he felt. He and Ark had been friends. Ark knew Madeleine. Henry knew he had to stop measuring everything by how it related to his ex-wife but he couldn't help it. Henry and Madeleine and Ark had once had dinner at "21" in New York. Now Ark was the producer of the moment. He had a string of hits. Most of them were special-effect jobs. SFX to the trade. Ark smiled and waved. Henry threw Ark a salute and turned away, trying to think about the story he had told Maggie. A salesman is going through a rough patch. He's losing his customers to the Internet. Anybody with a computer can outsell him. His head is barely above water. Kids are running wild. Wife is divorcing him. He wants to run away. He's in his car, out in the middle of nowhere, and there's a flash of bright light. He's caught in the beam. Then everything starts going right—his job turns around, his wife loves him again. He's got the touch. Then there's temptation. He'd push the part about how the guy got more than money, how he found inner peace, though not till the temptation part got a good workout. He wasn't exactly sure how much he had told Maggie. He ran through the major beats in his mind, identified the act breaks. They all loved act breaks and a little babble about rising action. Henry could sell it. And he could write it too. It had sex. Not too much. He'd call it love or romance. These things need sex, but it's better not to use the word. They go for the hot stuff but they like to think of themselves as having good taste about it. He'd call it passion. If she didn't respond to that, he'd call it erotic. There weren't a lot of special effects. There was the flash of light—sort of Saul on the road to Damascus. Better not mention that. Probably sound too ethnic. And Damascus, that'll set her off. Just call it a beam of white light. Maybe he could toss in an explosion. A big one that gets out of hand. Or a helicopter crash. Henry ran through other pos-sible elements that were popular. He didn't have any demonic possession, no serial killers. Maybe he should put in a serial killer who stalks the salesman and his family.

"Mr. Wearie, Miss LeMay's office called. She's in the car." Henry looked up to see Alphonse delivering the news of Maggie's schedule. "More iced tea?"

"No. Thank you." Ark's lunch date had arrived. A willowy blonde in black, almost as tall as the waiter. Probably another studio executive Henry didn't know. The round table held a certain sociological fascina-tion for Henry. The winners circle, he called it. If he was feeling extrava-gantly poetic, it was a faerie ring where bandit-bards breed. Today he was just feeling anxious, reminding himself that he was always outside its perimeter. He could understand its ways and the intricacies of its rit-uals, but he never had his own place at the table. Here he was, trotting down the long corridor of middle age, still an acolyte, never a full partic-ipant, always on the margin. The long blonde glanced over at him with what Henry thought was a look of pity. She did it and still stayed focused on Ark. Quite a skill. Henry wasn't sure if that was a skill of business or dating. Whichever, when there was no response from Henry, she looked away.

Henry heard Maggie before he saw her. She was streaming through the dining room dispensing her greetings like flowers—a hello blossom here, a hi-hi bud there. Henry took a tiny bit of comfort in that she wasn't stopping to talk to anyone. She knew she was twenty minutes late and for a few quality seconds nothing was more important to her than getting to Henry Wearie. He rose to greet her just as she saw Ark at the big table. She couldn't resist. She reached out a hand to Henry—taking his when he was not quite out of his chair. With her other hand, and all her attention, she waved to Ark, blew him a kiss, and then mimed holding a telephone, as if she were playing a quick round of charades. Finally, as Henry was concerned that his knees might lock, she turned to him and managed a kiss on each cheek. "I am so sorry. The traffic was crazy. I thought I'd be five minutes. I am never late, per se."

"I received regular bulletins on your progress." Careful Henry, he thought. Don't get sarcastic. And what's with this per se business?

"Oh, good." That was something new in her. The old Maggie, the one who shopped for electric drills at odd hours, was moderately funny. This woman seemed irony-proof.

De Gaulle was back, assisted by another guy who was tall enough to play for the Lakers. They were there before Maggie's bottom was in the chair. A bread basket and olive oil were on the table. Henry realized he'd been there for a while without such grace notes, as if they were keeping the bread until they were sure someone who could pay the tab arrived. The Laker waiter was making a show of opening menus as if he were a magician and the food itself was about to fly out of his oversized leather-bound books. Maggie ignored him and said, "I'll have the lettuce *assorté* with jicama."

"Very good. Today I'm showing frisé, baby arugula, mâche, radicchio, romaine, bibb, red oak, and I believe the chef has some tatsoi, an Asian leaf."

"Yeah. Okay. Lemon juice on the side. And bubble water," she said, uninterested in the fine points of lettuce taxonomy. At least she didn't insist on an obscure brand of water. And what the hell was jicama?

"And you, sir?"

Henry would have appreciated a look at the menu but asking to see it seemed like a tactical error. "I'll have the screenwriter's special. Bread and water." Maggie didn't hear that joke either. She was scanning the room, checking on the competition. The waiters' faces were too high up for Henry to read any reaction there. He managed to ask for a Cobb salad without amendments because that's what Howard Lathrop's date, the Asian temptress who hadn't seen *Finding Home*, had ordered. He couldn't think of another dish sure to be on the menu. Maggie looked more put together than he remembered. She had always been fleshy and all her squirming had kept her slightly disheveled. Her socks tended to droop. Not anymore. Maybe with her new eminence she had put a hair and wardrobe wrangler on her staff.

Maggie complimented Henry's story so effusively that it made him uneasy. He well knew that if someone wanted to buy an idea they made a point of telling you what was wrong with it to establish their authority and make you nervous lest you try to argue. Enthusiasm was the preface to rejection. "I've worked on it a bit since we spoke. It's fuller now. I've got back stories for the central characters." He seemed to have her attention until her cell phone chimed a few notes of "Twinkle, Twinkle, Little Star."

"That's my office. Sorry." Then she mouthed the words, "Frank Rosato" as if she were evoking a name so grand that Henry couldn't possibly find it rude that she was taking the call. Frank was Maggie's immediate superior at the studio. Henry had known him years ago when they were both starting out. Frank had always been a comer, had always known how to associate himself with the right people, was always able to get the most out of whatever came his way. He didn't take Henry's calls anymore. From the side of the conversation Henry was forced to listen to, it seemed that Frank wanted Maggie's opinion of a casting decision for what sounded like the love interest in an action movie. "What's her FQ? What do the boys say?" Maggie asked. "Do they want to fuck her?" Ah. FQ. Fuckability quotient. It's exactly what feminists complain about. They're right, of course, but what they don't know is that the women executives use the standard as much as the men. If beagles or bloodhounds bought the tickets it would no doubt lead to the petting quotient. The PQ. Oh, me-oh, my-oh. While Henry tried to stay cool, he noticed Mickey Resnick going from table to table, working the room. Mickey ran an agency and he was something of a public figure, regularly commenting on the state of the business in newspapers and on television. There was talk of running Mickey for governor, no doubt started by Mickey. When Henry first knew him he was an idiot and he was probably still an idiot, though Henry had to admit, he now had better tailoring. He was dressed in pin stripes and looked something like a diplomat. He was a handsome rascal, with a strong face and an easy smile. Henry wondered if Maggie had noticed him. Mickey saw her and came straight to the table, smile in place. By the time he noticed the phone, it was too late. He was already babbling her name and extending his hand. Nothing fazes guys like Mickey. When Maggie didn't jump up, Mickey just started talking to Henry. Then he saw Ark at the big table and was about to pounce on him. That got Maggie off the phone, but by then, Ark was on his feet. My God, Henry thought, it's a collision of barking alpha-dogs. For a pathetic moment, Maggie was reaching across Henry's head to shake Mickey's hand, and Mickey was stretching toward Ark even though he was several tables away. Henry probably should have stood up, but that now seemed risky. He could get caught in the crossfire.

For Maggie, this was a potential error. Frank was her boss, so she had to talk to him whenever he wanted. But Mickey was a big agent. She needed him to carry out Frank's orders and to conduct the studio's business. As the action swirled around Henry's head, he realized that one of the nasty revelations of middle age was that who got ahead often didn't make any sense at all. It just seemed to happen. It was the same with the writers. Henry would have thought that at least in his own racket talent would have meant more. A guy wrote a script or he didn't. It was good or it wasn't. And that counted, but again and again people without much to offer wound up with the big-ticket gigs. They were usually rewritten so much that you couldn't tell who wrote what anyway. Henry didn't think he was the best screenwriter in town, he knew better than that, but he did know that he was better than some of his colleagues who weren't worried about their health insurance or the state of their lapels. Was it luck? Maybe, though Henry knew that whatever part luck played, he lacked some gene or spark. He was too sarcastic maybe, too studied. He was always measuring his life instead of living it. Actors called it being in the moment. Henry was usually in two moments at once, which meant not being in either. If it were otherwise he wouldn't be huddled in his chair while all the action was just over his head.

Mickey moved on and Ark turned his attention back to his business.

Maggie made a little show of speed dialing her office and snapping, "No more calls." She turned to Henry with a toothy smile that seemed real enough, at least the teeth seemed real. Henry might not be quite in the Mickey Resnick league, but he was an old boyfriend and that was always of interest. She wanted her old boyfriends to be successful. It reflected well on her.

"Your lettuces, Miss LeMay." The waiter's presence intruded upon Henry's thoughts and brought him back to the table. Only one waiter this time. Maybe Maggie's stock had dropped since she ordered. Maybe this was the way executives were fired. It used to be that your name on a parking space was painted over. Now the number of waiters was reduced and they were made shorter. The really tall ones were probably reserved for the people on top. Henry glanced at Maggie's plate trying to see the jicama. It looked like slices of apple. Maybe it was a code word. If you called it an apple you would never get to sit at the big table. You had to say jicama. "Won't put an ounce on you," Maggie said as she sprinkled lemon juice on the roughage. "I'm an eight. I was an eight when we were going out, right?"

"Maggie, you're always a ten with me."

"No, no. Not that. Size eight. You would go out with an eight, right?"

"You looked great then, and you look great now." Maggie smiled at the compliment and at the memory. Henry told himself to ease up. Don't overdo it.

"I need to be a six. I'm going out with this hot lawyer. He won't date anyone bigger than a six."

"Sounds like a real charmer."

"Yeah. He is. I'll get him."

"Right. You're on top, Maggie. You deserve it."

"It's Margaret now. Maggie sounds like a puppy or something. Tell me about the script again."

"Salesman. Aliens."

"Oh, yeah. I don't know about that. Does it have to be a salesman?"

"What would you prefer?"

"You're the writer, not me. We had some trouble with a salesman script. Maybe he could be a counterfeiter."

"I think that would work."

"What happens? Tell me a story, Henry."

"A counterfeiter, a guy who travels around the Midwest. He's having trouble. The counterfeiting business is changing. A kid with a scanner and a computer can do it. He's scared. Then there's a big flash of light out on the highway. Starting then, everything goes right for him. He can't do anything wrong. It all turns around."

"The aliens, right?"

"Yeah. I'll put in a chase. That's pretty much it."

"I like it. We'll get some numbers together. I'll have business affairs call your agent," she said, getting up to leave. Henry got to his feet, confused but polite to a fault. "I have to go," she said. "I have another lunch. I hate to double-book lunches. I knew you'd understand. I loved seeing you." She blew a kiss his way and was gone. Henry sat there trying to replay it in his mind, wondering if there was something he might have done differently. He decided that it was all just too odd for that. What the hell did she want? Not the salesman now, a counterfeiter and aliens script. Nobody says yes that casually. Henry wondered if he could leave La Plume without appearing to be skulking away.

The next day Henry's agent, the always pretentious and rarely available Murray Marden, a man Madeleine used to call the secret agent, called to announce that Maggie's studio had made an offer on what Murray called the alien project. Henry avoided sarcasm and instructed Murray to negotiate lightly, improve what he could, and accept the rest forthwith. He threw in the forthwith because Murray often used legal terms of that sort. What Henry meant, and what Murray understood, was this is a bloody miracle and please grab it. Henry had to deliver an outline, then a treatment, then a first draft. At any of those points the studio could fire him without going on to the next step. It was called a cutoff. Henry didn't need reminding that top screenwriters didn't have to live with cutoffs. On the other hand, the start money was enough to get his health insurance back and fix his car. Henry had himself fitted for a new jacket and then got down to work.

A few days later Margaret called. Henry assumed that it was to discuss the script. She didn't mention it. There was a screening the next night and a dinner. She thought Henry might like to go with her. Henry had been around Hollywood and Margaret LeMay enough to know immediately what it all meant. She'd bought the counterfeiter-salesman-alien idea. In return Henry would become her escort. Her walker. Oh, me-oh, my-oh. You had to love this place. No matter what you think is going to happen, no matter how sure you are, something else comes bouncing through.

Over the next few months, Henry and Margaret went to screenings, parties, dinners, and benefits. Margaret always paid the tab, saying it was on the studio. For Margaret, Henry was the right man for the job. "You know Henry Wearie," she would say in a way that suggested that if they didn't it was their fault. A walker was usually a gay guy. Margaret didn't want to be known as a fag hag. She wanted people to assume they were dating, and in a fashion, they were. Now and then, after an evening, Henry would take Margaret back to her house in Benedict Canyon and he would spend the night. It helped that they had once been lovers. None of it would have worked but for that. They were like a divorced couple still comfortable with one another.

What surprised Henry was how easy it was for him to start enjoying Hollywood again. When Henry was younger, in his new, new, new period he had gone out most every night, always to the latest restaurant, the grandest opening, the hottest party. It was what everyone who was in the game did. Escorting Margaret reminded him that he had once been happy to participate. It didn't take him long to get his party chops back. It wasn't complicated. You met someone you might want to do business with and you talked about everything but business. People in Hollywood always worried that they only thought about business. That's exactly what they did, but they didn't like to admit it. You could talk about movies, but usually something so preposterously obscure or highbrow that no one else knew what it was. Henry found himself in deep conversation with agents and directors and actors and producers about everything but employment. The only sign that this was an elaborate ritual was that Henry never spoke to another writer at any of these gatherings. That was reserved for a lunch or a phone call and always devoted to complaining. Every writer knew this, so there was never much danger that another of what Henry liked to call his co-religionists would do much more than nod at him. At one Brentwood dinner party, while Margaret occupied herself with a writer she had been chasing, Henry spent the better part of the evening talking about Italian neorealism with a guy who had made millions producing pimply teenage farces. They had argued about De Sica's influence on *The Tree of Wooden Clogs,* which was the guy's favorite Italian movie. Henry had seen it once years ago, couldn't recall much of it, except that it was three hours long and about a cow. Still, he had no trouble criticizing it as ersatz simplicity and therefore anti–De Sica, who had genuine simplicity. The guy nodded and repeated "ersatz simplicity," probably filing it away to use at another dinner party. Later, when Henry thought about it, he felt bad because he had slighted a picture finer than anything he had ever written.

At an Academy reception after a screening, Margaret worked the room talking to one of the actresses in the movie they had just seen and then chatting up the director. Henry knew exactly what he had to provide Margaret on these occasions: Be at her side if she needed help, or stay clear if she was working, and always, always be engaged in something that looked serious. It would reflect badly on her if her escort seemed out of his depth. Henry delivered on all counts. At that Academy reception, he spent a long time with an agent discussing the state of the apple industry in the Pacific Northwest. The woman seemed to know a lot about it. Henry didn't care much about apples but after writing scripts for years he could fake anything. When Europeans were around, they were always disappointed not to hear vapid Hollywood talk. They were always so pleased when the requisite smart-chat was over and they could listen to gossip and deal-talk. The goal of these conversations, with men or women, was that they spin themselves out like miniature dates. Some flirting, some probing, some possibility. If all went well, the serious phone call and the offer of work would come later. A job was the equivalent of sex. Henry did it with practiced ease—whether he knew anything about the subject or not. It made him feel great again, giddy and if not exactly new, at least he didn't feel old.

After Henry and Margaret had been seen together a few times, Ark, who was always one step ahead of other producers in these matters, began to cultivate Henry. He said it was a shame they had fallen out of touch and why didn't they get together again? It was Ark's great skill to become close to the people that it was in his interest to know. It wasn't fake. Ark really meant it. Instead of talking about obscure Italian movies or produce, Ark took Henry to the fights at the Forum. Two Mexican welterweights were on the card and Henry enjoyed it more than he thought he would. Afterward they went to the Pacific Dining Car. Henry, who appreciated Ark's generosity, pronounced the evening, "An all-red-meat-and-testosterone adventure." Ark listened to Henry muse about boxing, a sport he had only seen on television. "Pretty basic, isn't it? There's manly blood on the floor and at the end one guy's standing and the other guy isn't."

"You're a screenwriter to your bones, Henry. You see everything like a script."

"Everything is a script. Or it could be." They were both relaxing into the evening and over the steaks and a better bottle of wine than Henry was used to, Ark talked about himself a bit. He had grown up in the Valley and after Van Nuys High School had gone into the army. "I don't know how it happened," Ark said. "Pretty soon I was booking USO acts in Germany. I was good at it."

"I don't doubt it," Henry said, glad that Ark was talking about himself. Henry had heard some of it before, even the same phrases. A few impressive facts, a little self-effacement. It was probably his set piece for talking to writers. I must have some heat, Henry thought. When a guy

like this gets chummy it means you're in business. Ark's story was interesting enough, even the second time around, and it meant Henry didn't
have to do much more than listen and eat a perfectly grilled slab of
pricey beef. Usually when these guys were trying to become your friend
they acted like high school girls on a date, professing great interest in the
details of your life. Ark wasn't pushing anything, he was just talking and
Henry was happy to listen.

"It led to the agency business. I booked variety acts for a couple years.
Mostly for the Vegas hotels. They needed a singer or a juggler or a damn
trapeze act, they had to call me. Then I went over to Metro for a while.
What a pain in the ass that was."

"Weren't you the head of it or something?" Henry asked, all the while
trying not to stare at Ark's silver hair. How do these guys get hair like
that? My hair just gets thinner. Maybe there's some secret silver tonic
available only to these rascals. Henry didn't worry all that much about
his appearance, which he knew full well was not exceptional. He sometimes thought he would have made a good extra. He could be background without trying. On his best day, he could play a neighbor or a
sidekick. An attendant lord. Guys like Ark would always be the king, the
general, the tycoon.

"I was a vice president of the studio," Ark said. "They've inflated those
titles so much that it's meaningless. I didn't like it. So I started producing.
And here we are."

"Yeah," Henry said. "About a half-billion dollars in grosses later."

"I've done okay. I like producing pictures. Working with the writers. I
know how to fix scripts, but I could never write one. I admire it though.
I wish I'd gone to college and all that."

"You didn't miss that much. I never graduated, you know."

"Reading books is an ordeal for me. I didn't learn how to do it when I
was the right age. Guy like you, you read for the pleasure of it. That's
from college—graduated or not. It's like a big hole in me." Henry suspected that it was at least partly an act—appear vulnerable to the weak
and they'll do what you want. Maybe it was the fights or the steaks, but

Henry decided that was too cynical even for him. He'd heard the truth as Milt Arkadine knew it. Henry found it unexpectedly moving.

During the time Henry spent with Margaret, at all the cocktail parties and screenings, she continued to work at losing weight. When she finally got herself down to size six she began going out with her lawyer again. That was about the time Henry delivered the first draft of the script now called *Funny Money from Space*. Margaret told him she thought it was great. He knew she never read it, which meant that her colleagues let alone Frank Rosato never read it either. Someone in the story department probably made a summary and checked it against Henry's outline to make sure the studio was getting something like what they bought.

Henry knew that would be that for the walker business with Margaret. He didn't mind. The whole crazy thing had made him solvent. If he was ever going to get out of Los Angeles, this was the time. He'd miss Margaret in an odd way or at least he'd miss going to the screenings and the parties. Left to his own, as he well knew, Henry could burrow into his apartment and not come out as long as he could have movies and food delivered. Ark knew all about the situation. He called Henry and told him to just stay cool. Even if he couldn't make a studio deal without Margaret, for a while he'd have enough heat to make independent deals. "You have to do that right away," Ark said, "before the heat evaporates, because that's what heat does if you don't take care of it." Henry knew Ark was right. Ark was always right, but Henry just didn't care any more so he thanked him and assumed that would be that. Henry started musing about the pleasures of London. He thought he'd go to New York for a while to see his father. Henry found their visits difficult and their phone conversations limited to Felix either sounding annoyed or being silent. It had been easier to see him when Madeleine was there to run interference. Felix was nearly ninety now and Henry knew that if he was going to make peace with him he'd better not wait much longer.

Ark called again the next day, concerned that Henry wasn't acting sensibly and in his own interests. Before Henry could explain that his own interests didn't interest him all that much, Ark invited him to lunch. Henry must have sounded surprised when he accepted, because Ark said, "Do you really think that because you and Margaret LeMay aren't going out anymore, I'm not going to talk to you?"

"It crossed my mind." For a moment Henry thought he might have insulted him.

"Please. La Plume tomorrow. One o'clock."

Henry puzzled it through overnight. It couldn't be as simple as that. Nothing with people like Ark was simple. There was always some deeper game being played. Still, if part of it involved helping him, why question it?

The next day, Henry and Ark sat at the round table in the back and talked things over. Henry was amused to be sitting at the big table. He enjoyed watching everyone else in the room take note of his presence. Soon enough though, after the initial kick, he had to admit that it didn't seem all that different from any other table. More space, but that was about all. Henry felt vaguely unsettled at not having a bigger reaction to the real estate. No flash of light, no alien interference. Ark, who was used to sitting at the best tables everywhere, began his brisk and gentle lecture, offering Henry hard practical advice about how best to take advantage of his friendship with Margaret despite the fact that it had cooled off. "You don't want to push this too hard," Ark said. "She's a former girlfriend. Two times. If you think of her as a meal ticket, you'll get nowhere. You want to get yourself positioned. Your scripts are good. *Streets of New York* was good. That's why it sold."

"So why is my career so rocky?"

"Is it?"

"Ark, I have been hot and cold more times than my oven." Ark laughed at that and Henry said, "When I say that to screenwriters they just grunt."

"Of course they do. They know. What are you hanging around with writers for anyway?"

"Friends of mine. Why not?"

"You don't have the right relationships. You ought to be able to see that. For the last few months you had an A-relationship. You must have talked seriously with twenty people who could hire you. You didn't follow up on any of them, did you? Your agent should be making calls, but you have to tell him who you met. You have to work as hard at that as you do at the writing. It's a club, Henry. Not a literary society. You can be in it if you want, but not on a pass."

Henry knew Ark was right. He also knew that his career was uneven because in his heart Henry just couldn't take the whole thing seriously. Counterfeiters? Aliens? He was thinking about London. Ark, who often surprised him, asked, "Are you thinking about quitting the business again?" Henry nodded and said, "I'm not so good at that end of things—working at being in the club. I just can't stay interested in it. I don't mind writing the scripts, but that's about it."

"What does that mean? Half the dry cleaners and pool guys have scripts. Some of them aren't bad. They write them, they show them to their friends, and they put them in envelopes and send them to guys like me. I won't even open them unless they send a release. It's an amateur's idea of how the business works. I need to know writers who can deliver, you need to know producers. Studio executives come and go. I'll get your script back. They'll give it to me."

"Then what?"

"It needs some work. That counterfeiter stuff is crazy."

"Originally the guy was a salesman."

"That's better. With the aliens though, right?"

"I don't know. I've never been sure about that part."

"Aliens are baked in the cake. That's what'll sell it. What if he's a professional baseball player? Triple A. Losing his fastball. He's twenty-eight. Very castable age. It's not happening. Young guys coming up throw harder, faster. He's getting worried. Then the aliens. That lightbulb stuff. Bang. He's in the majors. Throwing ninety-eight miles an hour."

"Can you sell that?"

"If you can write it, I can sell it. I'll get it in turnaround. You put up a down-and-dirty rewrite. Two weeks' work max. I'll put up my office's time and energy. I'll sell it right back to Margaret. I'll get you more money than you got in the first place. You think I won't?"

Henry watched him, thinking that Ark was rehearsing how he would sell the script, what song and dance he'd give Margaret. She wouldn't even remember the counterfeiters. Baseball player, salesman, counterfeiter. What was the difference? "I believe you, Ark."

"You don't sound like it. You don't like baseball, come up with something else."

"No. Baseball's fine. Good an idea as any." Henry wondered if he was being cynical again, accepting whatever someone said because what was the point of arguing when everyone knew the script would go through dozens of arbitrary changes anyway. Something felt a little different today. It wasn't that making the character a baseball player was a good or bad idea. The character had been pushed around so much that he was all but incoherent, so who cared what his occupation was? Usually thoughts like that made Henry feel cut off, shut down. Today he felt open and encouraged. Maybe it was the big table after all. Why question it? Just enjoy it.

When de Gaulle asked if Mr. Wearie would be having the Cobb salad, Henry said, "Keep the lettuce for the rabbits. I'll have a steak. I think they're lucky for me." Ark agreed, ordered one for himself, and in a goofy French accent that Henry hadn't heard before, told the waiter to bring the *carte des vins* because he and Mr. Wearie were going to have a bottle of the best merlot that the Napa Valley and La Plume had to offer. After the waiters had scurried and fussed, changing the wine glasses, and once Ark had performed the sniffing and swirling song and dance, he toasted them both, saying they would have many lucrative adventures.

"I hope so," Henry said.

"The iron's hot, Henry, but it won't stay that way." Henry nodded tentatively, wondering where this was headed. "There's no law against working on two scripts at once, you know. Push the odds your way."

"I don't know, Ark . . ." Henry said, letting his words drift.

"You need to come up with at least one more."

The idea of writing another script while he was wrestling with the aliens made Henry pour himself another glass of merlot. He steadied himself, ready to tell Ark no, he wanted to go to New York to see his father and then to London. One script at a time was his limit. What came out was, "I'll get started right away."

3

Take the Backlight

As *Henry was puzzling through* his marching orders and his inability to say no to Ark, it occurred to him that after nearly thirty years of writing scripts he surely had something in his files that he could fob off as new. If Ark was right, and he usually was, Henry was just hot enough to make a deal off something that might have failed once or twice in the past. So Henry was poking through the closet he called his files. It was a hodgepodge of old scripts and notes, some without covers or even titles. He came across a dog-eared and coffee-stained first draft of *Streets of New York*. He had spent months of obsessive work on that script and had been paid all that money for it. When he accepted the famous $250,000, he gave up all claims of authorship. This copy was contraband, probably illegal for him even to look at it. The money had been spent long ago and the script had vanished into rewrites and squabbles. Henry usually just opened the closet enough to throw something more onto the pile. Sorting through that Fibber McGee mess would surely exhaust him. Even thinking about Fibber McGee would probably get him in trouble. The youth department of the Writers Guild would bring him up on charges of knowing about radio. Oh, me-oh, my-oh.

Henry was living in a Spanish revival apartment building on Harper Avenue that in a cross-cultural confusion was called El Palladio. Given the enthusiasms of his West Hollywood neighbors, Henry had taken to calling the building El Fellatio. There were dusty Mexican palms and a grim, gnarled cactus in the courtyard, though the rooms were sunny and generous and decorated with Spanish tile. The rent was manageable. Henry hardly noticed any of it. This was his sixth apartment in the years since his divorce. He still missed Madeleine, though less and less as the years piled up. Sometimes he thought what he really missed was their lovely old Spanish house in the Hollywood Hills. Considering that a flash of heat had come his way, courtesy of Margaret LeMay, Henry knew he had better stop brooding and face the closet. He couldn't recall writing several of the scripts he uncovered, but there was a love story that was pretty good. The problem was it was owned by Paramount. The executives who had commissioned it had long since been fired and the present bunch had no interest. The last thing they were going to do, however, was let Henry set it up at another studio. If he succeeded, the Paramount crew would look like idiots for letting it go. Of course he could rip it off—tell the same story with the same characters but just different enough to slip it past them. The idea of scheming to steal his own script threatened to give him a headache. He found a modern Western that wasn't bad and that he owned outright but when he suggested it, Ark laughed and said that market had dried up long ago. Henry needed a finished script that he could dust off and that Ark could sell. He found his notes for a version of *Othello* set in a suburban high school. Othello was the captain of the football team. Desdemona was a cheerleader and Iago was a kid running a sports book out of the cafeteria. Seemed like a lot of work. He did find *Hard Drive,* a not quite finished first draft set in Silicon Valley. As he read through it, he perked up. An engineer with a gambling addiction gets mixed up with the mob who think they can tap into the computers of big businesses by getting their hooks into him. It had a star part for a man in his mid-thirties. Henry knew Ark would say, "Very castable." It was the story of a good man under pressure, about to go wrong. Instead, he rises up and outwits his enemies and prevails. There could be guns and gambling casinos with cocktail waitresses. The computer stuff was out of date but he could fake that. The unfinished part was the third act. These days all third acts were little more than chases. He could use the chase from the Western. Just cut all that sage-brush crap and set it in Palo Alto.

Henry and Ark had taken to going for hikes in Runyon Canyon on Saturday mornings. It was Henry's nod to exercise. Ark had a guy who called himself a personal trainer who turned up at his Brentwood house two mornings a week to personally train him. Ark had urged Henry to join him for a session just to see what it was like but Henry declined. He had once tried exercising at a joint in West Hollywood called the Work House. It was after he and Madeleine had split, when for a few mis-guided months Henry had tried dating. He hadn't liked it any more than the exercise. The Work House was filled with astonishing specimens who made Henry feel inept and inadequate. He declared it the lumpy in pursuit of the exquisite. That was it for the Work House. The hikes with Ark were quite enough.

Runyon Canyon, which had been the site of one of Errol Flynn's houses, overlooked the city in a peculiarly Los Angeles way. The trail went up to Mulholland Drive, almost as high as the cloud line, which meant Henry and Ark shared their hike with circling hawks, coyotes, and the occasional rattlesnake. There were a few places along the twist-ing trail where you could look back at your fellow enthusiasts who were trudging up and down the hill below. At the same time the city itself was visible. It always amused Henry to work his way through the chaparral and at the same time look out at tall buildings, which from this height looked like architectural models. Ark always claimed that in the far dis-tance he could see the ocean. Henry couldn't see it but the thought of looking all the way to the sea seemed to fill Ark with optimism, so Henry just went along with it. The trails could be quite busy on Satur-day mornings, filled with little groups of people huffing along or strid-ing without apparent effort, all talking about scripts and deals with their dogs yapping, sniffing, and occasionally brawling. The hikes provided a good chance to talk about their projects. Ark agreed that *Hard Drive* was promising. "It needs to be packaged. Maybe a director," Ark said, mus-ing on the possibilities.

"Fine," Henry said, thinking, thanks for the news flash.

"Better with a star. Then we can control the director."

"I've yet to meet a director I can control," Henry said.

"Rennie Leaf's looking for something like this. He could play the shit out of that part."

"Little old for it, isn't he?" Henry said, thinking of Rennie, who had been about fifty-seven for several years now.

"You'll make the character older. A studio won't go for it, but I can raise money from European exhibitors on his name."

"The European exhibitors haven't heard about his age?"

"It can be done." Henry knew that when Ark ignored his wisecracks it meant he was seriously conjuring. "Rennie Leaf's ageless. He's a star," Ark said.

"Yeah, and fading fast."

"To you. Not to ticket buyers," Ark said, exasperated. "Humphrey Bogart was always just sort of an adult." Henry couldn't think of what Rennie Leaf, who was a mushy ex-playboy with a suntan, had to do with Bogart, but Ark seemed convinced and he was the one who had to sell it. "I'll set something up," Ark said. "We'll sit down with him."

After the hike, Henry went over to Rocket Video on La Brea, a store where the clerks wore gold nose rings but knew enough about movies to make Henry comfortable, and rented an armful of old Rennie Leaf movies. He invited Ark to join him but Ark said he didn't need to be convinced and besides he'd already seen them all. Henry put a bag of popcorn in the microwave and settled in for a Rennie Leaf festival. As he watched parts of romances, comedies, gangster stories, and a Western or two, he was sorry he had been so harsh. Rennie was wonderful on screen, always himself and yet always the character, which is a real star trick. His age was going to be a problem but there wasn't any doubt that the man had charm. It wasn't simply luck that he had lasted nearly forty years. Henry looked at the movies in the order they were made. He got caught up in watching Rennie age. As creases appeared in his face, his torso thickened and his belly slipped south. As he got older, his performances took on a certain grace, or maybe it was wisdom. It wasn't in the writing, though as Henry well knew you couldn't be sure about that. Henry skipped through the dull parts, sort of skimming the pictures, some of which he knew well. He thought about what he had been doing when he first saw these films. *Deep in Love,* Rennie's biggest hit, was made when Henry was in high school in New York and already mad for the movies. Years later, Henry had shown the movie to Madeleine, and when he saw that she liked it as much as he did, he knew he could marry her.

*   *   *

Ark picked up Henry at his apartment for the drive to La Plume. Henry knew that this chauffeur service was because Ark wanted to be sure that they were seated before Rennie arrived. Ark acknowledged as much and added that it was also so he could be sure that there was no trouble with the table and he could survey the dining room.

"What do you think you'll see?" Henry asked as Ark gave the keys to his giant black Mercedes to the valet.

"I don't know. That's why I want to have a look around. What if some guy who Rennie hates is sitting there? What if there's a guy at the next table I know will come over and try to hustle him?"

"So what do you do?"

"I'll see what the situation is and I'll deal with it."

As they entered the restaurant, Alphonse all but bowed to Ark and greeted Henry by name, a first since the Gaston incident. "Mr. Leaf hasn't arrived yet. The parking lot knows."

"Knows what?" Henry asked as they started the stroll through the dining room to Ark's big table in the back.

"Rennie'll come in through the kitchen."

"He doesn't use front doors?"

"Less fuss this way." Henry wondered why Rennie would go to a restaurant at all if he felt like that, but he didn't say anything. As they walked through the dining room, Ark nodded to everyone, spoke the occasional name, and even patted one guy on the back, but he didn't stop, he didn't even slow down, and yet he managed to be polite to each person he passed. They had picked up de Gaulle and a few other giant waiters Henry didn't recognize. Alphonse was leading the way, as if there was a danger they might get lost in the dining room where Ark had been having lunch three or four times a week for years. Henry realized anew that Ark was good at restaurants. Headwaiters always knew his name, or if they didn't, they seemed to know that he was a personage, to be catered to, fawned upon. Henry was always slightly uneasy in La Plume, never sure if he would remember names or if anyone would recognize him. He was always ready for some minor humiliation. Good at restaurants, Henry mused. They can put that on his tombstone. Good at restaurants and he produced pictures. As he was about to sit down, Henry wondered what might go on his own tombstone. "He wrote movies and messed up his marriage, which he couldn't stop brooding about, and he never called his father." Hmm. Too harsh. "He wrote movies and his wife was unfair and his father was impossible." Better. He sat down.

"Not there," Ark said, pointing instead to the adjacent chair.

"He has a favorite chair?" Henry asked.

"He'll want the backlight," Ark said, referring to Henry's first choice. Henry nodded and took another seat. Chair number one was beneath a high fan-wheel window and the afternoon sun spilled down, just behind it. "Stars always take the backlight," Ark said.

The table had a little gold plaque that said, "Reserved for Mr. Milt 'Ark' Arkadine." When they were finally seated, Alphonse started to remove the plaque. "Leave it," Ark said, and Henry knew that Ark wanted Rennie to see it. "You have somebody out there to bring him in?"

"All set, Ark."

"Speaks English? Knows his face?"

"Yes sir."

"His guy in the kitchen? That's all okay?"

"Under control," Alphonse said, removing himself. It was like a military operation, Henry thought. *The Invasion of La Plume.* Maybe he could trick up a quick treatment and sell it as a cable movie.

"Stay focused," Ark said, interrupting Henry's thoughts, knowing that his mind was drifting. "You've done this before. All you have to do is remember everything is about him. The only time you should disagree with him is if he says he's not the greatest actor of all time." Henry was laughing at Ark's counsel, which he knew to be true, when he felt a change come over the room. Heads moved slightly, the noise level diminished, and attention turned to the kitchen door where Rennie Leaf, attended by waiters, had appeared. He stood in the doorway for a moment letting everyone see him, allowing those with their backs to him to turn casually, alerted with a whisper from their better-placed companions. Rennie absorbed the adoration like a sponge, letting it flood into him. He was wearing blue jeans and running shoes and he had an old sweater tied around his neck and draped over a blue-and-white striped shirt so exquisitely tailored that Henry thought it deserved a round of applause all its own. Henry had thought of Rennie Leaf as a good actor but a bit of a lightweight. Now he could see there was something more mysterious there. You just couldn't look away from the guy. Even the lines in his face, at least the ones that hadn't been shot full of collagen, seemed firm and direct. The good looks were a given, a kind of genius, really. What Henry hadn't expected was that Rennie's face gave off a relaxed intelligence that seemed to say, Yeah, I'm a handsome rascal but that's not all I am. As Henry stared, he thought about Rennie's charmed life. He had played football at USC. He hadn't been big enough for the pros, but he was a college star. He'd been one in high school too. That marks a man, shapes him as surely as who his parents were. All through Rennie's adolescence, Henry imagined, girls must have thrown themselves at him and younger boys must have wanted to carry his gym bag or wash his car. Oh, me-oh, my-oh, Henry thought. Everything goes his way. After college, Rennie had lazed his way into the movies on a cloud of handsomeness and charm. There was something boyish about him, even though he had to be at least sixty. It was the grin, Henry supposed, all happiness and shy delight. It seemed enviable, maybe even admirable. Then why did Henry want to punch his lights out, kick him in the balls, and stomp on his neck? Henry knew why, of course. How could he not be jealous of this guy? Henry wondered if he should stand up in greeting but before he could make up his mind, Rennie loped over to the table and said, "Hey, guys. How you doing?"

"Rennie, Rennie. How great you're here," Ark said, rising and embracing his guest with a full *abbraccio,* while Henry was still trying to decide if he should stand up.

"Hi," Rennie answered, as he extricated himself from Ark's grip. He said it almost shyly, certainly diffidently. He reached across the table to Henry and offered his hand, saying, "I'm Rennie."

"Of course you are," Henry managed, making it sound as if Rennie had just answered a hard question. Rennie sat in the remaining chair. He moved it a bit, adjusting it to take full advantage of the light that floated down from the high window. Henry had to admit that the backlight kept Rennie's face a little mysterious. Rennie could see everyone else clearly, but he stayed shadowy and elusive. His wrinkles were masked and he was in command.

"Now how's Julie?" Ark asked. "I'll bet she's a great mother." Henry had met Rennie's wife years ago, when she was an agent. She had seemed like a lunatic to him. He had gone to her office once with his hat in his hand and found her babbling into the telephone with white powder dribbling from her nose. Now, as the wife of a star and the mother of two, she was something of a social figure, photographed at charity events and openings.

"Julie's great, the kids are great. I turn out to be pretty good at marriage. She makes all the decisions," Rennie said with a wry smile. "So? You guys order?"

"Not yet," Ark said, as Alphonse, de Gaulle, and a few deputies appeared with two menus. One went to Ark and the other to Henry, and at that moment Henry understood Ark's earlier question to Alphonse about the guy in the kitchen. Rennie would be eating, but he had brought his own chef. Henry decided he had better follow Ark's lead in ordering lest he offend Rennie's sensibilities.

"Cobb salad," Ark said.

"Same here," Henry said. Rennie didn't look disapproving so Henry figured he was in the clear at least as far as the food was concerned.

"So you in town for a while, Rennie?" Ark asked.

"Yeah. We're here," Rennie said and turned to Henry. "Have you ever been to India?"

"I was there once, a few years ago. Why do you ask?"

"Julie and I are getting into it. Hinduism. I think you have an old soul."

"Thanks, I hope."

"It's a compliment. I think you have *darshan*."

"I don't know what that is, Rennie."

"It's Hindu or Sanskrit or one of those. I'm trying to develop it. Julie has it. I don't know about the kids yet. It means meeting God, so you can see into the divine core of things. It's a gift."

"Sounds useful," Henry said.

"You're a star," Ark said. "Can Henry see into you?"

"I don't know. Can you, Henry?"

"Well, I've tried to look at your performances as deeply as I can, thinking about you playing in this picture. I felt a connection to your characters. Is that what you mean?"

"Yeah. It is. Wow. Great."

Henry was feeling light-headed from how well all this was going. He was still wary, but he could see that Ark was happy. He wondered if maybe he should shoot one of those little Indian prayer-bows over to Rennie. Before he could decide, the parade of waiters were back with two Cobb salads and a plate of mystery food for Rennie. "I'm on this diet," Rennie said. "Everything I'm going to eat for the rest of my life is already planned. This is Meyer lemons, tofu, peppers, onions, mushrooms, and this green stuff," he said, poking a fork at the concoction. It didn't look any worse than a Cobb salad. Henry was longing to ask if he really had his own chef in La Plume's kitchen, but he resisted, hoping to keep up the aura of *darshan* that apparently surrounded him. "You want to try it?" Rennie asked. Henry and Ark passed on that a little too quickly, which made Rennie smile. "We make it for the dogs too," he said. "Julie's got them on the same diet."

"Your dogs are vegetarian?" Henry asked, trying to keep astonishment out of his voice.

"Sure. I think it makes them gentler." Rennie seemed to be eyeing the bread and olive oil. "Talking about this," Rennie said, "it reminds me of Lakshmi Devi." Henry knew of Lakshmi Devi, once one of the world's great beauties. She was a little old now and out of the public eye, though for years she was one of the few Indian actresses to have an international audience. "She was the most gorgeous thing anybody ever saw. I ever tell you how I met her?"

"How was that?" Ark asked.

"I called her up. Told her how much I admired her, which I did. She said, 'Come on over.' I said, 'Okay.' She said, 'Right now.' It was fine with me but I was here. She was in Bombay."

"Did you know her? Before you called?" Ark asked, probably already knowing the answer. For all Henry knew, Ark had heard this tale many times. Henry hadn't heard it and he was interested.

"No. She knew who I was. I called anybody in those days. She said, 'Right now or forget it.' I went to the airport and went over there. Why not? We got together, went down to Goa, and stayed in some house she had with a palm-tree roof that had monkeys living in it. She was really hot. I called her Vindaloo."

"Sex and monkeys on the roof," Henry repeated. "Sounds like Hollywood."

Rennie laughed at that and said, "We didn't come up for air for a week. I think she gave me the clap."

"Do you still see her?" Henry asked.

"I get a Christmas card from her. It's about saving the whales. She's Hindu. Or she was. Julie gets a kick out of it."

Ark laughed, not because the remark was particularly funny, but as a way to punctuate that part of the conversation, to tie it off and get on to the business at hand. Henry admired the skill involved. Ark simply recounted the plot of *Hard Drive* as if he was making it up on the spot. The main character was called Dutch, though Ark called him Rennie, conflating the actor and the character. Rennie began to nod happily. Yes, he seemed to be saying, I've read that script, or at least someone has told me the story and I recognize it.

"You would be sensational," Ark said. "Henry must have had you in mind when he wrote it."

"That right?" Rennie asked.

"It's easy to have you in mind when I'm doing any leading character. You fit most of them. Makes it simple." Oh, me-oh, my-oh, Henry thought. Where did I get that crap?

"Yeah. I see what you mean," Rennie said. Henry thought he had laid it on a little thick, and perhaps he had, because doubts began to surface. "Can you make the guy a little older but, you know, keep him younger?"

"Of course he can," Ark said before Henry could ask what the hell that meant. "The public sees you in what you do. Young. You bring young to a script. We'll tweak it."

Rennie nodded, seeing the wisdom in that. Henry knew to keep his mouth shut and to trust Ark. Henry could see that Rennie gave the impression of being a careful listener. Listening and reacting are fundamental to a screen performance. Rennie would nod thoughtfully and agree with everything, then a moment later say something that suggested he hadn't heard a thing. It wasn't that he was stupid, Henry knew better than that. It was that he was a public man and had been one for all his adult life. So many people jabbered at him all the time that no matter how sincere he appeared, he listened only to himself. Henry was about to say something when the opening notes of Beethoven's Fifth Symphony issued from one of Rennie's pockets. Henry knew it was a cell phone, but what wasn't clear was just where the damn thing was. The lines of Rennie's shirt and trousers suggested that, like the Queen of England, Rennie carried nothing with him but his fame. "It's Julie," he said, as if his wife was somewhere on his person along with an orchestra. He took the smallest, slimmest cell phone that Henry had ever seen from his shirt pocket, flipped it open, and said, "Hi, babe. I'm with Ark and Henry Wearie." Henry was astonished that Rennie knew his name. It irritated him that he found it flattering. "They've got a great story. We're talking about it." Ark waved in the general direction of the cell phone until Rennie sent Ark's greetings to his wife and then put the device back in his pocket. It wouldn't have surprised Henry if Rennie had swallowed it. Then the Beethoven started again. This time Rennie ignored it, explaining, "She's trying to learn how to do messages. She's got this guy teaching her, the cell phone tutor. Big pain if you ask me."

"She has a cell phone tutor?" Henry asked. Ark shot him a look that said, Don't get cute.

"The electronics coach only works in the house. TVs. Computers. So this guy does the cell phones and some other outdoor stuff."

"Okay," Ark said, knowing they had lost the thread, determined to get back on track. "I think the key to the story is making Rennie not just a little older, which we agree would be nice but he doesn't really need, but giving him a job that's appropriate. In Henry's script, which we all agree is great—"

"Great. Absolutely great," Rennie said. Henry wondered if he should throw in a great or two just to show he was a team player, but he let it go.

"Great script," Ark said again. "If Rennie was bigger than a computer guy it would make more sense. I see Rennie as higher up the ladder."

"Sure," Henry said. "He's the guy running the company. The CEO." Henry couldn't remember what CEO stood for. It meant the boss, but what did the initials stand for? Commander? Excellency? What about the *O*?

"See that?" Ark said, when he realized Henry's mind had wandered again. "Great rewrite. Sometimes a simple change can make an enormous difference. Henry's not afraid to be minimal. Whole thing makes more sense now. He starts to gamble, there's more to lose."

"I was wondering about the gambling," Rennie said. "What is it, exactly? Craps? Blackjack?"

"Roulette and craps at the casinos and the sports book when you're in your office." Henry knew the answer right off because it was in the script.

"Does it have to be gambling?" Rennie asked.

"Well, if he's going to get in trouble . . ." Henry said, dribbling off, knowing what was coming.

"It's not very sympathetic."

"True," Ark said.

"What if I lose control of the company because I give all the money to charity? What with the kids, I'm really into that kind of thing."

"That's not bad at all. Good start. Now Henry's going to take all this back to his magic desk and come up with a few great answers using your input," Ark said, bringing the lunch to a close.

Rennie smiled, shook Henry's hand, and again said what a great script it was. As he turned to go back to the kitchen, four guys who had been waiting for this moment jumped up and came over to him, hustling one scheme or another. Henry watched it knowing that the rule they were following was that they wouldn't interrupt as long as Rennie was at Ark's table. A studio head could interrupt, but would be more likely simply to wave from across the room. A bigger star than Rennie might well come to the table, because stars liked to pretend they were above these customs. Once Rennie stood up he was in play and the hustlers pounced. Henry thought of them as parakeets, pecking madly at grain. As they were swarming around Rennie, Ark looked at Henry and could see that he was worried. "Don't worry about it," he said. "Say yes to everything and keep moving ahead. We can always dump him later."

* * *

Henry spent a week working on *Hard Drive*. He dropped the gambling and the mob. He made Rennie's character older, but not too much older. He changed the guy's name from Dutch to a generic Jim, because Ark thought that Dutch might be confused with Ronald Reagan. Jim worked at several vaguely liberal causes when he wasn't running his computer company. One of his employees had embezzled company funds and blamed it on Jim. *Hard Drive* became a story about a man unjustly accused who fights to restore his good name. Henry realized that in the strange way of scripts, it could also be read as the story of his own professional dilemma. Screenwriters always get blamed for the transgressions of others and always have to battle for credit for what they've done. Ark didn't know if Rennie would go for it, but he pointed out that the more pages he reads, the more involved he'll be and the more likely to say that they can use his name as a part of the package, and that means the money will start flowing. "More pages" rang in Henry's head. He'd been around these stunts long enough to know that when an actor, and certainly a star, began suggesting rewrites, there was no end to it. Henry didn't feel he could bail out at this point, but in his mind he began thinking about what diplomats call an exit strategy.

Rennie agreed to meet with Ark and Henry to talk about the new pages but he canceled the meeting twice and then kept changing the time. After several days of maneuvering, Henry and Ark went to Rennie's office to discuss the script. Rennie's digs were in an old stucco office building in Hollywood that was in an architectural style Henry always called High Chandler. There were bug-eyed gargoyles with lolling tongues in front and murky staircases within. It wasn't a sign of a top star, who would be at a film studio. Henry knew not to ask about such matters, and he also knew that if he did, Rennie would say something about not wanting to be too close to management, as if not having a studio production deal was a smart and independent move.

Rennie's office had been done up like a library in an English country house in an MGM picture of the 1930s. There were paneled walls, dark bookshelves filled with a mixture of art books and scripts, and no desk. They sat in brown leather club chairs. A young woman in tight jeans and a bare midriff that featured a jewel in her naval served tea. She looked more Melrose Avenue than Metro in the thirties. She was called Blaze, and the casual way she touched Rennie's shoulder as she poured the tea made Henry wonder about the exact nature of Rennie's blissful marriage. The tabloids had all been blaring, "Rennie: A Dad at Plus Sixty" or "Rennie: Happy at Last." Maybe for Rennie, marriage and a family meant compromise and sacrifice on the order of cutting down on the number of mistresses he kept on the payroll.

"The pages are great," Rennie began. "We're really rolling." A bad sign, Henry thought.

"I agree," Ark said. "Henry's got a grip on this. It's his. He knows it. And he knows you." They're both vamping, Henry thought. Ark's looking for a moment to get this guy to commit so he can go out and get money. Rennie's going to jerk me around some more.

"I love the stuff about the charities." Rennie went silent for a moment, looking through the script. That's it for the good news, Henry thought. Here comes the reality check. "It gave me some ideas," Rennie said.

"What's that?" Ark asked. Henry thought he sensed a little fear in Ark.

"Julie and I are taking these Kabbalah lessons."

"You?" Ark asked.

"Why not? Julie's Jewish. She was never much into it but now with the kids, she wants to learn it. There's one course called the Karma of Kabbalah."

"Perfect for you, I would think," Henry said.

"Are you raising them Jewish?" Ark asked.

"I don't know yet. Kids make you think about that stuff. Anyway, the Kabbalah teacher is this rabbi. He comes to the house. It's interesting. So I—I mean in the movie—I don't have any faith. It's not in there. Why can't I have religious beliefs?"

"You want me to add Kabbalah to the script?" Henry asked, edging toward sarcasm.

"I think what Rennie is saying is that the issue of faith should be raised—not necessarily the Jewish faith. Am I right?"

"That's it," Rennie said. "Belief. It could be Jewish or one of the other ones."

"You're not reading Hindu stuff anymore?" Henry asked.

"Mostly Kabbalah. Awaken the mystic within. The inner journey. Maybe you guys could come up to the house when the rabbi's there. You might learn something."

"That'd be great, Rennie," Ark said. Henry could all but smell the fear. That's all Ark needs—to start spending his evenings with some mystical rabbi.

"Your mentioning the Indian stuff is a good idea. What if I'm a professor of religion? An expert in all the faiths. When I'm accused of stealing the money, my faith is shaken. So I have to solve the crime and regain my faith. It's my spiritual journey."

"Not bad," Ark said.

"It might play," Henry said.

"Just a thought," Rennie said, hearing Henry's less than enthusiastic endorsement. Then he smiled his famous smile. Whenever he was through with one topic and ready to move on, he brought out that grin. It was like a gavel and Rennie was the judge. There was no appeal. "I knew Carolyn Fortner," Rennie said.

"Who?" Ark asked.

"The author. She wrote books about comparative religion. She was a Buddhist when I met her. We were in Tahiti together for a while. I couldn't stay away from her."

"Did you just call her up one day?" Henry asked with a smile.

"It was different with her. She was a consultant on a picture. We got together over that. She knew something about everything. I taught her some tricks." Henry knew that the meeting was over, which was fine with him because he didn't want to hear the details of Rennie's romance with Carolyn Fortner, who had been one of his heroes when he was a student.

As Henry and Ark were leaving Rennie's office, Henry said, "He's never going to do this script."

"You can't know that. This is just his way. He'll turn it around a few times and then come back to the way it was. That's how he is."

"He's jerking us around."

"Stars are like dogs around a script. He has to piss on it for a while to mark his territory. Just humor him. When he commits, we're two phone calls from the money."

"I don't think so. I think I just want to call this one a day."

"Jesus, Henry. If you withdraw the script, it'll be like firing him."

"So? Actors get fired all the time."

"Yeah, but not by writers."

"I own this thing free and clear. If he wants to buy it from me or option it and hire another writer, I'll consider it, but I don't want to hear about his girlfriends and his religions and his tutors or his addled script ideas." Henry knew that there was a time when he would have gone along with it. After all, that's what screenwriters did—cater to stars, change everything all the time, and all the while say things like, Wow! What a brilliant idea. No more. Maybe Henry was too old, or maybe the fact that he had a measure of his old heat back made him resistant. He knew that the heat was a result of Ark's interest in him and that Rennie would be angry at Ark, but Henry didn't care. To Ark's chagrin, Henry withdrew the script.

The letter arrived a week later. It was from Rennie's lawyer, Marilyn Woolf, aka the Wolf Woman of Century City. When Henry had waded through the goofy language of the law, the letter said that Rennie Leaf would sue Henry Wearie for stealing his material if he tried to do anything with *Hard Drive,* a script that Rennie Leaf had contributed to in a significant way. Henry called Ark and asked, "Why does he want my pathetic script? All he ever did was take it apart."

"He doesn't want your script," Ark said. "That's not what this is about."

"If he thinks suing me is going to make him some money, he's positively deluded. I don't have that kind of money."

"He doesn't want your money."

"Then what does he want?"

"You've insulted him. You've said, in effect, that his ideas are worthless. That you don't need him."

"He's right about that."

"He wants to scare you and he wants to make sure you can't take this script somewhere else. He's put a cloud over it. And he's going to make you spend some money on a lawyer."

"Great."

"The Writers Guild will handle this. Call the legal department. Explain it all. They'll answer the letter for you. They've seen this stuff before."

"Are you pissed off?"

"Why? Because a star is acting like a star? No. I'll tell you, though, a writer isn't acting like a writer."

"I like the script. We should be able to go somewhere else with it."

"Get the Guild lawyer to move on it and copy me on the letter. I'll sniff around. Rennie's pissed off and Marilyn Woolf's just blowing smoke."

"Wolf J. Flywheel, attorney at law," Henry said.

Ark missed the reference but recognized the sarcasm. "Take this seriously," he said.

"I thought you said they were blowing smoke."

"Yeah, but they're blowing it at you. You can't leave it to luck or chance, which is what you always do. I'll help you."

When Henry put the phone down he had the unsettling sensation that Ark might not be the best person to ask for advice here. It was in Ark's nature to cover all bases all the time. He could well be counseling Rennie as well. He had better be careful. The Guild was helpful because as Ark had said, they'd seen this problem before. The legal department had an appropriate letter and they sent it to Marilyn Woolf, assuring Henry that was usually enough. But it wasn't. Another letter arrived with yet new threats and new accusations. Henry was worried that this was too complicated for the Guild's overworked legal department and he would indeed have to hire some high-priced bandit of his own. Henry had been comfortable with his own lawyer, the late Tom Lewin. They had been pals, hanging out together, a couple of night crawlers of the

Hollywood saloons. They were easy together—Tom with his ponytail going gray and Henry in his tailored jackets—until Tom met a wonderful girl and got married. His life looked enviable to Henry and then, still in his forties and working late, Tom Lewin suffered a heart attack and died at his desk. Even now, several years later, it was too painful for Henry even to think about hiring another lawyer. Oh, me-oh, my-oh. Another fine mess, as Ollie used to say. Henry brooded, trying to reason his way out of his dilemma. He was stuck until he tried thinking of the situation as a script problem. How would a central character deal with this? Hmm.

Henry's friend Elsa Mallory was a reporter in the Calendar section of the *Los Angeles Times*. Elsa was really more Madeleine's friend, but she called Henry occasionally to ask his opinion about a story she was working on. Henry was glad to help, because Elsa told him what Madeleine was doing, which meant who she was dating, without his having to ask. Whatever information Henry gave Elsa was a well-turned guess. In the articles, she usually referred to Henry as "a Hollywood insider." Ha! Elsa Mallory owed him a favor beyond the reports of Madeleine's romantic life, and this was collection day. Actually, Elsa wasn't a bad reporter. She'd spent a year in film school at USC so at least she had looked at movies. As to what was going on in the business at any given minute, like most everyone at Calendar or anywhere else, Elsa didn't have a clue. Neither did Henry, of course, and Elsa probably sensed that, but Henry was the closest thing Elsa knew to an insider who could deliver a breezy quote on the spot. Henry told her the saga of *Hard Drive,* stressing that although Rennie was a wonderful actor he was too old for the part and they had worked hard to make the character a little older so that Rennie, who was older, could play it. Henry was afraid that that he'd laid it on too thick and Elsa might laugh. She didn't.

An article headlined "Rennie Leaf Sues Writer in Ageism Dispute" appeared a few days later. Elsa didn't use "old" as many times as Henry had said it, but it was in the article along with references to Rennie's age being hard to pin down. Elsa had called Rennie to give him a chance to respond, but Rennie had turned the problem over to his publicity agent who was better at getting things into the papers than keeping them out. Elsa ran an earnest quote from the press flack about the problems of ageism in Hollywood. For Henry it was like a bonus. He knew that the story was a two-day wonder and nobody would get it quite right, but they would forever link Rennie Leaf's name to "age" and "older." Henry knew that when Rennie had refused to talk to Elsa, he had lost the battle. Henry had assumed that a star would patronize him. That was typical of what screenwriters endured and for which they often received exquisite sums of money. Elsa Mallory was a different sort of writer. She wrote for a famous newspaper. Instead of money, she expected a certain deference. Rennie didn't give Elsa her portion of respect and that irritated her. After the article appeared, which Henry in his triumph was calling "Too Old Blues," the letters from Marilyn Woolf stopped.

To celebrate Henry's maneuver and his extricating himself from Rennie Leaf, Ark took him to lunch at La Plume. This time Ark didn't object when Alphonse removed the gold plaque and they didn't worry about the food. Henry had a taste for the bangers and mash that La Plume kept on the menu for its English customers who didn't pay much attention to Los Angeles food fashions. Ark ordered pork chops and they were happy to have a bottle of Napa cabernet. "I thought you'd go with Rennie on this," Henry said after the wine had relaxed him a bit.

"Why?" Ark asked. "He's washed up. Too old."

"I think I read something about that in the paper."

"You won."

"How do I know that? He didn't exactly make a concession speech."

"You won't hear another word about it. Don't do anything. Just enjoy it."

"Should we send the script to somebody else?"

"As long as we don't use any of that crap Rennie came up with, why not?"

"So who?"

"I had an idea. What about making him a woman?" Henry's face dropped and Ark started laughing. "Got you there, didn't I? When are you going to learn? Scripts open the door to everything."

"I've heard that before but usually from writers."

"I'd rather have your next two starts than Rennie Leaf's next two."

"Then why do I always get fired by guys like you and Rennie?"

"Did you hear me? 'Starts.' That's what a script does. Gets things going. Then you get stars and directors. They want to think they did it. That's why you get the big checks."

"Not for the script, is it?"

"That's part of it. Don't forget, you were the guy who was there when the pages were blank."

"Yeah," Henry said. "The trouble starts when there's writing on the pages."

Ark laughed at that and pretty soon Henry was laughing too. Oh, me-oh, my-oh. The ball goes up and it goes down. Occasionally it even bounced his way. When Henry was feeling mellow and even a little optimistic, he began to muse on his victory over Rennie Leaf, wondering if it was a victory at all. Ark, who understood him better than Henry realized, said, "You're starting to doubt it all, aren't you?"

"Doubt what?" Henry answered, even though he knew full well what Ark meant.

"Do yourself a favor. Enjoy it."

Ark was right, of course, and Henry stopped pretending that the whole thing had to mean something and decided he would take Ark's advice. Pretty soon they were laughing again and Henry's mood lifted. Ark declared Henry a master of public relations and called for another bottle of the cabernet.

4

You Know What I Mean

*H*enry *maneuvered* through the traffic on Fairfax making his way to the Farmers Market. He had been coming to the Market in the morning for almost as long as he had been in Hollywood. The place had grown on him and he had grown with it. He'd have coffee with his friends, gossip a bit, and look at the trades. The ritual of it was a bit of stability in an uncertain life. In the way of the media world, the table, as Henry called it, had become almost famous. New Yorkers and Europeans had heard about the morning gathering and when they were in town they angled for invitations. Documentary crews filming Hollywood often wanted to come by and see what one English twit had called "Working Holly-wood." Ha! Henry said the table's career was in better shape than his own. In recent mornings Henry had been distracted by more than the traffic. The seekers of wisdom and truth who ran the Market were tearing down part of it and putting up a mall. Just what Los Angeles needed, another mall.

Henry had trouble finding a parking space because yellow construc-tion behemoths were blocking everything. Henry knew that change was inevitable and maybe not so bad, but the idea that the place would be altered and not improved was upsetting. The Market was one of the few places where Henry felt comfortable. It was just a collection of produce and souvenir stands and food stalls and a lot of old tables and folding metal chairs. There were patches of tin and wood roof, but for the most part the Market was open to the sun and the rain. Over the years, the place had grown in an ad hoc way. The people who owned the various businesses were the ones who ran them, often helped by their kids. Henry thought of the Market as an *ur*-mall. For Henry, this mall, this new indignity, would be a place without a memory. It would have fancy commercial associations but there would be no sense of the lived past. He dubbed it the false Luxuria.

Henry found a parking space near the clock tower, which now had scaffolding around it as if it were in quarantine. The chimes, which in their certainty always gave him a measure of comfort, were ringing half past eight. Henry sat in his recently repainted Jaguar for a few minutes listening to the echo. He was unable to get out and yet didn't want to stay. Finally, with a theatrical sigh, though there was no one to hear it, he strolled in, greeting the morning regulars. He stopped at the Coffee Corner, the stall he favored, and ordered an espresso. The young woman behind the counter was new and she gave Henry a white plastic spoon, a device he found primitive. Once, the market used metal spoons but people kept stealing them. Everyone knew it was the old people from the Park LaBrea apartments, those towers and townhouses of enlightened geezerhood, who were taking them. The thieves were old and often confused so instead of making accusations, the Market switched to plastic. As a service to Henry, the Coffee Corner kept one of the old metal spoons on hand for him. Nobody had told this woman, who didn't see a significant distinction between metal and plastic. Henry kept his temper in check. He didn't want to start the day with a squabble. He took his coffee, spoonless. Before he was seated, a clerk from the doughnut stand who had seen the problem delivered a proper spoon, saying only, "She's new." It amused Henry that his flatware preferences were known at the doughnut stand, which he rarely patronized.

Henry joined Leo Verakos, a screenwriter who had been kicking around town as long as Henry had. Leo was a Southerner who regularly left town to decompress at a farm he owned in North Carolina. He was a big, fleshy man, well over six feet tall, who had lived in Paris and sometimes wore a beret. Henry often wondered how many years an American had to live in France before he looked comfortable in one of those silly hats. Leo had been single for years and then he married the lovely Liv, who was Swedish and twenty years his junior. Now they had two small children. The remarkable thing about it was how much more comfortable Leo seemed since his marriage. It made Henry wonder what would happen if he too were to join regularly conducted middle-class life. Leo's career hadn't improved all that much but neither had it suffered, and he seemed to take great pleasure in the children. Leo was asking Henry's opinion about a script idea. "A Korean girl about twenty. Carrying Korean currency—whatever it's called—a lot of it. She's supposed to launder it into dollars in L.A. She hooks up with a local boy, white kid. They steal the dough. It's from the Korean mob or the Russian mob or whatever the hell mob is around, and they wind up on the run through all the ethnic neighborhoods. What do you think?"

"Sounds like a movie to me," Henry said.

"Yeah, but should I spec it?" Leo's Southern accent was in evidence, which usually meant he was thinking really hard about something.

"If you get a couple of young television stars, maybe it could happen."

"Another firm opinion from Henry Wearie," Leo said. Henry knew it was true. Every movie idea sounded plausible to him and none of them ever seemed like they would happen. Before Henry could think of something a little more definite, Irwin Lasky and Wally Flagg sat down with their coffee, talking about the Dodgers. One of Henry's problems with modern life was that he didn't much care about professional sports. He got a visceral kick out of pro basketball and he tried to stay aware of things like the World Series, but the truth of it was that he couldn't see getting all that worked up and developing what seemed like statistical fanaticism over somebody else's commercial venture.

Irwin looked up at a few of the construction workers buying coffee. They were big, butch-looking guys in yellow hard hats. Irwin shouted, "Hello, Village People!" When there was no response, he warbled, "Why—Emm—Cee—A." Irwin was older than Henry, a director who had once had a significant career making pictures that were good and were often hits. He was a Brooklyn boy, Brownsville bred, though after years of celebrity and world travel, the sounds of his old neighborhood were gone. Irwin was built along the lines of one of Picasso's bulls. Sometimes when Wally wanted his attention, he called out, "Toro! Toro!" which gave way to "Torah! Torah!" Henry sometimes called Irwin the Aging Bull. For a time, a generation ago, when adults went to the movies, they went to see Irwin Lasky's pictures because they were comedies and dramas about adult life. That was a while ago for Irwin, and for everyone else at the table, too. Now it seemed a picture had a better chance of being a hit if it was stupid. The audience had turned into teenagers who wanted to see other teenagers having sex, outwitting their parents, and running from explosions. The situation put Henry in mind of the Market being given over to a mall. You could see what it once was and you knew it was only going to get worse. Irwin still had the respect of people in the business, but the young audience didn't know him and didn't have much interest in the sort of pictures he was good at. He spent a lot of time getting awards or being a judge at film festivals, but he couldn't ever seem to arrange financing for his own pictures. For all that, his lunatic humor was intact and he could be counted on to break into imitations of the people around him or to make surreal wisecracks when the mood was upon him. One morning *The New York Times* ran a story about the last two Jews in Kabul explaining that they'd managed to avoid the Russians, the Taliban, and the Americans. They ran adjacent synagogues even if there was no one to attend either of them. They hated each other. Well, it sounded like the setup for a Jewish joke, and Irwin declared he was going to make a movie of it to be called *Two Jews in Kabul*. He couldn't stop saying it. Then, for reasons known only to Irwin, the story changed into a restaurant in Kabul with the synagogues in the background. He'd snap his palm open as if it were a cell phone and say, "Yall-oo. Two Jews. Table for four at eight o'clock? Yeah. We can take you. Of course not by the window. I have a nice table in the bunker. You staying for services? Never mind. I need a home phone and credit card. Other line. Wait a minute. Yall-oo. Two Jews. What? You? Don't call me here! A dog is better than you. I spit on you. Pa-tooie!" He'd go on like that for a bit. Maybe changing it back to the synagogues for a while. It was as if he were trying out the jokes, sort of road testing the story. When invention faltered, Irwin might put a paper napkin over his face and stick his tongue through it. There was something about the desperate way Irwin's tongue broke through with bits of paper sticking to it that Henry always found funny. It was the sheer show-business lunacy of it. Irwin was a *tummler* and making jokes kept him going.

Wally was a painter and a descendant of the illustrator James Montgomery Flagg. Wally occasionally turned up in an Uncle Sam outfit as a sort of homage to his ancestor. He was about Irwin's age. Together they represented the table's wisdom of age, or as Wally put it, the depredations of mange. Wally usually had two or three pairs of eyeglasses strung around his neck, and he might show up in a straw hat claiming to be a scarecrow or possibly a plantation overseer. Wally had a loose-limbed gait that sometimes made him look a little tipsy. He was connected to the movie business because people in Hollywood collected his work, which at first glance seemed accessible—filled with strange trolls with large penises, biblical prophets with wary eyes, and commissioned portraits that always flattered just enough. Like the man himself, the pictures appeared lighthearted, but beneath the wit and the drollery there was an elusive darkness that was anything but amiable. Henry had been looking at Wally's pictures for some time before he saw the darkness and now he saw it almost to the exclusion of all else. Well, Wally wasn't dark this morning. He had a plan. He often had plans but you had to be careful— Wally wasn't given to exactitude. He got arrangements generally right though there were usually loose details that fell off the table. In a few days it would be what Irwin called Erev Chinese Rosh Hashana, which translated from the Irwin meant Chinese New Year's Eve, Wally's favorite holiday. He loved the paper dragons and the firecrackers in the parade. "We'll go to Monterey Park. Watch the action, ogle the Chinese dames, have dinner," he said. His enthusiasm was enough to sweep up the others. Leo would bring the kids, Irwin would bring his grandchildren, and because he had little else to bring, Henry said he would provide a running commentary.

Over the next few days, when the dust of enthusiasm had settled, Leo and Irwin had dropped out, which was what usually happened with plans of this sort. Henry was still up for the adventure and Wally had invited his friend Gloria Warren, who was a costume designer. Gloria was a girl from Louisville who had arrived in Hollywood with a husband and two kids and a passion for Italian cooking and American antiques. When Henry first knew her, during his marriage, Gloria wore tennis outfits and headbands. Her kids were now grown, the husband long gone, and the housewife routine abandoned. Gloria had grown fleshier since the days when she and Henry and later Madeleine used to hang around the director Rolf Shilling's tennis court. Gloria had become a deeply bohemian individual. Madeleine had introduced Gloria to Wally and over the years they had gone out together. It always made Henry a little jealous. Henry still had a crush on Gloria. He called her a recovering Southern belle. Gloria had decorated Henry's apartments. She never complained when, in his restlessness, Henry moved again and again. She always saw to it that there was comfortable furniture, rugs on the floor, and dishes in the kitchen. For this current West Hollywood joint, she had provided a brown Southwestern look with Navajo rugs and large clay pots and a cactus. There had been some loose talk of a steer's skull, but Henry said no to that. He called the place the hogan.

Gloria had invited one of the costume assistants from her workshop to join them. He was called Bo and apparently had an interest in Asian clothing. Gloria, like many women who worked around costumes, had become something of a fag hag. Wally was oblivious to such matters and Henry, who assumed Bo was another of Gloria's gay friends, didn't care either way. On the day of the parade, which was a Friday, Henry was waiting in his apartment for what he had taken to calling the Expeditionary Force. Wally and Gloria were similar in matters of arrangements, so there really was no telling if either of them would show. All three were meant to arrive at

Henry's apartment by three o'clock so they would be sure to see the parade. Dinner was to be at a fish restaurant that Henry favored. The actual name was in Mandarin and no Anglo knew what it was. The one sign in English, which was surely meant to advertise the house specialty, had been rendered as See Food. You couldn't make reservations unless you did it in Chinese. They would watch the parade and then take their chances.

By five o'clock when no one had arrived Henry knew that the parade was all but over and he didn't think there was much profit in hurrying to Monterey Park, which in good circumstances was forty-five minutes of freeway traffic away and during rush hour on Friday, pretty near hopeless. There was no hurrying Wally and Gloria anyway. They arrived at six. Gloria was in a red silk caftan with several necklaces made of metals Henry couldn't identify. In the midst of the clattering jewelry, perhaps as a nod to the young matron she once was, Gloria wore a string of pearls. She had on a tight black turban. She looked like a fleshy version of a Martha Graham dancer. She might be outrageously late without apology, but her presence always made Henry happy. If he hadn't met her when he was married, if Madeleine hadn't introduced her to Wally, well, who knows? Wally followed in her wake, wearing baggy white trousers with wide black stripes and a leather vest. As Henry was greeting them, Gloria said, "Hush," in her soft Louisville voice, and then pushed open Henry's apartment door. Henry thought she was about to leave. She'd done stranger things, though this time she was creating a drama. The lights hadn't changed, but something about the way Gloria waved her hand in a little flourish, a sort of salaam, seemed to create a spotlight or maybe it was a signal, because a delicate Asian woman with long dark hair and a shy smile entered. She was dressed in what Gloria later identified as a cheongsam—a tight, high-collared dress with a slit all the way up one side. The dress was lavender and it wrapped around and closed with little silk knots that Gloria called frogs. She wore earrings that hung like chandeliers and made a musical sound when she tottered in on her spike-heeled shoes. She was beautiful and though Henry didn't know much about cheongsams, he could see that any woman wearing one had better be perfectly formed because the thing looked painted on.

"This is Bo," Gloria said with pride of authorship in her voice. Bo dipped her head in a deferential bow. Gloria gave Bo's dress a tug. Oh, me-oh, my-oh, Henry thought, realizing that this was the costume assistant from Gloria's workshop.

"I'm Suzie," Bo said in a whispery voice that threatened to turn husky.

"Of course you are, dear," Gloria said. "Suzie Wong herself."

"Suzie's got Chinese New Year and Halloween a little confused," Wally said. Once Henry realized the situation, it became obvious. On second glance, this was a man, but one with smooth legs in white pantyhose, and a face with enough makeup and powder to cover the line of a beard. Her eyebrows were painted arches in a style that Gloria said was an homage to the Wongs, Suzie and Anna May. Her eyes had been made to appear slightly slanted, enough to make the point but not enough to insult any real Asians. The effect was not unattractive, but despite Gloria's handiwork and Bo's commitment to the enterprise, neither male nor female. There was certainly a bustline and a curved backside, though there didn't appear to be any sort of male bulge. It was a triumph of padding. She certainly brought to mind the prostitute who had bewitched William Holden in the old movie.

"Isn't she sublime?" Gloria asked, as she adjusted Suzie's bust.

"They'll just eat her up in Monterey Park. Or something," Wally said.

"We really ought to get going," Henry said, casting himself as the steady one in this assembly.

"Can we still go to Tryst first? You said," Bo whined. Henry realized that her breathy whisper was a mix of Marilyn Monroe and Jackie Kennedy, with a touch of a Chinese accent that reminded Henry of Charlie Chan movies.

"Of course we can, darling," Gloria said.

"Parade's probably over anyway," Henry said.

With Gloria and Bo in the backseat of the Jaguar, Henry drove the few blocks to the neon glare of Friday night on Santa Monica Boulevard in

Boys Town. They escorted her through the strolling romantics out for a night's adventure and into the throbbing light of Tryst, where metallic music was playing to the point of inducing pain. Sweaty men were dancing in a frantic style that put Henry in mind of aerobics. As Bo looked around, waiting for people to notice, he said, "Only call me Suzie. Bo isn't here." Gloria just purred at him, which Henry took to mean I'll agree with anything because this is all so wonderfully amusing to me if not to anyone else. Gloria knew her way around Tryst. For all Henry knew she came here all the time. Maybe it was just that gay guys understood her authority. Gloria was a priestess of design and design is the gay church. The waters seemed to part, or at least a whole crew of muscular men got out of her way. Henry's eyes blurred as he tried to take in all the well-groomed and well-formed men. Most of them were quite tall. Maybe, he thought, this is where the La Plume waiters hang out when they're off duty. Gloria arranged three bar stools around Suzie, who stood glowing in the attention. The dancing stopped as the denizens of Tryst fluttered around, admiring Suzie and the perfection of the job. Many of them knew that this was Suzie Wong, a character who seemed to live for them. Henry, like everyone else, knew gay guys were drawn to operatic personalities like Judy Garland or Joan Crawford. Suzie Wong was fictional, a hot-tempered prostitute next door if you happened to live in Hong Kong in the fifties. That she had a place in the gay pantheon was news to Henry. For her part, Suzie preened and made a grand show of ignoring her admirers, turning away disdainfully when anyone spoke to her. Henry noticed that Suzie spoke as little as possible. He assumed that was because her breathy Charlie Chan accent, unlike her outfit, wouldn't fool anyone.

As Henry was taking it all in, he heard a familiar voice asking, "Henry? Henry Wearie? It *is* you!" Henry turned to see Murray Marden, his agent, dressed in leather trousers and a T-shirt that showed off his surprisingly large biceps. Yikes. There was no mistaking it. Murray looked like one of the regulars. From the smile on his face, Murray seemed to think Henry might be trying to become a regular himself. Secret agent, indeed. It was a dilemma for Henry. Murray seemed to think a mutual secret had been revealed. Henry certainly wasn't going to start announcing his heterosexuality. What would he do, talk about cars or baseball? The hell with it, Henry thought. It'll probably be easier to get him on the phone now.

"Suzie, you're so gorgeous," Murray said. "I want you. I want you." Then he turned to Gloria. "I bet you're Alla Nazimova. You're so beautiful too."

"Absolutely," Wally said, starting to laugh. "Nifty Alla and the forty *gonifs*." Wally had about six generations of Protestantism behind him, but he enjoyed Yiddish and sometimes even got it right. Murray, who would never acknowledge he understood one word of Yiddish, let it pass. My God, Henry thought, realizing what Wally had already seen. Not only does Murray think I'm a fellow traveler, he thinks Bo and Gloria are both drag queens. "Great to see you, Murray. We're off now. Take care." Before Henry could whisk his party out of there, he saw that Suzie had stepped away and was now dancing with two muscled guys who made Murray in his T-shirt look overdressed. A crowd had gathered around Suzie and her new admirers and was beginning to suggest activities more vivid than dancing. She would pout at one of her partners, making her dark red lips a target, and then twist her backside at the other, offering a sort of second goal. The boys understood exactly what was on offer and the three of them writhed with a certain desperate pleasure. Henry remembered that Suzie Wong had danced up a storm in her Hong Kong saloon and now this Suzie was doing the same. Henry could see why the slit was in the side of the cheongsam. Without it, this sort of twisting about couldn't be done. Wally saw Henry's consternation. "Why don't you just cut in and we'll cut out," he said. Henry plunged in, took Suzie by the arm, and hurried her through the crowd toward the door. Gloria was making salaams to anyone who came near. Maybe she thought Nazimova was Egyptian. Wally was laughing and Suzie was flashing her legs. Two boys followed them out, but Wally told them to shoo, because it was Chinese Rosh Hashana and Ms. Wong was expected in Monterey Park. Henry wondered if Wally understood that Yiddish and

Hebrew were two entirely different things, but given the confusion, he let it pass.

During the ride, Wally, who was next to Henry, turned around so he could watch the show. Suzie had hardly spoken in Tryst. Now she was nattering happily. "Gloria and me are going to have a line of Suzie cosmetics and hair products. Revlon might buy it."

"That's right, dear," Gloria said. "Let's have another look at your hair." Gloria produced a brush and made a few adjustments. Suzie, absorbed in the possibilities, didn't seem to notice.

"Okay. I'm doing dresses too. Hong Kong sheaths. I have them in every color. I have them in black, I have them in gold, I have them in—"

"Yes, dear," Gloria said. "You do."

"I'll model them. Work the runways at the shows. Real silk. No nasty poly. Couture and off the rack. We'll design them together."

"Of course we will," Gloria said.

"I can do your portrait," Wally said. "Henry can write your life story. *From Hong Kong to Hollywood.*"

"No!" Suzie said, all but stamping her foot. "*The Suzie Way.* You said."

"Whatever you want, dear," Gloria said. "Remember what I told you?"

"I forget."

"This is your night."

Monterey Park is a very Los Angeles version of a Chinatown. It's not a few crowded blocks in an old part of the city. There is a Chinatown like that near Union Station, but this Chinatown, which Henry called Chinaburb, is one of malls and wide boulevards. The only way to know it's Asian is from the signs, none of which are in English. As Henry drove along Atlantic Boulevard, looking for their restaurant, he had to slow down and thread his way through the remnants of the parade. Young boys were dragging a battered paper dragon. One of them tossed a firecracker into the road and the pop startled Suzie. "Flashback to the Rape of Nanking?" Wally asked, but it didn't mean anything to Suzie. See Food was on the second floor of a strip mall. As the group climbed the stairs, Suzie said, "I wonder if I'll know anybody."

"They'll adore you," Gloria said. "Don't forget your entrance. Walk in fast and take the backlight." It reminded Henry of Rennie Leaf at La Plume.

As this was a holiday, See Food was crowded. It was a big room with easily a hundred tables and with the standard Chinese restaurant appointments—lacquer trim and red-flocked wallpaper and an enormous fish tank that took up an entire wall and had sections for shellfish, including lobsters, one for finned fish, mostly carp, and another for creatures Henry couldn't identify except for a few eels slithering about. It was like a series of dioramas in a museum. Or, as Wally suggested, a fish apartment building. Children were gathered around, fascinated by the display. The segregation of the fish made Henry think about the restaurant's seating policy. Asian people sat in the airy main room where the action was and where gentle Muzak played. The non-Asians sat in the so-called private rooms off to one side. See Food pretended those rooms were a special privilege. Every Anglo who braved the restaurant knew better. It was to keep them and their manners out of sight. The Chinese people, mostly large families, were dressed for the occasion and for a moment Henry was concerned that his gang didn't look grand enough. Suzie tried to walk in fast, but the room was crowded and it was so brightly lit that there wasn't any backlight for her to take. The staff was always looking for reasons to give Anglo customers a hard time, but when the captain or the official greeter or whatever he was saw Suzie, his reaction was no different than that of the boys at Tryst. He inspected Suzie's cheongsam and called to the waiters to come have a look. They spoke to Suzie in Chinese, probably Mandarin, though who the hell knew. Suzie just bowed her head and batted her eyes some more. It was enough, because they were shown to a pleasant table in the main room. These places always had a few waiters who spoke enough English to manage a dinner. They were the ones who worked the private rooms. The captain himself took their bar order. Henry looked the guy in the eye and asked for martinis for everyone. He knew Gloria and Wally wouldn't say no, and he wasn't about to get into the question with Suzie. He also knew the bar wouldn't be much good at cocktails, but given the last few hours he figured even a lousy martini would be helpful. Suzie waited, preening, aware that people at the other tables were looking at her. Henry wondered if any of them had ever seen the movie, or if they made the connection. Did they sense this was an American in drag? Did they care? Maybe they just liked the idea of the elaborate cheongsam, certainly the grandest one in the room. Maybe they were curious about this lovely Chinese girl with the three Americans. Henry was musing on the question when the so-so martinis were delivered.

Henry inhaled a couple of the drinks and then the food started to arrive, though he couldn't remember ordering it. The crabs in their delicate bean sauce were first, then a silvery steamed carp that the waiter filleted with a few swift slices of his knife, releasing the heady and seductive aroma of ginger. There was a bowl of bean curd in scallions and bamboo shoots and then a pigeon baked in salt and fish-head soup and more and more that Henry couldn't identify. See Food might not always be pleasant to those it thought of as foreigners, but when the kitchen was on its game, all the difficulty seemed worth it. As they ate, drinking martinis instead of wine, though Henry had asked for a bottle of the house white, they were all getting loaded. A few of the younger women were wearing cheongsams, though none of them were as vivid as Suzie's. Henry could sense the other diners watching them, glancing at Suzie and then whispering their opinions. It reminded Henry of being in a Hollywood restaurant with a film star. Everyone in the room glanced at you in a proprietary way. Well, at See Food on New Year's Day, Suzie was a star. She had started calling Henry "Robert," which was William Holden's name in the movie. "Do you want me to be your special girlfriend?" Suzie asked in her breathiest whisper, brushing Henry's face with her fingertips, drawing her crimson nails down his neck.

"Great idea," Wally said. "That way you'd always have a date for the prom. No more lonely evenings. Think of it."

"You know what I mean," Suzie said. Henry knew that the special girlfriend stuff was from the movie, but it still rattled him.

Henry blushed, possibly for the first time since high school, and said, "I don't think so. But thank you."

"Hush," Gloria said. "It's a sweet invitation."

"If I'm your special girlfriend, I don't go out with other men." Henry was feeling uncomfortable and it wasn't from too much to drink or eat. The truth that he was wrestling with was that despite himself, he found Suzie compelling. It was hard to look away from her. He had told himself it was the theatricality of it but he knew it was more. He responded to all that passivity even as he knew it was a contrivance. Hell, everything about her was a contrivance. Maybe it was her fingernails on his neck, but for a few overfed moments Henry was attracted. True to his ambivalent soul, he said only what deflected his feelings. "You know, Suzie, in the movie William Holden was an artist."

"Yes," she said. "He painted my portrait and sold it in London. It was beautiful."

Henry didn't remember the London part, but he could see that portrait in his mind's eye. Funny, how a movie with such dopiness in it could still lodge permanently in his memory. Maybe the first Suzie Wong had a bigger effect on him than he knew, but what he said was, "Wally's an artist. Maybe you could be his special girlfriend."

"Or his model," Gloria said. "You were William Holden's model."

"I want to be Robert's special girlfriend," she said in a tone that suggested she wasn't likely to change her mind. "I would be very good to you." Then, with her instinct for what worked, she put those fingernails back on Henry's throat. Henry kept his face neutral, but the skin on his neck broke out in gooseflesh that couldn't be denied.

As Henry was trying to get a grip on the situation and his runaway emotions, he could feel an odd and elusive change in the air as if someone had opened a window. At first he thought it was his own unexpected reactions that were causing disturbances, but he decided that his ego wasn't that grand. He glanced up in the direction of the private rooms and saw the former Madeleine Girard, once, for a time, Madeleine Wearie, and now, in some elaborate naming logic of modern women and despite her new marriage, once again Madeleine Girard. She was looking at him, taking in the scene. Oh, me-oh, my-oh, Henry thought. Please let this be someone who looks like her. Henry and Madeleine rarely spoke, though when they did it was never unpleasant. All their battles were in the past and Madeleine was now a psychotherapist. Henry thought about her too much. This was certainly Madeleine, but she looked different. The Madeleine in his mind was the one he had first known—small and sleek with large eyes and an amused smile. She was still a magnet for Henry; the briefest of glances, even in these circumstances, reminded him of that. She had short hair now, starting to go gray, and she had become a bit more matronly than Henry remembered. It didn't matter. Simply seeing her made the years fall away as Henry recalled a time that was, for him, a better one.

Madeline and what's-his-name were watching as Suzie draped her arm across Henry's shoulder. Gloria saw Henry's distress and looked up to see Madeleine staring at them. "Madeleine, well, hello," Gloria called. "You just come right on over here." Gloria turned to Henry and said, "Don't fret, dear." Then she told the table, which of course really meant Suzie, because Wally already knew, "It's his ex-wife." Then Gloria giggled, no doubt contemplating mischief. Henry wondered if Gloria had arranged the whole thing, including finding a way to get Madeleine to See Food. He wouldn't put it past her, but he decided that it would take more organizational skill than Gloria could manage.

As Madeleine, who was trying not to gawk, and what's-his-name approached, she said, "Hello, Henry. You know Duane, of course. This is Gloria and Wally." No one heard the politesse because they were all staring. Suzie might not have understood all the ins and outs of the situation, but she knew something was up and that she was once again the center of attention. She fluttered her eyelashes. Henry did his best to offer a firm hand to Duane, who to Henry's chagrin was a good-looking man.

"This is Ms. Wong," Henry said.

Suzie looked at Duane and said, "You're totally hot."

"Thank you," Duane said.

"You're welcome. You have nice muscles."

"Thank you again. Yours aren't so bad either."

"Want to see?" she said, sticking a leg out from under the table and offering everyone a more complete view than they had anticipated. Duane didn't know what to say about that. He was a television production manager. When Henry first heard about Duane, he remembered what Madeleine had said when they split up, about how she just couldn't stand being around the movie business. And in no time at all she was going out with this lunk and his below-the-line soul.

"Ms. Suzie Wong," Gloria added in case Madeleine had missed the point. Thanks, Gloria, Henry thought. Let's see if you can make this even harder for me.

"I see," Madeleine said. "Are you and Henry friends?"

"I'm his special girlfriend."

"I'll just bet you are," Duane said.

"It's not quite that," Henry said. "It's really simpler, or more complicated . . ." Henry got lost in his words.

"It's okay, Henry," Madeleine said. "It's a whole new world. Whatever you want. Your choices are your own."

"That's right," Duane said, "Your choice."

"Your outfit is very beautiful, Ms. Wong," Madeleine said.

"Gloria did it," Wally said. "Pretty hot, huh? You have to damn near paint it on. Show us, Suzie." Always glad to oblige, Suzie stood up and twirled, flashing a leg again and assuming a little pout in Duane's direction. He took a step back as if to hide behind his wife. Henry could see tension on Madeleine's face, or maybe it was that he could still read her thoughts. He knew she was upset by his predicament. There was at least a glimmer of concern. Henry took a little strength from that. Then Suzie turned back to Henry and ran her hand through his thinning hair. The activity caught the attention of the Chinese families at the surrounding tables. A few of them called out something to Suzie that was incomprehensible to Henry, though he assumed it was along the lines of Happy New Year. Suzie picked it up and repeated it back to them. When she raised her voice a bit, she forgot to use the breathy whisper and the sound was more male than she intended.

"Holy shit!" Duane said, apparently the last to figure it out.

Madeleine patted her husband on the arm to calm him. "You know, Henry, if you need someone to talk to, a professional person, I mean, I would be glad to give you a referral."

"I'll keep it in mind," Henry said, trying to end that line of conversation and find a way out of this morass. Gloria and Wally were no help. They were watching the entire encounter as if it were a movie. Henry wanted another drink, but before he could figure out how to arrange that, Suzie, perhaps spooked by forgetting her breathy voice, spun away and began dancing between the tables in the same aerobic style she had used to greater success earlier in the evening. The Asian Muzak was playing, but Suzie was listening to her own music. As she twirled, showing her legs to anyone interested, a few of the waiters were clapping in rhythm for her. Perhaps inspired by their enthusiasm, Suzie pushed herself between Madeleine and her husband and began grinding her pelvis at Duane. He turned bright red, which Suzie took as encouragement and began running her hands over his chest and squealing, "Oooh, oooh." When she dropped to her knees in front of Duane, Madeleine gasped and pulled her husband away and the two of them excused themselves, with Madeleine saying, "Henry, I hope it works out for you. Bye, Wally. Call me, Gloria." Madeleine and Duane retreated as quickly as they could without actually running out of the restaurant. After that, Suzie's dance might have just played itself out, but she was nothing if not excessive, and she couldn't resist jumping on a table where a family had just about finished their New Year's dinner. The kids were amused when Suzie kicked over a plate of fish bones, but a woman Henry assumed was the grandmother began to wheeze and shout in Chinese. Perhaps she was having a heart attack, Henry thought. Or maybe she was demanding justice for her family and their fish bones. Suzie seemed to like this new platform because she leapt to an adjacent table where a family was still eating. This group didn't have an offended grandmother. They seemed to think Suzie was part of a floor show that involved breaking plates and sending forks spinning like little pronged missiles. Among the many questions that were rocketing through Henry's mind were, Do these people know Suzie is a man in drag? Do they know she's not Chinese? Are they going to kill me when they find out? Suzie gave no sign that she found any of these issues significant. The staff didn't seem to know what to do about Suzie's aerial stunts. Then Gloria and Wally started clapping in rhythm, urging Suzie to greater heights. When Gloria tried to climb on a table and Suzie started to undo her cheongsam, pulling at the frogs, the headwaiter decided that was enough. Two of his men pulled Suzie down from the tabletop, an exercise she seemed to enjoy. Henry, Gloria, Wally, and Suzie were soon surrounded by the See Food staff, who threw the lot of them out of the restaurant, though not before Henry paid the bill including a charge for broken crockery.

*   *   *

On Monday morning, Henry got to the Market early only to see that the scaffolding around the clock tower was gone. The clock and bell and the entire top of the tower had already disappeared. They must have worked on Saturday, he thought. A bulldozer stood ready to start attacking the rest of it. The bell was really just a prop that didn't ring and the chimes were a tape, but the effort always amused Henry. He liked to call it the faux clock tower. At half its height and without the clock, the tower looked naked or at least vulnerable. It made Henry sad so he went into the Market and sat quietly by himself drinking his coffee and listening to the old Jews reminiscing in their tired voices about meals of the past. "Remember the butterfish?" one old gentleman was saying. "You can't get that anymore. I didn't have that since I came out here." His companions nodded and one of them repeated, "butterfish." Henry thought the guy sounded like Charles Foster Kane saying "Rosebud." The wistfulness of it gave Henry comfort until he heard rumbling from the parking lot. He knew that the bulldozer had started whacking away. Henry supposed the others were watching the destruction. And sure enough a few minutes later Morty Elfman, who had produced *Finding Home,* came in shaking his head at the activity. While Morty got himself some breakfast, Henry stood in the archway leading to the parking lot and watched the bulldozer plow into the tower, knocking it into scraps, grinding it to dust. Leo and Irwin and Wally were watching and Henry waved to them and went back to the table, thinking about how he wouldn't hear the chimes again. The Market itself seemed to be receding into the past. It had been there sixty years, not much even in California, but those years had seen Henry's productivity and now perhaps his decline. Leo and Irwin and Wally strolled over to the table and Irwin offered a round of applause to Henry. At first he thought it had something to do with the clock tower, but then Irwin asked, "Does she have a sister?" Wally had told them about Monterey Park.

"I don't know," Henry said. "She's a little young for you. More in Leo's line."

"Did she really look like a woman?" Leo asked.

"Was this thing in the trades?"

"Absolutely," Irwin said. "No secrets around here."

"The clock tower's gone," Morty said, joining them after watching till the last of the dust had settled.

"Yeah," Henry said. "The axes are on the cherry trees." Leo smiled but the others were already talking about the movies they had seen over the weekend and weren't paying attention. Henry knew that they would razz him a bit and then the weekend's escapade would be filed away, another story to dine out on. Then it too would fade into memory. Soon Monterey Park and Ms. Suzie Wong would be one with the clock tower. It didn't matter. Something else would come skipping along because this was Hollywood, the capital of change and chance. Henry thought he'd just have another cup of coffee.

5

The Art Deco Widow

*O*nce, *when Henry had hit a dry patch,* and he thought he couldn't bear the screenwriting racket for another minute, Rick Moses had urged him to put scripts aside and try something else. "If you don't like what comes out, you don't have to nail it to the church door." That was Rick. Decisive, like a director. Not like Henry, who would chew over the question until he was sick of it. Rick's ability to act carried over into his personal life. He had a new wife—his third—and a baby as well as two grown sons. It meant Rick didn't come to the Market as regularly as he once did. Henry was in awe of it, though he missed his friend.

On a morning when Rick was at the Market and Henry was feeling unsettled, Rick had an idea of what the problem was. "Work or love?" he asked.

Henry laughed and answered, "Probably both, but at the moment, work."

"Try some stories. You used to do that kind of thing. They'd be good."

"What would I do with them?"

"You'll think of something. You don't have to ask anybody."

"I don't know."

"What about Audrey Lewin? Weren't you going to do a script about how Tom died and all that craziness with his mother?" Tom Lewin had been Rick's lawyer as well as Henry's. After Tom's death, Henry had tried to spend time with Audrey. Neither of them called it dating, but that's what it was. They had known each other well during her marriage to Tom. This was different. After a few dinners and a few movies and long sessions of Henry just holding her, the possibility of sex was unavoidable. One night, when things looked as if they might turn serious, Audrey began to cry. She couldn't help herself. It all felt so incestuous. The closer Henry and Audrey got to the inevitable, the more vivid Tom's presence felt to them both. Henry backed away and apologized—he wasn't exactly sure why—and though he saw Audrey now and then after that evening, they were never again alone together. When Rick suggested writing a story about it, Henry knew that if he could write about Audrey and Tom, perhaps he could put a difficult memory to rest. And if he could do that, then maybe he could make peace with his father and even talk to him about his mother, alive now only in memory.

"Henry," Rick said, "Stop dithering and just do it."

*   *   *

The Art Deco Widow
By Henry Wearie

WHEN Alice Leone heard that the screenwriters who met at the Beverly Hills Gun Club called themselves Armed & Literate, she began fishing for an invitation. The only thing Alice knew about guns was that everybody had an opinion about them and that they figured in most of the scripts she dealt with at Paramount, where she was a reader in the story department. Her friend Sibyl, who was a screenwriter and like Alice was single, agreed that Armed & Literate might be an amusing way to meet people, which was their code for unattached men. Sibyl signed them up. When she canceled, Alice went anyway.

The gun club met in a warehouse on the Westside that wasn't even near Beverly Hills. There was a lobby where you rented guns and bought cartridges, which Alice was careful not to call bullets because Sibyl had looked into the terminology so they wouldn't appear as the rank poseurs they were. A line of firing lanes in the back gave the place the look of a bunker. There were single men but they were more interested in shooting their guns than in talking to Alice, so she made jokes and turned sarcastic, which is what Alice did when she was frustrated. She dubbed the evening Sip 'n' Shoot because when the gun-toting screenwriters weren't in the firing lanes they were drinking Diet Coke. Alice knew that actively looking for men was demeaning. She had decided it might be worth being demeaned a little if it meant she could find a serious boyfriend. Alice was pretty but in a way that could take a while to notice. Hollywood tended to trade in a more immediate kind of attraction.

The first thing Alice noticed about Ted Gruen was his hair. She didn't mind that he was balding, which Alice considered honest enough in a man she guessed was in his mid-forties. She had decided that if anyone asked how old she was, which was thirty-two, she would say she was in the three-oh area code. She tried not to stare at Ted's hair. He had pulled what remained of it into an Oriental-looking bulb, a style Alice called a dork knob. She also noticed he wasn't wearing a wedding ring. Alice tried not to glance at the left hands of the men she met, but it was a losing battle. He had come because a client of his who was a screenwriter told him that shooting a gun might make him feel less restless. Ted was an entertainment lawyer who had trouble even reading scripts. Ted never quite got the hang of loading the Glock 9mm semiautomatic he was using. His thumb was nicked from jamming in the cartridges, which he called bullets.

Alice had a small bottle of hydrogen peroxide in her purse and she offered to pour a little on his thumb. "I take it you're not exactly a sharpshooter," she said as the peroxide fizzed pink.

"Do you always have hydrogen peroxide in your purse?"

"I keep it handy because I am humiliatingly cautious."

When they discovered that neither of them was a screenwriter, Ted asked if she would like to get away from what he called "this noise and nonsense" and have a drink. "We can go armed if you want."

Alice, who knew when a man was flirting, said, "I'll settle for just literate. Two questions first."

Ted had been in Hollywood a long time, so he knew what she meant. "I'm straight and single."

They sat in a red banquette in the bar at the Santa Monica Grill, where they drank kamikazes and resisted the peanuts. "I thought screenwriters were all liberals," Ted said.

"I think they'd call themselves realists," Alice said. "That means liberals with guns." Ted laughed at her joke but didn't seem competitive about it, which could be a problem with Hollywood men. When she asked, he told her about his law practice and how he had been married briefly, long ago. Alice told him how she had gone to graduate school in Chicago for an unhappy year before she had come west to be a screenwriter. "Now I'm a reader. It's embarrassing. Everybody else is some kind of gunslinger. I'm on the slow track." Before they knew it, it was eleven o'clock.

At Paramount the next day, Alice was supposed to be covering a script about werewolves. Her job was to make a summary of the story and give an opinion about its prospects. Instead, she replayed the evening in her mind. He had insisted on paying for the drinks. That should mean she could now invite him for a drink. Ha! She turned her attention back to the werewolves. She was repeatedly told to be on the lookout for sympathetic leading roles for women. The women readers were told that, anyway. It was meant to keep them happy. The studio wasn't against big roles for women, but what they wanted were star parts for men because that's what made hits. Whichever sex it was, all the readers knew that the issue that really counted was sympathy, sympathy, sympathy. Alice said that Sympathy Über Alles was the Paramount motto. In the script, a werewolf attacked a woman surgeon and tore off her clothes all the way down to an NC-17 rating. The next victim was a woman architect in black mesh stockings. Hot babes still got kicked around, but now they had great jobs. This was the third werewolf script in two weeks. She wasn't even sure what a werewolf was. A regular wolf that was really angry at women, she guessed. Alice put the werewolves aside and made a list. He was older, which she didn't mind, but she thought it made him a little uneasy. He was a partner in a law firm, so he was probably solvent. He had that hair problem, but she'd fight that battle later, if there was a later. She amused herself imagining dork knob variations. Maybe he could braid it and wear it in a chignon. She had once seen a waiter in a restaurant with hair like that. Or maybe pigtails.

When Ted called, he said he had been thinking about her. Alice was thrilled, but because she was cautious, she didn't say he had been on her mind. He suggested that they drive out to Malibu for dinner at Geoffrey's, a romantic spot on the cliffs above the ocean. Alice had to will herself not to think about what to wear. She knew if she let herself, she'd think about the possibilities all the time, get no work done, and then be disappointed if the evening was merely pleasant and not life changing.

Ted had told Latasha, his assistant, to book a table on the patio overlooking the ocean. If there was any resistance, she was to tell him. Latasha used the imperious white woman voice she dragged out on such occasions. Latasha was an actress whenever she could get jobs. For a task of this sort, she identified herself as Natasha though once she said she was Muffie. It always made Ted laugh, though he wasn't sure of the racial etiquette of the situation. It worked and as a result, Ted and Alice were perched above the water, lulled by the rhythm of the waves below. They talked about the difficulties of romance, which Alice found a hopeful sign. He didn't pretend it was something he didn't care about, nor did it seem like a clumsy way to talk about sex. They both knew people who weren't well, which was the Hollywood euphemism for HIV-positive, and they agreed that whatever other problems that caused, it put a damper on dating. "I think the sexes are like ethnic groups," Alice said. "Vaginal-Americans and Penile-Americans." Maybe it was the joke, or maybe the wine, but Ted found himself touching her hand and saying he hoped he could see more of her. It pleased Alice, because it was what she wanted. In her cautious way, she asked if he would first get a test.

"I don't think you're sick or anything, but I would feel better."

He didn't say anything for a moment and Alice wondered if she'd offended him. Asking a prospective lover to get a test was pretty tame stuff. Alice hadn't done it before, because there hadn't been anyone she was interested in enough to ask. She thought she had been presumptuous until he nodded and said, "In the meantime, can we do a little intraethnic fooling around?" Alice laughed and smiled in a way that said, it was a possibility.

Ted's doctor was in Beverly Hills. He felt awkward about asking him about the test, so he went to a clinic in West Hollywood where it was done anonymously. You walked in, were asked for forty dollars, which Ted paid in cash, and were given a number. The waiting room must have once been used for pediatrics. There was a faded mural of Disney characters on the wall. Ted wondered if this clinic was aware that Disney was known to threaten lawsuits against nursery schools for painting unauthorized pictures of Snow White or Goofy. Studio lawyers sent stern letters to the teachers of three-year-olds. "Lovely business," Ted thought as he looked at posters about flu shots and condoms that partially covered Mickey and Minnie. The other patients didn't look like frightened gay men or drug users. People like that, he thought, probably didn't come to places like this. This was just a bunch of guys who wanted sex. Women have found a way to go back to not sleeping with you on the first or second date. He thought about how much he liked Alice, how funny she was. He pictured the way she sort of looked at the floor when she made a joke or a wisecrack. It was as if she knew it wasn't the usual way to a man's heart, but she couldn't help herself. He loved that because he couldn't do it. He was smart enough, he just wasn't very funny. He never told jokes and he certainly didn't try to make wisecracks. Sometimes he tried to make witty remarks, but they usually seemed forced. He had managed that thing about fooling around because it was a reply to a really funny thing she had said. Alice had brought it out of him. He knew he could love her for that. After he had been there for about twenty minutes, he was sent into a cubicle where a middle-aged Korean woman entered his number in her computer, took a blood sample, and told him that usually the tests came back overnight but there had been trouble with the computers. He should call in a few days.

When he told Alice that they wouldn't have the results for a while, he could sense she was relieved. At first that disappointed him, but as the few days became a week, Ted found that he liked it too. They saw each other every night, talked during the day, and thought about each other the rest of the time. Ted wasn't scheming ways to get Alice into bed, and she wasn't worried about how she was handling it. She called what they were doing El Courtship.

Because of his law practice, Ted was expected to appear at the screenings and dinners that seemed to go on every night in Hollywood. He was always looking for appropriate women to escort to yet another evening on behalf of the rain forest or a disease he'd only barely heard of. Alice, who hadn't been to many such evenings, was glad to go. As they walked into the Beverly Hilton, for a benefit for the Heart Fund, they caught sight of themselves in a mirror. They were quite taken by how striking they looked in evening clothes. Alice said, "The last time I got this dressed up for a boy I didn't sleep with was my high school prom."

The high point of the evening was when Harriet Kastle, a Paramount executive known to the readers as the Sympathy Queen, made a point of greeting Alice. Harriet, who all the readers agreed was certainly a gorgon and possibly a werewolf, usually treated readers like the help. Alice had known that partners in movie-business law firms were formidable, but it hadn't seemed real to her till tonight. When she told Ted things might be easier now with the Sympathy Queen, she knew that the best part was that she wanted to tell him. With a lot of men, that would be an acknowledgment of his power and an admission of her weakness. With Ted it was something to be pleased about. Talking with him never felt like the date-chatter Alice usually had to endure. She told him the best thing about El Courtship was that they weren't interviewing each other.

The next night, while they fed each other bites of sushi at

Matsuhisa, which was too expensive for casual meals but seemed just right to them now, Ted said, "I told my mother about you."

"Did you tell her I wouldn't sleep with you till medical science approved?"

"I went easy on that part. She invited us for tea. She wants to use her stuff."

"What stuff?"

"Tanya is deeply committed to Art Deco silver."

"I don't know anything about that," Alice said, feeling a trace of panic.

"It's not a test."

"Ha! Is she okay? I mean, do you get along?"

"Sure. Men get along with their mothers. It's women who have a problem."

"That's very encouraging."

"Tanya's a little eccentric. She sort of rattles around since my stepfather died."

"What happened with your real father? Oh, God! It sounds like I'm checking on breeding stock."

"I'm already older than he got to be." Ted touched her face and said, "I'll call the clinic tomorrow and see if it's ready."

"Wait till after your mother gets her chance to humiliate me. I can't think about both at once."

The next afternoon, as they drove to Tanya's apartment in Beverly Hills, Alice asked about the silver collection.

"The forks and stuff are James Robinson. Onslow. If you happen to recognize it, she'll want to adopt you."

"If you know about silver patterns I might kill you."

"That is the sum total of my knowledge."

When Ted introduced Alice, she knew from the way Tanya's face was pulled tight that she had probably had her share of cosmetic surgery. Her white hair was cut straight across her forehead like a helmet. And she was nervous about meeting Ted's new friend. Alice understood that Tanya was getting old and wanted to see her bachelor son settled. She fussed over Alice, twice saying how pretty she was. She meant well, but it was unsettling to be complimented so effusively. Before they sat down, a bell rang somewhere in the apartment. Tanya went to tend to it.

"What was that?" Alice asked.

"Probably to take a pill or something." Alice nodded and looked around. A display cabinet that she assumed had once been in a large dining room held candlesticks and tea services. There were platters and enamel bowls with inlaid silver on the end tables. Alice couldn't keep practical thoughts from running through her mind. How much was all this worth? Was it safe here? Who polished it? When Tanya returned with a tea tray that looked like cubist sculpture, Alice thought about *A Guide to Art Deco Silver,* a book she had skimmed in Book Soup. "Puiforcat?" she asked.

"It is!" Tanya answered, delighted. "Are you interested in silver?"

"I wish I had your eye." Alice held a spoon up to the light. "Onslow?"

Tanya nodded happily. Alice could see Ted's mouth in his mother. In Ted, the mouth was closed and a little tense. Tanya's was open in a smile that seemed as ornamental as any of her tea services.

When Tanya left the room to answer another bell, Ted said, "You're on a roll! How'd you know Puiforcat?"

"Not because you told me. I didn't get in James Robinson yet." As Alice looked around, she saw that Tanya also collected Mexican ceramics and pottery, the hand-painted cups and platters that everyone in Los Angeles knew not to use for food because of the lead in the paint. The ceramic figures were dancing skeletons and painted death heads.

Tanya returned with a silver basket that she offered like a prize. "It's Hoffmann. Wiener Werkstätte."

"Of course it is," Alice said, not about to wrestle with the name. Then a buzzer sounded, followed by a bell. Tanya went into the bedroom.

"What do you think?" Ted asked when they were alone.

"I think we ought to get out of here while I'm ahead."

The next day Alice met Sibyl for lunch at the Angeli Caffe on Melrose. Before she became a screenwriter, Sibyl had been a reader at Paramount and Alice's ally in the hunt for sympathetic roles for women. In those days they had eaten lunch here regularly. Alice was once quoted in a story in the *Los Angeles Times* about Hollywood restaurants, saying "The Angeli Caffe is where a generation of Hollywood screenwriters learned to eat like Umbrian peasants." Sibyl was the only person Alice had confided in about being glad the test results were late.

"Equity demands you get tested too," Sibyl said.

"For my needle-sharing ways? Or the wild nights with my bisexual lovers?"

"He didn't say anything about it?"

"It didn't occur to him. I don't think he reads *Cosmo*."

"You're going to make trouble with this AIDS test stuff. You are so old economy."

"I'm no economy!"

"Can't you just enjoy something?"

"The one thing is, he gets stress headaches."

"Only a man would think staying single avoids stress."

"The mother has crank possibilities."

"Because she has good silver? You want a man who doesn't care about his mother?"

"She makes him nervous."

"Stress headaches, yes. AIDS, no. I promise."

"The test is a way to say we're serious without saying it."

"Enjoy it however you want."

After two weeks of voluptuous anticipation, Ted collected the printout certifying his good health and faxed it to Alice with a sweet note asking her to go to Two Bunch Palms for the weekend.

"I just hope we don't miss the way things are," she said when she called to accept.

"We're going to have a great time. Don't worry so much." She did worry. What if they didn't like sex as much as they liked the evenings when they just talked and looked forward to sex? Then what?

Awash in longing, caught between restraint and desire, they drove into the desert for what they both hoped would be a romantic weekend. At first they were a little shy. It felt comforting but not passionate. So without plan or calculation, Alice took charge. She wanted it to be wonderful for both of them. The generosity in that made her know she was in love. The streak of lewdness that she discovered when she set her thoughts into practice thrilled them both. Their time together was a release of what had been pent up. They were amused to think that the few weeks in which they had gone from being strangers to lovers could be considered a long time. To them, it was as if they were already lovers, but ones who had been parted and were now once again together. Each gave to the other and in the giving each got what was needed and wanted. Neither could ask more, because they both knew that is what love has to offer.

After they had walked on the grounds, bathed in the grotto, taken mud baths and massages, when they lay in bed wrapped in their love, Alice told Ted her last secret. She couldn't bear the way he wore his hair. "It makes you look trivial." She hoped she hadn't ruined it. All weekend she had been telling him tenderly that she was so happy. Now she was worried that she had hurt him. He was quiet for a moment, then he looked in her cosmetics case for a pair of scissors. When he sat on the edge of the bed, she kissed the back of his neck, then snipped off the dreaded dork knob, letting it fall to the floor. Then they made love again, fierce and possessive, sure of what they were doing and certain of each other. The next day they drove to the Nevada side of Lake Tahoe where they were married at the Wee Kirk of the Heather Chapel, which was painted plaid and where once you could get married in a fever and now you could still do it without an appointment.

They thought about moving into Ted's apartment, but they both wanted a place that didn't have more of a past for one than the other. Alice found a house in Nichols Canyon that cost more than they had intended to spend. It had a guest cottage covered in bougainvillea. Alice knew it could be her studio. When Ted saw her reaction to the cottage, which she called a hut as a hedge against disappointment, he bought the house. He told her she should quit her job and think of herself as a screenwriter. As Alice's life settled down, she was often surprised by how contented she was. During the day she worked in her hut and sometimes had lunch with Sibyl. She looked forward to the evening when her husband got home. Alice found herself thinking about having a baby.

Ted and Alice began to give small dinner parties. "When I was single," Ted said, "I was always a guest. Now I can make that right." It meant a lot to him to be able to entertain, and Alice was pleased to see that it was done right. They often invited Tanya, who brought serving utensils and platters.

After tending to her silver collection, Tanya's main activity was making telephone calls. She called Ted at his office several times a day. Latasha spoke with her for a few moments, then said Ted would call back later, which he did at the end of the day. Tanya was glad to include her daughter-in-law on her telephone list. Alice soon discovered that Tanya called so often because she didn't remember when she had last called. "She could use those buzzers to remind herself," Alice said.

"Let the voice mail get it."

"I hear it ring, then I listen to the message. I might as well talk to her."

"I'll take care of it," Ted said, though he never did.

Later that day, when Tanya called, Alice tried to sound relaxed, though she felt tense when Tanya said, "Abell's auction has a Christofle vase."

"I know. You told me."

"I want to see how much it goes for."

"Why can you remember a vase but not your schedule?"

"Are you mad?"

"It would be better if you called after four. I mean if it's just a casual call. Okay?"

"Why didn't you say so?" Alice thought she had solved the problem, but Tanya just continued calling all day long. In her confusion, she seemed to think Alice meant not to call about auctions before four o'clock. When Tanya had run out of things to say, she had a default topic in silver polish. She liked to tell her daughter-in-law, "You should use Goddard's for your best things." Alice had found that the most practical thing was to just let her talk about it for a moment or two rather than give in to the temptation to say, "You may have mentioned that." Sometimes Tanya referred to it as "Goddard's of Regent Street," pointing out that it had to be ordered from London. Occasionally, Tanya sent a tin of the pink paste to Alice along with instructions for its use, which involved a damp cloth. Sometimes, when Tanya had talked herself out about the polish, she would start in about how wonderful Ted was. "The best. I can't believe how perfect. Nobody has a son like that." It made Alice uneasy.

"She says stuff like that about you," Ted said, when Alice told him about the call.

"She does?" Alice asked, flattered, despite herself.

"Plenty of women her age do nothing but complain."

"I keep thinking she means the opposite. She's really mocking us."

"I tune out when 'wonderful, wonderful' starts." What both of them were sensing was that the very idea of parental love, which is where everyone learns how to love, was undermined by Tanya. She was so effusive that she made love meaningless. Her anger could be equally baffling. Tanya developed grudges against her neighbors. For a while she believed that the elderly couple in the apartment above her were rolling steel balls on their wood floors. "It's awful," she wailed. "They do it to annoy me. They should put down carpet." Whenever Ted tried to discuss it with her, he got sucked into a debate about the trouble all that ball-rolling caused. There never seemed to be a discussion of whether it was happening at all. Ted had always dealt with his mother's eccentricities by ignoring them. Alice couldn't do that. Tanya wasn't her mother, as Ted pointed out, but she was her mother-in-law and she lived just a few miles away. "I have to deal with her," Alice said. "All you have to do is smile and be a man." Ted had no patience for the problem and got irritated when Alice brought it up. "So what? She's old. It's harmless enough."

"Today she said you were one of the greatest men in California. Did she think I was going to disagree? 'In California and Arizona. Part of New Mexico too.'"

"Just say, Uh-huh. She'll talk herself out."

"Do you think she can take care of herself?"

"Oh, come on!" Ted snapped. "Because she lays on the compliments, she should be put in a home?"

"You know what I mean."

"She's okay. She has her interests. Her silver."

"What am I going to do with this stuff? It's too Beverly Hills for this house."

"Just cool out."

"If I told her the house was on fire, she'd tell me how you quit smoking."

"You keep picking at this. Not every problem can get solved, you know." They had argued before and even raised their voices to one another, but each time they had resolved the issue. Alice knew this was different. Tanya's calls caused a rift between them. A chill came over the marriage. Ted's headaches seemed more frequent and he was given to unexpected fits of anger. Alice urged him to see a psychotherapist. Ted went a few times, but then insisted the man practiced Tibetan gong therapy and refused to go back. He began staying later at his office. Before Alice met Ted, when she was still in what Sibyl called her Sarcastic Era, she knew she had a way of holding grudges. Alice could feel herself slipping into what Sibyl called Sarcastic Era II.

"This isn't a script," Sibyl told her over lunch at Angeli. "You don't have to figure it out to fix it."

"She is totally oblivious. He's afraid of her."

"Ignore it. Be extra nice. She doesn't even know you're mad."

"She knows. It's what she wants."

"Don't get sucked in. Invite her to dinner. And you might invite me. Thank you."

Alice asked Tanya to a small dinner she was giving for a client of Ted's who was in from New York. The man was unattached. Of course she would invite Sibyl.

Tanya decided to bring a set of 1930s demitasse spoons. She had been meaning to give them to Alice and this would be the perfect opportunity. She told Ofelia to see that they were polished. Ofelia found several sets of spoons, none of them demitasse. "No, no," Tanya said, "Little spoons. *Poco.*" Tanya enjoyed using Spanish words. It only confused Ofelia. "They're by the Lladró," Tanya said, using the Spanish brand name of some ceramic statuary. To Ofelia, it sounded like *ladrón,* the word for thief.

"I didn't take it," she said, indignant.

Tanya had assumed Ofelia had misplaced the spoons or mixed them in with others. Now she believed the woman had taken them. Why else would she deny it? Ofelia presented her purse and shopping bag for inspection. Tanya saw that as a pathetic attempt to deny what she had done. She could have smuggled them out of the house at any time. "I've had enough of you," Tanya said, perhaps confusing her maid with her daughter-in-law. She fired Ofelia and threw her out.

When Tanya told Alice about Ofelia's treachery, Alice said, "Do you mean the Georg Jensen? In a leather case?"

"Yes, yes."

"You gave them to us. I'm using them for the dinner."

If Alice hadn't sounded so exasperated, Tanya might have reacted more sensibly to the situation. She felt cornered. "She steals. It isn't the first time."

"She didn't take them. You gave them to us. You better apologize to that woman right now."

"She stole my spoons!"

Alice could imagine Tanya repeating that complaint for years. The thought of it made her light-headed. "They're in this house," she said, biting off the words.

"Do you want them?"

"Nobody wants them! They're too small for anything."

"They're demitasse."

"They're hideous. Useless." Tanya was sniffling, but Alice didn't care. "Never say spoons to me again."

Tanya immediately called Ted, demanding to speak with her son, which she said was her right. Latasha, who could sweet talk most anyone out of their anger, told Ted, "Your mother is in a state and I don't mean Wyoming." When Ted finally got Tanya off the telephone, he called Alice to find out what it was all about. He expected his wife to be a little upset, but when he found her as angry as his mother, he blew up.

The dinner was canceled. Ted's client was staying at the Four Seasons and Ted met with him in the hotel's dining room. He cut the evening short but instead of going home he checked into the hotel. He was too angry to sleep and at two o'clock he called Alice. She was frantic with worry and not mollified when he told her where he was. "When there's trouble you don't have the decency to side with me or the courage to side with her, which is what you want to do," she said. "You just blame everybody else and run away." She was immediately sorry she had said it. So what if he went to a hotel? She didn't want to be right, she wanted her husband back.

Caught between his wife and his mother, Ted was angry all over again. He told the switchboard not to put through any more calls. In the morning he moved to a furnished apartment in the Del Capri in Westwood. He told himself, he'd rather be a bachelor than a pawn hammered in an absurd battle between the two women. The thought of listening to them complaining about each other gave him a stress headache.

The old, cautious Alice would have waited it out. The happiness of her marriage had made her bolder. She sent an e-mail to Ted at his office. "You're hiding behind this stress business. Everything has stress. Certainly your mother. You should come home and not put us through this." Ted couldn't get a grip on the situation. He would look around at the little apartment in the Del Capri with its anonymous furniture and wonder how it had come to this so quickly.

At his office, where he often worked late because he couldn't

bear to go back to the Del Capri, he was on the phone with a producer named Freddy Lutz. Ted was thinking what difficult clients
producers were. When things went wrong, producers blamed their
lawyers. Freddy was yelling about his financing that had fallen
apart. He had taken options with his own cash in the belief that
European money would be there to cover his gamble. Ted had
pointed out that it was the sort of risk producers had to take if they
wanted to be in business. "You said go ahead. You told me it'll be
there." As Freddy yelled, Ted could hear his mother. He thought the
phone lines must be crossed. As he was trying to make sense of it,
he heard Alice complaining about Tanya. All three seemed to be
shouting. Freddy was shouting. Alice and Tanya were quieter, but
no less insistent. The voices were saying, "I know your hand is out
on every side of this. I want my spoons back. You have to make her
stop calling me." The verbal jumble seemed to shoot into his ears,
pricking him with noise. He went dizzy as something pushed on his
chest. It was so insistent that he was sure that something had fallen
on him. As he bent his neck to look, what felt like a steel rod shot
up his spine and spread out across his shoulders. The pain stopped
everything but the voices. Ted couldn't catch his breath. He was
sweating and becoming nauseous. He gasped into the receiver that
he wasn't well, but Freddy wouldn't hear it. "You hang up on me,
that's it. You too sick to spell malpractice?" Ted knew this was the
very thing that had killed his father. That was long ago, now there
were remedies. Even as the weight on his chest grew heavier, he
couldn't believe he had arrived at life's last surprise.

*

THE dark wooden coffin sat on the stage at the front of the chapel
at Forest Lawn. The two widows were in the front row on opposite
sides of the aisle. They were grieving, but they still weren't speaking. Alice was with Sibyl, who had stayed with her since she got the
awful news.

Tanya had buried two husbands but this particular hell, outliv-
ing her son, had not been in her mind at all. She tried to remember

the age of Ted's father when he died, but it was too many years ago and Tanya couldn't summon the face of her first Mr. Gruen.

Richard Olwyn, one of Ted's partners, was giving the eulogy. Alice remembered going to Dick Olwyn's house for dinner. It was a Spanish house in Brentwood Park. She tried to remember if the Olwyns had been to their house. When she found no solace in dinner parties past, she listened to Dick, who was quoting from absurdly diverse sources, as if he had taken his remarks from Bartlett's. "The brittle thread is torn, the golden bowl is broken," he said. Alice barely heard him. Tanya, who was also drifting, heard the part about a golden bowl. She called out, "Silver. James Robinson." Her friends assumed Tanya's confusion was part of her grief, which it was. They also assumed it would pass, though it didn't.

Dick was speaking about Ted's brilliance in the law, asking, "Who among us could frame an issue and cut to the heart of a problem the way Ted could?" Tanya interrupted, saying, "Georg Jensen." It was a name Dick Olwyn couldn't quite place. The mourners strained to see as Tanya made her way across the chapel, saying, "I want my spoons."

"Oh, shut up," Alice snapped, then sat through the rest of the service in a daze.

Everyone knew that no matter what spoons might have to do with it, the stolen object in question was the deceased. Like the cobbler whose children had holes in their shoes, Ted left no will. When he was alive he hadn't wanted to think about not being so. When a married man dies intestate, his property goes to his wife. As Tanya pointed out, they were separated. Ted died a resident of the Del Capri. On the other hand, no papers had been filed or contemplated. The house, his partnership in the law practice, and his investments were the property of his widow.

Tanya didn't want any of it, but she did want to believe that her son had made a point of writing out a will that included her. He was a lawyer. She had paid his tuition at law school. She wanted to think of him writing something like, "To my beloved mother, to whom I owe so much, I bequeath whatever mementos she might care to have." After all, at Ted's insistence, hadn't she herself made out an elaborate will specifying which pieces of silver were to go to her son, which to friends, and which to various charities? She had hated doing it. Dividing it up had been amusing enough. It was the part about her death that she didn't care for and didn't want to think about. She knew they'd probably want to have her cremated. It seemed barbaric. Hateful. They all did that now. It was fashionable. Bury or burn? Burn or bury? She didn't want to be shoved into a furnace. It was like the Nazis. She wanted a grave on a quiet green hill. And a stone that they could visit. For a while, anyway. Until they forgot. She didn't want to leave the silver to them. No. She didn't want to leave it to anybody. What she wanted was to be buried with it all, every gleaming spoon and bowl.

As she sat musing on the bequest that was not to be, she picked up a silver tray and traced her finger along its design of concentric circles. She wasn't completely deserted as long as she had her silver, her little soldiers, there to guard her and keep her safe. She noticed that the tray was starting to tarnish. Where was that Ofelia? There was some problem with that girl, but Tanya couldn't quite recall what it was. Her mind wandered back to her son and his unwritten will. Tanya ached for the acknowledgment she knew he had intended. "To my beloved mother, to whom I owe so much." She knew that was now unlikely, so she called Alice to demand the return of her things. Alice wasn't there, which was just as well. Tanya left a message: "You have my Puiforcat tea service and you have two Serrière bowls and I don't know what all else. Send it back or I'll call the sheriff." She hadn't meant to be so harsh. The trouble with those machines was you couldn't go back and change something. Then Tanya remembered her spoons. So she called again.

Alice tried not to take the harangues seriously, but they still affected her. Tanya just kept repeating, "Give me back my things." There was no way to hear it and not think she was saying, "You failed him. You killed him." Losing Ted had been horrible enough, but to lose him while they were separated seemed more than Alice could bear. They would have gotten back together. She would have seen to it, even if it had meant going to the Del Capri and bringing him home. Married people fought. It didn't mean the marriage was over. Alice ached to tell Tanya off. She would say, "Each time you call I'm going to throw one piece in the garbage." She saw herself stuffing demitasse spoons into the garbage disposal, then holding the phone over the sink so Tanya could hear the awful grinding noise. Then she would say there was nothing left but silver dust that was now polluting the water supply.

Instead, Alice bundled the silver in a black trash bag and drove to the Heart Fund Thrift Shop on La Brea. The man at the counter was astonished when Alice spread out an array of Art Deco silver. "Do you have a value on this?" he asked.

"Whatever it's worth," Alice said, "it's not worth it."

"Don't you want the write-off?"

"I want to be through with it."

That night when Tanya called to leave her diatribe, Alice answered and told her what she had done. "I chose the Heart place because Ted gave them money."

Tanya's breath went short and she began to shriek, "You didn't. You couldn't." To Tanya, it was as if Ted himself had been given to the thrift shop. Alice had meant to irritate her in a way that was roughly equal to the way Tanya had harassed her. She had wanted to shake loose of her, not destroy her. Now she felt queasy. It didn't matter that Tanya was awful. She cared about those spoons and bowls. She also knew Ted would have been furious.

"You have to get it back," Sibyl said, when Alice told her what had happened. "You go down there first thing. Make a donation or something. I'll go with you."

The next morning at the thrift shop, the clerk was a woman who looked as if she might know about Deco silver. She noticed the hall-mark on a serving spoon and said, "Some of this is James Robinson. It's quite valuable."

"So is this," Sibyl said, taking the checkbook from Alice's purse. Sibyl wrote out a check, then put the pen in Alice's hand for a signature. Alice was relieved that her friend was taking charge.

Sibyl called around and found Ofelia and asked if she could come to Alice's house for one day. Ofelia was wary of working for anyone in Tanya's family, but she was sorry to hear about Ted and she needed the money. She spread newspapers on the kitchen counter and soon the familiar and slightly noxious odor of God-dard's polish filled Alice's kitchen as Ofelia polished the silver she had polished so many times before. Alice told her, "I know you didn't take anything. Tanya's getting old. She got confused." That was the first time anyone in the family had told Ofelia that they didn't think she was a *ladrón.*

When the silver gleamed again, the women wrapped it in tissue and packed it in cartons. Alice gave Ofelia extra money, and then she and Sibyl drove to Beverly Hills and left the boxes at Tanya's door. Alice wondered what she made of it all, but Tanya never called again. Alice found herself thinking about Ted before Tanya was a part of her marriage. She thought about the way they had met at the gun club, the way they had fussed over his AIDS test, and about their weekend at Two Bunch Palms. As the past became burnished in her mind, grief turned into memory. She put the Nichols Canyon house up for sale and moved in with Sibyl.

Alice's humor returned and she started writing a script. "It's about a beautiful young widow. It's called *Extremely Sympathetic Heroine.*"

"Let me guess," Sibyl said. "She has a fight with her mother-in-law. Also a widow."

"Right. The mother-in-law tries to ruin everything. She definitely isn't sympathetic."

"Call it *Extremely Sympathetic Heroine Triumphant,*" Sybil said.

After several months of work, Alice showed a draft to Harriet Kastle, her old boss at Paramount. Harriet didn't give Alice an answer for a long time but when she had finally read the script, now called *The Silver Wars,* she said that it needed some work but it was a good story with a sympathetic leading role. On Harriet's recommendation, Paramount bought the script and hired Sybil to do the rewrite.

* * *

Henry showed "The Art Deco Widow" to Murray Marden, who in his gentle way said, "What is this shit? Is this some new hobby? What happened to bookcases?"

"It's a story, Murray."

"Where's the movie in any of this? Everybody is going to know this is Tom and Audrey Lewin."

"It's not a secret."

"Is Tanya supposed to be his mother? I never met her."

"Maybe now you have."

"Are you going to show this to Audrey?"

"I don't know."

"Didn't you go out with her for about a minute and a half? There's going to be libel questions in this."

"I'm trying to say good-bye to the man the only way I know how."

"Yeah, yeah. Well, darling, he's dead, so I guess he can't sue."

"Very encouraging, Murray." Ever since seeing him at Tryst, Murray called Henry "darling."

"I didn't know you were interested in Art Deco."

"I just learned a little for the story. It's the characters who are interested in it."

"There might be a movie in that. Not this widow stuff, though. Pump it up. Make it hot. That silver is gorgeous. Shoot it in L.A. and Paris. International Deco silver thieves. You should spec it, darling."

"I'll think about it."

"If you have to play these little games and use real people, cock it up more so nobody knows what you're doing. So, have you been to Tryst lately?"

"Not lately. Listen, just forget about the story. I'll think of something else."

"Whatever you want. I'll see you soon, I hope."

"Right. Bye, Murray."

In Henry's Fibber McGee script closet he had a special box for things he cared about. In moving from apartment to apartment, some scripts got lost, but the pages in the box stayed safe. Henry had built his box in the Madeleine days, in his workshop in their house in the hills. He had made it of old pine with dovetail joints and only a touch of glue. He had painted it dark red, inside and out, and put nickel-plated handles on the sides. It was his private repository and although it was all but buried beneath forgotten scripts, Henry dug it out and dusted it off. Into the box went his story, his spent emotion. He closed it up and tried to forget about Ted and the two widows. Henry's crush on Audrey had made them both uncomfortable, so he wrote a story about her instead of pursuing her. It was Henry's prerogative but it was a poor substitute for what he had wanted. It was Henry's lot to live more in his work than his life, which sounded like something Madeleine might have said.

The next day, Murray called about a rewrite. It was quick work and the money was good. Later, when Henry thought about it, he wondered if Murray hadn't found the job for him to get his mind off writing stories and back to the movie business so they could both make some money. Well, Henry thought, it was one way to get an agent to work for you. Henry was glad to have the gig. It might help him stop thinking dark thoughts of death and mortality. And for a while it did.

6

Tomorrowland

Henry and his friends never had a name for their morning gatherings. When people asked if there was a name, Henry sometimes said that yes there was, but it could never be mentioned. In fact, any member was obliged to get up and leave the table if the actual name was uttered in his presence. It was all some salami Henry had picked up from a magazine article about Skull and Bones. The best part of it was how many people believed him and apologized for bringing up the subject, thanking everyone for making an exception and not leaving. If someone asked if he could join them, Henry would say they would have to discuss it. Then, in a day or two, the guy would be told, "You may come this Tuesday as guest speaker." It was amazing how many people got into a lather over being guest speaker, wondering what they were supposed to say and even preparing remarks. The whole business came to a head when the *Los Angeles Times* ran an article about literary and political salons. According to the paper, mornings at the Farmers Market constituted a salon. Henry said that each morning everybody had to make one grand statement about art and the world. Wally offered to design invitations that they could then make a point of withholding from anybody who wanted one. The salon business along with the construction of the mall led to yet more articles and TV interviews. A reporter for the *L.A. Weekly* took an interest in Henry's metal spoon. She saw his refusal to accept a plastic utensil as the last gasp of the *ancien régime*. All the stories had an

98

elegiac tone and most of them came and went, but the "tin spoon," as the *Weekly* called it, took on a life of its own. People stopped at the table and pointed it out or asked to see it. Henry never sought publicity. What benefit could it possibly have for him? He wasn't a performer. In his bemusement, Henry started telling anyone who asked that he had sold the film rights to *The Tin Spoon* to Milt Arkadine and even now they were working on the script. Then the reporters started calling Ark! He told them that the plans were still secret but an announcement was imminent. It made Henry wonder if his view of personal publicity was right. The studios don't have any real standards for hiring writers. A comedy set in Italy? Get so-and-so, he cooks a mean osso bucco. A Western? Get this one or that, he rides on the bridal path in Griffith Park. If there's a plausible name with any connection, no matter how remote, it gives them a reason to make their decision and an excuse for why it's not their fault if it all goes south, as it usually does. Maybe, Henry thought, he should hire a publicist and start wearing black clothes and going to clubs with twenty-two-year-olds, except he didn't know any. Eventually the spoon business was forgotten and everyone went back to talking about sports and movies and politics and women, which led to the one real change in the population of the table.

Liv Verakos said that the Market had "Too many men all the time." She was probably right but Henry couldn't help thinking what a sign of modernity that was. In the days when Henry was married, Madeleine took comfort in the fact that the table was all men. She never said anything about it, but when the occasional woman joined them, which Henry always reported, he knew it made Madeleine uneasy. She seemed to suspect that Henry wasn't telling her the whole story. Liv took a different view. As a result, Leo had recruited two women who had been around the Market to join the table. Lauren, who was even younger than Liv, was an actress who was amused by all the testosterone. She knew Fitzgerald's novels, which pleased Henry, who had thought that her generation's reading was pretty much limited to computer screens. He declared Lauren the table's youth representative and came to count on her to explain what the hell all the twenty-somethings were up to. The lads, as Henry sometimes called his pals, listened to Lauren's stories about the horrors of auditions and cheered with her when she got jobs. Woman number two, Jane, was a psychotherapist about Henry's age. She knew Madeleine and was kind about reporting her professional activities without Henry having to ask. Jane and Lauren looked a bit like mother and daughter, and they fit in without any noticeable bumps. Everyone had to admit that Liv had been right.

Not everyone turned up at the Market every day, but on an overcast November morning, when Wally had announced that Mack Donnelly was coming, the attendance was high. Mack was an underground celebrity. Henry had once declared him the winner of the Craziest Man in Hollywood contest, and there had been plenty of qualified candidates. Mack wrote the occasional film script, but his day job was writing jokes for television talk shows. The work was lucrative but even more anonymous than screenwriting. Mack's real life was as a speaker at celebrity roasts, those after-dinner attack sessions that were soaked in alcohol and laced with aggression. People would make donations to one fashionable charity or another just to hear Mack's scatological and surreal riffs. Henry had been to a few and he was always amazed at the way Mack tossed off lines about defecation, bestiality, and penis size, three frequent topics. Henry had once heard Mack go on about an actor who had grown up on a farm. The guy was seated a few feet away. Mack pointed at him and said, "He was thirty-one before he fucked indoors—and he didn't even own the sheep." Henry always wondered what the victim was thinking when he heard that. Probably, Lord, let me get through this without tears. Being around Mack Donnelly, Henry thought, was like slipping through the looking glass into a place where the id was given a verbal free-ride. Mack was big, well over six feet tall, with broad shoulders and a thick mustache. He was from the Middle West and as a young man he had been a hurdler on the Harvard track team. None of those credits were likely to turn up in the résumés of other joke writers, who tended to be short, desperate, and from the meaner parts of Brooklyn.

As everyone waited for Mack, a man not known for punctuality, Irwin was getting ready for the wisecrack session that would surely ensue. Irwin loved old jokes—Jewish jokes, certainly, but also saloon jokes, desert islands, traveling salesmen—the whole crazy quilt of American humor. Irwin was a one-man vaudeville revival. To warm up for Mack, Irwin started in: "Guy sees an ad on the Internet: Talking dog for sale. So, he goes to see about it. The owner says, 'Yeah. Dog's in the back room. Talk to him if you want.' So the guy goes back and sees an old schnauzer on the sofa. 'I guess you want to know a little about me,' the schnauzer says. 'Well, yeah,' the guy says. The schnauzer says, 'I'm fifteen years old. Not so young, I know. For the first few years of my life, I worked as a sniffer for drugs. At airports. Then after that, I was an earthquake sniffer. I traveled all over. Those were my best years. Then I got rheumatoid arthritis and couldn't get around so much. Now I work part time as a seeing-eye dog. Volunteer work. That's about it.' The guy is astonished. 'Wow! What a life you've had. Give me a minute, okay?' The schnauzer says, 'Sure.' So the guy goes back to the owner and says, 'That dog is amazing. Really something. I have to ask you, why do you want to sell him?' The owner grunts and says, 'Why? Why? Because he's nothing but a LIAR!'"

Henry knew it was an oft-told tale, but he loved the spin Irwin put on it. The Internet, the earthquake sniffing. Irwin told it with gestures, accents, sound effects, and spontaneous side riffs that included different barks—a high yip then a growl because, Irwin said, the schnauzer was bilingual. Irwin might tell a story more than once, but never in quite the same way. He could always make it new.

Mack finally rolled into the Market in one of the tweed jackets he wore year-round, chewing on a Cuban cigar and spewing his lunatic insults and wisecracks even before he'd had coffee. "I'm wearing Hitler's shoes," he said as he sat down. Jack Poland, who was there that day, said, "I don't think he'll miss them." Jack was a television producer who had once been a sportswriter. He was a great audience for Mack, breaking into delighted laughter at whatever unlikely thing Mack said. Jack had a journalist's interest in facts and statistics and a deep need to figure out where the fiddle was in every deal. He was also seventy-five pounds overweight. He was sitting next to Morty Elfman, who was also overweight though not as much as Jack. The two of them were catnip for Mack Donnelly. He started in tossing off a quickie: "Jack Poland and Morty Elfman are so big they applied for statehood. North and South Dakota." Henry thought it was a generic line that Mack had probably used many times before. "The way Jack Poland tells the difference between coming and farting is when he farts something comes out." Jack laughed, but Henry just sat there in awe of this turn into such breathtaking vulgarity. Big as a state? North and South Dakota? Okay, Henry thought, those are fat jokes. But the coming and farting? What was that about? Part of Mack Donnelly was permanently set at the age of eleven. Henry wondered if Mack would go after Jane or Lauren. Maybe he would make lurid mother-and-daughter jokes. Jack and Morty knew what they were getting into. The two women, probably not. Henry needn't have been concerned. Mack didn't directly attack anyone he wasn't sure about. His strange skill was in taking it farther than his victim might have imagined possible. In the private ways of Hollywood, it was a badge of distinction to have been abused by Mack Donnelly. To Mack, if you weren't a player of some sort, you were just wallpaper. He wouldn't touch Lauren or Jane, and he was just fooling around with Jack and Morty. Mack was eyeing Irwin, his quarry, and everyone knew it.

Mack and Irwin had worked on the writing staff of the old Jackie Day show, when it was a network hit. Mack was in the chips in those days, though he never struck Henry as a guy who much concerned himself with money. Mack began by talking about Jackie, who was semiretired but not beyond the laws of slander. Jackie was a national institution. The lovable clown, the song-and-dance man, the volunteer for all kinds of charities. The man was a saint, though perhaps not to his joke writers. Henry was hoping for some real viciousness. Irwin jumped in, claiming that Jackie never understood many of the jokes he delivered on the air. Mack, who never worried about being specific, ignored Irwin's opening and said, "Jackie's cock is so small, he fucks Cheerios." There was tentative laughter from the table. Henry glanced over at Jane, wondering what a psychotherapist made of this display. "Jackie's a great cook," Mack said. "Every Thanksgiving our families get together and fuck his turkey." People from the other tables started to listen. For Mack, that meant a bigger audience, which is what he craved. An older woman, one of the Park LaBrea stalwarts, made a show of leaving, as if she felt an obligation to be offended. Mack giggled, a breathy little laugh that sometimes popped out when he thought things were going right. "Jackie believes in the occult. He goes to a Gypsy woman who reads his hemorrhoids." All Henry could think was, what on earth does this have to do with Jackie Day? "Jackie goes to the barrio and takes little kids into the sewer and teaches them to bob for shit." One of the security guys from the Market was listening and looking kind of jumpy. Maybe he'd try to arrest Mack. Public indecency or something. In the name of the Farmers Market. Mack would destroy him and the guy probably knew it. Tired now of Jackie Day, Mack turned on Leo. "What are you doing? Why don't you go over to Cedars and wait for the birth of your next bride?" Lauren laughed the hardest at that one.

At a table of Israelis who had been coming to the Market as long as Henry and his friends had, an older guy said, "Ehh. I've heard worse." It made Henry think about the first time he had been in the audience at one of Mack's celebrity roasts. It was years ago at the Friars Club, for some long-forgotten television grandee. Henry had heard about these events and wangled an invitation so he could see for himself. After a few bland testimonials had been delivered, the ladies were asked to leave the room. And they did! Without seeming to question it, a parade of fashionable women just got up and left. Where the hell did they go? Henry wondered. To some retiring room to fan themselves and take valerian drops? Then the staff was told to clear out. If you didn't already have a drink, you were out of luck. Only members and their male guests were allowed to be present when Mack Donnelly took the stage. Mack came out and did the same lunatic stuff about toilets and cocks in knots and all the rest. Henry was amused, but he kept picturing those women—there must have been fifty of them—and the Latino waiters and busboys, all out in the lobby. Now Mack was yelling essentially the same stuff at the Market and at the old Jews of Park LaBrea. Public discourse had become so lurid since that earlier time that Mack didn't so much shock this crowd as give them an opportunity to compare him to what they had already heard from their grandchildren or on television. The guy who said, "I've heard worse," might have been speaking for all of them.

Irwin didn't want to drop Jackie Day before he had his own go at him. Irwin could be every bit as compulsive about joke telling as Mack, but his occasional ventures into the scatological were mild and his gags always had coherence. Irwin too could fire a barrage of one-liners. On a normal day, that is, one without Mack Donnelly around, if something Irwin said fell flat, he would just move on to something else. Then, later, he'd come back to the failed joke and turn it a little and adjust it and try it again until it worked. It was the way all writers thought. Not Mack. He liked people to laugh, but if he pleased himself, that was enough. Irwin said that Jackie Day stole his whole act from Menashe Skulnick. Henry had to think for a moment who that was. He vaguely remembered him as a comic actor from the Yiddish theater who used to turn up occasionally in mainstream shows. The Park LaBrea crowd probably remembered him. Henry didn't think Lauren knew about Menashe Skulnick. Irwin jumped out of his chair and began flailing his arms and dancing in mincing little steps. Henry could almost hear brassy music and tap shoes. Damned if it didn't suggest Jackie Day at his most antic.

"That's it!" Mack said, and he got up and danced with Irwin in an improvised Yiddish theater vaudeville step. Irwin pursed his lips and puffed out his cheeks like a blowfish. He evoked a particular person as he danced. Henry didn't have any idea if it was Menashe Skulnick, but it was a performance. Mack just stumbled around and yelled his insults. "Jackie Day looks like a condom filled with walnuts. Jackie Day's . . ." Mack went blank and couldn't form the next word. He said something like "ok-a-co." The word seemed to surprise him and he tried once more. "Jackie's ok-a-co . . ." He got lost in the syllables. Surely he meant to say "cock," a word that was usually at the center of his vocabulary. He tried again and stumbled again. Mack's face went pale and he began losing his breath and it seemed his balance. Irwin had stopped dancing and he helped Mack sit down. The audience at the surrounding tables applauded, but Mack didn't look good. He said his arm felt funny. Lauren went to the coffee stall to get water for him.

"Is it numb?" Henry asked.

"It's nothing. I can't feel . . ." Then he got lost again. He seemed to be trying to say that he couldn't feel anything in his arm but the words wouldn't come. Henry knew it had to be a little stroke, what doctors call a TIA, a transient ischemic attack. It was hard to get a grip on the idea of Mack Donnelly floating alone in his own vulgarity, unable to say "cock." Henry wasn't sure what the others were thinking, but there were enough old people around that thoughts of strokes, big or small, were never far from their minds. Jane was the person likeliest to know something about all this. She said he ought to go over to Cedars and see a neurologist. Mack just waved her off. Henry could tell Mack's powers were returning when he lit his cigar and started making jokes. "Well, Doc," he said, no longer shouting, "I was trying to say Jackie's cock was tied in a knot but it came out the Santa Anas blew a flame up his ass." He's better, Henry thought. It must be strange to live in that trapeze of a mind under what passes in Mack for normal conditions. What if his mind was now muddled? What would happen? As Henry watched him, he thought that sometimes the jokes were funny in a preposterous way, but other times, when they seemed interchangeable and untethered to anything, Mack just seemed nuts. Part of the excitement of being around him, Henry thought, was no one—probably not even Mack—had any idea what he might say even at those roasts, when he had a printed sheet of insults in front of him.

Mack sipped the water and then said he had to leave. Wally wanted to drive him over to Cedars for a checkup, but Mack said he felt okay.

* * *

A few weeks later, on a Monday morning that promised rain, Henry poked along in the morning rush making his way to the Market. The traffic had grown so thick and slow on Fairfax that he sometimes wondered if the trip was worth the bother. The drivers seemed jumpy. People in Los Angeles always reacted to the prospect of rain as if it had never happened before. Henry thought about turning around but he had grown dependent on the morning ritual.

At the Market, Henry joined Leo and Irwin, who were contemplating the dark sky. When the first drops fell they moved to a table near the doughnut stand under the tin roof. They were a front-row audience waiting for nature to begin her show. Soon enough, a fierce squall began as if the sky had been unzipped. Henry always wondered how the idea that it never rained in Los Angeles had taken hold. It was a near-tropical city and this was the start of the rainy season. The three of them sat there letting the rain's steady tattoo block any attempt at conversation. Henry's eyes glazed as he stared out at the pounding water. Time seemed suspended. He was oddly comforted by nature acting in a predictable way. It didn't last long, maybe fifteen minutes, maybe a little more. It washed the air and a cool, sweet smell came over them all that helped Henry back to the here and now. The Market cats who were there to control the mice that followed all that produce and who by day patrolled the tin roofs emerged from the private places where they had taken cover. It was said that some of them only came down after dark and had become feral. Leo, who had probably been dreaming too, looked up at one of them and said, "Cat on a wet tin roof," and that was enough to break the storm's spell.

Monday mornings at the Market—rain or not—meant Kenny Klaven would be there. Kenny was a reporter who at one time or another had worked for all the Hollywood trade papers. He was about Henry's age, a slender guy with a graying Mephistophelean beard that he tugged when he talked. Kenny had a wide knowledge of films that Henry appreciated. He also covered production finance, a subject so arcane that to Henry it might have been Sanskrit. Kenny was now a reporter for *Variety,* and on Mondays he brought a printout of the previous week's grosses. He had started the custom some years earlier when movie grosses didn't appear until Tuesday and then only in the trades. Having them in advance in those days was limited to studio executives. That Henry's gang at the Market got them on Monday morning was more a sign they were in the game rather than any sort of useful tool. Now, as everyone knows, movie grosses are everywhere. Henry once claimed that he had seen the damn things in *Junior Scholastic.* No one doubted him until Leo asked why had he been reading *Junior Scholastic.*

Kenny came rolling in with Ike Bretherton, who was the head of the story department at Paramount. Henry was always wary of anything to do with studio story departments, which was where the actual reading of scripts got done. Story departments couldn't say "Yes!" to a script, but they sure as hell could say "No!" Ike had gone to Jesuit schools, right through college, and had once contemplated the priesthood. The Jesuits had honed his mind to an almost brutal sharpness. The Church surely had something other than the analysis of film scripts in mind for young Ike, but that's where he now applied his formidable analytical skills. He was a big man, about fifty, who looked like an athlete gone soft.

Kenny handed the printout of the grosses to Irwin and continued an argument with Ike that had probably started in the parking lot. Ike always seemed to be wrestling with his education. At present, Henry believed, Ike was an Episcopalian. He and Kenny were talking about *Diary of a Country Priest,* which was apparently about to be released in a DVD version. Henry couldn't help but think that Kenny and Ike were surely the only two guys imaginable who on this wet Hollywood morning could or would want to debate Bresson's picture from both commercial and theological points of view. And if they were in the right mood, they could probably switch sides and do it all again for the sheer sport of it.

"It's a boiling down of the Bernanos novel," Ike said. "The priest is gentle. His face has no affect. His holiness colors everything he does. He dies young. Bring any particular historical and highly revolutionary figure to mind?"

"It's a push to call him Jesus," Kenny said.

"He's not Christ," Ike said with condescending clarity. "He's a fallible man with qualities of great goodness that reflect his devotion to Christ."

"It'll do better in DVD than it ever did in the theaters," Kenny said.

The others were ignoring them and discussing the merits of the movies on Kenny's Monday morning list when Wally came in looking upset. "Mack Donnelly had a stroke," he said. "He's a mess."

"When?" Kenny asked, sharply, for the moment forgetting about Bresson.

"Thursday, I think. In his car. He was just sitting in it like that. In some garage. Couldn't move."

"Who found him?" Ike asked.

"I don't know," Wally said, irritated to be grilled. "His son got him to the UCLA emergency room." Henry hadn't known that Mack had a son. For a moment, all Henry could think about was having Mack Donnelly for a father. It would make Felix seem like Father Flanagan.

"They're taking him to Woodland Hills," Wally said. Woodland Hills meant the Motion Picture Home. Sending a stroke patient there wasn't a sign of optimism.

Kenny moved away from the table and began making calls on his cell phone. Henry knew he was calling the news desk at *Variety*. The UCLA emergency room sees its share of celebrities, and there's always someone on the staff who knows to call certain newspapers when a famous person is admitted. They probably had no idea who Mack was. If it had been Cedars, Henry thought, someone would have known and called it in to six papers and expected checks from all of them. Kenny was working the story.

"Can we go out there and visit him?" Henry asked.

"Yeah," Kenny said, still on his cell phone.

"Can he talk?" Ike asked.

"I think he's goo-goo," Kenny answered.

Henry always called the Motion Picture Home "Tomorrowland." It was for people in the business who had retired and needed a little help. Like all such joints, Henry knew that they made you sign over your money and then they took care of you till you died. Henry couldn't help wondering about Mack's finances. Did he have an accountant or a business manager? It was hard for Henry to think about such things, so instead he tried to recall the Motion Picture Home from a visit he had once made there. Somebody—probably Irwin—had called it "Palm Springs without the fun." Henry had seen some pleasant cottages with palm trees and a few golf carts ferrying old people around.

A few days later, Henry and Wally and Irwin took the Ventura Freeway out to Woodland Hills to what real estate people call the West Valley, and what Wally called to Hell and gone, to visit Mack Donnelly. Wally volunteered to drive. They sped past countless malls, each with what seemed the same stores all offering discounted merchandise. Discounted from what? Henry wondered. They all charged the same amount for the same stuff, but it made people happy to think they were getting a bargain. So discounted it was. Henry particularly liked the Christian Discount Book Center. It was next to Futon World. No discounts there, Henry guessed. Henry realized his mind was drifting again. He turned back to Wally and Irwin, who were telling old tales of Mack, recalling his deeds. Wally asked, "What was the deal that time he insulted the Indians?"

"Which Indians?" Irwin asked. "Dot on the head or woo-woo-woo?"

"Dot," Wally said.

"It was supposed to be a commercial," Irwin said. "He had the gig to write it or do the voice-over or something. Out of nowhere—which is where he got his best stuff—he said, 'Today we celebrate the life of Mahatma Gandhi and honor him for freeing sixty thousand Hindus so they can work at 7-Eleven.'"

Henry laughed and, ever the logical one, asked, "Was it a commercial for 7-Eleven? Or did it have to do with India?"

"Who the hell knows?" Irwin said. "When did it ever have to make sense?"

"True," Henry said. "Mack lives in his own mind." That quieted everyone for a moment as each man thought about Mack being unable to speak.

"When we were doing the Jackie Day show," Irwin said, "Mack used to walk around the halls at the network saying 'Blow me' to every woman who walked by. Secretaries, actresses, cleaning women, executives. 'Blow me, blow me, blow me.'"

"What happened?" Henry asked.

"The ones at the network ignored him or just told him to fuck off or whatever," Irwin said. "So then he did it outside where people were waiting to go on the tour. Bunch of ladies from the buses and Mack is saying, 'Blow me, blow me, blow me,' right in their face."

"Any takers?" Henry asked.

"It just bounced off their heads."

"That's Mack," Henry said. "Always ahead of the curve."

"The thing he did that people who were there swear it happened, was at Thanksgiving about thirty years ago," Wally said. "He was married then and they were giving the dinner."

"Mack as host?" Henry asked, unable to picture it.

"His wife ran it," Wally said. "Anyway, Mack comes in with the big platter and puts it down in the center of the table. Very *Gourmet* magazine. He pulls off the dome-thing and instead of the turkey he's got the baby there. On the platter. The kid was about six months old. Bare-assed. He had little pieces of parsley around him." Henry laughed, but what ran through his mind was that being Mack's son was even more fraught with difficulty than he had imagined. That story was probably part of family lore. Ought to keep a therapist or two busy.

Irwin was laughing and asking questions about the baby on the platter, seeing it like a director, trying to determine if it was even possible. "How'd the kid breathe?" he asked. "What if he fell off?"

Henry thought of Swift's *Modest Proposal,* which suggested ending a famine by eating the babies of the poor. Mack probably knew of it, or once did. Henry realized that in the years he had known him, he'd never heard Mack make a reference to anything literary or historical. He'd never heard him say anything that wasn't part of a nutty joke.

"At dinner in some restaurant he waved the cork aside and sniffed the waiter," Wally said. That made Henry laugh. "Another time he said, 'Sex is natural but not if it's done right.'"

Irwin said, "I remember him saying about somebody, 'He can insert a Popsicle in his ass and tell what flavor it is.' I always liked that he said 'insert.'"

"Yeah," Henry said. "When Mack Donnelly starts in, nobody gets out alive."

* * *

The main buildings of Tomorrowland seemed to loom up on a cliffside overlooking the freeway. There was something unpleasant and ghostly about it. Or maybe it was just that it was a cloudy day. Henry was thinking, Is this the future for me? He supposed Wally and Irwin were thinking the same thing, though no one mentioned it. As they went from the parking lot to the entrance, an old guy in a wheelchair rolled up to them. "Irwin! Hey, Irwin, how are you? It's me. Marvin. Marvin Starr. Remember? I was with you at ABC. Remember?"

"How are you?" Irwin said. He didn't have a clue who this guy was.

"Great. I'm doing great. How's the family?"

"They're fine, Marvin. Nice to see you."

"I got one for you, boys," Marvin said, not about to be dismissed so quickly. "Couple of writers get together. First one says, 'So how's the negotiation going?' Second one says, 'Not bad. We're about a hundred grand apart. I want a hundred grand, and they don't want to give it to me.'" Then Marvin laughed at his joke, which was pretty funny, Henry had to admit, though he wasn't in the mood for it. "I've got a script," Marvin said. "It's a treatment, actually. Between a treatment and a first draft. More like a first draft, but an early one. *Bank Job.* Got dialogue.

Scene for scene. All in there. Hysterical. About these old guys who knock over a bank," Marvin said, determined to get it all in before Irwin cut him off.

"Why don't you send it to my office," Irwin said.

"I got it right here." Marvin had a canvas pouch hung on the side of his chair. Maybe it was filled with treatments. He gave one to Irwin, who thanked him. For a moment Henry thought Marvin might hand out more of them, but he was a show-business veteran and seemed to know that Henry and Wally couldn't do him any good. As they walked toward the main entrance, Marvin rolled alongside Irwin, telling him more about his treatment.

Henry was glad to be in sight of the door and he hoped soon free of Marvin Starr. No such luck. Why Henry had thought wheelchairs stopped at the door he couldn't imagine. Marvin rolled right into the lobby with them. Henry wasn't sure what to expect but what he saw was Mickey Resnick, of the manicure and cuff-link set and noted habitué of La Plume. There were always rumors around that Mickey was going to run for governor, a prospect that Henry found so ludicrous that he fig-ured it might happen. At the moment, Mickey, in pinstripes with a silk square in his pocket, was the center of attention for a television crew. They were making a video of him standing in the lobby babbling about how great the Motion Picture Home was. When Mickey saw Henry, he stopped and came over to shake hands. Henry was about to ask him what he was doing, but by then Mickey had seen Irwin, who was a big-ger fish than Henry. Since Wally wasn't in the business, Mickey just nodded at him.

"Isn't this a great and wonderful place?" Mickey asked, directing the question to Irwin. Just like Marvin Starr.

"Oh, yeah," Henry said, answering it anyway. "G&W. Absolutely."

"What does that mean?" Wally asked.

"Great and Wonderful."

"Exactly!" Mickey said.

"Are you making a television show?" Henry asked.

"Public service spot. Little young for this place, aren't you, boys?"

"We came out to see Mack Donnelly," Irwin said.

"Mack Donnelly? Maybe we could get some tape of me with him," Mickey said and then thought better of it. Henry could see the doubt come over Mickey's face. If he was running for office, if that's what this was all about, he probably wouldn't want to be associated with Mack.

"It's okay. You'll be safe," Henry said. "He can't talk."

"Well, maybe," Mickey said. "Let's get some pictures right here." Mickey stood between Irwin and Henry. Wally sort of stayed on the edge and one of Mickey's crew took a few photographs. Mickey changed his expression for each shot. A serious face, a friendly face, and an odd one that he may have thought was a wise face. Henry thought this guy is just trying on hats because he doesn't know who he is. When Mickey had run through his repertoire of faces a young woman with a clipboard wrote down their names. Irwin said he was King Vidor. Then he spelled it for her.

"Give Mack my best," Mickey said and then turned to his crew and said, "We're out of here." Marvin Starr decided Mickey was a better bet and rolled after him, telling him about the old bank robbers.

"Hey, I'd vote for him," Irwin said.

"Right," Henry said. "A man to lead us into the future."

A woman at the rehab desk took them to Mack's room. Henry was surprised by the silence. Not only in the hall, but from his pals. Henry was scared, and he assumed Irwin and Wally were too. They found Mack sitting in a wheelchair in a sunny room that looked out toward the lawns and the cottages. Mack seemed immobile. An arm was stretched out and his face was drooping to one side. It had been ten days since the stroke, and his hair and mustache had gone white. He seemed to look at them as they came into the room. They greeted him, trying to sound upbeat in the inane way people do around the deeply damaged. Henry was glad that nobody told Mack he looked great. The questions on Henry's mind were, Did Mack know who they were? Could he hear what they said? He gave no sign and a nurse who looked in on them said, in a cheerful voice,

"Oh, he knows something. He's just not saying." Henry considered punching her in the face. As they stood around, trying not to gawk and quickly running out of small talk, Mack's arm, the one that had gone stiff, shot up in the air, lolled to one side, and then dropped back again. Did it mean something? What raced through Henry's mind was that Mack was trying to hit his visitors. Finally, Henry spoke to him. "Mack, I'm going to assume you can hear me even if you can't answer. I'm very sorry for the situation you're in. It breaks my heart to see it. They have the best doctors and neurologists here. They're working on it. What can be done, will be done." Henry knew it was the right thing to say and the others were relieved that he had said it, but it didn't make Henry feel any better. And of course he didn't know if it was at all true or if Mack heard any of it.

As they were trying to decide how long they should stay, an orderly, a young guy as big and as powerful looking as Mack had been ten days earlier, wheeled in another patient. It was a double room and this was apparently Mack's roommate. He was an old man, small and vacant-eyed. Like Mack, he said nothing and gave no sign that he saw anyone. It was Irwin who recognized him. "Is that Harold Strauss?" he asked.

"You hear that, Mr. Strauss?" the orderly said. "Here's a friend of yours."

"Hello, Harold," Irwin said, his voice subdued. Henry had to make an effort not to gasp. Harold Strauss was a producer who was famous for making earnest movies about race relations (could be better) or nuclear war (against it) or the Holocaust (dreadful). It was subject matter now relegated to television. Henry never much liked his pictures, but Harold Strauss was a big player. Whenever Hollywood had to offer up an example of a responsible citizen, it was usually Harold Strauss. Henry had never met him but he knew him to be a vital man who got what he wanted in the world. His movies might have been sappy, but nobody messed with Harold Strauss, at least not twice. Now he was shriveling into death. If Henry had ever thought about it, he would have assumed a man like Harold Strauss, in this condition, would be in a Bel

Air mansion surrounded by private medical help. There was a Mrs. Strauss, in fact he still had the original model, which was unusual for guys like Harold. She must have felt that he was so far gone that only this place could take care of him. Henry wondered if Tomorrowland got all of Strauss's money, too. Mack probably didn't have much, but Mr. Strauss might well have plenty stashed in Switzerland or the Cayman Islands. If he did, Henry wondered if he was aware of it. Henry was fascinated by the irony of Mack Donnelly, the wild man of Hollywood, the king of lewdness and vulgar insult, and Harold Strauss, the master of the earnest, being linked in this terrible way. If Mack had been able, he'd probably spend his days abusing his roommate just for the sheer pleasure it would bring him. That wasn't possible. Henry knew, and he didn't think he was the only one who knew, that soon enough Mack would grow thin and frail. He too would become a shadow. Henry also knew that after this day he would have bad dreams and they would continue for a long while. All he could hope for Mack and Harold Strauss was that neither of them was aware of their state. Henry couldn't say about Mr. Strauss, but he knew in his gut that Mack was aware of enough of his circumstances to make him want only one thing more from the world and that was an early death. For a brief moment Henry saw himself turning up a morphine drip and helping Mack float away. But there was no drip. Mack was all but immobile, though there was no sign that he felt physical pain. When Mack had suffered the TIA and couldn't say "cock," he had felt some numbness but that was all. There wouldn't be any morphine drip for Mack and no opportunity for Henry or anyone else to play angel of merciful death.

As they left the rehab building, going back to the car, no one was talking. Marvin Starr and his wheelchair were waiting in the parking lot. "How you doing, guys?" Marvin asked.

"Not so great at the moment." There was such sadness in Irwin's voice that even Marvin Starr knew to back off.

During the drive home they talked a little about Mickey Resnick. "Is that putz really going to run for governor?" Wally asked.

"He could win," Henry said. "He's got money, a big smile, and he's too dumb to know he'd be terrible at it."

"He'll keep ten percent of all the taxes," Irwin said.

"And never return anybody's phone calls." Henry said.

"He'll lie about everything," Irwin said. "He'll say he's the governor of Pennsylvania."

The jokes were funny enough, and they each tried to laugh but it didn't quite work. After they were finished with Mickey Resnick, they grew quiet, each pensive in his own way. Henry looked at his pals, each gone deep into himself, and felt a love so intense that Henry knew if he willed it hard enough his love could sustain them all and protect them from strokes and wheelchairs. Henry thought more about Mack, about his tweed jackets, the only remnants of his long-ago student days, about the way he might announce that he was wearing Hitler's shoes and about his taste for Cuban cigars and tall glasses of amber ale and how he liked to go out to the track at Hollywood Park and make rude jokes about the jockeys and the horses. He thought about how Mack wor-shipped at the vulgar god of offense, how he immersed himself in ni-hilism and indulged his passion for pushing, pushing. Henry wondered if anyone had ever told Mack to shut up, to not say another word. Prob-ably not. It was fashionable to be insulted by him. It was Mack's own body that finally had the last word and told him, enough.

"Do you think that's the right place for him?" Irwin asked. Henry knew that Irwin meant well, but he also meant, whether he knew it or not, Is that the right place for me when the time comes or should I just kill myself right now?

"I don't know," Henry said.

"Who the hell knows anything?" Irwin said.

"It's okay, I guess," Henry said. "He's in the capable care of Nurse Vim and Doctor Pep of Tomorrowland. Who could ask for more?" Henry found himself thinking about his little speech to Mack. He knew he had been precise at a moment when the others were unable to find words. He should have felt good about that, but he didn't. In the hum of the freeway traffic, it occurred to him just why that was. His remarks in their very precision, the articulation that Henry was so proud of, were a rebuke to Mack's surreal vulgarity. Henry had meant well, and perhaps even done well, but it was undeniable that there had been a note of hostility in what he had said. It was as if Henry were saying, See, if you hadn't been so loud and lewd, so out of control, this terrible thing wouldn't have happened. He kept his thoughts to himself and there were no more jokes, no more stories. In the privacy of his melancholy silence, Henry thought that he couldn't bear thinking about Mack's sadness for one more moment. Henry's sorrow took him back to a time that now seemed easier, to his own blithe days of carelessness where at least in memory everything seemed fresh and green. Henry found himself in the past.

Then

7

Down Mexico Way

Henry spent his thirty-fourth birthday in Mexico, where he was doing a production rewrite. He wasn't sure why he didn't tell anyone that it was his birthday. He told himself that he didn't want anyone to make a fuss, which he knew full well meant that what he really wanted was for people to set off fireworks. Oh, me-oh, my-oh. The picture he was working on was *Faster,* a romance set in modern Los Angeles with fantasy sequences in the Old West, which in this case meant the standing sets at *Estudios Churubusco.* There was a swinging-door saloon, a sheriff's office, a general store, and, Henry thought, every other cliché of a genre that had played itself out. He had been called to Mexico by his chum and sparring partner the English director Rolf Shilling. There was trouble on the set. Perhaps Henry could come down and have a look. Rolf made it sound oh so easy. Henry knew better. No one made a call like that unless the show was all but on fire. Blake Porter, the star, was unhappy. The studio had wanted to send Paul Baron, the original writer. Rolf couldn't bear the guy and his dopey wardrobe. Paul had screamed that Henry was trying to steal his credit and that he would ruin the picture. The more Paul complained, the more Rolf insisted on Henry being hired. Henry knew that by taking the job he would make an enemy of Paul Baron, but he didn't hesitate. When the maneuvering was complete and all the phone calls answered, Henry was in Mexico.

Hollywood location shoots have always been lubricious holidays.

Everyone is far from home and the only thing that matters is the movie. Diets and marriage vows aren't quite forgotten, but they often seem suspended. The nights can be enlivened by what in the trade were known as locationships. They tended to be brief. Henry was staying at the Posada Durango, a hotel that looked like a set designer's idea of a Mexican rancho with courtyards and fountains and a cactus or two outside each room. From the inside looking out, all the planting seemed a fine addition, but from outside the place looked like a cactus farm. Still, from the moment Henry put on a guayabera, he relaxed into Mexican rhythms. California—*el norte*—seemed far away. Henry was looking forward to working with Rolf, though he was wary. A director in production is like the dictator of a small country. If there are script troubles, then it's as if the country is at war. Henry was there as a one-man army, a soldier of fortune. The mantra that ran through his head was, Be ready for anything.

Rolf had recently turned fifty, an age when a sensible man is bound to start taking stock. He was tall, angular, and often had a wicked smirk on his face, as if he had just learned something about you that you'd rather he didn't know. Because Rolf was in a position to give jobs to others, he could have been as rude and high-handed as any other director, yet Rolf still made a point of being charming. There was calculation in it, of course. The general reaction was that he must really mean it, otherwise why bother? He had agreed to shoot Paul Baron's script without alterations, saying he had no intention of changing a word. Then he began improvising, which was what Rolf always did. It drove screenwriters and production managers mad. Henry found it amusing, at least when the script being mauled was Paul Baron's. Rolf's speech was often rhetorical, the syllables slightly extended and given equal weight as if he were speaking in French cadences, translated into English. His years in California hadn't flattened Rolf's accent. He habitually dressed in the director's uniform of blue jeans and running shoes, but because of that accent and his high forehead and slender nose, to Americans he might have been Mountbatten.

Rolf was divorced and had a checkered romantic history. He could accept fifty because his libido still ranged widely and was usually engaged. Henry assumed that though Rolf was working hard, he wasn't denying himself location pleasures. Henry had been eyeing the actresses sunning themselves at the hotel swimming pool, wondering which of those babes Rolf had claimed. Henry had to laugh at the naïveté of that. Rolf was sleeping with one of the actors! A young hunk called Chad or maybe it was Lad. The guy thought he had won the lottery. He went around saying Rolf this or Rolf that or me and Rolf or—now and then—Rolf and I. Henry knew that although Chad or Lad had a certain appeal, it was also a way for Rolf to let everyone on the picture know he didn't play by their rules. A few days later, Rolf dropped him and started inviting Bree Miller, who played a dancehall girl, up to his rooms at night. Always keep them guessing, that was Rolf Shilling.

Henry and Rolf had met over *Streets of New York,* Henry's famous $250,000 unmade script. Ark had shown it to Rolf, telling him that Henry was a hot new writer just out from New York. Henry didn't feel all that hot—he'd already been in Los Angeles a few years—but Ark knew Rolf would be interested in whatever was new. He also knew that if he could add Rolf's name to the mix it would make it easier to sell the script. As Ark knew he would, Rolf liked what he read and he helped Henry revise the script. They tightened the rambling scenes and let air into the truncated ones. Henry's version had three main characters. Rolf explained that one would do, thank you. With an antagonist. In his bone-dry way, Rolf had said, "Stars tend to like scripts in which they're the whole show." In addition to the big payday, Henry got a first-class tutorial in studio script construction. And he and Rolf became friends.

After Henry had spent the day lazing about, while Rolf was shooting, they met for a late drink in the hotel bar. It was an article of faith with Rolf that he never appeared worried. The more low-keyed he seemed, the worse the situation. "It's going quite well," he said.

"I saw some of the footage in L.A."

"Yes," he said, making it sound like "yeee-sss." "What I'm doing here is another movie entirely."

"It's a question of blending them, I suppose."

"Blake's never done a Western. He's not comfortable in the clothes. He sees himself as an urban man." This wasn't news, so Henry just waited. "You know the Calderón play, *Life Is a Dream,* I'm sure." Henry nodded, though he hadn't read it in years. Rolf and Henry were notorious for flashy literary debates. It was usually done to intimidate others and it usually worked. "It ought to serve as a model for the scene in the saloon," Rolf said. "The brawl. It could be a jumping-off point."

"I see," Henry said, trying to recall the play. Rolf wanted to see if Henry knew it, which was just the sort of obscure test Rolf fancied. Henry took a stab at it. "The king has kept the prince in chains for years. Then he frees him to put him on the throne. He changes his mind and throws him back in the dungeon."

"Yes," Rolf said, accepting the summary. "Then the prince is told he dreamed the entire episode and has never been out of the dungeon at all. It's bloody marvelous."

"I seem to recall that after Calderón wrote it, he took up the priesthood. Dropped out of show business," Henry said, rummaging around in his memory.

"Blake wasn't familiar with it."

"So what?"

"What matters is that suggesting themes of this sort has spooked him entirely." Henry hadn't seen any such theme in Paul Baron's script, though the idea of reality being a dream was certainly a possible way to play these fantasy sequences.

"He now questions everything I say. It isn't productive." What Rolf meant was he had lost Blake's confidence. That was not an easy admission. It was a measure of his comfort with Henry that he was talking about it at all, even in this roundabout way. It crossed Henry's mind that Rolf's pansexual antics might be another reason Blake was being difficult. By the time they had finished their drink, Henry knew his task wasn't to rewrite the script, but to renew Blake Porter's faith in Rolf Shilling.

Blake and his family were living in a hacienda between the hotel and the sets at Churubusco. It was a grand place made of dark beams and local tiles. Every room seemed to have a patio and a string hammock. Henry had met Blake a few times to talk about other scripts. And he knew Blake had approved hiring him. Henry had enough of a reputation for rewriting scripts under pressure that Blake probably hadn't been hard to convince. Henry's memory of him was that the man was stoned most of the time.

Blake came ambling out to the patio where Henry and Rolf were waiting, calling out "Hen-ree! Hen-ree Aldrich!"

"Coming, Mother," Henry answered, with a gulp in his voice that caused Blake to break into a wide grin. It confused Rolf, who was unfamiliar with this rusty bit of Americana.

"Pages, pages," Blake said. "Henry's here and that means pages."

"Trees fall so I may produce dialogue," Henry said as he accepted Blake's embrace. He acted as if they were old pals—a star's benediction, Henry thought. Blake's grin was in evidence and there were a few laugh lines around his mouth, but his forehead was drawn tight and was without a crease. It had to be the latest chemical injection or some bit of fashionable plastic surgery. There was a slight waxy look about his upper face, and nothing between his hairline and his nose seemed to move at all. Henry thought the guy might be preparing for a monster movie. Blake poured himself into one of the hammocks and rocked gently as he held forth, full of fervent intensity. "Trees in the forest, that's really it. The way we use our natural resources for things that seem important, but who can know what counts in the long run? Trees. Dialogue. Images and content. Is dialogue real or is it imagination? Do we say what we imagine or imagine what we say? How are we to know the dancer from the tap shoe? What's the ratio between comedic and trees versus dramatic? You know?"

Je-sus, Henry thought. He's high as a kite. He sounds like Professor Corey. Rolf saw it too. How could he miss it? Henry waited for some signal from Rolf before he mentioned the script. Before Rolf got the chance, Mrs. Porter, the former Lilah Lynn, joined them, distributing kisses. She used to be a famous model who once earned large sums pushing lipstick or maybe it was eyeliner. Lilah was beautiful in the anonymous way of a face on a billboard. She was now an actress of sorts. She had a part in *Faster,* though she didn't appear in the Mexico scenes. She played an ex-model who was now a famous actress. Paul Baron had written it for her, probably at Blake's instruction. Lilah was wearing baggy khaki shorts and a blue oxford cloth shirt of Blake's that had more buttons open than not. As far as Henry could tell, she wasn't wearing any makeup or underwear. Lilah's forehead had the same stillness as her husband's. She was followed by Charlie, their five-year-old son, and Tita, his nanny. Charlie was a tow-headed kid who squirmed a lot and climbed on things. Tita had a broad, surgery-free Indian face. She was Mexican but she lived in Los Angeles. She was the only one in the crowd who looked uneasy. Henry assumed she had a green card—the Porters had enough lawyers to be sure of that. Still, to Tita, it must have felt risky to cross the border so casually.

"I've been reading the script," Lilah said. Oh, me-oh, my-oh, Henry thought. Here comes trouble. Even Rolf, for whom everyone was a performer and who was never bothered by anybody's behavior, looked uncertain. "The el grande number, before the fight, where Blake goes through the swinging doors, I don't know how his subtext will be clear."

"It will be on his face," Rolf said with an icy reserve that managed to communicate what he was surely feeling, which was something like, I don't care who you're married to, this is none of your business. Stop using acting-class terms that you barely understand.

"Look at this page," Blake said, flipping through the script and then reading Paul Baron's directions. "'He knows a fight is brewing. He goes through the doors with a swagger.' That is unfucking playable. My character wouldn't swagger. The whole characterization that I worked out and developed is based on an inner aura that I have." Henry knew this had to be the sequence that had provoked the Calderón talk. He knew that he'd better not let it go unanswered. This was the moment he would either fail utterly or earn his considerable pay.

"That scene stopped me too," Henry said, looking at the script, trying to hone in on what bothered the Porters.

"It's so tough-guy hombre," Lilah said. Ah. A clue.

"The way this is," Henry said, "Blake barrels through those doors, practically stepping on people."

"That's right," Blake said with resentment in his voice. "My character wouldn't do that."

"We have to know where he's been and where he's going," Henry said. "That's what will create his reality."

"Yeah," Blake mumbled. "Like I said."

"If we're really trying to deconstruct the genre conventions of studio Westerns, this is where we start. A lot rides on this entrance." Henry glanced at his audience. Blake was nodding and Lilah was smiling. She was buying it, which meant Blake would buy it too. "This scene has to appear to be about the big man walking through the swinging doors," Henry said. "In fact, the effect should be a counter-swagger. Blake has to have traces of fear. Bold, yes, but vulnerable. It's the essential duality of the character's ethos. You know there's going to be a brawl. The audience knows it. What we don't know is what does that do to you? That's where the drama is. Inside your head," Henry said, tapping a finger against his skull. "It's as if for a moment you rip open your heart, you show us your soul, your fear. This is physical assertion, and at the same time your character has a nagging doubt that he's imagining his presence here. It's quite complicated, and of course it has to look simple. You weigh all those feelings, balance them on the peaks of confusion and clarity. Then, when your traditional masculinity overtakes the fleeting glimpse of your more feminine side, you tamp it down and return to strength. Now, with tempered testosterone, you look at that crowd in the saloon as your maleness rises up and you say, 'Move over, boys. The game starts here.'"

"Now that's a subtext," Lilah said.

"Cool," Blake said. "Minimal. I like it."

"You're welcome," Henry said. "The doctor is in." Then he ran it back through his mind. He'd covered the Calderón stuff and touched on the bisexuality. It seemed to be enough.

"In the rest of it, not so much dialogue, though. Give me more Gary Cooper shit."

"Sure." Henry said, glad to accommodate. Rolf understood what Henry had done and he also knew that Paul Baron couldn't have come close to Henry's little dance. Blake had painted himself into a corner over this swagger business. It might have been talk of seventeenth-century drama that had set it off, made him feel inadequate and resentful. He had seized on the vaguely related question of his saloon entrance. He'd gone too far with it and then he felt trapped. He needed the studio and Rolf to honor his difficulty, to justify the importance of it, by going to expensive lengths to help him out. In practical terms, it meant the studio had thrown money at Henry.

"Come here, Charlie," Blake said to his son, apparently through with the script for now. "I haven't seen you all day." The boy scrambled up into the hammock, glad to have his papa fuss over him. Blake tickled the boy while Lilah scrutinized the pages, perhaps hunting for more subtext, while Henry pretended that the filial horseplay was interesting. Blake, comfortable again, asked his wife to call for a round of *cerveza*. Lilah picked up the phone that was patched through to the hotel and asked the operator to get her the Michael Singer Agency in Beverly Hills. Then she asked her husband how many she should get. "Get six," he said. "Tecate. And chips."

"Mike Singer, please," Lilah said and waited till someone came on the line. "It's Lilah for Mike." She waited again and then said, "Hi. Things are looking good. Doc Wearie is getting this stuff sorted out." Then Lilah asked her husband's agent to call room service at the Posada Durango and have somebody come over to the hacienda with six bottles of beer and some chips.

That night, Murray Marden called to tell Henry that Paul Baron was still kicking up a fuss about Henry's rewrite. "'Sabotaging my script with a lot of literary bullshit' were his exact words."

"How'd he hear about it?" Henry asked.

"He's probably got spies on the set. He's worried about his credit. He offered to go down there and do it for free and God knows what all else if they'll dump you."

"I'm not exactly performing major surgery."

"Not according to him. Something about an Italian play."

"Spanish. Never mind. What happened?"

"Rolf said he'd walk off before he'd let Paul Baron on the set. That you were doing exactly the right thing and that Blake was happy."

"Good."

"Good? It's fucking wonderful. Rolf Shilling never went to bat for anybody I ever heard of."

"Did he talk to the studio?"

"The phone lines have been humming. Didn't he tell you?"

"Rolf won't say a thing about it."

"If they want you for one extra minute, the numbers go up. I'm putting this out everywhere. Your price is on the elevator."

Later, when Henry thought about it, he realized that this was Rolf's way of saying thanks. He knew if he voted for Henry loudly enough and to the right people, Henry's stock would rise. Rolf operated by indirection and code. If you couldn't follow it, too bad for you. Henry found it oddly endearing.

Henry did some cutting of the script at Blake's request and with Rolf's blessing. Paul Baron had overwritten some of the speeches, not because he didn't know better but because studio executives tend to think making the meaning numbingly clear is good writing. Then, when the money is in place, and the executives are busy improving some other script, the speeches get pruned into speakable dialogue. It was what Blake was talking about when he asked with such exquisite delicacy for more "Gary Cooper shit." Paul could have done it, he was a competent guy. Henry did it in an afternoon and cut three pages out of the script, which made the production people happy because it put them a half-day ahead of schedule.

The next day Rolf asked Henry to come out to the set. Henry knew all too well how deadly a film set can be unless you were the director, the cinematographer, or an actor shooting a scene, but as the studio was paying him thousands of dollars a week, he figured the least he could do was show up for work. The company drivers were a mix of local men and Los Angeles teamsters. God knows what kind of financial shenanigans had gone into that plan. The L.A. guys drove the equipment trucks and the company bus. The locals, using their own cars, did everything else. Rolf and Blake had their own drivers. The wardrobe mistress had given Henry a straw hat to protect him from the sun. He got into a gaudy old Buick held together with duct tape and bailing wire that had been cleaned and polished for this job. A woman he hadn't yet met was in the car. She too was wearing one of the wardrobe department's straw hats. Her name was Sister and she was down from L.A. She was a little vague about her purpose but she worked for Mike Singer, the organizer of the long-distance beer and chips. The driver was to drop her off at the hacienda and then take Henry on to Churubusco. Sister laughed about the hats and settled in for the ride. She was a leggy thing a bit taller than Henry, with strawberry blond hair and fair skin that might once have been freckled. She had a rural quality about her and what Henry thought of as a Southern drawl—it turned out to be a West Virginia accent, a relaxed, throaty sound that was new to Henry. He understood she wasn't an actress because she wasn't trying to be charming or full of personality or spirituality or IQ points, which was a relief. After a few years in the picture business Henry could spot actors as easily as he could pick out, say, collies or dachshunds. "Have you been to Churubusco before?" he asked.

"Where the sets are? Yeah. Way cool," she said.

"It's a first for me."

"When I saw it, I thought it looked fake. Then when I saw the movie that got made, it looked real."

"That's the movies all right." Henry liked this woman. She didn't seem to be working him or trying to impress him yet their conversation had a flirty edge. "How long are you here?" he asked.

"Couple days. Maybe a little more. So you're writing new stuff for Blake?"

"Yeah."

"I heard you did a great scene for him already."

"I think it'll help." He resisted telling her it amounted to one line of dialogue.

"Was that chick there?"

"Lilah? Yeah." Henry turned her question around in his mind. A chick? Nobody talked like that. Besides, Lilah Lynn was famous.

"With the Mexican words? 'Nice sombrero,'" Sister said, imitating Lilah and touching Henry's hat. "The kid's cute."

Henry decided to avoid gossip about his patron and asked, "Is Sister your real name?"

"Sure. My family's from West Virginia. Hillbillies."

"How'd you get to California?"

"My grandparents came out here, but I was born back home. Kind of like *Grapes of Wrath*." Henry smiled at the reference. "And yes, I read that book and I saw the movie." She said it as if she thought he wouldn't believe her. She had taken his smile for the patronizing gesture that it was. Henry knew Mike Singer wouldn't send her to Mexico unless he had faith that she could solve whatever problem was at hand. They were both here as troubleshooters. Neither of them was wearing a wedding ring. They rode in easy conversation and when that waned in a companionable silence. At the hacienda, which Sister called, simply, "the house," she gave Henry a knowing smile that suggested they were likely to see each other again.

Later that morning, Henry ate lunch in Rolf's tent shaded from the sun and reviewed the scene that was to shoot that afternoon. Trailers were in use on movie sets, but not yet in Churubusco. Rolf had an officer's tent with a Oaxacan rug, a field desk, and a day bed. Lunch was tortilla soup and then a local fish baked in banana fronds. The catering crew had set up an outdoor kitchen and turned out elaborate meals. It was too much to eat for lunch on a working day, but Henry appreciated the effort. As their meals were served, a guy Henry hadn't yet met followed the waiters into the tent. He was an overweight American, maybe thirty-five, sweaty and uncomfortable in the hot climate. He was carrying about a dozen shoe boxes in a mesh shopping bag, of the sort sold in every *mercado*. The way he lugged those boxes put Henry in mind of the young women who go office to office at the studios selling sandwiches out of a basket and who always seem to be looking for an opening to give you their picture and résumé. The guy reminded Rolf that his name was Louie and asked, "Ten and half, right?" Then Louie started opening his boxes, which contained running shoes. Louie was the product placement man. Rolf's plan to deconstruct studio Westerns had the characters driving automobiles from the 1940s and wearing up-to-the-minute running shoes. Money changed hands between the studio and the shoe company with the understanding that the shoes, with their brand name displayed, would appear in the movie. Louie was handing out footwear to the above-the-line personnel. He was starting with the director. Rolf mentioned that Henry was the writer. "I already saw the guy in L.A." Louie said, hesitating to give shoes to a second writer. "You're just doing a rewrite," he said.

"It's all right," Henry said. "I don't care."

"What the hell," Louie said, apparently sensing Rolf's disapproval. "What's your size?"

Henry told him and later that day, four pairs of fancy running shoes turned up at Henry's room. He didn't feel like lugging them back to California so he gave them to the maids.

Aside from the decision to shoot all the Mexican sequences in black and white, there wasn't all that much to talk about. If Rolf said he wanted to discuss the pages and then allowed Louie and his shoes to interrupt, it meant he didn't yet know what he wanted to do. It didn't bother him that a crew was waiting and that the actors were as ready as they were likely to be. Rolf wanted to talk, which really meant he wanted to appear occupied on official business while he waited for inspiration. Louie was a welcome diversion though Henry was ideal, because no production manager or studio functionary really understood what it was directors and writers talked about in their story sessions. Most directors work from storyboards with camera moves mapped out. Rolf rarely planned his shots before the day's shooting. Oh, he made a shot list the night before, because if he didn't the studio production managers all but called the police. He decided the dynamics of the shots at the last moment, always trusting to the charged atmosphere of production to provide him with ideas. His movies could veer from drama to satire to sudden sex. It was as he was. Whatever interested him did so completely, for a few minutes.

Henry couldn't read Rolf's mind and he knew that it wouldn't do to thank him for the enthusiastic vote of confidence with the studio, so he mentioned that he had met Sister.

"Unusual woman," Rolf said, trying to assess Henry's interest.

"Not your typical agent."

"She's not an agent."

"Mike Singer sent her down here. I thought to hold Blake's hand or something."

"She's Blake's delivery service," Rolf said, touching his nose with his index finger.

Directors can be like small businessmen, and for all his talk of spontaneity, Rolf could be shrewd. He owned the negatives to his early pictures and that had made him a lot of money. Henry had seen him issue orders as if he were a producer or an agent. But Rolf also had a mind that danced. The thought of cocaine must have been music enough for him because he left the tent and called for the first shot of the afternoon.

Henry invited Sister to dinner that evening. They went to a little cantina in Durango that the company favored when they wanted a break from the hotel. They were drinking home-brewed mescal. It had a touch of gold to it and a raw smoky taste. The waiter poured from a clear plastic jug that might have once held mineral water. They could see the worm—*el gusano*—nestled at the bottom. Henry thought the stuff tasted like rough tequila but Sister was partial to it. By the time they got to their second glass, Henry had placed the cantina with its clouds of cigarette smoke, Mexico City bullfight posters, and the occasional drunken campesino, at RKO about 1949. "This joint looks like a set. More film noir than Western." Sister laughed at his need to quantify everything. "Here comes the judge," she said, pointing at Henry.

"Yeah, but I don't have a courtroom," he said.

"It's in your head."

"So you going to tell me about your business?" Henry asked.

"Not on two drinks, that's for sure."

"I never even drink this stuff," he said as he signaled for another round.

"Order a martini. Let's see what happens," Sister said.

"How do you know I drink martinis?"

"Hey. I'm a stone expert on knowing what people do to lower the temperature."

"I'll tell you what'll happen," Henry said. "I'll say 'Martinis,' and the guy'll say '*Si. Si,*' and then he'll bring that plastic bottle of mescal anyway. Whatever your first drink is, that's it. That's how it's done, down Mexico way."

"Are all screenwriters funny?"

"They're all wisenheimers, that's for sure. So I understand you're a courier."

"What else do you understand?"

"You're a handful. I can see that."

"How did you get to be a screenwriter?" she asked, not at all ready to talk about the courier business.

"Just lucky. Tell you what. Let's trade honest answers. One each. Not just date shit. One real answer."

"Give it your best shot," Sister said, attacking her third mescal.

"Any question at all, right?"

"You're a screenwriter. I'm a courier. Two gigs where the truth gets wobbly."

"Touché. I'll tell you any damn thing that interests you."

"I'll say this, it's a lot easier to bring stuff into Mexico than take it out."
As Henry was contemplating that, Rolf and Bree Miller came over to the
table. Well, Henry thought, he's taking her out in public. Must be at least
a two-night stand. Bree, who had blond hair that didn't look like it came
as natural equipment, had a trashy and available air, which is why she
was cast as a dancehall girl and no doubt why Rolf was interested. "Ah,"
Rolf said, extending the tiny word and investing it with a quality of dis-
covery, as he looked at Sister and introduced Bree. Henry urged them to
sit down and see if they couldn't catch up on the home-brewed mescal
consumption. Sister was the first person in Mexico that Henry had seen
who wasn't in fear or awe of Rolf. She knew he was the director and she
knew what that meant, but she wasn't auditioning. Henry knew that
would make Rolf toy with her for a bit. He wouldn't mind if she wasn't
impressed with him. Quite the opposite. It would make him want to
know more about her, to find out what made her tick. When Bree saw
that her beau was interested in Sister, she turned to Henry and said, "I'm
a writer, too."

"What do you write?" Henry asked.

"I'm working on a poem about a nun in the twelfth century, but I
might turn it into a screenplay."

"You should play the lead," Rolf said, apparently listening after all.

"Cool," Sister said, offering a high-five to Bree.

"Nuns were treated really bad back then," Bree said as she slapped
Sister's palm.

"Sort of like screenwriters now," Henry said. He glanced at Rolf, who
was looking around the cantina, not paying any attention to Bree. Henry
knew that he would soon drop her.

"I want to know who Henry Aldrich is," Rolf said. It took Henry a
moment to make the transition from medieval nuns and Rolf's roving eye
to old radio serials. Henry Aldrich was what he and Blake had joked
about at the hacienda.

"He was a radio character. Sort of the primal teenager. I think there
were a couple of pictures built around him. That 'Coming, Mother' stuff

is how the show opened." Rolf nodded his understanding but he looked sad, as if he was sorry he too hadn't been an American teenager like Blake and Henry. "You didn't miss all that much," Henry said.

"Perhaps not," Rolf said, but he looked a little put out.

"Bob Smiley would know all about it," Henry said, trying to help Rolf out of his mood.

"Who's that?" Bree asked, probably wondering if there was another man around she ought to know about.

"Henry insists that's my American name," Rolf said.

"Not my idea," Henry said.

"'I am an American, Chicago born.'" Rolf said it in his flat declamatory tone. Henry glanced over at Sister to see if the reference registered. She gave no sign. For years Rolf had played with a fantasy, imagining that he had grown up in the Middle West.

"What's with you guys?" Sister asked. "You trying to impress the girls? I really don't give a shit. I think you're both pretty cool without it." She knew she had stepped into an old and bookish routine and felt no need to worry if she understood all of it.

"I was a cross-country runner at Northwestern," Rolf said. Bree wasn't sure what to make of that, so she just nodded as if she were offering sympathy.

"You should be proud of it, Bob," Henry said.

"You should both calm down," Sister said. "I want more." Henry waved to the waiter, gesturing for another round. The jug was almost empty now and the worm looked as if it had moved a bit. The waiter's face seemed to say, Let's see what these gringos are made of. He shook the jug, letting the dregs wash over the worm, and asked, "*¿Quien queras el gusano?*" Sister took it for the dare that it was and snatched the jug away, tilted her head back, and poured the remains, worm and all, straight down her throat.

Back at the hotel, Henry went up to Sister's room for a taste of what had brought her to Mexico. "So you going to tell me about your delivery service?" Henry asked, as Sister produced a gram of cocaine. She held it up as if it were a prize, taking pleasure in its presence. "If I feel like it," she said. The subject was cocaine, but Henry knew that it was also something else. Sister was saying, I might sleep with you, I might not. Henry knew to relax and let whatever might happen unfold. Sister dipped into the tiny bottle with an even smaller spoon and held it up to Henry's nose. It was the color of ivory and seemed more flake than powder. Henry had tried the stuff a few times. You couldn't be around Hollywood without running up against it occasionally. He wanted to know Sister better and this was a test. He snorted hard, rushing the cocaine into one nostril, then the other. Sister did the same. Henry's throat went dry and he could feel a numbing sensation in his mouth. "Wow!" he said. "That's quick."

"This stuff is the best," Sister said. Henry could sense her heart racing, perhaps because that's what his own was doing. He could feel his blood coursing and for a moment he thought his torso was transparent, like a mannequin in a science museum. He could feel his mood starting to fragment. He was feeling sexually charged but he was also feeling curious about this woman. He wanted to ask her questions. As he was sorting all this out and still contending with the buzz in his head that was making him ready to shout and run in circles, Sister laughed and said, "You get good blow in you and you find out what you really want."

"I'll let you know, soon as the report is in," Henry said, thinking he might levitate.

"I'll tell you," Sister said.

"What?"

"Don't get cute. You want to know what it's like and how I do it, right?"

"Yes."

"The customs guys down here are like doormen. If they think you're a tourist, they practically carry your suitcase. It's taking stuff out that's tough."

"Why would you do that?"

"You think Mike is going to pay for a one-way trip? I'm going to load up on weed."

"Very business school of him." Henry's high had changed to a pleasant rush. Sister dug into the cocaine and spooned out another round. "So is this Blake's stuff?" he asked.

"He gets what he's supposed to. If there's some left over, that's my vig."

"Does Blake pay you? I mean, do you collect money?"

"No way. Mike takes care of that. He probably charges it to the movie. I really don't know. You going to write a script about it now?"

"Why not? Bolivian marching powder. Hollywood loves it."

"We could write it together. I know what. You know how."

Sister was sailing. Henry wondered if he sounded and looked as high as she seemed to be. The question was of only moderate interest because soon enough she and Henry were in bed. He told her a little about himself, about growing up and leaving college and coming to Hollywood. About how he both loved and resented the place, and about how his mother was dead and how difficult it was for him to talk with his father. He always thought the worst part of dating was telling his life story to yet another woman. He didn't feel that way now. He wanted to know about her and if the price was a few details about himself, that was fine with Henry. Sister had spent a semester in medical school in West Virginia. A pregnancy ended that. She had two kids who were back in L.A. There were two fathers—one was an ex-husband and the other was just the other. Henry knew there was more and he waited while she stretched out on the hotel bed and snared him with her long legs. "I got busted for dealing."

"What happened?"

"I sold a couple of grams to a cop. It smelled bad. I knew he was playing me. I had to get home to my kids so I took the chance."

"And?" Henry asked, accepting the little bottle from her.

"Some chicks, if there's any doubt, they fuck the guy. Get him naked and you can learn something. If he's wired, if he's got a cop gun." Sister went silent for a moment. Then she said, "I did eighteen months at Terminal Island."

"Je-sus!"

"Possession with intent to distribute. Bargained down to possession. I lost my kids over it."

"I'm sorry."

"Yeah. It's okay now. I got one of them back."

"It must have been hard."

"I learned how to play chess. You play?"

"A little. That the only thing that happened at Terminal Island?"

"It's like everything. Stay on your toes. Give a little, get a little. I did my time." The only sign that the memory was raw was that Sister was all but inhaling the cocaine, using twice as much as Henry. The more she consumed the more she wanted to make love. When she was high, she broke into delighted laughter at intimate moments. Henry watched her, thinking she's hooked on having it and selling it and doling it out. She loves everything to do with this stuff. She was a deeply corrupted person and her story all but ignited him.

* * *

A week later Henry was back in Los Angeles, determined to sleep until all the cocaine was out of his system. On his second day at home, Sister called. Would Henry care to accompany her on a little excursion to Terminal Island to see a play put on by the prisoners?

"You want to go into the jail? Voluntarily?"

"It's interesting. You know you want to see it."

"You're right. I do."

"About that other stuff. I don't do that up here. My kids and all. Mexico was different."

Henry said he would handle the driving to Terminal Island, which was about one freeway hour south of the city, across the Vincent Thomas Bridge and not far from the docks at San Pedro. This expedition was the first time Sister had seen Henry's bright red 1959 Porsche Speedster. He had the top down and was looking forward to the drive with the wind blowing. He changed his mind when the first thing Sister did after she got in the car was fire up a joint. As they were already going to a prison, Henry

said he didn't think they should push their luck. She had told him she
didn't play around with drugs up here but Henry had seen the urgent way
she had breathed in the cocaine in Mexico and now the casual way she
smoked marijuana. Geography wasn't going to make much difference.

Henry had been to the Men's Central Jail in Los Angeles, for script
research, but Terminal Island wasn't a holding cell. It was a medium-
security prison where people were put away for years. Sister explained
that when she was a guest there, Terminal Island had a men's side and a
women's side and occasionally the two divisions bumped up against each
other in the exercise yard, which is where she learned to play chess. Passing through the various doors and gates required an elaborate choreography of identification and signatures. At the final door, their hands were
stamped with a blue *TI*, for Terminal Island. "Like the prom," Henry
said. "If you went to a really rough high school." Sister wasn't saying
much as they walked into a large room set with folding chairs and a temporary stage. Was it an auditorium? For what? Prison assemblies? Henry
didn't think he'd ask, just keep his eyes open and learn what he could.
Whatever the room's usual purpose, it was not air-conditioned, hardly
even vented. It was hot and close. The audience was divided into visitors—people like Henry and Sister who had come for the performance—
and inmates who were allowed in as a reward for what Sister called good
behavior, which apparently meant they hadn't stabbed anyone for a
while.

Guards, mostly white guys in blue uniforms, patrolled the back of the
room. They seemed less interested in the theater than their charges, most
of whom were black or Latino. They wore khaki work trousers and blue
denim shirts, which wasn't all that different from Henry's usual outfit.
The actors, who were prisoners, were performing *Waiting for Godot*. The
relevance to prison life wasn't lost on anyone, prisoner or visitor. The
acting was enthusiastic though Henry couldn't quite concentrate on it.
He spent the first act looking at the actors, wondering what had put
them in this place. He whispered to Sister, "They should have programs
with little bios. 'Jocko Jones, who is playing the part of Estragon, is mak-

ing his stage debut. He's doing fifteen years for armed robbery. His hobbies are reading Eastern philosophy and sodomy.'" Sister didn't seem to find it funny. The set—the simple tree Beckett called for—had been made by prisoners and the few lights were operated by prisoners. Henry thought that performing a play here was exactly the sort of thing Rolf would love. If he were to see all this, he'd want to get involved, going fearlessly into the midst of it and probably throwing out whatever script they had—Beckett's or anyone else's—and goading his actors to the edge of violence, improvising scenes about their lives.

At the intermission, the visitors were allowed to get up and stretch and walk around in the back of the auditorium. The prisoners in the audience stood up but didn't leave their seats. Sister introduced Henry to a few people she knew, explaining that he was a screenwriter. She meant well by it, assuming the others would be interested and perhaps impressed, but whenever someone mentioned his profession, Henry thought that saying he was a screenwriter always sounded like an excuse. A man Sister knew was talking about other plays he had seen here. He was with a small, dark-haired woman who wore serious-looking wire-rimmed glasses. She had a sketch pad and had been making quick impressions of the actors and the audience. When Henry asked, she showed him her drawings. She had caught the mood of this place. Henry asked if she was going to make paintings of her sketches. "Not really," she said. "I work at Fox. This is just something I do on my own." Henry was glad she hadn't called it her hobby. She explained that the studio had made a donation to the prison theater group and she was here to see what they got for it. Her name was Madeleine Girard and Henry found himself listening to her. "It's interesting to see this play here," Madeleine said. "You want a play to be good, but in these circumstances other things seem more important."

"Yes," Henry said. "In a prison everything is about prison. Certainly this play."

"That's right," she said, looking Henry in the eye, trying to gauge him. "Are you going to write a movie set in a prison?" she asked.

"I don't think so. I'm just keeping Sister company."

"If you do, you ought to think about including the theater group."

Henry was drawn to this woman, though he couldn't yet say why. Perhaps it was her calmness, which was a contrast to Sister, who was capable of most anything. Henry knew it was unlikely that Madeleine Girard would do anything odd. It didn't make her seem dull or predictable, but steady and straight ahead. He knew that in her presence he didn't want to sound like he was showing off or suggesting more knowledge than he had. "This is the first time I've been in a prison," Henry said. Without thinking, he glanced at Sister. Henry wondered if Madeleine knew about the activity that got Sister stuck here for so long.

When the play was over, when the lines "Well? Shall we go? . . . Yes, let's go" were still hanging in the dank air, everyone in that sweaty auditorium knew some people weren't going anywhere. Henry saw Sister make eye contact with one of the prisoners who was clearing the folding chairs. He was a tall, dignified black man about fifty, which made him old for this place. He made a tiny nod of his head, a fleeting acknowledgment. Henry started to ask Sister about it, but before she could answer, Madeleine Girard came over to say good night. "I enjoyed talking with you," Henry said.

"If you're interested, I can send you some stuff about the foundation," she said as she handed him her card. Henry thanked her and said good night. He realized that he was being slightly formal with her, on his best behavior. He decided that it was because her friend had probably told her about Sister's past and he didn't want her to think that he was of that world.

"She liked you," Sister said.

"Interesting woman."

"So you hit on me one way, and chicks like that another way."

"I wasn't hitting on her."

"I might be stoned but I'm not blind."

"It wasn't anything."

"Chicks like her with those glasses? Ms. worker for the good of man. All that bitch cares about is Italian shoes and hooking up with a rich dude, which is how she pegged you."

"You think she came to Terminal Island to meet men?"

"She met you, didn't she? Chicks'll do anything."

"May I quote you?"

"Fuck you. She was ready to."

Henry smiled at that, wondering what it must be like to be deep inside Sister's head. When they got to the car, he asked about the prisoner she had glanced at. "Did you know that guy?"

"No."

"So what was that about?"

"I was telling him to look under my chair."

"What would he find?" Henry asked, already suspecting the answer.

"I taped a joint."

"You took dope in there?"

"How else are they going to get it?"

"Why him?"

"He was doing the chairs. A trusty. Good karma."

"How did he know?"

"He knew I left something. When he finds out, I guarantee you he'll be very happy."

"What if they searched you?"

"They don't do that."

"You don't know him, you don't know what he's in for. You just gave him marijuana."

"You a cop now? Or a social worker?"

"Seems risky."

"I'll tell you what's risky, being in that place for years on end with nobody cutting you any slack. He might be waiting for Godot but he'll settle for a little weed."

"What are you, the Johnny Appleseed of dope?"

"Yeah, yeah," she said and lit up again for the drive back to Los

Angeles. Henry kept the Porsche within the speed limit, which made
Sister restless. He wondered what Madeleine Girard would think of his
racy little car.

*   *   *

Henry found himself thinking about Madeleine. He liked her wire-
rimmed glasses. He hadn't noticed her shoes, but he hoped they were
Italian and expensive. A serious woman who was attractive and who
knew something of the movie business? Sister's instinct was more right
than not. He didn't think he had flirted with Madeleine but he knew in
his gut that she was single and he knew that she understood he was too,
and also that whatever his relationship with Sister was, it wasn't permanent. Henry called Madeleine the next day and took her to dinner and
they started going out. Henry declared that the way they had met was a
new peak in the annals of meeting cute. When they talked about the theater group at Terminal Island, he told her his joke about the information
that should be in the program. She laughed and added a few details. "In
addition to founding the Terminal Island Jailbreak Project, he enjoys trying to con volunteers into supplying him with drugs," which was closer
to home than she knew. Madeleine liked a drink or two and she did wear
expensive shoes and she didn't know anything about the cocaine business and didn't expect to learn. It was a relief to him.

8

Cut

Rolf amused himself parsing the folkways of the movie business. He once told Henry, "Charm is what lubricates Hollywood." Henry laughed and reminded himself that even though Rolf was a director, he still liked him. "You can go a long way in Hollywood on charm," Rolf said, warming to his subject. "Careers have been built on it, though it's a coin best spent by the young. In the not so young, charm, which is the enemy of character, can be an excuse. 'He's quite charming' means he's a good dinner guest but his accomplishments are in the future. 'He can be very charming' means he's achieved a bit but is in danger of falling into the slag heap of the unperformed. 'I don't quite see his charm' means he's utterly lost."

"Surely there's more to it than that," Henry said. "What about talent?"

"Talent comes and goes with the jets at LAX, but if a fellow has the music of charm, the world will come dancing to him." Henry applauded, which was the only thing he could think to do.

Later, Henry thought about Rolf and considered his singular life. When he was a young man, tired of England's rigid ways, Rolf had longed for the classless kingdom of the cinema. He found Hollywood as stratified as Britain, but instead of family and school, what mattered was chance and the deal. Rolf loved that. Henry knew, without ever having been told, that Rolf was in the grip of America from the day he arrived. His pictures were psychologically astute, though Rolf wasn't introspective and he was untroubled by other people's emotional burdens. He turned out movies that were the ones he wanted to make. That takes an act of great will. Capable directors are always in demand, but usually to do what the studios want done.

Rolf was a romantic adventurer who thrived on the new but was nonetheless close to Eva, his ex-wife, who lived in London with their son. Rolf had long since decided dating was an activity for the young or the dim, preferring a succession of friends and lovers. He was fond of the polymorphous sex clubs of Silver Lake and West Hollywood. Club Fuck had been his favorite, but its name had gotten so much publicity that Rolf said tour buses stopped there. "Those Mexican boys with the maps send them." When Henry doubted that, Rolf said, "No one cares where Lucille Ball lived. They want Club Fuck."

"I'm sure you're right," Henry said.

"Put on your dancing shoes, Henry. We're going clubbing."

Henry asked Madeleine to join them. He expected her to refuse and he was thinking about how he might coax her. He would remind her that she could bring her sketch pad.

"It sounds great," she said. "I always wondered what goes on in those places." Henry felt silly for doubting her. If a place interested him it would interest her. Or she'd come along just to see what there was to see. Madeleine was always up for an adventure.

The plan was to go to Sin-Opti-Con, a sort of sexual vaudeville in a warehouse in West Hollywood. Rolf organized their visit in the spirit of a campy anthropological expedition. Rolf liked Madeleine and owned one of her paintings. Henry had taken him to her studio where he had glanced around and then pointed to what Madeleine knew was her best work and asked to buy it. Madeleine protested that the picture wasn't yet finished. She certainly couldn't bring herself to name a price. Rolf simply took it off the easel and then sent her a big check. Later, Henry told her that Rolf never had trouble acting on his impulses. "I can see that," she said. "But there was more to it. He wanted some part of me because he really wanted some part of you." Her insight astonished Henry.

As they stepped into the cavernous room at Sin-Opti-Con, a young woman dressed as a forties cigarette girl, in fishnet stockings, offered condoms from her tray. Rolf gave her money and said, "Give some to the condomless, in my name." Rolf led the way deeper into the fleshy crowd, amid people in leather jockstraps and diapers, with nose and nipple rings. "Fashion statements for the terminally libidinal," he said, breezing past the merely heterosexual, stopping to watch two women on a shaky platform, dancing in a sinuous circle. Madeleine pointed out that the women had what must have been a double-ended dildo inserted in themselves. It kept them at a certain distance, but as Madeleine said, had a closeness all the same. They moved on, and watched an overweight man stapling his scrotum to a board. "Interesting mischief," Rolf said. "Think he's union?"

"I.A." Henry answered, meaning the stagehands.

Madeleine was occupied making sketches of a man attempting to descend onto a broomstick. When the guy realized Rolf was also watching, he put more enthusiasm into his task. Everyone wanted to glow around directors, but it was also because Rolf had an eccentric sexuality that was changeable and encompassing. "Rolf," Madeleine said, "I think there's enough ambiguity here even for you."

"Très cher," he said, nodding to the gent on the broomstick in a lordly way, then lifting his arms in a sweeping gesture as if he were framing a panning shot that ended close on Madeleine's surprised face. She laughed and Rolf said, "Cut!"

* * *

After making movies, Rolf's passion was his house in the Hollywood Hills. It was Spanish, with a courtyard and a cherub fountain that was filled with yellow tulips. There was a tennis court and a pool house where one itinerant young actor or another was usually in residence. The house looked out to the east. In the mornings, Rolf watched the sun glint off the buildings downtown, making them look like a Deco movie set. It seemed fake but was real. He said it was perfect for Hollywood, a celestial joke. Rolf had bought his house from an actress who worked in pornographic films. When she realized she was selling her house to a legitimate director, a man who might help her get the one thing she yearned for, which was respectability and a career in traditional movies, she invited Rolf to tea. Rolf didn't tell her he hated the very idea of tea. He thought if he talked about movies and took her seriously, she might agree to more favorable terms. She wasn't at all shy about telling him that she wanted a part in one of his pictures. In return, she offered what Rolf always said she called "a famous blow job." What the lady didn't understand was that Rolf, though certainly not adverse to fellatio, was at that moment more interested in real estate. Henry always thought of that as a very Los Angeles attitude. Rolf had said that if she thought it would get her career out of the mire of pornography and into the shopping malls of America, she probably would have given him the place. When Rolf stammered that he wasn't quite prepared for her kind offer, she was perfectly willing to forget it and just talk about the house. In the end, the price wasn't any different than a less colorful negotiation might have produced. Rolf saw it as a sort of blessing of the house. "Who wouldn't want to live where such things could happen?"

The house had an elaborate aviary with dozens of brightly colored birds in stacked cages. Rolf enjoyed naming them in what he called his feathered inventory: wren, robin, grackle, oriole, cormorant, blue jay, toucan. Only the peacocks were allowed to roam, and they thought nothing of wandering into the house and crapping on the floor. Those strutting birds, always on display, seemed to be competing for Rolf's attention with the self-absorbed actors sunning themselves by the pool or the writers and producers who were waiting nervously for Rolf to approve their plans or just listen to their ideas.

Rolf was usually in some stage of remodeling the house. He never used blueprints or an architect. He decided what he wanted, then hired carpenters and started directing them, knocking down walls or cutting new windows. At first glance, the house had a bourgeois calm about it that was wildly misleading. It was a place of sunlight and laughing gossip, of fast romance, fanciful movie schemes, and screeching-peacock afternoons.

Rolf believed that spontaneity determined luck. He believed in luck. People in Hollywood all do, and why not? Who succeeds doesn't always make any sense. In his pursuit of the new, Rolf picked up and dropped colleagues without hesitation. Henry knew if the spirit moved him, Rolf would fire him and hire another writer. He'd done it already—to Henry and to others. Later, he'd hire Henry back. There were no apologies. He'd say the situation was now different and the script still wasn't right and after all, Henry knew it well, having already done a draft. And Henry would come. He'd tell himself it was just business, so he should put irritation aside. The real reason Henry went back was he knew he'd do good work. That's a powerful draw. Rolf had an instinct for the best, and he brought out the best in others, certainly in Henry. It had been Rolf's counsel on *Streets of New York* that had turned a promising but unwieldy script into a big payday. Rolf said, "Instinct is everything. A director must seize the true as it rushes by, pluck it from the air, and pin it down."

* * *

Rolf's son, Will, who was at Oxford, divided his holidays between California and his mother's house in Hampstead. When Henry first knew him, Will was a gawky adolescent with his father's angular features, but not yet his father's wit or engaging style. Henry had watched him grow. Will now seemed perched on a wobbly fence between the end of adolescence and the start of adulthood. His arrival for the summer was an occasion for Rolf to give a Sunday lunch, the last of his English habits. Grand lunches that ignored California's food fashions were no longer as unlikely as people outside the movie business thought, because being thin was no longer the good business it had once been. Weight was a sign of health.

When Henry arrived, Madeleine was already there, playing tennis with Gloria Warren, who lived nearby and often used Rolf's court. Madeleine would have come for lunch in any case, but Gloria's presence was an inducement. "I'll be sure to have somebody to talk to when they're all going on about movies they hate that I never saw anyway," she had said.

Gloria liked tennis, but Henry always thought she also liked to see the hunky young actors who were usually lurking. Gloria was Rolf's neighbor but their personal arrangements were complicated. She was married and had two young children, though that didn't prevent her from spending a lot of time at Rolf's. Gloria had a Southern belle's compulsion to flirt, certainly with Henry. She had gone far past flirtation with Rolf. Gloria was interested in antiques and Rolf cared only for the new, but neither of them had any interest in monogamy. Gloria was wearing a fancy tennis outfit and pearls. Even from a distance, Henry knew her face would be perfectly made up, her hair arranged in a fashionable style. Madeleine, to Henry's pleasure, was wearing cut-off blue jeans and a T-shirt with nothing written on it. She had a plain baseball cap on her head. Henry stood above the court for a moment, admiring her. She was small and slim, but her breasts were swaying under the T-shirt.

Henry waved to them and went to the pool where Rolf and Will were discussing the menu. Will was asking if there were going to be vegetarians, as if he were inquiring about Hottentots. When Madeleine and Gloria came up from the court, Gloria gave Henry a smooch. He had to laugh. It was Madeleine he was seeing and Gloria was mixed up with Rolf, but Gloria acted in a proprietary way toward Henry. Perhaps in response, Rolf asked where her husband was. "Out getting money, I hope," she said, and began making a gin and tonic for everyone whether anybody wanted one or not. She often served as a sort of de facto hostess for Rolf's gatherings, bringing glasses and linen or whatever she thought was needed.

Rolf must have been feeling mischievous because he ignored Gloria's fussing and asked Will to do his imitation of Henry. It embarrassed the boy terribly. "I can't think I'd be anything but flattered," Henry said, trying to get him to do it.

"It's the way the two of you argue," Will said. Then, in an irritated

American accent, which Henry found nasal and unappealing, Will muttered, "Hollywood is a directocracy. Film directing is the most overrated occupation of our time." Will had the family gift for mimicry with a touch of cruelty. Gloria laughed and said, "That is just marvelous." Madeleine smiled but Henry knew that she thought it was mean-spirited. Directors are always slightly at war with writers. Henry hadn't realized that this could extend to their children. It's not practical for either side to acknowledge the enmity, and in this case, Henry had genuine affection for Rolf. They had feigned good will in order to make their work productive and it had become real. Still, Rolf was the boss. Writers and directors talk about partnership, but it's mostly nonsense. They'd kill one another if they didn't need each other so much.

"I want to wash my face," Madeleine said, and went into the house. Henry knew she wanted to see if Rolf had hung the picture of hers that he'd bought. Henry went with her, which caught Gloria's attention.

Henry knew it would please Madeleine more if she didn't have to look for the painting. It was hanging outside Rolf's bedroom. The picture was of a black-bottomed swimming pool next to a house made of white geometric shapes. The sun was setting and shadows played on the walls and the water. The shadows seemed to have a texture that made them feel alive. Madeleine had spent a summer on Corfu painting when she was in college, and she and Henry had hopes of going there. Rolf had hung her picture near two early Hockney lithographs. Henry knew Madeleine was trying to decide if her work could stand on its own next to such heady neighbors.

"I think it was a mercy purchase," Madeleine said, squinting at her picture.

"Not Rolf. If he didn't want it, it wouldn't be here."

"I like where he has it. I want a quick shower." She said it with a little smile that was an invitation.

Henry followed her into the bathroom, still seeing the way her breasts had been swaying on the tennis court. He slipped his hands under her T-shirt, wanting to touch her. Madeleine said he was incorrigible and that she was taking a shower no matter what he had in mind. As they peeled off their clothes, Madeleine said, "It would be just like Gloria to come knocking on the door. 'Do y'all need any towels?'" she asked, imitating her friend's honeyed Louisville voice. The shower was in a tiled booth that had a half-moon window near the top. The afternoon sun was filtered by the steaming water. Henry and Madeleine rubbed soap on one another and then made love standing up.

When they arrived back at the pool, pink and toweled dry, Gloria handed them drinks and smiled in a way that reminded Henry of the way she looked when she was inspecting a prize vase. Henry knew that Gloria had no jealousy about his romance with Madeleine. Gloria thought of sex as something people did when they felt like it, with whomever they cared for at the moment. It was a remarkably unfettered view of love, and it was just the way Rolf saw such matters. They were made to be part-time lovers. If Rolf noticed that Henry and Madeleine seemed particularly clean, he gave no sign. He asked Madeleine to explain the eating customs to Will. "The local motto is, 'Use salt and die,'" she said. "What's the grub?"

"We've sent Jorgé to the market with a detailed note," Rolf said. "I've ordered a roast and a big salad. Someone will no doubt want white wine."

"Do they really believe the whites have fewer calories?" Will asked.

"It's a fact," Gloria said.

"A Los Angeles fact," Henry said. "But still true."

"There's a marvelous Napa cabernet in the cellar. We'll drink it if they don't," Rolf said. Perhaps when they were alone, Rolf and Will had more private conversations, but Henry doubted it. They probably always spoke as if others were present. They rarely talked about anything more personal than Rolf's movies or Will's Oxford adventures. Rolf was more comfortable when people were saying clever things. If something popped into his head, he might shout it from the roof whether there was anyone to hear it or not. Personal matters were usually disguised. For now, Will was content. Although neither of them fully understood it, Rolf was Will's model in such matters, and the boy was getting his lessons.

"Vikram Ghosh is coming," Rolf said. Henry realized that it hadn't occurred to Rolf to ask his son if he would like to invite any of his own Los Angeles friends.

"Isn't he your agent?" Will asked.

"No longer. He calls this house El Raj." Vikram, who stubbornly hung on to his Bombay lilt despite ten years in Hollywood, arrived with Brook Riesel, an unsettlingly lean woman in her late twenties. She was a production executive at Paramount who had great swirls of blond hair. When Rolf greeted her, he said, "'Only God could love you for yourself alone and not your yellow hair.'"

"Yeats!" Brook fairly shouted, with the authority of an expensive education and glowing yellow hair. Brook's success depended on how many directors and writers she knew. This lunch was a business opportunity for her. Henry predicted that in the Paramount staff meeting on Monday, she would drop Rolf's name. Vikram said if she played it right, she could conjure with Henry's as well. He meant to flatter, but still Henry said, "Do you know about the actress so stupid that she slept with the writer?" Only Will, who had never heard it, laughed. He seemed to be glancing at Brook. Henry saw Rolf watching them. He knew Rolf was wondering if it might be worth making a pass at her. The idea of being in a contest with his son for her attention interested him. Henry glanced at Madeleine. She was watching it too.

"Where's your water bottle?" Rolf asked, in his flat, unaccented way. Brook usually had a liter of Evian water in a leather carrying case from Vuitton, as if she felt in danger of being stranded in a fashionable part of the desert.

"I thought you might be able to take care of my needs," she answered, staring him to a momentary draw.

"The flirting lamp is now lit," Gloria said and moved a little closer to Vikram, which made Rolf smile. "'When the rose dies, the thorn is left behind,'" he said.

"That's Ovid," Gloria said, pleased that she recognized it.

"Yes. *Art of Love*," Rolf said, locking his eyes on Brook and all but ignoring Gloria.

Henry seemed about to add more literary arcana when Madeleine touched his hand. She had told Henry that he read so widely and perhaps even madly because he felt bad about dropping out of NYU, which had so upset his father. "It's show-offy," she told him. "Especially with Rolf. The two of you act like you're on a quiz show." It was true, but he couldn't resist. Madeleine had to suppress a groan when over the salad Henry challenged Rolf by saying he and Madeleine had seen a compelling production of *Electra*.

"The Greeks?" Rolf asked, sliding his glasses down his nose, as if he were Mr. Chips in the sun. "Henry Wearie? A proponent of the slash-and-burn school of dramaturgy?"

"This was hot. A storefront in Hollywood," Henry said with a deprecating shrug, the way screenwriters always defer to directors. It irritated him when he did that, so he stepped up the argument, saying, "It was vivid in a way only live performance can be."

"I can't bear those plays," Rolf said, taking up the challenge and dismissing Euripides.

"Rolf Shilling rejects the Greeks? Alert the media," Henry said with more sarcasm than was entirely wise. It made Gloria laugh, though not because she cared about *Electra*. She knew Henry was throwing down a gauntlet of sorts and she was hoping for a show. Madeleine nudged him under the table, but Henry just didn't care. Maybe it was the sex in the shower or maybe it had to do with Madeleine's uncertainty about Rolf's reasons for buying her picture, but Henry was into the game.

"They're so declamatory," Rolf said. "All that fuss about putting the action offstage. If there's action, is it asking too much that we all be let in on it?"

"Only in movies does action substitute for language."

"Oh, but *Electra*? Really, Henry. The girl goes mad. She stays mad for years. Then the wretched brother turns up."

"Perhaps you'd like a modern version? Set it in Malibu. Orestes returns, kills Clytemnestra, then he and Sis open a mental-health clinic on the beach."

"Wonderful," Vikram said. "Brook can put it in development."

"And Rolf can take credit as the auteur," Henry said.

"People fuss endlessly about the importance of the script," Rolf said, no longer interested in *Electra*. "Any interview with an executive, you can count on, 'It all starts with the page.'"

"Because a studio executive says something does not necessarily make it false," Henry said, enjoying himself and no doubt about it, showing off.

"The script is the most important element," Brook said, trying to engage Rolf and join the debate.

Vikram stopped her before she made a fool of herself and said, "If the substance eludes you, pay attention to the form. When they're through, they may switch sides and do it all again."

"Very Oxford Union," Will said.

Rolf ignored them and said, "I can look at fifty feet of Hitchcock or Ford and know the director. I'm hardly alone in this skill."

"The finest make their own rules," Henry said. "At your best, your pictures could only have been made by you. Not all your work is so particular. No one could say from fifty feet who made it. A few stars who can sell tickets to anything are more important than the director."

"Now you're talking about commerce," Rolf said.

"Trade? Oh, dear. I've sullied the air."

"Movie stars are children," Brook said, still trying to take part.

"Yes," Rolf said, noticing her again. "No studio trusts an actor with money. A director who can deliver picture after picture, no matter what, he's a man to follow."

"Directors are father, lover, and boss," Henry said. "You guys enjoy a *droit de seigneur* unknown since the Medici."

"Seems only just," Rolf said.

Henry laughed and, determined to top him, said "Directors are the true hustler-artists of the world."

Rolf bowed his head and conceded the point. Then he shook Henry's hand and said, "I wasn't keeping close score, though I think it was mine on points. Care for another round?"

Gloria said that was quite enough. She declared the whole thing a draw and opened another bottle of wine.

Vikram began telling a story about a parrot Rolf had once kept in the kitchen. "Pepé the screenwriting parrot. He could do rewrites. Dialogue polishes, actually. He had a great ear. He flew off one day."

"He didn't fly off," Rolf said. "He wouldn't do that. He was experimenting. It got out of hand." As Rolf was offering a toast to the disappeared parrot, Jorgé brought out the rest of the food. Brook was twitching her hair and glancing from son to father as Rolf began to cut the roast. Perhaps if he hadn't been laughing at the tale of the parrot, or if he hadn't enjoyed his debate with Henry quite so much, or if he hadn't had so much to drink, he would have been more careful. When the knife slipped, it went deep into the tip of his index finger. The cut created a little flap of flesh. It raised a tiny curtain. The message it revealed was clear to everyone. Rolf's finger was pumping out the cankered rose that no trope could illuminate, no joke alleviate, pulsing rich and red onto the meat.

Rolf had never acknowledged his condition, but he could see from the faces around his table that it was no secret. He himself had said many times that in Hollywood if there's something about yourself that you'd prefer be kept private, that's as good as putting it on a billboard on the Sunset Strip. Each person was staring at the growing stain, unable to look away. As Rolf's finger leaked out the perfectly colored red liquid, Henry did a quick mental tour of his own body, trying to recall cuts and abrasions. Madeleine, who had been sketching, put down her pencil and reached for Henry's hand. Gloria gave Rolf one of her linen napkins to wrap around his finger. Henry couldn't help but wonder about Gloria. Was she at risk? Was her husband?

Will couldn't quite understand what had happened, but he knew that the tension was greater than even a bad cut deserved. His father's romantic reputation wasn't something Will had been able to think about, and even now, in the face of the fear around the table that could mean one thing only, it seemed to Henry that Will alone could not yet acknowledge the truth. Rolf knew that appetites were gone. "Excuse me," he said, adding a second napkin to his finger, stanching the blood.

"Maybe we should go down to Cedars," Henry said. "Get a stitch put in that. We'll drive you."

"No," Rolf said, pressing the linen to the cut, holding back the blood. "Plenty of time for Cedars."

"Are you sure, P'pa?" Will asked, reverting to a childhood name for his father.

"I'm positive," Rolf said.

The little pun made Brook gasp. "Ohh . . ." she said.

"Why don't we get rid of this roast and open another bottle," Rolf said.

"I'll do it," Will said, about to clear the table.

"It's for me to do," Rolf said. With his good hand, he picked up the soiled platter and sailed it into the pool. The meat hit the water first, turning it dark from the gravy and the blood. The platter floated for a moment before it too sank. At that moment of spontaneous nihilism, Henry could see the ache of understanding come over Will's face. Rolf tilted his bloody finger into the air at an optimistic angle and Henry knew he had seen it too. A message had been passed. Will bowed his head in a gesture that was his father's, then steadied himself and poured the last of the cabernet.

* * *

In the months that followed, Rolf continued to work on scripts and to meet with actors until he began to lose weight and tire easily. Will took a leave from Oxford and came to stay with him. Rolf wanted no part of hospitals, but to remain in the house that he loved. Henry and Madeleine came to visit often. Sometimes Rolf spoke of his illness, which he called "a little gift from the pool house." He no longer could drink, but once he lifted his glass of water and said, "Here's to the last adventure." Later,

Henry explained that "the gift" was Rolf's way of telling them that he had been infected by one of the pretty actors who were in and out of the pool house. Madeleine didn't require an explanation for "the last adventure." Gloria was in the house, doing her best to make Rolf comfortable. She took Madeleine aside to answer the question that had been on Henry and Madeleine's minds since the day of the lunch. "I'm okay," she said. "I knew. We were careful."

On an afternoon when the bright Los Angeles sun was leaking through the blinds of Rolf's bedroom, he was sitting up, talking with Henry and Madeleine. The room was kept dark because Rolf's eyes had grown sensitive to light. It was unmistakable. He was sinking into blindness. The idea of Rolf without his eyes was too horrible to contemplate. He asked Madeleine if she would get her picture and prop it up at the foot of his bed. Henry thought Madeleine might cry but she simply went out into the hall, took the thing off the wall, and did as Rolf had asked. At Rolf's direction, Henry adjusted the blinds until the picture could be seen from the comfort of the shadows. When Rolf's condition took its final turn, Eva came from London to say good-bye and to help their son, who everyone agreed was handling the situation with great aplomb and even charm.

Henry had been around long enough to have lost other friends to that disease, men he liked and respected, but none of them were Rolf Shilling, who refused to make plans, who got giddy from spontaneity that fired his imagination, and who would do absolutely anything if only once. It had caught up with him and Henry knew that the loss would never be made up. On a night not long after Rolf's death, when some friends and colleagues gathered at Rolf's house, Henry offered a toast: "To Rolf Shilling," he said. "There won't be another." Henry spoke the words in a flat declamatory way, without accent or emphasis. He hadn't intended to evoke Rolf's voice but that's the way it came out.

Henry thought about how Rolf had helped him revise *Streets of New York,* which was the real beginning of his career, and about their time in Mexico and how Rolf had helped him raise his price and never cared if

Henry knew what he had done. And he thought about the way their book talk intimidated people. He wondered if Rolf had ever thought about Henry's crazy aria that had overwhelmed Blake Porter and got *Faster* back on track. Henry knew he wouldn't have done it so vividly if any other director had been in the room. Henry had wanted to please Rolf as if he were an older brother, or more likely as if he were Felix, his father, the first man Henry knew who remained silent, no matter what Henry did. Oh, me-oh, my-oh, Henry thought. Rolf and Felix. They couldn't be more different, except of course to Henry.

Soon after Rolf's death, Henry and Madeleine decided not to wait any longer. They were married downtown at City Hall. Rick Moses and Gloria were in attendance to get them through the ritual and to throw a little confetti. Henry and Madeleine went to Corfu for a honeymoon so Madeleine could revisit her old haunts and do some painting. They couldn't find the house that had been the source of the picture Rolf had bought right off Madeleine's easel. She found other models and she was content. Henry loafed in the sun and read a lot and took notes for a memoir of Rolf that he had been thinking about. They talked about their future and about having a family. When they got home they didn't want to live in either of their apartments. They both felt a need to start fresh. They moved into a bungalow in Hollywood and began their life together.

Thank You for Everything

*H*enry *drove* his new green Jaguar east on Fountain Avenue on his way to the Market. He knew the car was an indulgence, but things had been going well for him. He was working. He was feeling optimistic. Henry loved Fountain. Even at rush hour, traffic on this street always moved. He took a certain pride in the lack of traffic in Los Angeles. People complained about the freeways and Henry stayed off them at busy times, and knowing how to avoid the occasional snarl made him feel a part of the place. One of the pleasures of Los Angeles was that simple things were, well, simple. There was much to miss about New York, certainly, but rents were cheaper out here, shop clerks were relaxed, and the movie business provided him with a living. Henry had trouble getting pictures made, but every screenwriter had that problem. He could make deals though, and that meant a paycheck whether the picture happened or not. He was certain that his home was in the West.

Madeleine had grown up in Chicago and she was always interested in visiting New York and seeing her husband's boyhood haunts. She was now in the marketing department at Fox where she organized focus groups to look at early versions of the studio's pictures. She often spent evenings at screenings. Henry went with her for a while, but he had trouble with the people in the groups, who were recruited from shopping malls and, Henry insisted, from mental health clinics. After watching a film about love and murder shot in the Loire Valley that was so elegantly made that Henry could feel his heart beat as he watched it, he told Madeleine that the beauty of the land made the violence all the more shocking and unexpected. Then Henry heard a citizen say "Too many trees" and another declare it "A travelogue of the old country." Henry decided he'd best stay away from focus groups for any movie he hadn't personally written.

When they were first married, Madeleine said that their bungalow in Hollywood looked like a doll's house. She thought it was cute but soon enough she wanted something more substantial, something of their own. They were in that bungalow for almost two years before they bought a Spanish house in the Hollywood Hills. Choosing the house and enduring the difficulties of negotiating a deal and securing a mortgage had been an ordeal of indecision, mostly on Madeleine's part. Their house, their property, the emblem of their stability, was meant to make them feel settled. And at first it did. The house was built around a courtyard with a fountain. There was a swimming pool with blue tile and a ramshackle greenhouse that Madeleine planned to repair. She would learn to grow things and fill the house with flowers and always have fresh vegetables. There was an office for Henry and lovely walls that needed bookshelves. The house had an unusual octagonal dining room where Henry and Madeleine amused themselves planning dinner parties for people with octagonal connections. Henry VIII, certainly, and Pius VIII, who could say grace, though Henry thought that given the unpleasantness over closing the monasteries, it wasn't a good idea to seat His Holiness next to His Majesty. Claudette Colbert would be invited because she had played Bluebeard's eighth wife in the old Lubitsch movie, and Marie Dressler and Jean Harlow from the cast of *Dinner at Eight,* and Eight-Ball Brown, a Mississippi blues singer who Madeleine said Henry had just made up.

It surprised them both to put so much weight on real estate, to fetishize it, but that's what they did. They believed that this was the house they would live in for the rest of their days. Henry was coming to understand all the statistics that said married men lived longer than bachelors, though it wasn't entirely clear to him if that was also his wife's view. Lately there had been an elusive tension between them. Madeleine wanted to talk about "the marriage" as if it were a pet or an investment that required their attention. Madeleine was a mixture of the adventurous and the cautious. She'd go most anywhere without much thought, though it was her nature not to rush into big decisions. It was a while before she felt sure enough of Henry or of herself or of their future or God knows what before Madeleine decided she wanted a child. Once she decided, she thought of little else. Of course that was the source of the tension. How could Henry have missed it? It was a natural enough instinct. Henry hoped a baby might provide them with a goal beyond "the marriage," which Henry was starting to think of as one more thing he didn't do well. He knew he wasn't the easiest guy to live with. He tended to brood and live much of the time in his own mind. Madeleine said she knew Henry believed he loved her but he was absent so much, as she put it, it was hard to see how it was supposed to make her happy. Henry suspected that they were putting a lot of weight on this baby, who didn't seem interested in joining them anyway.

Madeleine liked her job, though she didn't much like the movie business. It had seemed glamorous at first, but now she was tired of all the egos and the screaming. If she were to quit to raise a child she didn't think she'd miss much. They enjoyed having her salary, and it was certainly steadier work than screenwriting. When Henry thought about it, he came to believe that buying the Jaguar was what had pushed Madeleine into wanting a baby. She never said it, but he knew that she worried that if they started buying expensive things that's all they would do for the rest of their lives. Madeleine was in her mid-thirties. If they were going to do it, now was the time. They went through a strange period of scheduled sex in positions dictated by science rather than passion or whim. When they didn't achieve the desired result, they began visiting doctors, one after another. Henry's Writers Guild insurance paid for some of it, but the effort began to depress them both. Madeleine felt the weight of her sadness all the time.

At the Market, Henry parked near the clock tower in time to hear the eight o'clock chimes. He was careful to find a wide space to avoid getting even the smallest nick in his car. Henry loved that Jaguar. Simply looking at it made him happy. He liked the Market too, though only in the morning, because when the delivery men unload their fruit and vegetables, bustling about with handcarts, the Market belongs to the locals. Soon enough, the place is filled with tourists admiring the grapefruit and buying souvenirs to take back to Osaka or Iowa City. The Market had started right here at Fairfax and Third in the 1930s when this corner was a field. Farmers sold vegetables out of the backs of their trucks. There was no clock tower then, faux or otherwise, and only a few tables. Now it was one of the landmarks of the city.

Henry joined Leo and Morty, who were talking quietly and looking at the trades. Irwin was absent, in the cutting room working on a film that he and Leo had written. The usual topic of the morning, women and sports aside, was the unrelenting malice of agents and film studios, though today Morty wanted to talk to Henry about something else. It was known at the table that Henry and Madeleine were trying to have a baby. They had decided not to keep it a secret. Henry wasn't so sure that was a wise strategy, as it made him the object of a good deal of razzing. The absent Irwin doted on his young granddaughter and he had been encouraging. Leo considered himself a spectator in all questions of married life. Morty had urged adoption. He had adopted his daughter when she was a toddler. She was the natural child of his now ex-wife. Morty loved his daughter, who was a teenager, but the kid was always mixed up in some difficulty, usually to do with odd boyfriends. Henry couldn't see where the pleasure was. Henry knew that his friends meant well, but he was sorry he had told them about this baby business. At the time, it hadn't occurred to Henry that they might have trouble getting pregnant. Henry left the Market a little early that morning.

Henry didn't tell Madeleine that Morty had urged adoption. Given Madeleine's anxiety it didn't seem wise to remind her that their situation was a morning topic at the Market. It didn't matter. She was thinking about adoption, too. How could it be otherwise? Henry thought. He decided if that's what she wanted, he wouldn't object, and he would do what he could to make it happen.

The adoption laws in California were difficult and it could take years to work out all the details. The state favored younger couples. The idea of going hat in hand to state agencies filled Henry with dread. He wasn't sure how he felt about adopting a child anyway. Madeleine said that was ridiculous. The world was filled with children who needed parents, and they were parents who needed a child. Just how to do it in a way that would be effective and not debilitating was the problem. They had heard about people who had adopted Latin American babies. It had involved nerve-racking trips to Mexico or San Salvador. That seemed like a possibility to Henry, but Madeleine said no because she wouldn't want a baby who would surely look more like any nanny they would get than either of them. Madeleine wasn't proud of that view but it was the way she felt.

One evening, after Henry had spoken at some length with Morty about the issue, he told Madeleine how they might accomplish their goal. Morty's daughter, who was apparently part of the adoption network, had told her father that one way was to place ads in small-town newspapers in the South or Middle West. "Something along the lines of 'Pregnant? Broke? We can make a deal.'"

"That's awful," Madeleine said.

"Morty gave me the name of a guy who handles it. There are forms for consent. It's legal."

"It's still horrible."

"That it is."

"Does it work?"

With the help of a gent who called himself an adoption attorney but who Madeleine called "The Beast," Henry put ads in newspapers in Alabama and Nebraska. The Beast, who was actually Sidney Aronson and who Henry thought wasn't so bad, handled it all. Tom Lewin was Henry's lawyer for his own business. Tom and Henry had both married late. In their bachelor days they had rambled through all the Hollywood saloons. Tom looked into the legal aspects and recommended that Henry see Mr. Aronson. Sidney's office was in a modest part of Hollywood. Henry came to see that one of the reasons Sidney had developed this specialty was that he believed in it. That gave Henry a measure of comfort. The man was a little older than Henry and he didn't look like someone who worked out at the gym. His suit had probably been purchased when he was about ten pounds lighter. Sidney had sad eyes and he wasn't a fast talker. There were pictures on the wall of happy parents and infants. Henry thought that was pushing a little hard, and for a moment he wondered if they were all actors. It was Hollywood. It was possible. He put those thoughts aside and tried to let the pictures be reassuring. Part of Sidney's services involved finding a lawyer for the person he called the birth mother.

"Oftentimes these kids don't know about getting legal help," Sidney said. "Their parents are the same. If they don't have independent counsel, the whole thing can come back and bite you in the ass."

"What does it cost?" Henry asked.

"Five grand to the birth mother is usual. My fees are about the same. Plus medical expenses, the other attorney, and incidentals. You're looking at twenty thousand, give or take."

The amount was about what Henry had guessed. What made him slightly uneasy was that term "birth mother." Henry thought it would be best to keep Sidney and Madeleine apart as much as possible. Sidney suggested that they use his office phone number in the ads, but something about that struck Henry as wrong. He knew Madeleine would want to talk to whoever it might be before lawyers were involved. He instructed Sidney to place the ads but at least for now to use the Wearies' home phone number. Sidney said that was unwise and urged Henry to install a separate phone to be used only for this. "When it rings," Sidney said, "you'll know it's important." Henry thanked him and sanitized the conversation when he reported back to his wife. The idea of a special phone line charmed her. She seemed to see it as a sign of their seriousness.

The pressures of the adoption business sent Henry out to the garage to his workshop. Madeleine could see that the harder things got for her husband, the likelier he was to build more bookshelves. Henry tried to explain the satisfaction he found in the effort. "When shelves are done, that's it. A script gets kicked around and changed and if I'm lucky, maybe something like what I wrote becomes a movie."

"People want scripts. That's why you get paid."

"If I tried to sell the bookshelves, I'd probably hate them too." Henry decided to beef up his shelf-making equipment. He went on an expedition to Westwood Tools in Culver City. It was an important place if you were a cabinetmaker or had aspirations to be one. It was a storefront, from a time before malls and chain hardware stores. It was where Henry shopped when he felt the need for the best. He went in search of a new router. He took his time, talking tools with a salesman who had worked there for years, and then selected a top-of-the-line Delta model and more router bits than he would ever use. He had a perfectly good router, but his need to spend some money was great. He shopped for old pine planks, not the young wood that the rascals at the lumberyard tried to sell him. He cut his planks to the required length and then ran them through his joiner and his planer until all the irregularities were gone and they were square and true. With his new router he made dovetail joints and then using only glue—not a nail, not a screw—he assembled his shelves. He stained the wood and then he lacquered it, coat after coat. It took a long time because each coat had to dry and be sanded before he could apply the next. He was proud of the result, but all Madeleine said was, "We don't have more books to put on it."

* * *

One night, a few weeks later, while they were having dinner, the hot line, as Henry had taken to calling it, rang. It was a collect call from Towson City, Nebraska. Her name was Nikki Ann and she sounded frightened. Henry spoke to her for a few moments but all he could recall her saying was "I saw your thing in the paper."

"But you talked longer than that," Madeleine said, after Henry had put down the hot line, looking a little spooked by the brief conversation.

"She gave me her phone number."

"Give it to me. I'm calling back." And she did, talking with Nikki Ann in a reassuring voice that Henry hadn't heard in quite a while. Madeleine established what was needed, asking Nikki Ann how old she was, how pregnant she was, and did her parents know about any of it.

"Do they?" Henry asked when his wife was finally off the phone.

"She says she's twenty-one, five months pregnant, and her mother knows."

"Anything else?"

"The only part I believe is she's pregnant, and I won't be sure about that until a doctor here examines her."

"How'd you leave it?"

"We're sending her a plane ticket."

Nikki Ann was to arrive on a Thursday on a flight from Omaha. Henry and Madeleine would meet the plane. Neither of them had any idea of the social protocol required. Henry asked Sidney Aronson about it. Sidney pretty much repeated what he had told Henry earlier. Henry wondered if he should get a discount for hearing the same stuff twice. "Put her in a hotel near your house," Sidney said. "Having a pregnant teenager around is difficult enough."

"She's not a teenager."

"They're never teenagers on the first call."

"Madeleine's wired. I don't know how I feel."

"Other people have done this," he said, gesturing to the happy pictures on the wall. "It's not always easy, but it can work. In a few months, you'll be parents." Henry knew that was meant to be encouraging, but all he could think about was who the hell was Nikki Ann and who had knocked her up and what were their genes like and how on earth had he got into this?

A few days before her flight, Nikki Ann called again. She wanted to know if she could trade her ticket for two Greyhound bus tickets. She wanted to bring a friend.

"For what?" Madeleine asked when Henry told her the news.

"Moral support, I guess," Henry said. "She's never been anywhere before."

"What'd you tell her?"

"I said we'd meet the bus."

Then Madeleine started to cry. It wasn't a big cry, but there were tears and she didn't know why. Henry held her and tried to comfort her but he was scared too.

Henry had never been to the Greyhound station. He assumed it was downtown, but he asked Madeleine to look it up in the *Thomas Guide,* that compendium of maps which was the only way anyone could find their way around Los Angeles no matter how long they had lived there. The bus station was downtown, all right, and not in the stylish part by the Music Center. Henry and Madeleine sat in the fluorescent-lit waiting room on a plastic bench across from a vending machine that featured watery coffee. Their companions were several desperate-looking stragglers who for all Henry knew lived in this bleak place. "I think we're in a Hopper painting," Henry said. Madeleine smiled but Henry could see it was an effort for her. He couldn't recall her ever being quite so tense.

"How are we supposed to recognize her?" she asked.

"We'll just rope off the pregnant ones and interview them all."

When the bus arrived, just a little late, there wasn't much question as to which passenger was Nikki Ann. She was a little round thing, with her growing belly. She was wearing blue jeans that wouldn't quite button and a baggy sweater. Her companion was a boy about her age, skinny with a little tuft of a beard and sallow skin with acne scars. He was a white boy. Nikki Ann was black. Henry knew that Madeleine was making genealogical calculations as well as social ones in her head. Henry felt a strange numbness coming over him as he offered his hand to Nikki Ann. Her friend stepped forward and said, "I'm Joker." The Wearies understood that this was the father. Oh, me-oh, my-oh, Henry thought. Happy trails.

When Madeleine put the pair of them in the backseat of the Jaguar, she slammed the door so hard that Henry thought the window might break. It was a sign of just how tense she was feeling, though slamming that door was an irritating habit of hers. Henry didn't think he'd point that out just now. They drove back to the Westside in an awkward silence punctuated by Henry's feeble attempts to point out sights like the Hollywood sign. He felt like an inadequate tour guide. After entirely too much of this, Madeleine twisted herself about so she could face the back-seat and asked if they had any questions.

"Can we see Universal Studios?" Nikki Ann asked.

"Not from here," Henry said. Madeleine shot him a look that said, Don't be sarcastic. "Maybe later," he said.

"Is this a new Jaguar?" Joker asked. Henry ignored the question.

Madeleine stayed in the car while Henry helped their guests check into the Sunset Plaza Hotel, a modest joint on the Strip, not far from the Wearies' house. Henry worried that he was deserting a frightened young woman. He hadn't counted on Joker, of course. On balance, he decided, it was good to have them nearby but not in the house. In the lobby, after Henry got them checked in, Joker said, "We used up our money." Henry gave him some cash for which the boy thanked him, calling it an advance.

At home that night, over a nightcap, Madeleine said, "I don't mind about the race. It takes some getting used to. I would like a coffee-colored baby."

"That's what it'll be," Henry said.

"Especially after the Latina baby business. I still feel bad about how I felt . . ." She seemed to get lost in her unhappy words.

"Right."

"That boy is horrible. Did he ask for money?"

"I gave him some."

"She's sweet. He's running the show."

In the morning, Henry, Madeleine, Nikki Ann, and Joker went see Dr. Pamela Riley, an obstetrician in Westwood. She was upbeat in a way that made Henry think she was auditioning for a television gig. Nikki Ann called her "The lady doctor." She expected to be called Dr. Pam, which

Henry couldn't quite bring himself to do, though once he almost called her Dr. Pampers. Sidney had made the arrangements because Madeleine didn't want to go to her own gynecologist. When Dr. Pam, who had handled similar cases for Sidney, spoke to Henry and Madeleine, they felt like Nikki Ann's parents. How could it feel any other way? Dr. Pam declared the patient in her second trimester, about five months pregnant, just as Nikki Ann had said. She also said the pregnancy appeared uncomplicated. "At her age, a woman can do this without much strain." Nikki Ann took that as a compliment and smiled proudly. For Madeleine, it was yet another humiliation. Henry could see both reactions. He held his wife's hand and they left the office, though not before the receptionist asked for payment. Henry gave her his Visa card. Sidney had explained that the medical expenses would not be covered by Henry's Guild insurance." She's not a family member," he had said.

Henry and Madeleine, feeling stressed and confused, decided that they would take their guests for a look at Los Angeles. "All they want is the Universal tour," Madeleine said.

"I don't go to Universal without a firm offer," Henry said.

"Maybe we can take them to Venice. Show them the ocean."

"Couldn't we hire somebody to do all that?" Henry asked, knowing the answer.

"If this is going to work, we have to take charge."

As Madeleine had hoped, the beach interested them. They walked along the skaters' path and stopped while Joker looked at the T-shirt stalls. He seemed impressed by shirts that advertised sports teams or beer. Nikki Ann waited patiently for him. Henry was beginning to see that the entire business from becoming pregnant to answering the ad in the newspaper had so spooked Nikki Ann that she wasn't likely to complain about anything. She was a gentle soul, certainly frightened at her situation. It brought out maternal feelings in Madeleine. She had wanted that, but of course she didn't think those feelings would be directed at her hoped-for child's mother. Madeleine tried hard and in her way so did Nikki Ann. They broke into pairs, with Nikki Ann starting to hang on Madeleine, looking for protection, Henry thought. As they were strolling, Joker started in on Henry. "So, you ready for a black baby?"

"I assumed the baby would be coffee-colored."

"Depends on the father, don't it?"

Henry could see where this was going. Joker had him pegged as a liberal and now he was going to see if he couldn't make him feel guilty. He probably thought it would help him squeeze more money out of the deal. It made Henry wonder if Joker and Nikki Ann or perhaps some other girl had done this before. All Henry said was, "I thought you were the father."

"Maybe I am, maybe I'm not."

"That narrows it down."

"I'm not afraid of black. White, black, all the same. How about you? You big enough for this?"

Henry wanted to slug this little prick but he was determined not to rise to the bait. He told himself that this idiot wasn't the battle. The baby is what counted. It calmed him a little but he still wanted to take a poke at him. They walked for a bit in silence, both of them looking out to the sea.

"When do we get the five thousand?"

"There are papers to be signed. They're from our lawyer. You'll have to have someone look them over. Then after the baby's born, she'll get the payment."

"How we supposed to live?"

"I think we can arrange an advance, but the papers have to be done first."

"No problem. I'll take care of that part."

"Our lawyer will want to see proof of Nikki Ann's age. Her birth certificate."

"I'll get it from home. I'll call them up tomorrow."

"Good. You be sure to do that, Joker."

For a moment when the sun was setting and the sky had turned crimson with streaks of yellow, the four of them stood looking out at the lapping waves. Henry thought that they must look like a family out for a walk. A racially imaginative family, but a family still, enjoying the lush Venice Beach sunset.

That night Henry and Madeleine took their guests to La Plume for a special meal. It was meant as an act of generosity on Henry's part, though Madeleine predicted that they wouldn't like it. La Plume in the evenings was a little more relaxed than at lunch. There were over-dressed people in the movie business but the deal making wasn't quite as raw as in the afternoons. Joker kept his eye out for movie stars and though there were a few well-known actors in the dining room, they weren't well known to Nikki Ann or Joker. Madeleine said she was going to have grilled fish and vegetables and maybe Nikki Ann would like the same thing. She nodded and said okay but it was apparent that wasn't what she was used to eating.

"I want a T-bone steak and a Seven-and-Seven," Joker said to the waiter. When he was asked how he would like that cooked, Joker seemed mystified. The waiter tried to help by suggesting the three likely possibilities. Joker went for the well done. Henry asked for another mar-tini, saying he'd order food later.

"I want a Seven-and-Seven, too," Nikki Ann said.

"I don't think you should have alcohol," Madeleine said.

"Maybe a Six-and-Six would be safer," Henry said. Madeleine giggled, her first laugh of the evening, but Nikki Ann just shrugged.

*   *   *

The next day "the kids," as Henry had taken to calling them, walked up the hill to the Wearies' house. Joker wanted to talk with Henry again. They went out to the courtyard and sat by the pool. Joker was quiet for a moment, looking at the blue water. He asked a few questions about the price of houses in the Hollywood Hills, then got down to it. "We have to have the money," he said. "Your doctor looked. She's okay."

"You have to either prove she's of age or she has to have her parents' consent."

"I told you, she's twenty-one."

"It's not a matter of telling me. It's a matter of proving it. I think you can understand that. Documents have to be signed and you have to have them examined first."

"I know how."

"No. If you haven't had competent advice, there are grounds for a lawsuit."

"I don't want to sue you."

"We can agree on that."

"Whatever."

Henry could see that Joker's mind was racing. He wasn't a genius, but he was shrewd enough to recognize that sweet talk about Los Angeles might have been enough for Nikki Ann back in Nebraska, but he was out of his depth here. The two men just sat and stared at each other. Henry now understood why Sidney Aronson had suggested that the ads use his office phone number. Henry went back inside. He felt uneasy about leaving Joker unattended. God knows what that kid will put in his pocket, but Henry needed a break. As he walked back toward the bedrooms he heard his wife and Nikki Ann talking. He couldn't help himself. He edged closer to listen. The bedroom door was open and he could see that the women were doing something with clothes.

"Why did you wait so long?" Madeleine was asking.

"I don't know." Henry noticed that when Joker wasn't around, Nikki Ann spoke up a bit more.

"Did you want to have the baby?" Madeleine asked. Henry admired the way his wife managed to keep disbelief or frustration out of her voice. Henry knew Madeleine was pressing as hard as she dared.

"Sort of."

"Did you think you'd raise it?"

"Yes."

"Were you and Joker going to get married?"

"Not really. Lots of people do it alone. Can I tell you something?"

"Yes."

"You're nice."

"Thanks. You're pretty sweet yourself. Was it Joker's idea to come here?" Then Henry could hear Nikki Ann start to cry. He couldn't see her but he knew Madeleine was holding her and possibly crying herself. Henry wasn't feeling so hot either.

Later, Henry asked his wife what they had been doing in the bedroom. "We were looking at my clothes, seeing if anything fit her."

"Did they?"

"A couple of things. She doesn't have anything. I'd take her shopping, but it's weird. Giving her some stuff feels okay."

"Good."

"I feel like a grandmother here."

"It's complicated. The baby's real."

"I know. I can't just change my mind because it's uncomfortable. What kind of parent is that?"

"I don't know," Henry said, feeling bleak. Madeleine told him that she had been discussing the situation with her friend Bridget Bosco. They were colleagues at Fox. Henry never quite trusted Bridget. The few times he had met her, she had been wearing very tight clothes. She was sexy, that was certain, but she didn't strike Henry as someone who would have a sensitive view of a complicated situation. He felt bad because Madeleine told him whom she had talked to and he hadn't been forthcoming about his talks with Morty and Tom Lewin. "Does she help you?" was all he managed to ask.

"Not really. She sees everything as a practical problem. She's more into strategy."

"It's harder than that."

"Yes," she said and rested her head on Henry's shoulder. He comforted her as best he could, but he was confused too. And then thoughts of Bridget Bosco and her tight jeans bounced unexpectedly through his head, unsettling him entirely.

By late the next day, no progress had been made on the question of the birth certificate. Henry told Joker there was no point in their seeing a lawyer until that issue was settled. Madeleine suggested they do something that Nikki Ann might enjoy. The Comedy Store was a club on the Sunset Strip that Henry usually tried to avoid. Joker and Nikki Ann were excited at the prospect of going there, as if they had been told they were going to the White House. No, Henry thought. They probably don't care about the White House. The Comedy Store crowd was a little more to their liking than the people at La Plume. It was a couple of dark rooms with a stage at one end. Overworked waitresses moved about trying to fill the two-drink minimum before the acts started. Henry and Madeleine were relieved when they noticed a few people older than themselves. Joker ordered a hamburger but Nikki Ann waited till she heard what Madeleine wanted, which was a chef's salad. The entertainment was a few comics telling stories about how they couldn't get laid and their troubles with the airlines as they flew about the country. Joker laughed at the sex jokes. It was hard to tell about Nikki Ann. When Joker seemed happy she looked relieved. As for her own reactions to the comedy, Henry could see that Nikki Ann kept an eye on Madeleine. If Madeleine was amused, Nikki Ann was amused. Then, just as Henry thought the evening might be winding down, the announcer, a guy in a shiny tuxedo and ruffled shirt, all but shouted, "Here, tonight, a Nirvana moment. Ladies and gentlemen, put your hands together and give it up for Mr. Richard Pryor!" Joker didn't believe it. He seemed to think that the man with a look of fearful surprise on his face who had strolled out onto the stage was some sort of imitation. Mr. Pryor was twitching, blinking uncontrollably. His face and body were a whole symphony of compulsive tics. He had the face of a man who seemed aware that he needed a better excuse. After a few false starts, he launched into a riff about the life of a black man. It was funny enough, but when he began to assume a white voice and personality he was inspired. He walked like a white guy, told a few lame jokes like a white guy, asked for some white-guy food, and came on to an imaginary woman in a white-guy way. Henry was enchanted. He had heard stories of Pryor, unannounced, working on new material at local clubs, but no one he knew had ever actually seen it.

When Henry wasn't laughing, he sneaked looks at Nikki Ann. He watched her come alive. She radiated astonishment. Her skin seemed to change hue and he could feel her breathing. Henry knew that he was watching the very moment when a young person's world opened up to possibilities that seconds earlier were unknown to her. He tried to nudge Madeleine but she had already seen it as well. Their eyes were bouncing between the stage and Nikki Ann. Henry knew she had certainly seen black comics on television, but they were few and for the most part they studiously avoided talking about race. This was Richard Pryor. He knew that when a black man got on a stage all alone the subject, whether anyone said so or not, was race. Instead of skirting it, or taking a few polite pecks, Mr. Pryor flew into the belly of the beast, no caution, no net. Henry tried to imagine how powerful that was to someone like Nikki Ann. Whatever else might happen with this poor benighted girl, Henry had given her something she would remember. Henry knew that after this, Joker wasn't likely to leave Los Angeles. He wondered if that would complicate his own life, but then his life had become so complicated that a few new turns wouldn't make that much difference anyway.

Late that night, when neither Henry nor Madeleine could fall asleep, Henry told his wife what he thought. "They haven't produced a birth certificate."

"Maybe it's just late. You know the mail."

"It means she's underage."

"You don't know that."

"I work every day in a business more venal than anything that miscreant could even imagine. I know what it means. If her parents, whoever they might be, were going to give permission they would have already done it. He's here for a good time and to try to collect five thousand dollars. He hasn't thought it through very well, but so far he's had a trip to Los Angeles."

"Nikki Ann is pregnant. Look at her."

"Yes. And whatever happens to that baby, I'm sorry to say I don't believe it's going to grow up in this house." Madeleine started to cry again. This time she wouldn't let her husband comfort her. Henry knew that there wasn't any good solution to the problem. He also knew that Madeleine had grown attached to Nikki Ann. He thought that his wife wanted a daughter she could help guide and talk with, try on clothes with, and do whatever the hell else mothers and their nearly grown daughters did. She wanted a baby too, but not as much as she wanted a companion. That's why she told her woes to Bridget Bosco. He knew his wife loved him, or at least she believed that she did. He also knew that she expected him to solve this problem. She didn't want to hear that some problems couldn't be solved. Bridget Bosco and her tight jeans and all her strategy didn't make any difference. He would do what people in Hollywood always did when situations got dicey. He would spread some money around. He would take them aside and offer to pay for their tickets back to Nebraska and for the baby's birth. He knew Nikki Ann might be persuadable but he doubted that Joker would go for it, unless it was a very big check. The hell with him, Henry thought. He would just ignore him and make his deal with Nikki Ann. If she gave the money to Joker, well, it wouldn't be the first time such a thing had happened. Henry wasn't sure just how much of his view he ought to explain to his wife. It didn't give Henry any comfort that he didn't know how to discuss it. Madeleine already seemed fragile. It would be better if he could just get rid of these two. He knew that wasn't the best way to conduct a marriage but he didn't see any other way out of it. If Madeleine and Nikki Ann spent much more time together, he'd never get them apart. Madeleine would want to keep her here and think of herself as the baby's grandmother. If that happened, Joker would hang around long enough to steal Henry blind and then he'd probably go looking for another girl to knock up and start the whole thing again with some other well-meaning childless couple. Eventually, Henry fell into a fitful sleep, berating himself for all that had happened. He knew that no matter the outcome, in the end Madeleine would blame him.

A few days later, when matters had gone pretty much as Henry had expected, though he hadn't yet been able to find the words to tell Nikki Ann to take some money and go away, he was kicking himself for seeing the future but being unable to act upon it. Henry's deliverance came in the ample form of one Marvel Johnson. Mrs. Johnson, who looked to be in her mid-fifties, was a black woman who when she appeared at the Wearies' door seemed dressed for church, in a dark blue dress with a fur collar and a matching hat with feathers. She had an enormous bosom and an air of rectitude. Her face was darker than Nikki Ann's and though there was a physical resemblance, there was no shy diffidence, no frightened uncertainty. This woman was a general. One look at her and Henry had a pretty good idea who she was.

"Mr. Wearie?" she asked.

"Yes."

"I think you got my granddaughter here."

"Not at the moment. But come in." Mrs. Johnson, who looked ready for any battle that might come, followed Henry into the house. He could sense her taking a silent inventory of the furniture and making a judgment about the cleanliness of the place. She didn't seem like someone who would give you the benefit of the doubt when it came to housecleaning. "I'd like to call my wife. Are you Nikki Ann's mother?"

"I told you, I'm that child's granny. Her mother's worthless. I'm who looks out for her." Henry didn't doubt any of it. He called Madeleine, who wasn't in, and left a message to call home. Mrs. Johnson followed every word. "That boy with her?"

"He is."

"He's a shiftless bum. Her troubles started when he got in the picture. Where are they?"

"A hotel. Near here."

"You paying, I suppose."

"Yes."

"You make a habit of buying babies?"

"It's not quite like that."

"More like it than not. That child's not of age. She can't be doing this. I know the law same as you."

"How old is she?"

"Nineteen."

"I take it you're not here to negotiate."

"Let me tell you something and you listen now. That's my great-granddaughter she's carrying. If she can't raise that baby up, I will. Nothing's for sale here, not for all your Hollywood money. You go make your own baby."

"I'd like to help with the expenses." It was all Henry could think to say, and he regretted the offer. His motives were more complex than Marvel Johnson cared to acknowledge, but she wasn't wrong and Henry knew it.

"Don't want your money, don't want your pity, and I don't want you messing with my family."

Henry offered her a cup of tea but she wasn't interested in that either. He drove her over to the Sunset Plaza Hotel. Nikki Ann was surprised, but not too surprised, to see her grandmother. Joker sort of moved away and hung back. Marvel Johnson told Nikki Ann to pack up her things, they were going.

"I don't want to go. We saw Richard Pryor. I'm staying."

"We're going home."

"They're nice. They took us places."

"Pack up your bag and no back talk. Now!"

"Yes, ma'am," Nikki Ann said, bowing to the will of a powerful woman who had right on her side.

"I'm not going," Joker said, which was his version of digging in his heels. Mrs. Johnson ignored him. As Henry had guessed, Joker was going to try his luck in Los Angeles. Why not? Henry thought. Worse people have made a go of it here.

"Let me call my wife again. She'll want to say good-bye."

"Run up the phone bill all you want."

This time Madeleine was in the office and when Henry explained the situation he knew her feelings were a mixture of anger and relief. Like her husband, she felt ill-used and well out of it, but the end didn't make her happy. The sadness that Henry knew they would both come to feel would never be shaken off. Madeleine said good-bye and Nikki Ann was quiet for a moment and then she said, "Thank you for everything, especially Richard Pryor." When Nikki Ann gave the phone back to Henry he could tell that Madeleine was crying.

Henry offered to take them to the train or the airport, but Marvel had driven from Nebraska and was ready to start driving back. Henry went down to the lobby with them and Marvel watched to be sure that Henry paid the bill. She asked for a copy, which at Henry's request the desk clerk provided. She wasn't taking any chances that she'd eventually be stuck with the cost of this place. Joker hung back watching, and for a moment Henry thought he might want to go with them after all. Instead, he gave Nikki Ann a quick kiss and then touched her belly. It was the only paternal gesture Henry had ever seen him make. He left the lobby before them, disappearing into the Sunset Strip and God only knows what sort of West Hollywood future.

Henry drove Marvel and Nikki Ann back to his house where Marvel's car, an enormous old Chevrolet, was parked. When Henry saw that car, which was sparkling clean, he realized that Marvel wasn't dressed for a twelve-hundred-mile drive. She must have arrived, had the car washed, and changed clothes for her call on Henry Wearie. Henry could feel the righteous anger in that. She was going to look as formidable as she was. No one in Los Angeles was going to have reason to think ill of Marvel Johnson. Henry was in awe of her though he didn't see how he could mention it. He said good-bye and Nikki Ann thanked him again for everything, especially Richard Pryor. Henry gave her a fatherly peck on the cheek. Her grandmother told her to get into the car and then had a last word with Henry, which he had been dreading. "I'm sorry if I was sharp with you," she said.

"I think I'm the one to apologize."

"You're not what I thought."

"We'd still like to help."

"You got the address. You want to send something, I won't say no."
Then Marvel Johnson, with her granddaughter and future great-grand-child, drove away.

* * *

A few months later, a picture of a coffee-colored baby boy arrived in the
mail. His name was Henry. But by then the whole affair had put such a
strain on the Wearies' marriage that Henry and Madeleine were trying it
apart for a while. Madeleine had sent the photograph to Henry at the
Oakdale Apartments in Burbank where he was living in a suite of furnished rooms. He kept it on the mantel in his living room for a while
until it started to make him feel bad about his marriage. He put the picture of baby Henry in a drawer and tried not to think about it.

10

The House of Woe

*T*he Oakdale was like a condo fortress, a developer's dream of white stucco and red-tile roofs poured over a Burbank hillside. The condos had never sold and the dreaming developer went bust, which put a bank or two in the month-to-month rental business. There were two hundred apartments, many of them, like Henry's, furnished right down to the teacups. The complex, as the rental agents always call the place, was near the studios, and in January and February, which is television pilot season, the Oakdale was filled with child actors and their mothers. For the first week Henry found himself in residence he was too numb to so much as walk around the grounds. He kept asking himself the same questions. How had it come to this? How had they gone from wanting a child to not wanting to live together? Madeleine had said it could be temporary, but Henry knew there wouldn't be any going back. He missed Madeleine but he also missed their house in the hills and his study. How could he work in this anonymous place? He was without his books, his supplies, and soon, he feared, his grip.

By the second week of his tenancy, he resolved to take a look around. In the early evening he walked over to the "Health Club Ranch and Spa," which he had resisted because of the name, as if they were trying to convince people it was a combination of Gene Autry's house and Baden Baden. Whatever it was called, it was in the midst of some eucalyptus trees and had a pleasant view of the San Gabriel Mountains. Why couldn't they just call it the swimming pool or the hot tub, which is what it was? As Henry was coming to see, a second week standing on rarified linguistic principle was ridiculous. It was a cool evening, so Henry didn't expect to see swimmers. He put on a sweater and went for a stroll. What he saw was a tangle of teenagers fooling around. A few were in the hot tub, but most were just hanging out on the deck. He could smell the sweet acrid aroma of pot. He saw the kids fussing with the joint, snuffing it out. Henry was amused that they felt obliged to ditch the drugs. Maybe they think I'm the principal and if I catch them I'll make them stay after school. Henry had so little to do with teenagers that anything they did was news to him. Maybe he could get a script idea out of it. As he got closer, he could hear their conversation. One hulking lad who was wearing a baseball cap backward, a style that Henry always associated with gross stupidity, was saying, "You have to make your agent work. Talk to him. Grease him."

"He's supposed to work for me," said a long-legged redheaded babe in a green bikini, seemingly indifferent to the cool night air.

"There's lots of us and not so many of them. You do the math."

They were talking show-business strategy. My God, Henry thought, they're already in the game. These kids were here for pilot season, he was sure of that. They all had the anonymous pastel quality, the hue and flavor of Necco Wafers, that populated the sitcoms. They must have a parent or two somewhere. The girls had careful hair, even for the pool. The well-muscled boys were surely veterans of the gym. Well, actors have always been like that. The surprise for Henry was that they sounded like a junior version of his table at the Farmers Market. Once they had put out the joint and decided he wasn't a talent scout, he become background for them. Backward Cap was going on about the difficulty of dealing with producers. "They're trying to juggle everything. If they have to sell you out, they'll do it. It's not personal." As he spoke, the redhead unwound her legs in his direction and stretched her back, like a cat. The choreography of that little pas de deux was pretty clear. The boy was probably a director in the making. The two of them were playing director and actress, but in a more extreme way than Henry had seen it in the adult versions. They had probably read about behavior of this sort or perhaps seen it on television, and now that they were in Hollywood they were trying it out. They weren't wrong, but what irritated Henry was the received quality of all the chatter. The head boy was describing conditions he hadn't endured and delivering synthetic opinions as if it was wisdom acquired on the battlefield.

"My audition's set," one of the girls said, apparently picking up a thread of an earlier conversation. She wasn't quite as spectacular as the redhead and Henry could sense that she felt like the understudy, hoping for a little attention.

"Is there an offer?" This from the future director. Henry could now see that his cap had "Technicolor" emblazoned on the front, which of course was in the back. He seemed to be the authority here, the alpha male. The other boys listened to him, probably waiting to see which girl he claimed before they asserted themselves. The redhead was first prize.

"It's just a reading," the understudy said. She seemed embarrassed that whatever she had been promised was now seen as inadequate.

"You should negotiate the deal first. On an if-come basis."

"I didn't know," she mumbled.

"Is the reading for the producer or the network?" Backward Cap asked, all but flicking a towel at the poor girl. She dipped her head and didn't answer. "Network is what counts," he said. "It doesn't matter. TV is all crap. I'd rather have a little feature than the biggest TV anything."

"I just want to work," she said.

"TV is shit!"

"I'm sorry," she said.

The other kids listened and nodded. Backward Cap had managed to browbeat her and boast, all at once. He's a director, all right, Henry thought. How did they get so worldly so soon? Is everything in Hollywood strategy? Of course it is. Strategy about strategy. The only difference between these kids and his chums at the Market, aside from the fact that his pals weren't teenagers, was that these scamps weren't writers. At least a screenwriter can do something without asking permission. As these kids had already learned, an actor can't do a thing until someone else allows it. Henry knew they would be good at ingratiating themselves. They would want adults to like them, to think they were talented. Actors never lost that pathetic quality. Even stars had it. Henry guessed that Backward Cap was the only one of those kids who wasn't an actor. When he'd heard enough for this evening and was about to go back to his charming apartment, a woman he assumed was the mother of one of the kids strode over to the pool. She was about forty, Henry guessed, and attractive but with worried eyes. She had big hair that he associated with the South.

"Hi," she chirped. It wasn't exactly a Southern accent, but a sort of enthusiastic drawl. Before Henry could manage a reply, she had turned her attention to the kids. "Gretchen, you have to be up early." Gretchen was the leggy redhead. Henry assumed Gretchen would put up a fight, but instead she smiled in an unconscious imitation of her mother and put on a denim shirt that just covered her bottom. The effect was to make her appear even less dressed. The obedient child. As Gretchen was saying good night to her pals, Mom offered her hand to Henry. "I'm Sally Jill. We're from Dallas." Henry shook Sally Jill's hand, saying his own name and wondering if Jill was part of her first name.

"You have a kid here?" she asked.

"No."

"Then you're getting a divorce?"

"Do I have a sign on my back?"

"People here have kids for pilot season or are splitting up. Come on back with us. We can have a drink. Hurry up, Gretchen."

Sally Jill's apartment was two bedrooms larger than Henry's, though the furniture seemed identical. The Oakwood must rent white sofas with big pillows by the boxcar. Even the framed prints on the wall were the same. It looked like a chain motel, which is probably where they got the stuff. Henry had been indifferent to his furniture, but now that he realized all the apartments were the same, he felt even more uncomfortable. Oh, well, he thought, what's one more indignity? Sally Jill poured white wine and introduced her second child, who was called Rudy Junior, though there was no sign of a Rudy Senior. The kid was about ten with bangs and a cute smile. He looked like a sitcom moppet and he reeked of self-importance. Henry offered his hand and thought the boy was going to give him his card in return.

"Are you in the business?" Rudy Junior asked.

"Yeah. I am."

"As what?" he asked, apparently not ready to take Henry's word for it.

"I'm a writer."

"What did you write?"

"Maybe I can give you my credits some other time," Henry said, looking for the door.

"You go do your homework," Sally Jill said.

"I don't have any."

"Don't you lie to me."

"I'm not," Rudy Junior said and wandered out of the room.

"Do they go to the Burbank schools?" Henry asked.

"Yep," Sally Jill said. "While we're here."

"They just drop in for a month or two?"

"Until they get jobs. Then it's studio tutors."

Henry wondered how often they went to school and whether it much mattered. Gretchen already had a pretty good understanding of the power of her long legs and red hair, which was as useful as anything they were likely to teach her in the Burbank schools.

Sally Jill poured more wine and began telling Henry about her life. She spoke quickly and in a disjointed way, and as she drank her drawl got thicker. She explained that Rudy Senior—was he called Mr. Jill?— was back in Dallas where he was a contractor. As she was going on about her son's theatrical abilities and sitcom promise and her daughter's accomplishments in the world of junior pageants and talent shows, Gretchen joined them. Sally Jill announced that Henry was a screenwriter. Gretchen didn't seem to require a list of credits to take an interest. She and her mother were both touching their hair and squirming about, smiling in a display of teeth that must have put some Dallas orthodontist's kids through school. Henry couldn't quite tell if Gretchen was flirting with him independently of her mother or if this was an activity they did together, the way other mothers and daughters might bake cookies.

"Me and my friend," Gretchen began, unaware of the effect of her grammar on Henry, "we wrote this script. It's for me to star in and him to direct."

"Very ambitious," Henry said, dreading what he knew was coming.

"It would be way great if you would read it. Give us some tips."

"It's a difficult time for me right now, Gretchen."

"It don't have to be like right away or anything."

"Well, maybe sometime." Gretchen's language confirmed all Henry's snobbish assumptions. Maybe that's what Madeleine didn't like about him. Maybe he should try to be more generous about these things. Who cares about her damn grammar, and what difference does it make what they call the swimming pool? Sally Jill could see that Henry's mind was wandering. "How lovely," she said, trying to tug him back.

Each time Henry would make a move to leave, Sally Jill poured more wine. Henry had stopped after the second glass, but his hostess was still knocking them back. At some point, Henry wasn't quite sure when, Gretchen left the room, perhaps to join Rudy Junior and the no homework. When Sally Jill was all but batting her eyes, Henry stood up and excused himself, thanking her so very much and agreeing that yes, now that they were neighbors, they would see each other often. My God, he thought, is this the single life? She's not even single. He'd best take care. The boy was a horror. He supposed the girl had a sweetness about her somewhere, or maybe it was just that she was good-looking. Henry mused on the evening as he hunted for his apartment. Since every door looked alike, he had trouble finding his. He found himself walking back in the direction of the pool. There were still a few kids at the hot tub, but off to one side, in the privacy of the eucalyptus grove, he could see two of them wrapped around each other. As he got a little closer, he saw that it was Gretchen and Backward Cap, no doubt her cowriter, the future director. The other kids must have been aware of them, though they didn't seem to pay any attention.

As Henry continued wandering, wondering what would happen if he never found his apartment, and still a little rattled by the eucalyptus grove exhibition, he came to a sort of meeting hall or community center or whatever the hell they called it in a joint like this. He peered in an open window and saw six children all about Rudy Junior's age. Several women he assumed were mothers were watching while one of them ran a rehearsal. Henry listened to the dialogue for a moment.

"I want to sleep over at Brenda's," one little girl was whining, as the others watched her with critical eyes.

"Her brother dresses up like a girl," a little boy replied. They spoke in the slightly artificial manner of television comedy. All it lacked was the laugh track.

"I don't think you should go over there," said an adult women, reading the mom's role.

"It's all right. He lets me try on his dresses," the little girl said, punching each word.

"Try it again, Ashley," the woman running things said. "More oomph." More? Henry thought. The roof will come off. And who was that adult? A director-mom? A new hyphenate, perhaps.

"I want to sleep over at Brenda's," Ashley whined with more oomph.

"Better," the director-mom said. "Sell it!" Ashley, a little beauty queen, barked out the line again. "Jordan, come in fast. Big!"

"Her brother dresses up like a girl," Jordan fairly shouted.

"It's all right. He lets me try on his dresses," Ashley shouted.

Henry wondered how Rudy Junior missed out on this deal. Here they were, mothers and children, come from all over at great expense to try to achieve mediocrity. Henry thought they seemed to be succeeding.

* * *

The next morning when Henry was trying to figure out where he was supposed to put what little trash he had accumulated, he ran into Bob

Desantis from Warners. Bob had supervised *Finding Home,* Henry's hit. Henry could tell from the dark look on Bob's face why he was at the Oakdale. He began to tell Henry the story of the breakup of his marriage. "She just didn't want to live with me anymore. All of a sudden all the things I always did were awful."

"I know what you mean," Henry said. When they had worked together, Bob had been energetic and wildly ambitious, not this crushed-looking sad sack. At least he wasn't using black street slang. Henry wouldn't have been surprised if Bob turned up wearing a baseball cap on backward. He had lasted through various purges and calamities. Well, Henry thought, he's good at staying out of the line of fire.

As they were standing there while Bob continued to moan about his marriage, Sally Jill seemed to materialize. She must have radar for needy men who might be able to help her kids. Or maybe they were just near her apartment. Henry still got lost every time he stepped outside. He didn't need a shrink to point out that he wasn't about to allow himself to get comfortable here.

"Henry, hi," Sally Jill said as she came over to the trash cans. Henry introduced Bob, letting drop that he was a studio executive. As the words were out of his mouth, Sally Jill stepped away from Henry and closer to Bob. And why not? Henry had made it clear that he was barely interested in a friendship and certainly not more, and Bob might be able to help her kids more than Henry could anyway. If Henry could tell that Bob was a wreck and available, Sally Jill certainly could. Right on cue she said, "Now, Bob, you have to come by for a drink tonight. I won't take no. Henry, you too."

"I'll have to take a rain check for tonight," Henry said.

"Well then, Bob, I'll just be expecting you. You can meet Gretchen and Rudy Junior."

"Okay," Bob said, ready to be led anywhere.

When Henry got back to his apartment, Gretchen was sitting in front of his door, script in hand. "I know you can't read it now," she said. "My mom thought if I left it off with you, then when you could it would be handy." Gretchen was wearing jeans with two buttons open at the waist. Henry could see the top of her green underwear. Her eyes seemed to get larger as she looked at him. It was one of her mother's moves. Henry had seen this child at the pool in a bikini, at home in a flirting duet with her mother, and in the bushes screwing her boyfriend. Now she was at his door unbuttoned and asking for a favor.

"You should show it to Bob Desantis," Henry said. "He's at Warners. Your mother knows him."

"Sure. I'll give him one." She handed Henry the script, saying, "Whenever you can." She gave him a little kiss on the cheek, brushing her breasts against him, and then she was gone.

He put the script aside, determined to get to work. He had made a space for himself in what the Oakdale called the dining area, which meant the part of the living room nearest the kitchen. As he didn't think he would be giving dinner parties, Henry had made it into his study. He flipped through *Gorgeous Gretchen* by Cody Malone and Gretchen Jill. Well, that settled the last-name question. Sally Jill wasn't like Jim Bob after all. At least now when he spoke to Sally he could use her name. Cody Malone, he was sure, was Backward Cap. *Gorgeous Gretchen*. Well, Henry thought, if it's for her to act in, why not? It was something about a young girl from Dallas who wins beauty contests and her overbearing mother and impossible little brother and her father who isn't around. My God, Henry thought, they're writing about her life. The other times he had been dragooned into looking at a script that somebody's kid had written he hadn't been able to get past the first few pages. They were usually about drug dealers and hit men, or characters who said, "fuggedaboudit," all of which these suburban kids knew of only from movies and television. *Gorgeous Gretchen* was awkward and Gretchen's grammar was in evidence, but it had modest ambitions and seemed able to fulfill them. Henry didn't know if he should be happy or sad. He didn't think Gretchen and Cody Malone were necessarily going to start churning out studio scripts, but at least what they wrote was from the planet earth. It didn't make him jealous, though he doubted that he would be able to get any work done. What Gretchen and her script did was fill him with wonder at how unpredictable the world was.

Henry thought he would be more comfortable in his new surroundings if he had more of his gear. He didn't need much. He'd always kept a supply of the Blackwing pencils he liked. They had stopped making them and he had forgotten to bring his stash. And he wanted some clothes, too. He knew enough to call first to tell Madeleine he'd stop by the next afternoon, when she was at work.

"Could you do it the next day?" she asked.

"I need the stuff."

"Some people are coming over."

"What does that mean?"

"Some of my girlfriends."

"You're having a party?" Henry asked, a sinking feeling coming over him.

"Bridget thought it would do me some good."

"Is this to celebrate?"

"Henry, please. This is hard on me."

"It's been a real walk in the park for me. I'm the one living in a dump."

"I'm not going to fight with you. Please don't come tomorrow. Now good-bye." She hung up on him! What else could it be but a party to celebrate his leaving? And in his house. Henry imagined himself peering in the window and watching while *les girls* mocked him, discussing his many flaws and telling Madeleine how lucky she was to be free of him. It had to be the wretched Bridget Bosco. She had been married to a screenwriter some years ago and Henry had always assumed she and Madeleine commiserated about the difficulties. Henry tried to stay clear of Bridget, though the real reason for that was that he found her attractive. That stubborn and inconvenient fact had always spooked him, but there it was. She always wore tight clothes that showed off her figure, particularly her well-rounded bottom. The clothes were probably from an expensive shop, but on Bridget they had a slightly trashy look that held a secret appeal for Henry. He knew Bridget had seen him looking at her.

She was waiting for him to do something about it. Henry always felt it was safer to keep his distance. Well, he thought, I guess I made an enemy out of her. Henry knew that this party wasn't something Madeleine would have thought of herself. No, it was Bridget taking her revenge. As Henry brooded he could feel himself slipping into the blues. The telephone jolted him out of his ennui.

"Henry? Hi. It's Bridget."

"Ah. The party girl."

"It's not what you think."

"What do I think?"

"That this is about you. It's about Madeleine."

"Well, in that case I don't mind," he said, unable to keep a lid on the acid in his voice.

"Don't be like that. How are you, Henry? I mean how has it been going for you?"

"Just peachy."

"Yeah. You know I always liked you."

"Interesting way of showing it."

"We're both single now. Isn't that something?"

"Well, I'm not sure what. I'm a little ragged these days."

"Whenever you're ready. It can be our secret."

Oh, me-oh, my-oh, Henry thought when he got off the phone. "Our secret." She's such a treacherous little bitch that she's likely to tell Madeleine I hit on her. What to do, what to do? He knew that he would do nothing at all, except of course wonder about the party and what terrible things they would say about him. He saw himself at the window again, his nose to the glass. This time it was a snowy night as if their house in the hills had migrated to the East Coast. There were Christmas lights and a snowman in front, though Henry wore only a thin sweater. My God, he thought, I'm rewriting my own fantasy. Now it's some Norman Rockwell calendar. He couldn't stop wallowing in his unhappiness. Inside they were celebrating Christmas and agreeing about how thoughtless and manipulative he was, how he took

Madeleine for granted and his only concern was himself. Bridget Bosco was leading them. Madeleine should get a medal for putting up with him. He didn't want a wife, not a full partner. He wanted someone to provide food and sex when he felt like it. The others oohed in agreement as they drank his red wine and passed a plate of Christmas cookies with white icing and red sprinkles. He was an ego-ridden, self-centered horror. Henry wanted a drink and one of those cookies. It was cold out there. He was lonely. Bridget Bosco in her snug leather trousers was starting to look pretty good.

Henry knew he wasn't as awful as that but he tried to review his marital sins. He probably shouldn't have complained about Madeleine's car-door closing technique. It had irritated him the way she always slammed the Jaguar's door. She had never approved of that car or maybe it was that she resented the way he fussed over the damn thing. Once, in Musso's parking lot, she had slammed it so hard that Henry could feel it in his teeth. He was sure she was challenging him in some obscure way. Now, he replayed the scene in his mind. He had asked her to be more careful. He tried to recall his tone of voice. Maybe his anger had showed just a little.

"I do not slam doors," she had said. He should have just let it go but he didn't.

"Just car doors. This car. You put your shoulder into it like you're winding up to throw a fast ball. Then you swing your arm."

"My God, Henry. It's a car door."

"All you have to do is touch it and it closes. It's a Jaguar." Then he demonstrated how easily it closed and pointed out how it made a soft, satisfying thud. He crossed some sort of line with her when he did that. "If someone slammed the front door like that, you'd think they were demented." Oh, me-oh, my-oh. Why couldn't he just let it rest? She said he loved that car more than her. Actually, he loved them both, but he let it go.

That night, unable to work and unable to sleep, Henry did what he always did when he was sad. He got out his hammer and nails. Madeleine had always said it was her payment for her husband's moodiness. At least she got house repairs out of it. The Oakdale didn't provide bookshelves. Even if he didn't have his special pencils, he had his toolbox. It gave him comfort to have it around. His table saw, his planer, and his new router were still in the garage so he wouldn't be able to do a complete job, but he could get started. Making shelves might make him feel better. The difference between a hobbyist—which is what Henry was, though an obsessive one, it was true—and a cabinetmaker was doors. That's what separated the men from the boys in the shelf game. Henry had once considered getting out of Hollywood and learning cabinetry, apprenticing himself to a master for however long it took. The guy he went to see built furniture that might have been sculpture. He told Henry to stick to screenplays. His feelings were hurt, but as he thought about it, he knew that was right. Henry gave up his dream of building perfectly balanced cabinets with marquetry and doors that slid or rolled or swung. He decided to stick to simple bookshelves made as perfectly as he was able. Henry didn't much care what went on the shelves. It was the form, the perfect lines of a well-made shelf, that always drew him in. He tried not to think about what that might mean, but it was hard not to see that he didn't have anything worth keeping, nothing that he was proud of and wanted to display. In time, Henry came to see that doing adaptations, taking a novel apart and putting it back together in a different form, was something like cabinetry, and he tried to take pleasure in that.

It was eleven-thirty at night when the urge to build came over him. Bookshelves, even incomplete ones, required lumber and paint, not items that might be found at the Burbank 7-Eleven. Only in Hollywood, Henry thought, would this be as the locals would put it, No problema. The Home Depot stayed open almost all night. Henry made his measurements and took the green Jaguar with the easily closed doors over the hill, deep into Hollywood.

Henry loved to walk the Home Depot's wide aisles examining power tools and checking out the transformers and generators. It always brought back memories of the hardware store of his youth. Until Henry was eight, his family spent summers in a cottage on Long Island Sound, near Port Washington. Felix must have been flush in those days. Henry had fragmented memories of barbecues and the fire station and of digging for clams in the sound with his father. Henry and his father spoke less and less as the years wore on. It was hard for Henry to say just why that had happened, but as Felix got older, mired in being a widower, he grew less communicative and so taciturn that phone calls were an ordeal. When Henry was in New York he tried to visit him in the family apartment but even those visits were uncomfortable, and sometimes when Henry was in New York for a brief time he never quite got around to calling Felix. What he wanted to remember now, what came back to him most clearly, was going into the village with Felix on Saturday mornings to Rubio's Hardware Store. Henry remembered the white garden furniture displayed on the sidewalk in front and the wide plank floor inside. It was bowed and worn and it creaked when men walked through the shop. There were women in Rubio's, though they always asked for something specific. "I need a quart of shellac and a brush, please." They completed their business and left. Women didn't linger at Rubio's. Henry had thought there was probably a rule about it. He remembered the open bins of nails from little tacks right up to mean-looking items that he learned to call spikes. If his father wanted nails, a clerk would use a metal scoop to gather the right amount and drop them onto the scale. Henry admired the off-hand accuracy and felt bad if the clerk had to make adjustments. The better hand tools were displayed in flat glass-covered cases. Henry's father would lift him up so he could look down at the chisels and knives, laid out like the tray of butterflies in the library of the Columbia Grammar School where Henry had recently endured the third grade, learning all about the Pueblo Indians and how they lived in caverns dug into hillsides, which Henry thought of as primitive apartment houses. In his mind those knives and nails and dead butterflies were all jumbled together with the Pueblo Indians. If his father was in the market for something serious, Mr. Rubio himself, who knew his father by name—a fact that always impressed Henry—would open the case with one of the keys he kept on a big ring at his waist. Mr. Rubio would point out the virtues of one blade or another. On those occasions, Henry was encouraged to pick up a screwdriver or a fishing knife and give it a heft. His father and Mr. Rubio were serious men when it came to tools and Henry absorbed their view. Tools meant you could do things. Henry knew, in the inchoate way of childhood, that if he had a hammer or a drill he would have power. He wouldn't be helpless, he could be in control, which was surely why all these memories were flooding through him now.

The Home Depot was built like a studio soundstage. The ceiling was thirty feet high and the aisles were stacked with Henry's delight. It was, he often thought, an elephantine version of Rubio's Hardware Store. Late at night, the crowd was a mixed lot of contractors getting a jump on the next day's work, husbands getting around to what their wives had been asking them to do, and young actors checking each other out, and like every place movie people gather, talking strategy. Henry would wander the aisles picking up this and that. Nails no longer came in open bins, but he might buy a package or two just to have them around, and he always looked at the power tools. He was inspecting table saws when he noticed a young woman with thick unruly hair looking at electric drills. She didn't have a clue and Henry was just in a loose enough mood to start talking to her. "I take it you're not exactly in the machinist's union," he said.

"You're right about that. I am Ms. Ditzomatic." Henry liked that. He repeated the word, trying it out. "You have to be a writer," she said. "Only a writer would think that word is worth repeating." Her name was Maggie LeMay and she was a reader at Paramount. Henry guessed that she was in her mid-twenties. She knew Henry's name, or she said she did. Either way, it pleased him. She was a chatty thing who didn't seem bothered by talking about language or tools in the Home Depot. "Which one should I get?" she asked, as she examined the drills. "I need to hang some pictures."

"In that case, the cheapest one. They're all from the same factory in South Korea."

"Sold!" she said, plucking a drill from the shelf. "I think we just met cute."

"If we did, it's a first for me," he lied. "I've written it, but I've never done it," he added, ignoring where he had met Madeleine.

"I think I read a script of yours. Did you do a modern version of a Shakespeare?"

"*Henry IV* set in a college. The name appealed."

"I read it. The Falstaff guy couldn't graduate. All he did was smoke pot and hang out. Hotspur was a student radical."

"Something like that."

"I think I passed."

"It's all right. Nobody liked it."

"It was very well written."

"When people say that, it means they didn't like it but they don't know why. Nobody buys a script because it's well written."

"Wow. That's great. And you know about tools?"

"Regular Renaissance neurotic."

"Are you married?"

"Separated. You're the third woman I've flirted with since I ran away from home."

"Who were the other two?"

"A lunatic neighbor where I live and a friend of my wife's. They don't really count because I didn't flirt back."

"Where do you live?"

"The Oakdale."

"You're separated," she said with satisfied finality. "Nobody would live there for any other reason. So can you hang my pictures?"

"Sure."

"Then I don't need this dumb thing," she said and tossed the drill back on the pile.

A few days later Henry brought his drill along when he took Maggie to dinner. Afterward he hung her pictures, which were framed posters, remnants of a student life which was, for Maggie, in the recent past. She lived in a remodeled garage that she called a guest house. It was behind a beat-up Craftsman bungalow on Argyle Street in Hollywood. After the posters were up, Henry and Maggie started going out. It wasn't all that unusual for her. She was a single woman and she was young. Dating is what she did. For Henry, it was all news. Maggie found that funny and kept giving him campy dating tips. If they were at a movie, she would say, "You don't have to fold down the seat for me, but it would be nice." Once, when she said, "A girl likes bon-bons now and again," Henry thought he had made a mistake, until she laughed. Another time, in a restaurant, when Maggie wanted to pay the bill and Henry almost fainted, she pointed out that he should pay most of the time because he had more money, but that she should pay some of the time because it wasn't 1957 anymore. Henry recognized that Maggie was an ambitious woman. He liked that, since he wasn't feeling very ambitious himself. He watched her worry about what moves she was making at Paramount and how she might get promoted. Strategy, strategy. At first he resisted inviting her to his apartment, telling her that any time spent away from the vile Oakdale was a victory. She insisted on seeing it. On the evening she came over, Sally invited them to come by for a drink.

As they strolled over to what Maggie was calling "the party," Henry told her how it took him two weeks before he could find his way around the Oakdale.

"Only a mental case or somebody who doesn't know thing one about L.A. would live here for more than about a minute," she said. "There are plenty of furnished places cheaper and better. This is the House of Woe." From then on that's what Henry and Maggie called the Oakdale. "So who is it we're going to see?"

"Sally Jill and her fabulous children. The boy is a fugitive from a sitcom and the girl wants to be a screenwriter-actress-slut."

"Ought to be room for one more."

"They're here for pilot season. Bob Desantis will probably be there."

"From Warners?"

"Yeah. His wife threw him out."

"Into the House of Woe."

"We did a picture together. *Finding Home.*"

"I saw that. About this cop who did something."

"That's about it."

"I can't remember the plot anymore. It was a hit, though."

The population of Sally Jill's apartment was greater than Henry had expected. It was indeed a party. There were several of the women Henry thought of as the sitcom moms and their kids. Gretchen was bouncing between Cody Malone, backward cap in place, and Bob Desantis. He must have said something promising about their script, Henry thought. Sally had put out bowls of sour cream dip and potato chips. The plonk was flowing.

"Interesting crowd," Maggie whispered to Henry. "Hope I can keep up." As Maggie surveyed the room, Henry saw her eyes stop at Bob Desantis and Gretchen, as the only two people worth bothering with. Desantis because he was a studio man, and Gretchen because she had beauty, which in an actress is gold. Henry knew she was writing off everyone else as useless to her. One of the little kids might be valuable, but she had no standard for judging them. That was Maggie, he thought. Everything was business. Bob Desantis looked more relaxed than the last time Henry had seen him. Sally, Gretchen, and Rudy Junior were clinging to him. Cody was sort of hanging back, keeping his eye on Gretchen, apparently concerned that she was cozying up to Bob.

"I have an announcement, you all," Sally said as she handed Henry and Maggie glasses of wine. Henry was about to introduce Maggie, but Sally Jill must have thought he would take too long so she shook Maggie's hand and shouted out a slew of names and said, "Warner Bros. studio has bought *Gorgeous Gretchen*!" There was a moment of quiet as the news took its effect. Then the moms cheered and the children started yapping questions: "Is there a part for me?" was the central refrain.

"Easy, sister. It's not nailed down yet," Bob said.

"Gretchen's going to star in it, and Cody's going to direct it, and there's going to be a part for Rudy Junior just as soon as they do the rewrite," Sally said.

"It has to be real. Important," Rudy Junior said. "I'm not playing just the kid. I need a back story."

"You're ten," Cody said. "How much back story can you have?" Henry liked that. Cody was surely the engine in this writing team. Gretchen provided the raw material and, no doubt, some serious encouragement.

"There are a few things that have to be worked out," Bob said, though no one was listening to him.

"I haven't agreed to any rewrites," Cody said. "I want to see all the notes first."

"Good plan," Maggie told him.

"Right," Henry said. "You don't want them buying your script just any old way."

Cody could see that Henry and Maggie weren't taking this thing as seriously as he was. He scowled and took Gretchen's hand. "You can laugh," Cody said. "This is my shot. I'm not letting some studio asshole hack it up. I approve all script changes. And final cut. There's more than one studio, you know."

"You stick to your guns, Cody. The studios respect that," Henry said.

"Well, we'll see," Sally said, not sure if Henry wasn't being just a little sarcastic.

"I'm not doing any nudity unless it's artistically justified," Gretchen said.

"I don't blame you," Maggie told her. "I tell my boss the same thing all the time."

Gretchen, who was comfortable in her obliviousness, excused herself. She took Cody with her, explaining that they wanted to do some more work on *Gorgeous Gretchen*. No doubt in the eucalyptus grove, Henry thought.

Maggie finally got a moment alone with Desantis. Henry couldn't hear what they were saying, though he assumed Maggie was working hard to imprint herself on Bob's brain. The moms had been doing that, too, though none of them had Maggie's skill. They all tried to flirt with him. Maggie knew the task was to show him what a capable, clear-thinking young woman she was. If she also let him know she thought he was intelligent, charming, and sexy, well, that couldn't hurt. He was a big shot at a studio and knowing him was like capital for her. Henry was admiring the ease of it when one of the moms started to chat him up. Her name was Dorene and she was another Texan, one of Sally's home girls. She said their kids were friends. They had written *Gorgeous Gretchen* together. So this was Cody Malone's mother. She looked like a folksinger from the sixties, with freckled, sun-worn skin and a long gray braid down the center of her back. For a moment Henry wondered if she was an Indian. A squaw, maybe. He couldn't remember if asking someone if they were an Indian was now an insult, so he just let it go. "I know you read the script," she said.

"I've had a look at it."

"Cody wouldn't show it to me for the longest time. I had to practically kidnap it. Do you think it's any good?"

"Bob must have liked it."

"Did you, though? As a writer?"

"It's about their lives. Or Gretchen's, anyway. That's good."

"I hope so. I just don't know about all this."

"All what?"

"Coming here. Taking Cody out of school. He'd have just run off without me."

"It's the circus. He wants to join."

"It's Gretchen Jill."

"That too." They both smiled at the unspoken part of their conversation. Cody and Gretchen were in heat and their mothers knew it and Henry knew it.

"I don't know if he'll thank me for this or hate me. Someday, I mean." That surprised Henry and made him think, here is a thoughtful woman.

"Is Cody an actor?" he asked.

"He wants to be a director. That's all he wants." Then, perhaps thinking of Gretchen, she added, "Well, maybe not all."

"How old is he?"

"Seventeen. He's a senior."

"Stranger things have happened, Dorene."

"Not to me."

Henry liked this woman. She didn't have any loony ambitions for her son. It couldn't be easy being Cody's mother. He was intense and bull-headed, with a nascent talent. Just like a director. Henry was wary of being encouraging, but at least Dorene didn't give him a headache the way her friend Sally Jill did. Henry shook her hand, wished her well, and looked around for Maggie. A couple of the children had learned that she did something at Paramount and they had surrounded her, asking self-serving questions. Henry knew it was time to leave the party.

Maggie stayed at the House of Woe that night, but they spent most of the time laughing about how Bob Desantis must have promised Sally Jill the moon. "He wants to get laid," Henry said. "That's all this is."

"With Sally, if that's what he wants, he wouldn't have to ask," Maggie said.

"Daughter, too."

"Can I read their script?"

"You mean *'Le cinéma de Cody Malone'*? Why?"

"You said it was good. Bob thought there was something there. He doesn't have Warners lined up. I can slip past him. Paramount's always looking for youth stuff."

"You are some piece of work, Maggie."

"Do those people have an agent?"

"They're always talking about agents and deals."

"Yeah. But do they have one?"

"I don't know and I don't care."

"Maybe I should read it right now."

"Maybe you can read it tomorrow and we can find another activity tonight."

"What was that about a piece of something?" she asked, giggling as they fell into Henry's rented bed.

Maggie called the next day after she had read *Gorgeous Gretchen.* "So?" Henry asked. "What did you make of it?"

"It's a piece of shit. I think I can sell it to Paramount."

"They in the market for a nice piece of shit?"

"It's about kids. It's by kids. It could be my ticket out of the story department."

"What do I do in all this?"

"If they pop for it, you do the rewrite. Everybody gets a payday. Tell them I love it. Best script ever written. The boy can direct, the girl can star. Earthly happiness included."

"I don't know if it's for me."

"You don't want the gig?"

"It's not that. That script is what it is. It's naïve. That's its charm. If it goes through the chop shop it won't be anything."

"You don't have to write it. Hire somebody. We'll take your profits and go to Paris for a couple of days."

"I guess."

"That a yes?"

"Jesus, Maggie."

"It's time to make a move. Now what are you going to do, shelf man?"

* * *

It was never clear if Bob Desantis had presented *Gorgeous Gretchen* to Warners at all, but it didn't matter because Maggie moved fast. She talked it up to Frank Rosato, the youth expert at the studio. Henry laughed at that, because what youth expert meant was that Frank chased young girls. Maggie knew he'd go for Gretchen if not her script. Before he became a studio man, Frank was a writer, and he and Henry occasionally read each other's first drafts. After Frank became an executive, he had offered to help Henry do something similar. "You could run the story department," Frank had said. "And then move up." Henry didn't think it was for him. "Careful," Frank had said, "or you'll be a writer all your life." That was a line from one of Fitzgerald's

Pat Hobby stories, but Henry didn't see any reason to point it out.

Frank didn't buy *Gorgeous Gretchen* outright, but he did get the studio to take an option. It wasn't a lot of money but it was more than Gretchen or Cody had ever earned. There was a lot of back and forth about the directing and starring business. Cody wouldn't take the deal until Paramount agreed to some salami called "Best efforts." Bob Desantis told Sally and Dorene, who had to sign for their kids, that was the most they could get. Cody hated it but Gretchen talked him into it in private. Maggie became a story executive, whatever the hell that meant, reporting to Frank. They soon became known around town as "The Youth Patrol." Henry got the gig to rewrite the script, and Maggie found a writer she thought could handle the job and who knew how to keep his mouth shut. He got 20 percent of Henry's fee. Henry delivered the pages to Maggie, who told Frank they were fabulous and released a check to Henry. Cody flared up again when he learned that the script had been retitled *Burn It Down,* but by then not even Gretchen was paying any attention to him, because she was dating Frank Rosato.

Maggie helped Henry get out of the House of Woe and into an apartment in a pale green Moderne building from the 1940s in the singles district of Beverly Hills. Henry turned a second bedroom into an office. It had a glass block wall that faced east and filtered the morning sunlight. The clarity of that light made Henry hopeful that he might again be productive. He signed a one-year lease, which was harder to do than he expected. He said if he knew only one thing about Los Angeles, it was that when you changed your real estate, you changed your life.

11

Definitely Denim

*H*enry *never could bring himself* to read *Burn It Down,* the former *Gorgeous Gretchen,* though, to his chagrin, he didn't have any trouble taking Paramount's money. Maggie read it and the news wasn't good. Henry had long ago learned that to studio executives, even recently minted ones, there were only two kinds of scripts and this one had bounced between "greatest script ever written" and "piece of shit," ending up securely in the second category. Maggie said she was trying to push it at the studio, but by then she and Frank Rosato weren't getting along. "According to him, I'm too ambitious," she said.

"He might as well blame fish for swimming," Henry said. "What did you do?"

"I'm not a fish."

"You're certainly not."

"Screw Frank Rosato," she said. "He screws everybody else."

"You?"

"None of your business." Henry took that as an affirmative.

Frank Rosato wasn't interested in the script, probably because he had lost interest in Gretchen Jill as well as in Maggie. There was also a problem with Cody Malone. Maggie said he called all the time, once threatening to occupy Paramount, as if he were an invading army. Maggie couldn't remember what he had been so exercised about. Henry knew, even without reading the script, that Cody surely had plenty of legitimate complaints, starting with the new title. Cody's fuse was too short to remind Henry of his own younger self, but watching him blunder made Henry think about the days when he too had more ambition than skill. Even then, Henry had always had an instinct for getting along, for figuring out how things worked. Of course Cody was seventeen and Henry had been in his twenties when he sold *Streets of New York*. His instincts in those days were certainly better than Cody Malone's but not good enough to get that picture made, though it did get his career started. Of course, that was a while ago, in the days before Henry hired other people to write his scripts.

Burn It Down had become too much bother so Frank dropped it, which left Henry in a bad odor at the studio. Henry expected it. When things went wrong, the solution was always to blame the most recent writer. That was Henry, at least as a matter of contract if not actual fact. He absorbed the blows because he had cashed the check. Cody and Gretchen apparently believed that if Paramount had lost interest, they could reclaim their script. Henry contemplated telling them how unlikely that was. If Cody and Gretchen were to somehow make a success of it, then Frank would look bad. No, their script, under either of its titles, would languish at Paramount until the option ran out, by which time no one at the studio would remember any of it. And no matter how many times Cody called no one would answer. Maggie told Henry that it wasn't his job to educate them. He should keep his mouth shut.

Despite his new apartment and its lovely morning light, and no matter that he could amuse himself building bookshelves, Henry felt listless. The trouble at Paramount was the sort of thing that in the past he would have shrugged off. Paramount didn't want his script, which wasn't his anyway. They'd forget they were angry with him soon enough and in the meantime he'd spec a new one. He'd had his ups and downs before. It was the nature of the business.

Henry started spending more time at the Farmers Market. How had it happened? One minute he was happy or at least not unhappy. He was productive, comfortably married, and with a career that was on track.

Now he was a single guy in an apartment that cost more than it was worth, and he was unable or unwilling to do the routine hustle that he had managed for years. He would linger at the Market in the mornings, even after everyone else at the table had left. In the hour or so before the tourists filled the place, eating lunch at eleven o'clock, the Market belonged to the residents of Park LaBrea, where old Jews went before they graduated to assisted living, a name Henry always found amusing. Henry found himself worrying about money. Madeleine had always worked, and that gave them an income during the inevitable dry spells of a screenwriter's life. He wondered if it was worth paying so much rent just because his apartment was in Beverly Hills. What the hell did he care about Beverly Hills? That had been Maggie's idea, and since the collapse of *Burn It Down* she was around less and less. Henry was glad for the residuals checks that arrived once a quarter. Most of them were for television movies he had written over the years. He could hardly recall the pictures. One night when he was channel surfing, flipping relentlessly from one station to the next, unable to concentrate and unable to stop, a patch of dialogue floated past that made him perk up. A gruff masculine voice said, "I don't care who told you what, I'm telling you, you're wrong." A woman's voice answered, "You don't know anything about me." Henry flipped back a few channels. It took him another moment to realize why those lines had caught his attention. He had written them. The scene was from an uncredited rewrite he had done several years earlier. The picture was a backdoor pilot, which meant it was a television movie that with a lot of luck might become a television series. He couldn't remember much about it—a sensitive cop, some angry bad guys, a thwarted romance, and a lot of guns. What he did recall were the battles that went into getting it on the air. That's where the drama had been. At first he found it unsettling and then he decided, no, it was simply amusing. If he could forget about something that had once seemed so important, then perhaps he should stop taking himself and his ennui quite so seriously. He would shake off the blues and do something with himself.

As he was congratulating himself for his new enthusiasm, Henry got a note from Madeleine. That seemed odd enough—this person he had spent most every minute with for the past five years was now sending him letters. Not even an e-mail, but a letter on her own stationery in an envelope with a stamp. Seemed quaint. Perhaps, he thought, she's doing it for the historical record and she'll send a copy to the Library of Congress. She had decided to list his many faults. "You are so self-absorbed that unless I told you I was in pain you wouldn't notice." Henry didn't think that was quite fair. She always kept up such a composed front that he didn't see how anyone could know what she was feeling without being told. "You do nothing to help this marriage. You don't pay enough attention to it to even have a problem. All you do is build shelves. There are shelves all over this house. Remember when I asked you why you did that? What you thought you needed them for?" Henry didn't remember her asking that at all but he kept reading. "You said, and this is exact: 'Empty or full shelves promise adventure or at least a good time. They're always useful, always ready to serve'! I think you were talking about yourself. If that's what you want, to be useful, then you should forget about building shelves and try being somebody's father. That's useful! You don't get to be that by going to horrible lawyers and paying off desperate naïve kids. I think you want to put yourself on a shelf so all you have to do is look out and watch. That's you, Henry the Watcher."

She might have a point there. He couldn't see any profit in arguing, so he kept reading. "Whenever I say anything to you I never know if you're even hearing me. Your mind is a million miles away from wherever I am. It's insulting." Guilty as charged, but he didn't have any idea how he might correct it. Besides, it wasn't only Madeleine he was a million miles away from, she was just the one around the most. He didn't think he'd try to make that particular point to her. "You stare at my friends like an adolescent. I've seen you looking at Gillian Royce. You just gawk at her. It's humiliating for me and pathetic for you." Gillian Royce? Who the hell is that? Henry couldn't even picture her. Bridget Bosco, yes—he'd have to plead guilty there. He had always been both worried and hopeful that

Bridget, who was well aware of his interest, would do something about it besides give him smoldering looks. She'd already called him once. "Whenever you're ready," she had said. Was he supposed to answer Madeleine's letter? Argue with it? Correct the errors? Oh, me-oh, my-oh. It didn't take him long to decide what to do. He would call Bridget Bosco and perhaps finally scratch the itch that he had tried to ignore for all the years of his marriage. As he was musing on the possibilities, he reminded himself that Bridget would find a way for Madeleine to hear about it. Good, Henry thought. Let her find out. I'll tell her myself. If I want to go out with Bridget Bosco, why the hell shouldn't I? He might even go out with Gillian Royce if he could remember who she was.

Bridget was one half of Bosco & O'Brian, a publicity firm that handled what were called "special situations," which Henry said meant movies with unattractive subjects without stars that the studios won't touch. She was usually selling pictures about village life in Sicily or about how hard it was to be a Chinese rice farmer in the sixteenth century. Before Bridget had gone out on her own, she was in the publicity department at Fox, where she and Madeleine had worked together. Madeleine knew that Bridget was cultivating her to stay plugged into the Fox sales department. She didn't mind. She enjoyed Bridget and her studied clothing. Madeleine clearly didn't understand that her husband found Bridget interesting too, though for different reasons. Bridget had come to Los Angeles to be an actress and she had spent a few years chasing that elusive goal. That was before Henry knew her, though he often thought that her theatrical style was a souvenir of that unhappy time. She had told Henry all about it one night at a dinner party at her apartment. He had tried to pretend he was interested and not stare at her breasts. She pretended she didn't notice he was staring and kept arching her back, which pulled her blouse tighter.

Bridget was quick to accept Henry's dinner invitation. She suggested that they go to Nick's in West Hollywood. If anybody not in the movie business ever went there, Henry hadn't noticed. It was a small clubby room that made a point of being seedy. When the roof sprung a leak,

Nick, the snobbish thug who ran the joint, nailed a coffee can to the wall to catch the drip. It became a part of the decor. Nick kept the place dark supposedly to ensure privacy. Henry believed it was to keep the electricity bill down. People didn't want privacy at Nick's, they wanted to see who else was there. Bridget was going to make a public statement here and although Henry was a little nervous, he wasn't about to say no. He knew that without this step, the payoff he wanted would not be forthcoming. He waited for her at the bar, sipping a martini. He tried to glance casually at the dining room to see who else was there. He waved vaguely to two agents. Madeleine knew one of them. The question in Henry's mind was, did either of them know Bridget and that she was Madeleine's friend? Even if his marriage was kaput, this adventure still seemed like some form of adultery. He ordered another martini.

Bridget strolled in wearing tight jeans and a fitted blazer over a black cashmere sweater. Her straight blond hair had a touch of darkness at the roots, and she wore silver rings and a bracelet made of a miniature string of pearls. If Henry had been pitching her as a movie, he would have said: East Side call girl meets the Darien Polo Club. People looked up, even in that room, which saw a regular parade of good-looking women. It wasn't her great beauty, but rather her boldness. She exuded possibility. Henry wanted to touch every bit of her.

"So hello," she said, giving him a quick peck on the cheek. "Am I late?"

"I'm the one who's late, by about five years," Henry said. That made her purr. As they were shown to their table, Henry saw Paul Baron, fat as ever, in one of his preposterous outfits—though instead of a Hawaiian shirt and overalls he had on what looked like a tailored Turnbull & Asser number. His evening wear, Henry thought. Paul's electric hair was sticking out enough to annoy his companion, who was dressed in all-purpose black. Now and then she pushed a wayward strand from her face.

"Henry Wearie," Paul said, unable to keep the surprise out of his voice. "The thief of old Mexico. And Miss Bridget Bosco, herself." Well, there it was. Paul Baron had every reason to be pissed off at Henry. And he knew Madeleine and he knew Bridget. And he was something of a gossip. It'll probably be in *Variety,* Henry thought. Nu to U: Henry Wearie Dates Wife's Gal Pal!

"Hello, Paul," Bridget said, with a note of triumph. She was probably hoping to be recognized by someone more distinguished than Paul Baron, but she would take what she could get. Paul moved his hair aside and introduced his date. Her name just bounced off Henry's head, though Bridget made a point of saying, "Nice to see you, Gillian." The name meant something to Henry but he was too tense at the moment to try to figure it out. Paul pronounced their names again, savoring the connection, until Henry steered Bridget toward a waiter who had pulled out a table for them. "Does it bother you?" Bridget asked after they had ordered drinks.

"I think Paul Baron and his friend there just hit the trifecta of gossip. We had a little squabble over a script once. I think I did him a favor by going to Mexico to rewrite him. For some reason he thinks I stole his script and had a fancy holiday that should have been his. I think he sees the two of us together as an opportunity for revenge."

"What can he do to you?"

"I don't know. Nothing really."

"Then why do you care?" Bridget said, looking a little hurt, knowing full well why Henry cared. And it didn't have much to do with Mexico.

"I don't." Henry got up and moved around to her side of the table, so they were seated next to each other, looking out at the room. "How's that?" he asked.

"Cozier," she said. "So you know who that woman is? With Paul?"

"If you tell me she's Madeleine's secret lover I wouldn't be surprised."

"She's in marketing at Disney. She used to be at Fox."

"Is that Gillian Royce?"

"You've met her. She knows you." Bridget was a publicist and she understood how this bit of intelligence would be spread. Paul Baron would tell the above-the-line world, and Gillian, from marketing, would inform Madeleine's every colleague. What Bridget didn't know was that

Madeleine was a tad confused about which of her friends interested Henry. He looked over at Gillian and tried to see what Madeleine thought would appeal. She looked lethal in her black costume, but so many movie-business women dressed that way, Henry thought it made them invisible. Beyond the undeniable fact that Henry considered the possibility of sex with every woman he ever met or saw, some were still more desirable than others. Gillian didn't make the cut, no matter what his wife thought. And she says I don't understand her?

"What are you thinking, Henry?" Bridget asked.

"Madeleine may have mentioned her."

"They're friends."

"I have other interests now," he said and put a hand on Bridget's knee.

"Tell me," she said, opening her legs slightly, allowing Henry's hand to slide along the denim.

"You may have noticed me looking at you."

"So I know how to get your attention. So what?"

"How do you manage that? What gets my attention?"

"I wear something tight across my bum." Bridget had lived in London and had picked up the habit of using English slang. Henry never thought of it as her best quality. "I liked it when you looked at me, blah, blah, blah." Had she always ended sentences that way? It was a Los Angeles habit, this sticking "blah, blah" on the end of everything as if there was no point in finishing a sentence because there wasn't anything new to say about anything. "Are you still here?" Bridget asked. Oops, Henry thought. Pay attention. Who cares about her language. "So what are you thinking right now?" she asked.

"About something tight across your bum."

"That's more like it." The purr had returned to her voice. "For instance, what?"

"I'll think of something."

"If you have trouble, I'll help out."

"How do you get your jeans so tight?"

"You really want to know?"

"I've spent enough time looking at them. So?"

"I buy them too tight to close. Then I get them on, sort of. Then I get in the bathtub. When they're wet, they stretch enough to close."

"Amazing."

"Does knowing that spoil it?"

"Nothing could spoil it."

"I'm glad we've got that sorted," she said, laughing.

Henry ignored the Brit-speak and slid his hand further up her leg. "Definitely denim," he said.

* * *

Henry followed Bridget from the restaurant and parked in the street in front of her West Hollywood condo. He had been to her apartment once before, with Madeleine, for the dinner party where she had told him about her life. He sat in the Jaguar for a moment, thinking about putting a note on the windshield: "Owner may be committing adultery. Definition unclear. Please forgive me. CC: Madeleine Wearie." He was rewriting it in his head, putting a little more emphasis on the "forgive me" part, when Bridget came up out of the garage and tapped on his window.

As he followed her into the building, she stayed a step ahead, so he could enjoy the view. She's cooperative, he thought, that's for sure. In the elevator, he kissed her or maybe she kissed him, but whichever it was she melted into him while they smooched. "My apartment's a little roomier," she said when they pulled apart in order to breathe.

Henry remembered her living room as spare and modern with a lot of chrome and glass. As he was about to sit down, two white pugs waddled over to him, rolling and pitching as they moved. They looked like sausages on legs. Their abundance put Henry in mind of their mistress. She wasn't fat, but she was certainly excessive. "Pet them," Bridget said as she started to make drinks. Henry did as instructed. "That's Nancy," she said. The other one wanted the same treatment. "That's Sluggo." As Henry was considering the names, Bridget took them away. To the kennel perhaps. He wondered if they had been around the night he and

Madeleine had dinner here. He thought it best not to think about Madeleine when Bridget returned and got started on another round of martinis. Henry sat on a sleek leather sofa and watched. Bridget was making a show of twisting about as she brought Henry his drink, his third, or was it his fourth, of the evening? When she pretended to drop something so she could turn around and bend over in front of him, Henry laughed. "Do I have your attention yet?" she asked and opened a few buttons of his shirt, slipping her hand inside and leaning over him. She lingered there for a moment as he inhaled her perfume. Henry didn't know one scent from another, but this had a delicate citrus aroma that made him light-headed. She nudged him with her breasts and murmured that he had a wandering mind, which was true indeed, but that she thought she might be able to help focus his attention. Where men were concerned, Bridget usually did everything. She made the plans, she bought the tickets, called for the reservations, and held them to the schedule. If she didn't, nothing got done.

Soon there was music of the sort usually billed as "Romantic" or "For Lovers Only." What the hell, Henry thought. So she's not a music critic. Then Bridget had a joint in her hand. She took a puff and held it to Henry's mouth. Henry was more a martini man, and his Mexican adventure had put him off drugs of any sort, but he thought he'd make an exception tonight. Henry was pleasantly surprised to be reminded how gentle and lovely a marijuana high was. With Sister it had been a matter of getting paralyzingly loaded as fast as possible. As he was drawing the smoke into his lungs he remembered that before Sister, for years he had only done this with Madeleine. Before he exhaled, he told himself it was ludicrous at this moment to be thinking about Madeleine. Or Sister. Such confusing thoughts made him laugh as Bridget was taking another drag.

"Got the giggles already?" she asked.

"Guess so," he said. And then added a blah, blah, blah just to see what it felt like.

Bridget's bedroom, where Henry soon found himself, was done in a different style. There was flowered wallpaper in a pattern of tea roses. Flowered pillows were scattered on the bed, which was a four-poster with a frilly white canopy and a white duvet that was so puffed up it looked as if it might float away. Henry perched on the edge, telling himself he very much wanted to be here, yet still keeping his feet on the floor. Henry thought of the bedroom's style as Laura Ashley, though he had never been to a Laura Ashley store, if that's how they sold their flowered merchandise. He was thinking about just who Laura Ashley might be as the marijuana sent waves of warmth surging through him, making him tingle. He looked around for Bridget, wondering if she had changed into something flowered and was now indistinguishable from the decor. His mind drifted back to thoughts of his wife. Henry couldn't help thinking that there would soon be three people in this bed even if one of them was invisible. That meant Bridget would want to show off, or compete. Who could resist that? Certainly not Henry. He wondered if Madeleine's spirit, if not her corporal self, would put up a fight. No, probably not. She'd just get pissed off as usual and blame him. Didn't seem fair. All he wanted was a little harmless fun and to humiliate his wife, make her sorry for everything including throwing him out and slamming the car door, and make her miserable for the rest of her days. Ought to make for an interesting evening, he thought, as waves of erotic feeling came over him, induced by the marijuana and his wife's specter hovering beneath the white canopy, like a mirror.

"So . . ." Bridget said, letting the word drift. Henry followed the voice until he saw her standing near him. She had changed into an outfit that fairly screamed Victoria's Secret, though at the moment, given his state, Henry couldn't quite get a fix on the differences between Laura and Victoria, though he knew they were mixed up with Madeleine and Bridget. Sort of the good witch and the bad, or maybe it was a movie-business version of the Madonna and the whore. Henry knew that distinctions of that sort were not useful at a time like this and he tried to put them out of his mind while he watched the show. Bridget was wearing white stockings held up by silk garters that disappeared into a lacy black top that even Henry knew was called a bustier. This was the first time he had ever seen one outside of an advertisement or a movie, if you didn't count teenage girls on Melrose Avenue. In his fragmented and stoned state, bustier jokes ran through his mind. Bustier Keaton, Bustier Brown, Bustier Melrose. Bridget, who certainly didn't seem to have jokes on her mind, stood in front of him and then turned around, offering the angle that always got his attention. "So, see anything you like?" she asked, glancing back over her shoulder and letting the tip of her tongue poke out at him.

"I don't think I can speak right now," he said.

"Excellent," she said as she pushed him back into her imperial bed and produced what looked like velvet handcuffs. She slipped them onto Henry's wrists and snapped them shut. Henry had written scenes of this sort but he had never actually experienced one. Bridget seemed intent on pinning him to the bed with her knees. Those silky garters were all but in his face. He was unable to move his hands, which of course was the idea. She could do whatever popped into her head, a place Henry thought of as terra incognita. Bridget seemed so self-assured, so certain of what to do, that Henry began to think she had planned every moment, laid it out all in advance. Choreographed it. Perhaps there was a diagram somewhere. She had probably discussed it with her advisers, a panel of pornographers and Victoria's Secret bustier executives, who felt a little roughness would be good for this dreadful man who wanted to humiliate his wife, who never did anything bad except throw him out, which he deserved.

Bridget had arrived at the showdown of their tryst, not only in costume and with her velvet cuffs, but with a warm lotion that she was now rubbing on Henry. His mind was spinning between an intense eroticism that had his every muscle humming and an unsettling fear that made his body unwilling. Bridget whispered soothingly to him and did what she knew how to do to solve this problem. It warmed him up for a moment or two but it wasn't quite the flattering response she must have had in mind when she selected her wardrobe for this evening.

"Be with me, Henry. Don't stop. Be in your body, Henry. Be in mine. It's about struggle. Empowerment," she said, hijacking the political lingo of a generation she was only vaguely aware of, and mixing it up with self-help talk. Forget about language, he thought, and let this woman do what she's trying to do. It means so much to her. He knew that if this evening ended in the debacle it seemed headed toward, he would be made to pay and the price would be high. As Henry was trying to will his body to participate in this adventure, he heard Nancy, or maybe it was Sluggo, calling dolefully from the depths of the apartment. Perhaps the prospect of Bridget's pugs joining them was enough to nudge Henry forward. With an image bouncing around in his head of the cartoon character Mighty Mouse unshackling himself, breaking free of all restraint with pure mouse power, Henry yanked his wrists apart, breaking the velvet cuffs. It turned out they were only attached with Velcro, but it still seemed a very manly thing to do. "No more babble," he said and pushed her back on the bed and assumed a dominant position, hoping his own plumbing would operate as well as his act of bravado. Bridget gasped with what Henry supposed was meant to be a swoon, though it seemed manufactured. It occurred to Henry that these bedroom stunts were probably the only acting she did now. Maybe this is what happens to all failed actors. Henry made an effort to clear his mind and rolled Bridget over and made his entrance by way of that part of her anatomy that had interested him for so long.

* * *

Henry didn't call Bridget the next day or the day after that. It was his wife who was on his mind. He wondered if the gossip had got back to her yet. Finally, he called Madeleine just to see what would happen. He wanted to explain it to her, or maybe he wanted to figure out what it all meant. He thought that with Madeleine that might be possible. Maybe they could laugh about it together. When she answered the phone, before she even knew it was Henry, he could tell that she knew just from the way she said "Hello." It reminded him that they could read each other's mind.

That used to be a pleasure. What Henry read there now was dark indeed. "I wish I felt worse about it, but I just don't," Madeleine said, when he told her it was true, he had gone out with Bridget Bosco. "I hope you're happy with her," she said.

"I'm not with her."

"Please, Henry. I don't want to hear the details."

"There aren't any."

"With Bridget? No details? I doubt it."

"There's nothing to tell," he lied.

"There never is with you."

"For God's sake, Madeleine."

"I hate the movie business. The people are horrible."

"You may have mentioned that."

"I want out. I'm going to quit my job."

"And do what?"

"I want to be a therapist. I'm going back to school."

The idea of Madeleine becoming a therapist was too much for him to absorb. Did she want to cure the world? Or him? Or herself? She had always complained about people in the movie business, saying how awful they were. The directors and producers she had to deal with were monsters of ego who seemed to thrive on terrorizing everyone around them. She's more right than not, Henry thought. Not everyone though. He wondered if he had become awful. Henry hadn't come to Hollywood to be horrible. He came because as a kid he had been mad for the movies. He would ditch school and go to Times Square. In those days, Forty-second Street was lined with theaters where you could get cheap tickets for first-run pictures. Henry would often spend the day lost in those theaters, going from one to another—the Amsterdam, the Victory, and others whose names he could no longer recall, all old palaces gone to seed with rowdy back-talking crowds. "Kill that suck-ah, mash him up!" Henry could gorge on four of them in an afternoon, starting when the sun was bright and not leaving until Forty-second Street was lit by neon.

Later, he had spent his two unhappy years at NYU, scheming ways to go to California, where people didn't worry about "Survey of World History." At twenty, Henry had little interest in history. It was the future that beckoned. He wanted to be where people spent their days in the sun making movies. Felix had talked himself hoarse trying to change his son's mind, arguing that Henry should graduate and then go to law school. Doing what his father wanted seemed a guarantee of a timid life. Trying his luck in California was dashing and raffish. He had a vague idea of becoming a director, more because it was the top job than anything else. Directors were figures of glamour. They made huge sums of money and beautiful actresses lived to please them.

The signal event of Henry's still-forming life was the death of his mother at forty-five, ten years younger than Henry's father. It was cancer and it came fast and raged through her. Selma had introduced Henry to the movies in the days before video, taking him with her whenever she went. When she was sick Henry, at twenty, was young enough to believe she would get well. When that didn't happen the shock was pure and what ran, unbidden, through his head till he thought he might explode was: Who is going to take care of me now? Though he never put the answer into words, he knew that it was not going to be Felix. When Henry was twenty-one he ran away and went west.

He arrived in Los Angeles in what seemed a different world. It was before the Internet and video games or whatever other crap now so completely absorbs the young. Henry was scared out of his wits for the first year or so. There were fewer writers then and more pictures. Everyone had told him scriptwriting was the best way to become a director. He found that his temperament, which grew more ruminative as he got older, was exactly wrong for a director. They made decisions quickly, whether they knew what was best or not. Henry turned every question in every direction, contemplating the possible results. That was fine for rewriting, but not so great when fifty people were standing around and the company was hemorrhaging money. Some directors were artists, but they were also generals or politicians or businessmen. Henry was none of those things and no matter how much feeling he might have for the form, he wasn't likely to change. Felix couldn't understand why he would be paid for his scripts if no movie was ever made. Henry thought his father believed he was doing something illegal—selling drugs, maybe—and this screenwriting song-and-dance was a front. Felix worried about Henry's lack of formal education. He seemed to think, as his late wife had, that without spending four long years at Washington Square a young man would fail in life. It was simpler than that, of course. Henry knew "Survey of World History" or "Introduction to the Calculus" would wait. If things didn't work out in California, he could always come back. Hollywood was right now. It was a carnival, teeming with ambition and money, driven by anger and charm. Sex and drugs were the common coin. It was a flatterer's paradise. Fortunes were made on the basis of friendship and ever shifting alliances. Deals and pictures were done on instinct, not on the views of the preposterous focus groups that were now run by his soon-to-be ex-wife. Henry learned Hollywood's ways while he was still young enough, in the philosopher's words, to accept the world as he found it. Henry assumed that the world would be that way forever.

A few days later, Bridget called. She was cool to him, surely irritated that he hadn't called her. As always with men, she did whatever she thought needed doing. Henry told her that he needed a little time.

"Space? So is that what you're saying? You need space, blah, blah, blah?" Now she was correcting his language. The space-time problem was reduced, or perhaps elevated, to a matter of dating etiquette.

"Well, it's time I had in mind, blah, blah, blah." She knew he was mocking her, though she didn't know why. Hadn't she offered him sensational sex? What else did men want? It was what they talked about all the time. She didn't know if she should cry or get a gun. Henry knew he wouldn't be talking to Bridget Bosco again any time soon.

He heard later that Madeleine had indeed quit her job. He didn't know if she was going to shrink school, but several people let him know that she was dating. Bridget had probably fixed her up with some hunky actor and then made sure Henry heard about it. And why not? Bridget was angry at him and this was a way for her to take her revenge. It wasn't Bridget Bosco who was on his mind. It was Madeleine he thought about and who was tucked into his brain on what promised to be a permanent basis. Should he apologize? For which of his many sins—building shelves instead of a family? Caring too much about his car doors? Sleeping with Bridget? Really liking sleeping with her? No. He knew no apologies would be accepted, no matter how sincere or abject. He knew what Maggie LeMay would have to say about the whole sordid adventure. If she was still talking to him, which she wasn't, she'd say that there was a hot script in the story of his one-night stand with his wife's friend, and he ought to stop examining every little thing that ever happened to him and get to work on it.

Now and Then

1 2

Felix at Home

*H*enry's *style of proposing* to Madeleine had been a little eccentric. He thought about marriage and he assumed Madeleine did too, though it wasn't something he yet felt comfortable talking about. Still, they were growing closer and that gave Henry a kind of calm he hadn't felt. Henry came to realize that what brought him to propose was his father. Felix lived alone in the apartment on West Eighty-sixth Street in New York where Henry had grown up. In the days when Felix still had his accounting practice, his office moved around. For a while he was in the Empire State Building, which little Henry had adored, and later he was in the Lincoln Building across from Grand Central Station. The apartment, six rooms in a prewar building, was the center of the family's life. Selma, Henry's late mother, believed in few things but high on her list were the value of "Eighty-sixth Street," which in the New York manner was how the family referred to the apartment, and the value of an NYU degree, which Selma believed was a ticket to Easy Street.

After Selma's death, Felix married again, precipitously, and divorced in less than a year. It happened while Henry was at NYU. Madeleine was sure that the real reason Henry never finished college was that he wanted to get away from the mess his family had become. Henry insisted that no one could remember his stepmother's name. "Felix never gave up Eighty-sixth Street. He moved in with what's-her-name, but I don't think he ever moved his socks."

"Did he sublet it?"

"It was rent controlled. He just kept paying for it. Now it's a co-op. We own it. He spent more time at Eighty-sixth Street than on the East Side where she lived."

"The no-name bride."

"Right."

"I want to meet him."

"Sure," Henry said, without much conviction.

"Why not?"

"If you think there's a chance I'll be like that, you won't want to marry me."

"You have to find a backdoor into everything, don't you? Is that a proposal?"

"Yes." Henry could understand how Madeleine might not see it as the most enthusiastic proposal she had ever imagined, so he added, "Please marry me. I know we can be happy. I love you." It sounded like he was ticking off story points for a script, but Madeleine found the earnestness of it endearing.

"Yes, thank you, I will." And that was how they decided that a new part of their lives would start.

Henry was about to go to New York to meet with Ark, who was living there, preparing a picture. He wanted Henry to adapt a novel, a love story set in New York. Henry found the novel cloying. Ark wasn't someone Henry could just blow off so he said, yes, he would get on a plane. Ark made studio deals, so the gig would be well paid. He'd find a way to work around the tiresome novel. Henry made trips of this sort a few times a year. Madeleine had never lived in New York and she had never been there with Henry. She would take some time off and they would make a holiday of it, and she would meet her future father-in-law.

When Henry told Felix he was coming to town, he said Madeleine would be with him. He hoped they could take him out to dinner. He treated Madeleine's presence in his life as an already established fact.

Felix hadn't asked any questions. It wasn't quite like bringing a date home for approval, though that's the way Madeleine saw it.

"If he thinks anything, it's that he hopes you'll like him so he can have another person to lean on."

"Nothing like a cozy relationship with your father," Madeleine said. "How long since you've seen him?"

"We talk on the phone. He's not what you'd call chatty."

"How long?"

"It's been a while."

"Henry, that's not right. He's your father. You only get one."

"The key thing in Felix's life, even more important than my mother, is that he grew up in an orphanage."

"You never mentioned that little fact."

"Like Baby Snooks said, 'You never asked me.'"

"Who is Baby Snooks? Never mind. I want to hear about this orphan business."

"Later. I can't concentrate on more than one personal failing at a time."

When Henry told Ark that Madeleine would accompany him, and that she would be meeting his father, Ark knew that the romance had taken a serious turn. He told Henry, "Don't let this one slip through your fingers." Ark booked them into the Carlyle. It was a lavish gesture and Henry appreciated it, but he also knew that the Carlyle could figure in the script Ark wanted him to write. He had probably made a deal with the hotel, assuring them prominence in the movie, for which Ark would get a room rate so discounted that putting up Henry and Madeleine there was a bargain. Whatever Ark's motives, Henry knew it meant that he and Madeleine would have a lovely time.

The Carlyle was swank and it was stately but it certainly wasn't hip, which was fine with Henry. He checked them in, and then took Madeleine across the lobby to Bemelmans Bar. They settled into a cushy banquette that was like a holiday in itself. Madeleine knew about the animal murals there, and the combination of whimsy and luxe was just what she needed to shake off the stress of the flight. Henry explained that the murals had been painted as payment for Ludwig Bemelmans's considerable tab. Or maybe not. It was all part of New York legend. When Mr. Bemelmans hadn't been running up hotel bills, he had written and illustrated the Madeline books. Every little girl with that name, in all its various spellings, had grown up on them.

Ark had seen to it that they had one of the romantic rooms with the big windows that looked out over Madison Avenue. While Madeleine unpacked, Henry called Felix and announced their presence. "He wants us to come over there tomorrow night," Henry said, when he put down the phone. "Yvette's going to make dinner."

"Who's Yvette?"

"I don't have the slightest idea."

"How long since you've been in that apartment?"

"Few years. Could be more." Henry could feel Madeleine's exasperation.

"Didn't a woman ever answer the phone?"

"She could be the housekeeper. I don't know. Do you know all your mother's business?"

"Every bit of it."

That night, Ark took Henry and Madeleine to "21." What amazed Henry was that the maître d' fell all over Ark, saying Mr. Arkadine this and Mr. Arkadine that. The fussing was reminiscent of La Plume, Ark's regular hangout. Henry took to referring to the maître d' as the grandee. "It's like eating in the FAO Schwarz Museum," Henry said, looking at the model airplanes and toy soldiers hanging about in the barroom. Henry wasn't sure about the seating rituals in "21," but he assumed that if a table was given to Ark, it was a good one. Henry had dined in his share of famous restaurants, but "21" was in a league of its own. He had put on a suit for the occasion. The moneyed crowd here was older and quieter than at La Plume, and no one was cutting deals in any obvious way. With his thick dark hair flecked with silver and his tailored suits and the Windsor knot in his tie, Ark always looked like a generic rich man to Henry. An adult, a boss—conditions not usually ascribed to screenwriters.

"The food here is good, not that that's why anyone comes," Ark said. "Let's have a drink." Henry didn't see Ark order anything but soon enough a round of perfectly made martinis arrived.

"Is there any restaurant where they don't know you?" Henry asked.

"I come here from time to time," Ark said.

"I always wanted to ask you something about that."

"Ask away."

"It's about slipping cash to guys in these places. When do you do it?"

"It depends. At La Plume, I just do it at Christmas time. For a place where I only go now and then, I fold a twenty or sometimes a fifty and palm it to the guy on the way in. Place like this, if I know them, I do it on the way out."

"What's the difference?" Henry asked.

"In L.A., it's a flat-out bribe. In New York, it's how you say thank you."

Oh, me-oh, my-oh, Henry thought. I'll remember that but I'll never be able to do it.

As a bottle of burgundy from an earlier decade was being poured, Ark asked Madeleine if Henry had yet bought her an engagement ring. "Oh, God," she said. "That kind of thing isn't for us. If he doesn't skip out on me, we'll get wedding rings."

"In both my marriages diamonds were involved," Ark said, sounding a little disappointed.

"Ark," Madeleine said, holding up her tiny hand. "I don't want some rock. I'd feel ridiculous."

"The modern way," Ark said. "We can threaten to use that detail in our picture, and I'll let the diamond dealers association talk us out of it."

"I do," Henry said. "Just practicing. Don't want to forget my line."

"Now that you know about my jewelry preferences, maybe Henry will tell us about his father. I'm going to meet him tomorrow. Felix." She said the name as if it were a secret she was revealing.

"Is he from New York?" Ark asked.

"He grew up in the State Home for Waifs in the Bronx. I swear that was the name of the place. His parents died in the flu epidemic of nineteen-whatever-it-was. He was a ward of the state."

"That's terrible," Madeleine said.

"It shaped him. How could it not?" Henry said.

"Is he retired?" Ark asked.

"He was an accountant."

"'His parents' means your grandparents, right?" Madeleine asked.

"You old genealogist. Felix never knew them. He's not in great shape. He waits around for another heart attack. He was never Señor Warmth and now, I just don't know."

"He has a girlfriend," Madeleine said in a conspiratorial tone.

"There's an Yvette involved," Henry added.

"It's capital for you," Ark said.

"Money in the bank?"

"That kind of capital gets more valuable the longer you keep it. This is the writer's kind. Use it or lose it."

* * *

The next afternoon the city seemed to bristle with all the self-important energy of the dynamo of the world, which was the way Henry always thought of his hometown. He and Madeleine walked through Central Park to the West Side, enjoying the cool air and looking at the maple leaves that had turned red and were starting to fall. Madeleine had acquired a bouquet of out-of-season anemones from the Carlyle florist for Felix and perhaps Yvette. Henry had told her not to bother, because Yvette could turn out to be a parakeet. As they strolled, part of the swirl of lovers and tourists, Madeleine said, "I thought Central Park was supposed to be dangerous."

"Not if you're with me."

"Did you play here when you were little?"

"Sure. I caught rabbits and went down to the old swimming hole and chased Becky Thatcher around the maypole."

"Did you catch her?"

"Yeah. She gave me the clap, the bitch."

Madeleine took his arm and said, "I want to look at NYU with you. Let's go down there tomorrow."

"They moved it. Didn't you know?"

"Henry, stop."

"It's in Delaware now. They got a better deal on the taxes or something."

"I might dump you in the old swimming hole."

They came out of the park at Eighty-sixth Street and Henry pointed to "the building." It was dark brick and seventeen stories high, with a dark green canopy and an Irish doorman in front. It looked out at the north side of the Museum of Natural History. "Selma called that 'the north façade.'"

"What did Felix call it?"

"The museum."

"I get it," Madeleine said.

The building's lobby, which Henry insisted hadn't changed since he was a kid, had a black-and-white marble floor, a fake fireplace, and a couple of rubber trees in large pots. Henry said it looked like all the other lobbies on the West Side. "They get them from a lobby supply store down on the Bowery."

"When you start making compulsive jokes it means you're nervous."

"Yeah, I know," he said as they waited for the elevator. Henry was irritated with himself for being so tense. He was in New York in flashy circumstances, staying at a fancy hotel, and he had Madeleine on his arm. That should be enough ammunition to handle Felix.

And then there it was, the black metal door to Henry's past: 8-F in raised letters and in a wire frame, a white card yellowing at the edges. "Felix Wearie" was written in blue ink in a spidery hand. "That's my mother's handwriting," Henry said. Before Madeleine could absorb that, a woman Henry had never seen before opened the door. She was in late middle age, with theatrical lipstick and curly hair tinted with henna. The scent of powder hovered around her. "Come in. Come in. I heard the elevator. You are Henry. I'm Yvette." There was a French accent. She was wearing a silky blue dress that flowed over her ample figure. Her brows were black arcs done in pencil. Her face is a canvas, Henry thought. Eyebrows are her art. "And you are Marilyn," she said, offering her hand to Madeleine as she accepted the flowers. Henry corrected Yvette, gently, and they followed her into the living room. Henry realized that he had been expecting a sick room. Instead, there was the beguiling aroma of well-seasoned meat slowly cooking. And there was Felix, camped out under a blanket in a reclining black leather chair. He was eighty. His frame, once lean and sinewy, now seemed frail. He had gone completely bald or perhaps he now shaved his head. His collar was too big for his neck and it made his head seem to shoot up out of his shirt, like a turtle from its shell. As Henry tried to focus on greeting his father, an image of Yvette shaving Felix's skull ran through his mind. A straight razor, a lot of soapy lather, and a leather strap were involved. Felix's shell-rim glasses, half-moons, were the only thing that Henry remembered. He waved to his son, saying, "Hello. Hello." Henry glanced at Madeleine, who also had heard the double greeting from each of them. Any doubt about the intimate nature of their arrangements was now gone. If they talk the same babble, Henry thought, she's no housekeeper. Madeleine reached out her hand to her prospective father-in-law and said, "Hello, Mr. Wearie. I'm Madeleine Girard. Thanks so much for inviting me." God bless her, Henry thought. I'm considering jumping out the window and with a few words she's got this running right.

"Look at the lovely flowers," Yvette said, showing Felix the bouquet. He looked at the anemones and, it seemed to Henry, sighed and dug himself deeper into his chair, which was a recent addition, which meant it had been purchased during the years since Henry had lived here. The beige sofa and abstract prints on the wall were as they had been in Henry's youth. There were a few spindly end tables in a style that Selma had called Danish modern, as if they had been sent from Copenhagen instead of Gimbel's department store. Against the wall across from the three windows that looked out toward the museum was an elaborate bookcase made of cherry wood with a compartment for a stereo, a bar, and storage cabinets. It had been made for this spot to Selma's specifications. "The Unit," Henry said.

"What do you mean?" Madeleine asked. Before Henry could answer, Yvette rustled back into the living room with a bottle of champagne and a plate of foie gras canapés. "To celebrate," she said, opening the champagne as deftly as any sommelier. Soon they were eating and drinking and if Henry wasn't exactly relaxed, he was less tense than he had been. Felix wasn't saying much, but there was nothing unusual about that. Madeleine and Yvette were keeping a conversation going. They weren't saying much either, but having polite words in the air seemed to make things right. The champagne may have been meant to celebrate but it also served to relax everyone. Well, maybe not Felix. It was hard to tell if he was even listening. There was talk of the flight, the beauty of the hotel, and yes, they had seen the murals. As that line of discussion waned, Yvette said, "Isabelle and Tracy are coming. They want to meet you." Madeleine managed a quizzical look, which was enough for Yvette to add, "My daughter and granddaughter. I thought Felix explained."

"Oh, I'm sure he did," Madeleine said.

"Yeah," Felix said, which was the first sign that he had been listening at all.

"May I show Madeleine the apartment?" Henry asked and steered her toward a hallway. "Maybe he's running a rooming house," he said as they left the living room.

"Shh."

"And he 'explained' nothing. Marilyn."

"It was a mistake. She wants this to go well. He's a little on the quiet side."

"He thinks speaking is like giving away money."

"Don't get worked up. I thought there would be a lot of bookshelves."

"Only the Unit."

"The bookshelves in the living room?"

"Not bookshelves. The Unit." Henry invested the word with as much meaning as he could, though the exact nature of the meaning was unclear. The awe in his voice, which was only partly a joke, was meant to convey the totemic power those shelves once held for Selma. "It was built in a workshop in Brooklyn and put together right here. I watched it all."

"That's where your building shelves stuff got started."

"I tried to take it apart when I was about ten. The Unit."

"Please stop saying that."

"What's with the foie gras? He's supposed to have a heart problem."

"So what. She's nice. She's good to him. I can tell."

"She's no parakeet, that's for sure." Henry's bedroom, which now seemed the room of a little girl, was filled with dolls and lacy items and posters of popular musicians unknown to Henry, though he insisted that a babe in a leather bikini was Bessie Smith. Henry looked for a sign of his own tenure. "This is now the Tracy-a-torium," he said.

"Either that, or your childhood was a lot different than I thought."

"I think Colette in there is going to raise his cholesterol until he keels over. She'll claim the joint in the name of Isabelle and Tracy."

"Oh, stop," she said, stifling laughter.

"It's New York. Real estate is a blood sport." Henry opened a closet and found a few cartons amid the little-girl clothing hanging there. He poked around until he found a black-and-white photograph of a woman in her early thirties. She had an optimistic smile. "Ooh-la-la. Selma," he said as he handed the photograph to Madeleine. She scrutinized it, perhaps looking for a clue to Henry's personality.

"She looks lovely. See anything unusual?"

"What?"

"Look at this picture. She looks like me. Or I look like her."

Henry looked again at the photograph of his mother when she was a young matron. Both women were small and slim with dark hair and large eyes. Their mouths were different but both smiled in the same way. "Does this make me Oedipus or something?"

"I think it's very flattering and wonderful. I might cry. I'm taking it home."

"Let's ask King Laius about it."

In the living room, Henry handed the photograph to Felix, who nodded as if to say, I once knew that person. Henry held it next to Madeleine's face. "Notice anything?" he asked, expecting Felix to deny the resemblance.

"Yeah. I saw it when you came in." Then he called to Yvette, who was in the kitchen. When she joined them, he said, "She looks like his mother."

"How sweet," Yvette said. "Both so lovely."

Madeleine was charmed. Henry just felt confused. "You know the card on the door?" he asked. Madeleine said later that he sounded like a detective who finally broke the case. "That's my mother's handwriting."

"Let's look," Yvette said, helping Felix to his feet. His fragile state was more apparent now and Henry found it upsetting. The four of them moved toward the door. Madeleine looked as if she thought Henry might start frog-marching Felix, determined to reveal the evidence of a crime. Felix looked at the card for a moment, then said, "I never noticed." He reached over and touched it, saying in a gentle voice, "Selma." There was silence for a moment, then the specter of the late Mrs. Wearie seemed to materialize. Henry saw her and he wondered if his father did. She was the age she was in the photograph. It wasn't a ghost exactly, but she did seem a black-and-white visitor from another time. Henry knew Selma wasn't really there, but for a moment he was once again in his mother's presence. Instead of upsetting him, or prompting a skeptical remark, it gave him comfort. "She's lovely, dear," Selma said. "Did you meet her in Hollywood? She's not an actress, is she? I hope she makes you happy, Henry. That's no easy thing. I sometimes wonder if you even want to be happy. You should have finished college. She looks like me. Thinner. That's very flattering, dear. You're not usually good at compliments. Well, it's her turn now." Henry didn't answer. He wondered if Selma was also speaking to Felix. As he was considering that possibility, his mother's image evaporated.

As the others continued looking at the card, the elevator opened and a younger version of Yvette, accompanied by a girl of about ten, joined them. Madeleine, who was really on her game, said, "Hello, Tracy."

"Hi," the child said and embraced Felix and Yvette. Yvette seemed pleased but Felix betrayed no emotion except for the slight annoyance that was always on his face.

Isabelle, who looked harried, said "Sorry. I wanted to be here when you arrived." Then she gave quick kisses to her mother and Felix.

"Hello. Hello," Henry said.

"Why don't we go inside," Yvette said and helped Felix back into the apartment. Henry wondered just how long it had been since Felix had seen that door. Henry found himself clinging to Madeleine, as if he thought he might lose his balance. As he was considering the visitation from his mother, wondering if he should tell Madeleine about it, he realized that she had established that Tracy was in the fifth grade at Columbia Grammar. It was Henry's old school. Because Isabelle and Tracy lived in Queens, during the week the child stayed at Eighty-sixth Street. It didn't seem all that complicated, though Henry knew that without Madeleine, the arrangements would have remained vague. Isabelle was divorced and worked as an office manager at a printing company in Long Island City. Henry thought Madeleine could have been a census taker.

Yvette's menu for the evening was a good deal richer than Henry and Madeleine were used to. She served beef with a béarnaise sauce and potatoes that had been roasted in the fat from the meat. There was a cheese tray on the sideboard next to Madeleine's anemones, which were in a round glass bowl that Henry recognized. There were a couple of bottles of a pleasant cabernet from Chile. Felix ate so little that he didn't seem in danger of a fat attack. Henry knew that Madeleine would make an effort to draw him out. Good luck to her, he thought. She started by complimenting them on the food. It gave Henry a moment to inspect Isabelle and little Tracy. Isabelle looked to be in her mid-thirties, bosomy in the way her mother was, though she didn't have an accent and seemed thoroughly American. Henry sensed that Isabelle was the nervous one in this crowd, which confirmed his suspicion that the great unspoken subject here was real estate. Henry thought that after his psychic experience or whatever the hell it was, nothing of what Isabelle or Yvette did would mean much. Henry could see Madeleine trying to figure a way to ignite things a bit when the telephone rang. Yvette said, "The machine will get it." Before the ringing stopped, Tracy announced, "Hello. To provide you with the highest order of service this call may be monitored or recorded for quality-control purposes. Thank you for your cooperation." When Henry laughed at that, Felix said of his son, "He was always a wise guy as a kid." Henry couldn't tell if that was criticism or a fond memory or a point of comparison with Tracy, but it seemed to finally break the ice. Isabelle asked how Henry got interested in the movies.

"It's hard to say. I think it was my mother. She loved movies and used to take me all the time."

"How interesting," Yvette said. "I can't get Felix to tell me anything about her."

"Nothing to tell," Felix said. "It was a long time ago."

"He talks about Rachel sometimes."

"I never met her," Henry said. Ah, he thought. That's her name.

"Sure you did," Felix said, sounding irritated, which reminded Henry that that was his father's usual manner. "You were at the wedding." Before Henry could deny that bald-faced lie, Madeleine pressed his arm under the table.

"I guess I forgot," Henry said.

"Do you know Power K?" Tracy asked. "In Hollywood?" The name meant nothing to Henry.

"The singer," Madeleine said.

"She's a recording artist with a good butt."

"Oh, that Power K," Henry said.

"That's enough," Isabelle said. "She's showing off. Don't say things like that."

"Sure," Henry said. "Madeleine and I play golf with her at the club every week." Tracy wasn't so sure about that. Madeleine kicked Henry under the table. "Dad, I was telling Madeleine about the orphanage today."

"Why?"

"I'd love to hear about it," Madeleine said.

"It was all crap. I don't remember."

"How long were you there?" Madeleine asked. Henry knew that if anyone could get information out of Felix on this particular subject, it was Madeleine. She wouldn't sound aggressive, the way Henry might, but she would keep asking until he said something about himself. Henry wondered if Yvette or Isabelle knew that a fencing match of sorts was about to start.

"I don't know," Felix said. "Long time."

"Did you go to school there?"

"P.S. Eighty-two. Tremont Avenue. Around there." Yvette perked up at that tidbit of information. Henry knew that meant Felix had been no more forthcoming with her than he had been with his son. Tracy was squirming in her chair, apparently unaware that something significant to the adults was going on. "We went on the bus," Felix said.

"Do you still have friends from there?" Madeleine asked. Oh, me-oh, my-oh, Henry thought. She's going to keep burrowing till she hears what I want to know. She's trying to give me a present. How could I not love her?

"No. No," Felix said.

"You used to," Henry said, joining this little duel. "When I was a kid. I remember some of them."

"Maybe," Felix said, unconvinced.

"Is it still there? The orphanage?" Madeleine asked.

"The Home is gone fifty years," Felix said. "I don't know if they have them now." Felix fell silent. Henry suspected that he was rooting around in his mind, looking for a memory that might please her. If that was so, it was an act of generosity that Henry couldn't have predicted. "They took us ice skating in the winter," Felix said, dredging up the memory. He seemed surprised that he had said it. "Mount Morris Park.

There was a pond. If you had the grades you got to go. On the bus."

"You must have been good in school," Madeleine said.

"Yeah," Felix said, extending the word, letting it call up more. "I got on that bus."

"Was it fun?"

"There were other kids. From families. You know."

"How did that make you feel?"

"Lousy. In the Home we were all in the same boat." Then, as if one memory brought forth others, Felix said, "Secret fudge."

"What was that?" Madeleine asked, speaking for everyone.

"In the winter, we got sugar from the kitchen. And cocoa and chocolate. Not candy bars. The kind you cook with. Probably stole it all. We melted it on the radiator. It got soupy in a pan. We put it outside on the window sill. Secret fudge."

"Was it good?" Madeleine asked.

"It was better than nothing," Felix said, starting to sound annoyed again.

"Can I go ice skating?" Tracy asked, apparently listening after all.

"Oh, I don't know," Isabelle said, stroking her hair, trying to make it easier for the child to hear no from her mother.

"I'll take you," Felix said. Yvette seemed the most astonished of all, probably wondering how Felix thought he might manage such an expedition.

"Where you went?" Tracy asked.

"Who the hell knows what that place is like," Felix said in his put-upon voice. "We'll go to Rockefeller Center."

"*Merveilleux,*" Yvette said, so pleased that she slipped out of English.

"It'll be fun," Madeleine said. "Tracy, have you ever been to the top of the Empire State Building?"

"Nope."

"Felix used to work there. When I was about your age," Henry said.

Tracy, still doubtful about the Power K business, asked, "Is that true, Papa?" Papa? Oh, me-oh, my-oh, Henry thought.

"Where'd you get an idea like that? I never worked there. It was a dump. I was in the Lincoln Building. Sole practitioner. Now it's all big firms. It was just me. I took on temp help for tax season. I had some artists and a few galleries. I did their payrolls." Combined with the ice skating and the fudge, that was the most Henry could remember Felix ever saying about himself. And it had come out in a rush. Maybe it was a response to Selma's presence by the elevator.

"That is how you met Rachel, yes?" Yvette said.

"She was a bookkeeper. It happened."

As the conversation lurched along like this, with Henry learning about his father's second marriage, Madeleine cleaned her eyeglasses. Henry saw it as an act of metaphor as much as hygiene, but he didn't think he'd mention it just now. Then she reached over and took Henry's glasses and cleaned them as well. He was glad to have them attended to, but he thought, What's next, buttering my toast?

"Could you get Power K to give me a picture? With her autograph."

"I'll try," Henry said.

"'To Tracy, who is so cute,' it should say."

"Why not?" Henry said, thinking that if he couldn't arrange it, he could just buy a photograph of the dame and sign it himself.

As they lingered at the table, Yvette explained that she had come to America after the war, with Isabelle's father, who had been stationed near Lyon, which is where she was from. Isabelle, who had been watching the conversation between her mother and Madeleine as if she were scoring it, said that Tracy was learning French at school.

Yvette hinted at a second marriage but didn't seem to want to talk about it. Probably studied at the Felix school, majoring in withholding, Henry thought, all the while wondering why his own voice seemed to be drying up. Madeleine nudged Yvette toward the question she and Henry wanted answered. Yvette had been a temporary tax-time bookkeeper for Felix, years ago. Ah, Henry thought. The same as the elusive Rachel. Surely this meant Felix had a history of sleeping with the help. At least during tax season.

"I knew your father for a long time," Yvette said. "Before we got together." It was her way of defending her behavior. Henry understood that she meant to be saying, Our love affair didn't begin during either of his marriages. She didn't mention if it started during one of hers, but Henry was willing to cut her all the slack she wanted on the subject. He thought how strange it was that his father, a man who would never tell anybody anything, was now present as his secrets were put on the table along with all that cholesterol.

As the evening was winding down and after Isabelle had put Tracy to bed, and Henry and Madeleine were saying their good-byes, Henry could see that Yvette and Isabelle looked relieved. They felt they had passed a test of sorts, and perhaps now Felix's son and his fiancée wouldn't object to their presence in the apartment and in Felix's life. As Madeleine was repeating to Felix how much she had enjoyed meeting him, he said, "Take a cab," as if Henry might have been planning to make her walk back to the Carlyle.

"Good idea, Dad."

Tracy, in her pajamas, came back to the living room. She went to Madeleine and kissed her on the cheek. For a moment, Henry felt left out, but then Tracy kissed him too. She had probably been listening to the adults, unable to sleep. Henry didn't know many ten-year-olds and he was enchanted.

Before they left, Henry leaned over to embrace his father and assure him they would take a cab. Felix, who had spoken more than Henry had predicted, but who by any other standard was chatty as a rock, clutched Henry's arm, digging into it with his fingers that were like claws, and said, in a hoarse whisper, "Keep me alive."

* * *

In the cab back to the East Side, Henry was trying to decide if he should tell Madeleine about his vision or whatever the hell it was. Instead, he said, "He was positively yakking. I'm usually the one who can't shut up."

"Your mother was younger than your father. He's older than Yvette."

"Guess he likes young women."

"I'm younger than you."

"That would make my mother happy to know." He thought about explaining the ghost, but Madeleine was so taken with the age business that he decided not to risk it. Instead, he told her how pleased he was at her ability to draw out Felix.

"I did what anybody would do. You think it's a big deal because you get nuts around him."

Henry had trouble sleeping that night. He often couldn't sleep, though it was less of a problem now that he was with Madeleine most nights. The Carlyle was nothing if not romantic and inviting, but Henry just sat up, leaning against the hotel's plush pillows. It had started to rain and Madeleine had opened the curtains so they could watch the water beat against the glass. Henry said that his interest in the rain made him feel like a visitor in the city.

"You are a visitor," Madeleine said. "This is about what Felix said. You don't know him well enough to know what he meant."

"'Keep me alive'? I think we can figure it out."

"In your heart. He meant keep him in your heart. He's not good at saying things like that but that's what he meant. Don't forget him."

"He meant give him grandchildren."

"He has Tracy."

"That's why he said it. He wants his own."

"How do you know that?"

"Whatever I haven't done for him, that's what he'll bring up."

"You're so hard on him."

"It was talking about my mother. That's probably the most he ever said about her since she died. Think about that." Henry grew quiet for a moment. Madeleine could see that he had gone inside himself. She put a comforting arm around him and just waited him out. He knew he should try to explain what he had seen, but the whole evening was so confusing, he thought that for now he would stick to talking about his father and keep his mother for another time. Selma, gone so long, was perfected now in Henry's memory in a way that she could never have been in her fallible life.

"Where are you, Henry?"

"That's the most I ever heard about his childhood since mine. The Home. Ice skating. Secret fudge. It must have been a real treat to be married to him. You got it out of him. One try. Certain hostility toward me in that, don't you think?"

"I didn't get it out of him. Think how he started. A ward of the state. He had a career. A family. If you talked to him more, you'd probably both feel better."

"I talked to him. More than usual. I feel okay about it."

"He never talks about the orphanage? The Waifs Home?"

"It's not a happy memory. My mother's death isn't a happy memory. I'm not a happy memory."

"It means he never had an example of a parent. So if he's not so good at that himself, you can see why." Henry didn't answer. It seemed obvious now that Madeleine had said it, but it was a new thought for him. "Are you still here?" she asked.

"That's really good. I'm going to try to let that help me."

"I think he enjoys Tracy. That's healthy."

"Columbia Grammar's my old school."

"It's a compliment."

Henry wasn't so sure about that. He was always so ill at ease with his father, and Felix was so damn silent, that he never quite knew what anything meant. Was it a compliment that they were sending Tracy to Columbia Grammar? Or was it because Henry had never finished college and now Felix with his new helpmeet was going to try to get it right? That seemed ridiculous for a man in his forties to be worried about, but all Henry said was, "He's taking care of them all."

"I'm sure. Do you think he's happy?"

"Felix and happiness never go together."

"Maybe she loves him. Not as part of a deal. For him. It's possible, you know."

"There's something between them. You could see it. At his age people don't even like new TV shows. A new lover is complicated."

"Well, he seems to have managed it."

"I turn my back for a few brief years and look what happens."

"He's known her a long time."

"His second bookkeeper. Felix's harem. I bet he was doing that when my mother was alive."

"Sweetie, let it go. If he didn't have her, he'd have to hire people to take care of him or go to a nursing home."

"He could start with assisted living. A great term. A big place with lots of other people like him where they give you all your meals but it's still anonymous. Remind you of anything? An orphanage, for instance?"

"Henry, please. Who cares if they want the apartment? I mean, really."

"It's worth a small fortune."

"So is knowing your father is okay. How could you not know about her?"

"If you don't ask him a direct question, you get nothing. It didn't occur to me to say, 'Dad, have you acquired a French mistress with a family?'"

"I guess not," Madeleine said. "When you went to the movies with your mother, did he ever go with you?"

"I don't remember that ever happening."

"No wonder you're a screenwriter. Your Oedipal conflict got worked out by going to the movies."

"What's that mean?"

"You went with her. To please her. You were probably trying to top Felix in your mother's affections."

"My mother held things together. After she died, I sort of came apart. Felix? I don't know. He got married. I went west."

"It doesn't matter anymore. Wish him happiness for whatever time he has left."

"How'd you get so smart?"

"It's human, Henry. Children level things. He knows he's cranky. He didn't want to be like that in front of Tracy. He doesn't want her to reject him. Like you."

Henry knew she was right. He didn't want to live there. Running into his mother's ghost once every few years was fine, but he wouldn't want it to be a daily occurrence. If they ever decided to live in New York, they could worry about it then. Still, he felt bad. It wasn't about the value of the real estate. He had no relationship at all with Felix. Now there were these people he didn't know. It was even more complicated because he knew that Yvette and Isabelle and little Tracy were decent people with their own problems. Who was Henry to say what his father should do? He had ignored the situation for years. Now, through no fault of his own, there was a solution. "That kid's adorable," is all he said.

"We can give him a grandchild, you know."

Henry smiled at the thought. He was too churned up to think about what for Madeleine was a simple solution to part of the situation. "You're right. You're always right."

"Remember the name of your movie?"

"Which one?"

"*Finding Home*. Felix has his. Now it's your turn."

"You should have been a shrink."

Madeleine smiled at that and rolled into Henry's arms. The rain was letting up and they could see the clear night, which reminded them both that the Carlyle was a very romantic place.

*   *   *

The next day, Henry spent a few hours with Ark talking over the novel he wanted Henry to adapt. Ark didn't have a deal for it yet. If Henry could see his way to doing a treatment, Ark was sure he could set it up at a studio and then Henry would get a big payday. In other words, work on spec and maybe something will happen. Work of that sort was worth more than a few nights in a fancy hotel, but it had so pleased Madeleine that they were staying at the Carlyle that he didn't see how he could say no to Ark. No such thing as a free ride, Henry thought. Not with Ark, not

with Felix, not with anything. The bill always comes. Doing the treat-
ment and if that worked out, the script, would mean coming back to
New York a few times over the next months. If Madeleine could get the
time off, she could come too. He'd write the Carlyle into the thing so that
Ark could arrange for them to stay in the fancy digs. He knew he'd see
Felix and Yvette. He wondered if Selma would be hanging around. Felix
and Yvette still felt more dutiful than pleasurable, but he would also see
Tracy and that was appealing. He would tell her the story of the Unit and
how he had got in trouble for trying to take it apart when he was her age.
Maybe he could go with her to Columbia Grammar one day. He didn't
think Isabelle would object. Hell, if she thought it would help secure the
apartment, she'd probably offer to chauffeur them. He was curious to see
what he would make of the school. When he realized that Tracy was the
draw, he knew that was probably how Felix saw it, too. In an odd and
unexpected way, Henry felt a surge of closeness to his father.

13

It's All True

When *Henry and Madeleine* were first married they lived on Vista Street in a yellow masonry bungalow. When the pepper tree in the front yard was in bloom, dozens of dark red peppers hung low over the tiny lawn. There was an avocado tree in back and Henry entertained Madeleine by planning meals around their expected harvest: peppers in avocado sauce followed by a terrine of peppers, an avocado salad with grilled peppers, and for desert, a pepper tarte and pepper and avocado sorbet. Henry kept inventing dishes until Madeleine got the giggles. Vista Street was their first home and the rent was more than they had planned to spend, but Henry's career was going well and moving into that little house felt like a vote for themselves and their future. Henry built bookshelves for the living room and their bedroom and for his study, which was in the garage. He spent weeks on those shelves, finishing them with coat after coat of dark lacquer. Henry wanted to call the house Two Trees. He said he was going to make a sign for the front door. Madeleine told him that was ridiculous.

"Okay," Henry said. "How about Three Trees?"

"There's only two."

"We better start planting for the future."

Madeleine had held several positions at Fox, all to do with marketing and distribution. For now she was in the advertising department. She bought radio and television time for the studio's campaigns. Her title was

Assistant Time Buyer. Henry loved that and couldn't resist making jokes about buying and selling time because, as he liked to say, in the words of Artie Shaw, time is all we have. Henry and Madeleine were happy together and they began planning for a family.

Henry had been so wrapped up in building shelves that he was late delivering the New York script. Word had got around that Ark was irritated, which was enough for the telephone to stop ringing for a while. Henry decided to use the situation to solve a larger professional problem. He needed a hit of his own. Not a rewrite, not something from a skilled technician, but an original script that had his own style. His great success was a $250,000 script that was never made. He told Madeleine that if he didn't make something happen soon, he'd be known as a "no-hit wonder." Morty Elfman had been after the rights to a magazine account of some murders in Hollywood and he wanted Henry to get involved. It sounded interesting.

Three children from different parts of the city had disappeared. Parents were tense and frightened. Then the bodies turned up, or at least the torsos did. The heads were never found. The crime was eventually solved and the murderer convicted and sentenced to die. Morty was one of several producers chasing the story. He had a good shot at getting the rights then making a deal at Warners, if Henry would hammer out a tight story line. Without the rights, any treatment Henry would cook up would be worthless, or in the language of the law, "sterile." Henry didn't think he'd mention that linguistic detail to his wife. Madeleine told her husband that this was the time to gamble.

Morty wasn't quite Ark, but in the end both men had asked Henry to do something similar, and Henry was determined to make this opportunity pay off. Morty was trying to persuade the arresting officer, one Lionel Detweiler, that he and Henry were the best fellows to tell the story.

Officer Detweiler was a blue-suit lifer with the Los Angeles Police Department. Morty's guess was that if he got Officer Detweiler's rights and cooperation, the other principals would fall in line. If they didn't, Morty and Henry could work around them. Without Detweiler there was nothing. Lionel Detweiler wasn't quite ideal material for a movie hero. He was a dour, unhappy man who appeared to Henry to be on the verge of anger. He had dull gray eyes and a vein on his forehead that stood out in a way that looked as if it might burst. He had a weightlifter's build with a back like a shovel and biceps that strained the short sleeves of his pale blue shirt that he wore cuffed, the better to show off his muscles. He was without, as far as Henry could see, a single introspective impulse.

As part of Morty's campaign for the rights, Henry went on patrol with Lionel and his various partners, took them out for meals, and tried hard to show he meant to tell the story honestly. Lionel worked out of the Rampart Division and Henry loved cruising Echo Park and Silver Lake in a Black-and-White with the department motto on the door: "To Protect and to Serve." Henry soaked up real cop talk unfiltered by another screenwriter. Henry noticed that Lionel seemed happiest on patrol, rousting some pathetic miscreant. Henry would jump out of the car with him, assume a stern look as if he was a plainclothes supervisor, and watch as Officer Detweiler put cuffs on some fool for selling plastic baggies of marijuana or boosting a couple of steaks from a supermarket.

Henry asked Lionel personal questions of the most benign sort but after saying that yes he was married and that his children were grown and out of the house, Lionel didn't do much talking. It didn't matter, because simply being in that Black-and-White, with the occasional blast of the siren, made Henry giddy. For the first time in the years Henry had been chasing movie deals, he was convinced that he was doing the right thing for himself. "You're riding the wave," Morty told him.

Henry and Morty spent time at the Detweilers' house in Mar Vista, an area that had once been solidly blue-collar, but was now becoming fashionable. Their house was a 1940s cottage on a street that an overheated architecture critic had called "Retro-chic." Lionel was worried that the place would be declared a landmark and he'd never be able to so much as paint it. Jo Detweiler described herself as a housewife. She seemed unaware or maybe just uninterested that "housewife" was a fighting word for even the most moderate of feminists. She was a big, raw-boned woman who might once have been attractive in an earth-mother way but now seemed to be in a losing battle with her weight. Morty was overweight too and he tried to joke about it with her, but it wasn't a subject she cared to discuss. Jo wanted the wife in the movie to be a geologist or what she called "a high-class fashion designer." Henry tried for a brief moment to contemplate what sort of inner life Jo Detweiler had, but the effort threatened to give him a headache so he dropped it. They settled on a high school civics teacher. Jo wanted the character to be played by a television star Henry had never heard of and who turned out to be twenty-six years old. Henry intended to make the Detweilers younger, but not that young. Morty simply said he would try. Henry stressed how unusual it was for a uniformed officer to break such a big case. "Don't the detectives usually steal these things from you guys?"

"Not from me they don't," Lionel said with a certainty that surprised Henry.

With the movie money the Detweilers hoped to get, they would sell the Mar Vista house to an architecture lover and say good-bye to Los Angeles. Henry and Morty knew that if the Detweilers were already spending the money, they wouldn't present any problem that couldn't be negotiated. Things seemed to be falling their way until a bad bounce threatened to stop everything. It was Morty's luck to be selling a story of child mutilation during one of Hollywood's occasional bouts of good taste. Every time a senator with trouble in the polls attacked Hollywood as the well of evil, the studios put on hair shirts, berated themselves, and vowed to make pictures about wholesome families with cheerful kids and loyal pets. It usually lasted about a month, but it was Morty's month.

With Warners slipping away, Officer Detweiler announced that he had made a forensic error in the original arrest. Evidence had been overlooked and new evidence had come to light. Officer Detweiler cursed his luck, took a deep breath, and reported everything to his superiors, who in turn informed the district attorney. The case was turned upside down and though it took a while, the convicted man was set free.

Lionel thought he had blown his deal, but Henry knew that a winning movie had dropped into his lap. He turned what had been a grisly crime story into the story of one man's moral choice. In Henry's version, Officer Detweiler met with great resistance from his department and from the district attorney. Threats were made. His life and career were endangered, but he did the right thing, because, as Henry knew, that's what heroes in studio movies do best.

Henry told Lionel that the cop in this new version would be mostly but not entirely him. He explained that even if the district attorney hadn't actually objected to reopening the case, it would make better drama if he did. Lionel just grunted, which Henry had learned was the way he indicated agreement.

"He's a little on the silent side," Henry told Morty.

"Just give him a square jaw and make him kind to old ladies, and we'll all go to Cancún for the holidays," Morty said.

The executive at Warners who was now chasing this story with Henry and Morty was Bob Desantis, a young guy who was getting a reputation at the studio for having a good sense of gritty urban dramas, or as Henry called them, GUDs. Morty believed that if anyone could ram this story past the senior management, it was Bob Desantis. He was a tall, bony guy who was building a studio career on his supposed knowledge of criminals and the legal system. Henry had once run into Desantis late at night at the World News Stand in Hollywood. He was buying an armload of underground 'zines printed on smudgy newsprint and featuring the low-down on street life, much of it surely made up. Bob was no doubt hoping to acquire more of the slang that he used around his superiors. It must have worked because he had convinced them that a middle-class white boy from Oak Park knew about "the street."

Morty proposed that he and Henry take Lionel to Warners to meet Desantis. Henry thought the idea was genius. "Desantis will go crazy to meet an actual cop," Henry said. "It'll be money in the bank for him."

"I know, I know," Morty said.

Lionel had never been on a studio lot, but he had been in some tough scrapes and had fired his service revolver in anger more than once.

Henry figured Lionel could handle Warners and Bob Desantis. Lionel showed up in a jacket and tie, which was a disappointment to Henry, though he hadn't thought to tell him to wear his uniform. It was because when Henry thought about Lionel he always pictured him in his blue bag, as Lionel called it.

Desantis's office was on the second floor of the administration building, not quite the high-rent district for studio executives, though Lionel didn't know that. It was a big room, furnished with a buttery black leather sofa and deep, comfortable chairs. Posters from pictures made before Desantis was born were on the walls. As he shook Lionel's hand, Bob apologized for the office, saying more and better furniture was on order. That's what studio executives always did. No matter how preposterously overdone their offices were, they always said bigger things were on the way. It meant nothing to Lionel. Henry and Morty knew to avoid the big leather chairs, but Lionel, who wasn't quite so familiar with posh furniture, sank down into its expensive depths. He had to struggle to keep his knees from pointing up.

A young man who looked worried that he might make a mistake took the drink orders. Morty went for the Perrier. Henry, feeling frisky, said "*Eau de la cité,* please." Lionel passed on the drinks, probably not caring to risk any unfamiliar words. A young woman, almost as tall as Bob, joined them. She was carrying a yellow legal pad, which meant she was the designated note-taker. "This is Angela Randazzo," Bob said. "She's going to keep track of the brilliance I'm expecting."

"Razzle Dazzle," Henry said, still feeling loose. Angela smiled at him and rolled her eyes as if to say, you and I are the only ones who know how ridiculous all this is. The deputies who took notes in these sessions were on track to become executives. They were allowed in the room with the talent. And they didn't have to fetch drinks.

"Razzle Dazzle it is, from now on," Bob said, and then got down to business. "So, I have to ask you, Lionel. Are you packing?"

Lionel looked blank for a moment and then realized what Desantis meant. "I'm off duty. But, yeah. I am."

"Show me," Desantis said, with what Henry thought was a porno-graphic note in his voice. Lionel didn't hesitate. He opened his jacket and revealed his service revolver tucked into a wide band of white elastic strapped across his chest. "Can I see that?" Desantis asked. Lionel took out the thing and made a little show of removing the cartridges before he handed it over. They were in. Henry could tell Bob loved the part about emptying the gun. The man would dine out on that detail alone.

"You've been in the papers lately," Desantis said, as he returned the gun.

"Yeah," Lionel answered, as he reloaded.

"Not the first time, either, huh?"

"I was in when the case broke the other time."

"How'd that go over with the guys? They mind you getting publicity? A movie deal?"

"They didn't give a shit. They wanted to know how much I was get-ting."

"We'll take care of you," Desantis said.

The magic words, Henry thought. Bringing him here did it. Henry glanced over at Morty, but his face was impassive. With Bob smiling at Lionel, and Lionel sitting in his trap of a chair like a large knot of wood, Henry outlined the amended story line. The picture wouldn't be about the horrible murders, which was subject matter best left to a company that didn't have to deal with issues of government regulation. Bob Desantis certainly agreed with that. The murders, Henry explained, will have occurred offscreen, before the action of the movie begins. Perhaps a simple montage of the funerals under the credits with little coffins, which is how the audience will know children are being buried. The story would focus on Officer Detweiler here who broke the case and then found new evidence. He would do the right thing, no matter how much pressure was put on him from the district attorney to leave things alone. He would acknowledge his own forensic error and right a grievous wrong. The drama would be Lionel Detweiler's struggle toward his moral decision. Henry pointed to Lionel as if there might have been doubt as to which one he was and said, "This man, Lionel Detweiler, a good cop, is enmeshed in a moral dilemma. Does he do the right thing and make waves that could cost him his job and possibly his life? Or does he ignore a miscarriage of justice that he unwittingly caused and let an innocent man die at the hands of the state?"

Razzle Dazzle wrote it all down, and Morty pointed out that there was a star part to be had here. Finding big roles that male stars would want to play was what Bob Desantis worked at all the time. The studio would eventually forget about the good-taste stuff, and in public they would always talk about how they were looking for good parts for women, but they would never, ever stop scrambling for male star vehicles. That's what sold tickets and that's what they were in business to do.

Armed with Henry's new approach to the story, all set down in clear beats by Razzle Dazzle and no doubt with tales of his great friendships in the LAPD, Desantis pushed the project through. The studio turned on the money fountain. Morty got a check, Lionel got a check, and Henry got a contract and a big check when he signed the deal memo. The arrangement included a bungalow on the lot. Morty staked out the biggest room for himself and gave the smaller one to Henry. A secretary named Lulu, a middle-aged woman with dyed red hair and a smear of lipstick and a gravelly voice, who had been at Warners for years, came with the deal. She placed calls for Morty, scheduled his lunch dates, and typed the pages as Henry wrote them.

Madeleine marveled at how engaged her husband was. Henry was at the studio all day and then he stayed out at night, chasing around with Lionel Detweiler until Madeleine decided that the whole business wasn't healthy. "It's pathological," she said. "It's like a drug for you. I think it makes you high."

"It's exciting," Henry said, and then did an imitation of Lionel and his stolid humorless manner when he was on patrol. "'Hands behind your back. Legs apart! Am I going to find anything in your pocket I don't like?'" Madeleine tried to understand her husband's fascination, but his zeal confused her.

"Should we have them to dinner?"

"We've already got him locked in."

"I thought you liked him."

"I need him more than I like him."

"You are out of control. That's a terrible way to look at it."

"If this thing gets made, we get a monster bonus and my price triples."

"Do me a favor."

"What?"

"Don't become a Hollywood asshole over this."

Henry laughed, because Madeleine rarely used language of that sort. He promised that he would stay his own sweet lovable self.

In the script, Henry gave Lionel family pressures that weren't exactly the truth. Jo Detweiler had objected at first, but during one of the Mar Vista sessions, Henry explained that if she would accept it, he in turn would give the wife a bigger part. She would be more than a high school civics teacher. He would make her a gifted amateur geologist who took kids rock climbing. He was about to suggest that she was also a part-time fashion designer but Morty stepped on his foot beneath the Detweilers' kitchen table. Henry understood that to mean, Don't lay it on so thick. Not only did *Finding Home,* which is what Henry had titled the movie, have to be approved by the Detweilers, it also had to be vetted by the studio lawyers. The wrongly convicted man, one Dupree Lewis, who had been rightly convicted of other crimes and had been in and out of prison for years, had been kissed off by the state of California. At the time, he was so happy to be free that he didn't push his claims as hard as he might have. Warners wrote him a check, though not as big a one as he wanted. Dupree answered only to the one name, sort of like Cher, Henry thought. Dupree had no rights of approval or consultation. After he got the Warners payment, he had disappeared. It was something of a high-wire act, but Morty had managed to keep everyone else happy and was now trying to cast the picture. The studio had given him a list of acceptable male stars. Morty's job was to sign up one of them. He was chasing Blake Porter because Henry and Blake had worked together in Mexico, on *Faster.*

"Mike Singer's a guy I can do business with," Morty said of Blake's agent. Morty explained to Mike all the reasons the picture was right for his client. Henry was sure that the most important reason was that Morty probably gave Mike an under-the-table payment for himself. Whatever Morty did, it was enough for Mike to tell Blake Porter that the picture was a great opportunity and he ought to grab it.

When Henry and Morty met with Blake, he called Henry "The hero of the battle of Churubusco" and passed on loving greetings from Lilah. Morty closed the deal the next day.

Morty had been resisting putting a director on the picture. When Henry asked about it, Morty said, "What do we need one for yet? He'll just auteur the thing all up." Henry could see the logic in that, but once they were working on the lot, Warners insisted that the decision not be delayed any longer. Morty and the studio, with Blake's approval, settled on Art Lesser, who had made several cop pictures. He was about forty-five and had been kicking around for a while. Art had been an actor and he had solid good looks. Actors tended to trust him. One of the reasons Morty chose him was because he knew that Art would keep his hands off the script. Art recognized that Morty had already done the major casting and had chosen several of the locations. The heavy lifting of preproduction was done. Henry called Art the Duke O'Details because no matter what he was asked—Should the dishes be clean, or have toast crumbs and bits of egg? Should the trousers have cuffs? Should it be a sedan or a convertible?—Art always had a crisp reply, filled with certainty. The Duke O'Details.

Henry was churning out pages, working from morning till night. Madeleine said it was as if part of him had moved out.

"I'm just working hard. That's good."

"I know. But, still, why do you have to be in a trance or whatever it is you're in?"

"Everything is falling my way on this one. When something goes wrong, it always turns around. It feels blessed."

"I guess." She didn't sound convinced.

"Remember what Morty said? About riding the wave?"

"Yeah. Can't I ride it with you?" Henry laughed and said of course she could. He knew that wasn't the problem.

"This is for us," he told her.

"I know."

"But what?"

"You may have noticed, I'm still not pregnant."

"Oh. Should we see somebody?"

"I did."

"Why didn't you tell me? Never mind. What'd he say?"

"She. It was inconclusive. We should keep trying."

"Should I go to somebody?"

"If you think so. Okay."

"I'll do it. I'm sorry if I've been too absorbed in this thing. It's almost done."

"That's fast. That's the good side of you working all the time."

"Just a little longer." Henry vowed to himself to spend more time with his wife and to talk about the baby more. Just as soon as the script was done, just as soon as the wave subsided.

* * *

As Henry was arriving at the Market one morning, a man stopped him and asked if he was Henry Wearie. That wasn't unusual. People knew where Henry could be found in the mornings and they often sought him out, sometimes leaving scripts or messages at the Coffee Corner. This guy, however, didn't look like he was in the movie business. Henry knew it had to be Dupree. He was a knife-thin black man with a little patch of a beard below his lip. He was dressed in black jeans and T-shirt and a black leather coat. He wore a black crocheted feedbag of a hat that cascaded down one side of his head. Henry imagined it filled with tight black curls, like a snood. The man looked wary. Henry knew where that dark look came from. Dupree had prison eyes. He may have been innocent of the child murders, but he had twenty years of felonies on his record. "I'm Dupree," he said and waited for a reaction.

Henry bought him a cup of coffee and they sat near Henry's regular table. Irwin and Leo and Wally were there, and they knew that this was no ordinary business meeting and kept an eye on Henry. He wished Morty was around, but he was off having breakfast with Mike Singer, who probably didn't even know where the Market was. Bob Desantis had instructed Henry and Morty to stay away from Dupree. Henry knew that if Dupree had been white, they might have made room for him in the movie. The studio was nervous about making a black guy with a long rap sheet a felon, even if for once in his battered life he turned out to be innocent. Desantis didn't say that, but it was pretty clear. A black felon was acceptable in an independent movie, but not in a studio picture, where black people were more likely to be cast as stern but fair judges or overworked but fair government officials. It was a limp sort of liberal racism that Henry pretended he didn't notice. Henry had wanted to speak to Dupree before he wrote the script, but Desantis had said the story was about Lionel Detweiler and Henry should just leave it that way and not court trouble. Dupree spoke in a prison patois that was a mixture of West Indian lilt, Haitian French, and street slang.

"You the mon telling what went down?" Dupree asked, in a voice so musical that at first Henry thought it was a joke.

"Yeah. I guess so," Henry said.

"Tell it right, we be friends." He didn't say what the alternative was in case he didn't think Henry told it right. Part of Henry wanted to get out of there fast, but another part wanted to talk to this guy, to listen to his voice. One of the problems Henry had in writing his script was the character based on Dupree. He had only sketchy newspaper accounts to draw on. Lionel Detweiler came alive in the script because Henry had spent time with the man, gotten to know him. The script was out of Henry's hands now, but no one knew better than Henry that a script is never done. "It must be good to be out," Henry said, signaling that he was willing to talk.

"Beats death row, I tell you that." Dupree wasn't exactly relaxed, but he seemed to be settling in for a talk and to size up Henry Wearie.

"I don't doubt it." When Henry interviewed someone who would be the basis of a character in a script, he tried to establish something like rapport, chatting up the person before asking questions. It's the way reporters operated and the way common sense would dictate. This situation was unplanned and Henry sensed that Dupree was just taking a flyer by coming here this morning. Henry thought he'd try to take advantage of it and see what he could learn. The particular questions he might ask were less important than learning how the guy thought. It would help any rewrites he might have to do. Henry didn't see that he had to report it to Warners. "Can I ask you some questions?"

"What you got?"

"Did you ever think you weren't going to get out at all?"

"I thought they going to take me out in a box. Had me all measured up."

"When did you know you might make it after all?"

"I don't believe nothing till it happen. Detweiler, he spend a lot of time busting me, and then more time getting me free. Now who going to count on that?"

"I guess nobody." Henry was fascinated by Dupree's accent, which became less musical the more they talked. Henry guessed it was Jamaican or something like that, though it struck him as a contrivance.

"I got a lot of stories, don't you know? Better than this one. Lot of movies there, you know what I'm saying?"

"Sure. I'm kind of working on this one for now."

"I done things. I don't kill those babies. Why do that? Nothing in it. People say, Dupree, he a mean motherfucker, scare you up. Nobody say he crazy."

"That's right," Henry said. It was true. For all the bad things Henry had heard about this guy, everyone said he was smart.

"Crazy person done that. I going to kill me somebody, I get plenty out of it and I don't leave nothing behind. When do I read this movie script?" The lilt had faded and in its place a harsher street voice was emerging.

"That's not up to me. Warners owns it."

"You wrote it up, didn't you? You got copies. You give me one. Don't hurt nobody. I like to see what you got to say. Maybe I write my own movie script. You think I can't?"

"Part of my deal is I don't show it to anybody."

"It's about me. The miscarriage of justice that happened to me. I was on death row. A man don't come back from that. I'm here. You see that, don't you?" As he spoke, making his point about his own significance, he began using finger gestures, the odd pointing, the dipping and poking of a gang punk.

"You got paid, I think."

"Same as you. Same as Detweiler."

"He hasn't seen it either," Henry lied.

"But he talk with you."

"Can't do it, Dupree."

"That don't make me happy. I'm a free man. I got my rights," he said, as if reading Henry's script was part of the Constitution.

"Maybe somebody at the studio can do it for you."

"I don't know nobody there. I know you. Why you giving me a hard time?"

"It was nice to meet you, but I have to get going."

"You think about if you want Dupree for a friend or something else."

"I'm an employee of the studio. It's their money. They call the shots."

"This movie you making is about me. You don't want to forget that." Dupree never raised his voice but the menace was clear and it made Henry uneasy. As they talked, Dupree slipped the packets of sugar from the coffee tray into his pocket.

*   *   *

When Henry explained what had happened, Morty told him to try to avoid the man and if he popped up again to let him know. They both hoped the whole thing would blow over, though in his heart Henry knew it wouldn't. He mentioned it to Madeleine, but she was absorbed in the question of pregnancy and simply nodded when he told her about Dupree. He wondered if she had heard him at all. Then Dupree started calling the Wearies' house. Madeleine tried to be helpful. Dupree wouldn't leave a number and said he would call back. When Madeleine told Henry about the conversation, she was surprised that he was upset. The next time he called, Henry answered. He was polite but he told Dupree not to call again. "I'll stop calling when you start accommodating. You understand what I'm saying?"

"There's nothing I can do for you. I've explained that. Please don't call again."

"You listen to me, you jive-ass motherfucker, you are making *beaucoup* bucks off my life. Now I ain't going to roll over here."

"If you call again or in any way try to speak to me, I'll get a restraining order. You're a convicted felon. I think you know what will happen. Good-bye." Henry tried to reassure Madeleine, saying, "He's just blowing smoke."

"He knew you were at the Market. He knows where we live."

"We're in the phone book. It doesn't mean anything."

"It's creepy. I hate it. I have enough on my mind without this."

Henry tried to comfort her but it didn't work. Madeleine's failure to get pregnant had her looking for reasons. She saw this Dupree business as a bad omen. "It's not an omen," Henry said. "This has nothing to do with our situation."

"It scares me." Henry took her in his arms and stroked her, trying to soothe her. She finally smiled when he suggested that he might be able to demonstrate an old-fashioned technique for getting pregnant.

The next morning, when Madeline went outside to pick up the newspapers, she got a rude surprise. At their door there was a white shoe box lined with red tissue paper. It contained a doll in a blue-and-white checked pinafore. It had been decapitated and the head shoved between the legs. The doll was surrounded by rusty nails, pointing toward the torso. A double-edge razor blade was jammed into the neck where the head had once been. How the box got on their doorstep wasn't much of a mystery, at least not in the sense of who-done-it. The question was, what did he hope to achieve by doing it? If his goal was to terrify Madeleine, the gambit was a success. She wouldn't have the box in the house. Henry regarded it as evidence to be handled carefully. He put it in the trunk of his car so his wife wouldn't have to see it. Madeleine seized on this bizarre incident, determined, Henry thought, to connect it to her current difficulties. Henry knew that had almost anything else been in that shoe box, she might have shuddered, but she would have gotten over it. A mutilated child was just too much for her. Henry was afraid she might unravel.

Madeleine went to the Gardner Street library and began reading about voodoo. The books didn't give her comfort. She became convinced that Dupree had known something about her in the same way he had known how to find Henry. Instead of the relief she sought, she came to believe that the shoe box and its ghastly contents were connected to her failure to become pregnant. Henry knew that the two had no real connection, but he also knew he wasn't dealing with a question of logic. He came to believe that her problems with getting pregnant were so overwhelming to her, so very hard to bear, that she was looking for a reason, something that might help her understand her misfortune. In her frazzled state, voodoo seemed as likely a reason as any. Henry wanted her to see a therapist but he didn't know how to suggest it, fearing that she would think the suggestion was an accusation. She was fragile and Henry didn't see any sign that she might get better. He tried to reason with her, but he could feel his wife sliding from fright to despair and into depression. She stopped going to work. She lost her appetite. She came to believe that Dupree, whom she thought of as her tormentor, was trying to speak to her in what she called "the language of unborn children," which Henry assumed was something in the voodoo books she had been reading. "Unborn children don't have language," he said.

"How do you know that? I know about people who were in jail. Remember? Give him the script. Do what he wants."

"I would if I could. He's not somebody you can look up in the phonebook. He'll call eventually and I'll work it out with him." But Dupree didn't call and Madeleine didn't get any better. She refused to step outside their house until Henry first checked and made sure there weren't any surprises. Henry told Morty the whole story. "We better tell Desantis," Henry said.

"Not yet. He'll get spooked."

"I'm already spooked. Madeleine's just about around the bend."

"Let's talk to Detweiler first."

When Henry showed Lionel the shoe box, he pointed out that he'd been very careful about fingerprints. "Any prints are probably decoys," Lionel said.

"What's that mean?" Morty asked.

"He got somebody else's prints on the box or the doll before he put it together. He could have a couple of hands in his refrigerator for something like this." Henry made a mental note of that, filing away those hands in the fridge for use in the next cop script he wrote. "This is just worthless Haiti crap," Lionel said.

"I thought he was from South Central," Morty said.

"Yeah. He probably picked it up when he was inside. This guy is some jacked-up mix of conjure-man bullshit and jailhouse ju-ju. Dupree don't believe in nothing but cutting a deal for himself." Henry thought that wasn't a bad description of Lionel Detweiler too, but he let it pass.

"He believes in money," Morty said.

"He wants more than money and more than to see the script," Henry said.

"What would that be?" Lionel asked, unable to keep the anger from his voice.

"He doesn't want to be ignored," Henry said. "He wants in."

"Maybe, maybe not," Lionel said. "For sure he wants money. He's a greedy little pissant."

"So what's the move?" Henry asked, wondering if Lionel might now be developing mixed feelings about having worked so diligently to free Dupree.

"First thing is we do not tell this to Warners," Morty said.

"Yeah," Henry said. "Who the hell knows what they'll do with it."

"Like what?" Lionel asked.

"They could want to hire Dupree to do a rewrite," Henry said. He knew that was unlikely, but he also knew it wasn't impossible.

"Right," Morty said. "Desantis'll say, 'Just a polish. Your credit is safe.'"

"Sure," Henry said. "He'll say it'll give the script street cred or some crap like that."

"That right?" Lionel asked, taking it more seriously than Henry or Morty intended. Lionel didn't know that a morbid sense of exaggeration about film studios was just normal chat for Henry and Morty.

"Another new hyphenate," Henry said. "Rewrite man–felon."

"Anything that puts us at risk, we're going to stop," Morty said.

"What do they care?" Lionel asked, starting to take the matter personally.

"These things get tainted, jinxed," Morty said. "This won't help."

"Could that little shit close us up?" Lionel asked.

"We need him to calm down and stay that way," Morty said.

Two days later, Bob Desantis called to inform Henry that Dupree had gotten on the Warners lot and caused enough trouble that the police had been called.

"What did he do?" Henry asked.

"He broke a window in the Administration Building. I think he was trying to see me. You wouldn't know how he got my name?"

"Of course not," Henry said. Henry hadn't mentioned Desantis to Dupree, but he also hadn't told Desantis about the ju-ju box and the phone calls. "Where is he now?"

"He's inside. Parker Center." Desantis said it as if he were a member of the police force passing on privileged information.

"Has he got a lawyer?"

"Public defender."

Morty already knew about the situation though he hadn't yet spoken to Lionel Detweiler. Henry reached him first. Lionel knew all about it. "Is this going to shut us down?" Lionel asked, not for the first time. Good, Henry thought. Let him be worried enough to do something.

"It could," Henry said.

"No balls at that studio," Lionel said. "They let a guy like that push them around?"

"They don't see it quite that way," Henry told him.

"We'll hose him down." Something about the terse way Lionel said it made Henry uneasy, but he put it out of his mind.

The next day, Dupree was moved to a one-man cell at the Men's Central Jail. Soon after that, when a guard came by to check on him, he was dead. A carotid artery had been cut with a double-edge razor blade. The blade was still in his cold hand. There was a lot of blood. Lionel mentioned to Henry that there were lacerations on the side of Dupree's head. The police were calling it a suicide. Henry wondered if he had knocked himself out before he killed himself. Because of Dupree's notoriety and connection to the child murders, his death got a couple of days' play in papers and on the local news. It was reported that he had been arrested for disturbing the peace at Warner Bros., the studio that was making the movie about the child murder case. The head lacerations didn't make the evening news or any of the papers. Henry knew that little tidbit of information had been a special message from Lionel to him. He didn't mention it to Morty, to Madeleine, or to anyone else.

Finding Home starting shooting a few months later. The advertising agencies that follow these matters turned the picture into a product placement bonanza. Morty got various payoffs each time he agreed to show, on screen, the label on a bottle of beer, or mention the brand of a cigarette, or linger on a billboard as a car drove past. Henry got cases of beer, cartons of tissues, and a great deal of aspirin. Henry was willing to write that when a character offered a cigarillo to someone the line would be, "Want a Palmetto?" He drew the line at adding, "They're really smooth." They still sent him what seemed like a boxcar load of the damn things. Madeleine wouldn't have them in the house so for a while Henry handed out Palmettos to everyone he met.

With Henry's production bonus, the Wearies closed escrow on their new house in the Hollywood Hills. Madeleine stopped reading about voodoo and she didn't mention the ju-ju box again, though Henry wondered if she still thought about it. The Detweilers used their money to leave Los Angeles and Henry never heard from Lionel again. In time, what the newspapers and magazines called "Arthur Lesser's *Finding Home*" was in the theaters. Art had shot it carefully. He got good performances and the studio didn't stint on postproduction, so the picture had a wide-screen gloss. It was a big enough hit to make Henry a hot writer for a while. Henry and Madeleine decided they would let nature take her course and not work so hard at getting pregnant. Henry filled the rooms of their new house in the hills with bookshelves, and Madeleine was happy there for a time.

14

Old Times, New Times

There were often nights when Henry couldn't fall asleep in a way that pills didn't help. Once that would have meant he'd get out of bed and build something. After Madeleine called him Henry the Watcher who wanted to sit on his own bookshelves, he gave his Delta router away. He had his toolbox but even if he'd felt the urge to start building he didn't have any lumber, and it was usually too late for the Home Depot, which now closed at ten o'clock because the neighborhood association had complained about the noise from all that late-night shopping and romance. He couldn't sleep, he couldn't build anything, and he had no taste for television, for fear that he'd stumble on another of his old movies.

Henry sat by his bedroom's open window and looked up at the starry sky. It was a clear, perfect Los Angeles night, illuminated by icy light from the white moon. Even though the city might be turning into one giant unbroken mall and the traffic threatened to choke the pleasure out of the days, the vast southwestern nights were still untouched. At another time, the certainty of the sky might have calmed him, but on this night Henry couldn't stop thinking about the morning at the Market when Mack Donnelly had his TIA. Thoughts of Mack made Henry wonder if he too would wind up in Tomorrowland, unable to do anything for himself and sharing a room with some unlikely character whom he would hate and resent if he even knew the guy was there. Is that what happened? For everybody? Henry tried to see into the future but of course he could not. Like all such attempts, it forced him to look back instead, into the past, a place just as deceptive and uncertain, but one that Henry could conjure up.

He heard banjoes and muted horns. It was ragtime. New Orleans jazz, full of anticipation, though he couldn't see where it might be coming from. Then, to his delight, a lively parade approached in the street below his window. Madeleine was first. He thought he saw her smile. He wondered if she was happier with Duane than she had been with him. It turned out that Duane had two children, so Madeleine at least got to be a stepmother. He wondered if it gave her satisfaction. She had a new career now. She had made a complete break from her old life with Henry. He wondered if she thought about him from time to time the way he thought about her. If she spoke of him, she probably said, "My first husband." That was Henry in his middle age, somebody's first husband. As Henry was threatening to wallow in thoughts of his broken marriage, he realized that Madeleine was alone. Where was the dreary Duane? Henry knew that this was his dream, so he could scrap Duane if he felt like it. Still, this could be a positive development. Maybe Madeleine had come to her senses and dumped that character. She did seem to be looking around. Of course, she could be looking for Duane. What kind of man would let Madeleine wander away? Well, Henry had done that but he regretted it, and that ought to count for something.

Then Henry saw Ark and his silver hair. The scripts Henry wrote for him didn't get made, so Ark had moved on. That's how producers operated. Always on to the next. Henry thought Ark was calling to him, but he was gone before Henry could hear what he was saying. This is a treacherous little dream, Henry thought. Behind Ark were Gloria and Bo, still in his Suzie Wong drag. Henry knew this was a parade of memory, but it still felt vital and real. He willed himself to stop analyzing and just enjoy it. Gloria was in one of her caftans, making adjustments to Suzie and smiling with pride of authorship. Henry knew she wasn't thinking about anything except how splendid her creation looked. Bo was beaming as he minced along absorbed in being Suzie, perhaps pretending his feet were bound. Rick Moses came by with his children of two generations and his wives. Rick waved to Henry, calling "Come on down and join us. Don't miss your own parade." Henry smiled at his friend and waved back. Then he saw Blake Porter and Lilah, on display, absorbed in their own beauty. Sister was a few steps behind them, smoking a joint and walking with Rolf, who was admiring her long legs. Henry hoped he would see Nikki Ann and her grandmother, Marvel Johnson, and perhaps her baby, the little coffee-colored Henry. He was afraid he wouldn't be able to find them, to call them into momentary presence. Even with the passing of years, the adoption mess felt like one more time he hadn't helped someone as much as he had meant to, and now he would be denied their company, even in memory. That was such a harsh judgment, and made him so sad, that he willed himself to see them, and then there they were. Marvel was in her blue church outfit with the fur collar and the big hat with feathers, the one she had worn when she came calling on Henry. Her vast bosom seemed to protect her family. Nikki Ann was wearing a dark red skirt of Madeleine's and she was pushing baby Henry in a stroller. The three of them looked safe and serene and it gave Henry comfort. Marvel knew what was right. If she had judged Henry too harshly, she would correct herself. She would correct the whole world, whether the world wanted it or not. Maggie was with them, telling Nikki Ann something. Henry knew she was saying there was a cable movie in their story, maybe even a feature, and she was just the girl to help them take advantage of it. To get rich. To be famous. To see your life on television. He knew Maggie was assuring them that she would be faithful to their story, that she would tell it with the honesty it deserved, and if they would only trust her they both might discover their true selves. Nikki Ann was interested but Marvel wasn't buying it. Just as well, Henry thought. Marvel knew that getting mixed up with Hollywood again would mean more men like Joker, and in the end it would break Nikki Ann's heart. Henry knew Maggie would make her pitch, and when there was no sale she would move on to something else. Then he saw Cody

Malone, no longer with Gretchen, no longer with his option deal, but still with his Technicolor cap on backward, still looking angry, walking purposefully to nowhere. Here was a young man with some talent, though probably not enough, with some ambition, but not the right sort, and as Henry had expected, he was utterly lost.

Lionel Detweiler in his Black-and-White came cruising along keeping an eye on all the people. To Protect and to Serve. Lionel still wasn't talking much. He was staring straight ahead when he passed beneath Henry's window. Henry tried hard to summon Dupree but he couldn't manage it. Henry wanted to call to Lionel and ask, Why did you do that? Don't you know you did that in my name? I didn't mean for that to happen. Then Henry saw Bridget Bosco in her tight jeans looking to find a man she could please nearly to death, and Mack Donnelly from the days when he could walk and talk and insult people. He and Bridget looked like a couple. Why not? Henry thought. They're both so excessive they would probably enjoy each other. Mack's stroke had been banished and he was wearing a tweed jacket and chewing on an unlit Cuban cigar as he ambled in Henry's parade. Then Henry saw Madeleine again. She was walking with Felix and Yvette and little Tracy. Felix was still as silent as Lionel Detweiler, but he looked at ease with himself. Madeleine was keeping an eye on Tracy, making sure she didn't wander off. Henry thought seeing them together was promising. Then he noticed Selma behind them, keeping her distance but watching. Henry couldn't tell if Madeleine knew that Selma was there. It was hard to hear what people were saying, what with the syncopated music filling the air. He knew that Selma was trying to say something to him, but he couldn't make it out. For a moment Henry imagined that he was back in Room Ten at Warners. He adjusted the volume until he heard his mother say, "She's a very good person, dear. You can tell that by looking at her. You shouldn't have let her go. That's the sort of thing your father would do." Actually, Felix's situation looked pretty good, but Henry knew what his mother meant. "You have to hang on to the good things that come your way," she said. "You don't always get a second chance."

For a moment Henry thought of them all as a script. He wanted to revise their lives, to fix their problems, to make them happy and content and perhaps even make himself feel useful and, as his mother said, able to accept what pleasure came his way.

When the parade had passed and the music faded, Henry found himself no longer at his bedroom window but once again at the Farmers Market. The headache-inducing mall was there but it didn't seem so bad today. If Henry felt the need for a pair of socks or some expensive stationery after his morning coffee, why they would be available. And the clock tower was back. It was part of the mall, an attempt at a little historical reconstruction. The chimes were ringing again, marking the irrevocable hours. Henry dubbed the new model a faux faux clock tower.

Henry sat at his table and laughed with Irwin and Wally and Leo and Morty as they ogled the girls and outdid one another with tales of the perfidy of movie studios. Henry waved to the old people from Park LaBrea and to the Israelis, who were slipping back and forth between Hebrew and English. Henry knew that even if he didn't sleep on this night or any night, he would feel better now. Henry would always consider what had gone before. That was his nature. Perhaps now that he had made his report, honored his friends, and rebuked his enemies, he might be able to revise the past in his memory and organize a future that would pull him forward because it was time to face a few facts. Madeleine wasn't coming back, and when he looked at his career he had to admit that no sane person would put himself through any more of the picture business. He had better get ready to pack his bag. New York would be first and then London. What better use, he thought, for a lifetime of rewriting scenes than to be able to leap over heartache and banish sadness. Henry just had to laugh until the clatter of the Market in the morning dissolved into the sound of a ringing telephone. It was Ark. There was about to be a big change at the studio. "Remember your old pal Angela Randazzo?" Henry tried to place her. "You called her Razzle Dazzle when she worked for Bob Desantis all those years ago. That's her lucky name. She's going to be made head of production. The boss! She wants to work with you. She loves the aliens script."

"Then we'll call it *Bolt from the Blue*," Henry said, which made Ark shout with pleasure.

"One hundred percent Henry Wearie great," Ark said. "You just added ten million to the domestic gross. Be at La Plume tomorrow. One o'clock. You, me, and Razzle Dazzle."

Ark's excitement lifted Henry out of his reverie and pushed away his thoughts of other cities and different faces. He could feel his old optimism returning. He would dust off the script, do his best to charm Razzle Dazzle, and try his luck once again. And he would call Madeleine. Just to talk. He'd find out if she had come to her senses and dumped the dreadful Duane. He wouldn't put it that way but she'd know what he meant. He wanted Madeleine back but he also wanted the past, which he knew was harder to come by. He would settle for Madeleine. He knew his mind was drifting because Ark was calling to him again, telling him not to get lost in daydreams. "Stop worrying about what you can't control," Ark said, which sounded like the sort of thing Madeleine used to say. "The past is over. That's why it's called the past, you know?"

"No," Henry said, wanting to believe that the past might yet be corrected and a future built.

"Sure, sure," Ark said. "Stay focused, okay? There's a studio deal to be made here but you have to pay attention." Henry collected his thoughts, about to explain to Ark that he had other plans, but what came out was "Yes, he said. Yes. I will. Yes." It would have amused Rolf but it went by Ark. No matter. Henry would go to La Plume with Razzle Dazzle. He would do the dance and sing the song. And he would put a lid on the show-off literary references and he would call Madeleine and be as charming as he could be no matter how long it took. He would take himself for another walk along the twisty path. As the excitement surged through him, the years fell away because Henry knew it was the right thing to do and it might even be true.

About the Author

David Freeman is a screenwriter and the author of six books, including *A Hollywood Education*, *The Last Days of Alfred Hitchcock*, and *One of Us;* and the play *Jesse and the Bandit Queen*. He has been a contributor to *The New York Times*, the *Los Angeles Times*, *The Wall Street Journal*, and *The New Yorker*. He lives in Los Angeles.